DE MARKIES VAN WATER

Hilarius Hofstede

DE MARKIES VAN WATER

20TH ANNIVERSARY EDITION

WITH AN AFTERWORD BY THE AUTHOR

Zip Records

MMXVIII

À mon ami

Patrick Healy

WAN OWAH ONE OWAU BEFOAH HAW AURÂH ONE OWAU
BEAFOA HOW AURÂH ANUS MUNDUS OURANOS SOLANAS
SORANUS WÂWTÂW WÂWTÂW EVERYWHORE UNUS MUNDUS
ANUS MOONDUSCH MÚNSHOWER OWAH-WAH OWAH-WAH W
AN YOURANOS MÚNDUSCHAMPOOL UP TO CHIRHOSHIMA
LE NAGRASOKEANOS MINNEOTOURUSH IN THE BIKINI
THERE WAS THERE THE WORD ATOLL ATOLL ATOLL B
ULBUMBABILLA TOUR DEMOLITOUR POOLABULLY BAAL
ABILLÀ-BASS TERROR FUNK SHUI WIND OVER WATER
AQUAVATARKOVSKILOTON HIROSHIMALAYA MOUNT KAI
LAS MARQUESAS MILES DAVISHNUKU SHIVA COBRAHM
ARQUISES ORANGEL FALLSDE MARKIES VAN WATER E
XPLOSHIVA-DIONYS.O.S. OLLANDA ANADOLL EL MAR
QUESAN MICHELORANGELEAU WÂWTÂW WÂWTÂW EVERYS
HORE TABULLARTAUD BULGAUD H-BOMBARDEMENTIA P
RAECOX UP YOUR ARSCHIZOFRENIAGARA FALLSDELIT
TERRATIONILEXILE THE MOTHERTONGUE CONNECTION
ONE OWAUDIONIETZSCHAMANTRA VENUSSUELLASERRUB
SPACE BASSOLLEAUDIONYSOS PENISSUELLAS MARQUE
SAS THE MAGICK FLOOD KING GEORGE WATERFALLSD
EFUNKT THERMONUCLEAR SCHWITTERS MERZBAUBOMBO
OTSHIROSHIMALE FIATMÜL FLUX H-BOMBUANDIONYSO
SSMATOSS OFF ECCE HOMONO BIKINIETZSCHE ATOLL
AQUAPOKA'ATEATEATEATEATEA URQUELLE DIEU BLEU
VASERLAVER WATERLOVER MEET THE BLUE SEA HIRO
SHIROKLITAURUS ORANGE WARHAMMERZBAUBOMBUANDY
ONASSAU WAU WAU WAU MASTER BATESON DÉLA NAVE
N VASSOULLINGAMPÈRE UUBUTTON PENIS PROTEXPLO
SIVE MARQUISLOGANTRA IATMÜLTRAMONAVEN ORANGE
ORANGE EVERYWHERE HOLANDA DARKENING THE AQUA
FACE TONICCARROLLCLONE ALONE AT SUNSET H-BAM
BA LAMPÀPUASSUNSONG SUN RÀ THE BEGINNING PAL
AEO FUNKÀDELIC BÀSSÎSM IN SUNSET MARQUIS HOT

ELLAR-LO-WAYS & WATERS SUNSET TRIP ORANGE SU
NSHINE EXPLOCEAN MELT-THE-SUNDOWN WELT-THE-S
UNDOWN TO A SUNLESS SEA ALLSDE MARKIES VAN W
ATER PAPUTA'A TA'TACQUA NEU GUNNATRIX W/AR W
/AR DOMINAVEN WATERFALLEN POE-FUNK A DESCENT
INTO THE MAELSTRÖM ORANGINASSAU DROP THE BOM
B THE BASS GODDISSEA ORANGEL FIREFALLS LUNAS
EA MWAN OWAURAPE EL MARQUESSUNNY SIDE UP HOL
LAND AQUÀ CAM AQUÀ CAM BOOTSHIROSHIMMALAYSIA
MESOAPOOL PAPUA NEW GUINEANDERTHALES ÎLES WA
TTICKA PRICKACQUAPHONIAGARA FALLSDELUGEOMATE
RRE INUNDADATA BASSPACE BASSOLLEAU & LORANGE
ATOMIC BOMA YE MOHAMMED ALISUN IN WUNDERLAND
NARANZJÊWAWA SMELL MY FINGER UP YA DIKĒ OWAU
PIG PANGLADUCHAMP SUNSETBECKADELICATE BIKINI
ATOLLAMOURQUELLE MARQUIS DE SADHU FREUDFONKI
NG THE HÉROSHIRAKLITTERROR BUTT TO THE BUTTO
N UNCLE JAMDUNKELNASSAU GRAND MALE MARQUIS E
PILEPSYCHO UNDER THE SUN SPAESSIBASSI SPAESS
IBASSI THE MARQUESSUMANTRA MOTHERMILK FLOWIN
G INTO THE HEAVY WATERS HOLLAND DADALAI LAMA
RANATHALATTA MARANATHALATTABOOTSHIVA-DIONYSO
S & BOOTSILENUS STONE H TO SPACE H SUNNERSET
MORONSON PLUTONICCLONIC BASS WATERROR SPASSI
BASS SPASSIBASSEXPLOCEAN NORTH SEA DELTABOOT
SHIROSHIMARQUESSOUNDTRACK MWOORDZEE BOMBORAN
JEBOOM! MURDER MOST FOULTRANCE WATER WATER I
VORYWHORE HOLLAND HERE COMES THE SUN MICHELL
ANGELORANGELEAU MW DE MARKIES VAN WATER MÊMM
ÊMMÊMMORY DAIMONDE LO LOW LEAU LÀ-BASS MÊM M
ÊM MEMORY MÊM MÊM MELODY DIVE-INAKIN DEEP WA
TER ARANCIA NÄSSEAU DIONYSOS FLOODING HOLLAN
D FLOODING DIONYSOS HAMMERING THE SPACE ABYS

S M. COLLINS W. COLLINS EXP-FUNGWE POETAM HE
AVY WATER EVERYWHERE ZURBARANCIAQUALIASPARAG
US WE ARE GOING DUTCH HUANG HO HUANG HOLLAND
URHINNERIVERRISE PISS EVE & AMSTERDAM'S ON T
HE OCEAN DEEPILEPSEAS WELLECTROSHOCKWAVEFRON
T JJ/FF/PP-FUNK ALL-STARKOVSKIWASSERBOMB FAB
RICATION HÂPI HÂPI HOPI HOPI INSTANT SPERM B
Y RADIOACTIVITY IN THE ELECTRONICCLONIC BRAI
N CIRCUIT TOHOTAUA HAAPUANIJINSKI DIONYSOS F
LOODING DIONYSOS ORANGE 9MM HIGH SPEED CHANG
E COURANT DE FOUCOULT YOURQUELL'ORANGE UP YO
UR ARSCHLOCHNESSAU FLOAT FLOAT ON BIG BANGLA
DUTCH PSYCHOPATRIA TRANSSEXUALLSDE MARKIES V
AN WETT WETTÈRAKLIT MW/RATIONAL DISORDER IN
THE VENUS HIGHWAY HOTEL GOD ANUS MOONDOUCHAM
ANTRA EL MARKIESKIMOHAVE SCHIZIUMANIESMOUSSU
CKSTRÖM CHAPPELSÍNASSAU OLLANDA ANADOLL 6000
ORANGES FLOWING ON WÂWTÂW WÂWTÂW EVERYWHORMO
NDOUCHAMPAPUA NEW VAGUINEA WAU WAU WAU SHE-M
ALE SEIZURE MICHELANGELORANGEL FALLSUCKSTEAM
CHAPPELSIINILE WAH-WAH DE BAPTISMOHAVESITRÚN
NAVEN MARANATHALATTABOOTSÍTRÓNASSUCKSTRÖMPAD
ELICKAOS PORTAKALVINNENRAUM THE MARQUESSOLAR
ANUS MÚNDUSCHAMPÈRE UBULLUTSCHIZOFROMMIATÜL
TRA WAVEMAKER NEW ATLANTIS KUNG FOO-FIGHTIN
G OH, GEORGE CLINTONTON JAMPÈRE UBOOTSZINÁSZ
APPAPUA GAUGUINEA ORANGE H-BOMBASSONNÉORANGE
UP YOUR ASSEXPLAUDDING IN ORANGADELICUNT NAZ
ZALBERTEXTUALLITTERRA ORANG VAGINASSAU DE MA
RKIES VAN WATER ONE MAN SHOWER P-FUNNAGRA TH
E BOMBISONNEMILCHAMANIAGUARA GLITTORISE & FA
LLSUCK OR FUCKALL ORANG-UTANTRA WAVE MEGA GO
TT BRAINFALL UP YOUR ARSCHWEPPILEPSEA DRY OR

ANGE BOOTSINISTERRA HANGAQOGNITHALATTA PSI-F
ONKUDOPPELGANGGANESHAMALEMONDE MARKIES VAN W
ATER WATER MASTERBURNER BASS TERROR BULL NIC
HOLASWELLEN BOOTSHIVAGINASSAUDIONYSOS MWATER
WATERRORRUN ORANGE NOISEA SLIPPIN' INTO DARK
NESS WAR ANGEL FALLSUCK ORPHEOS BAKKIKOS ORI
ONYSOS-KIDD FUNKADELICKA PRICKASKADATABOOTSY
BILLASWELL BUDDHA FIRE WASSERMONO BIKINI ATO
LL STRANGELOVE LOVE WIDO WIDO VISHNUKE HIROS
HIVA WATERIAL UPRIVIRABHADRA KRISHNAGASAKI H
IROSHYDROGEN BOMB THE BASSPASSAGE NUCLEAR TI
DAL WAKE NORTH SHEROSHIMALE BUMBRELLA BOMBRI
LLO WARTOWAH WARTOWAH HOLLAND CALVINNATRIX D
UNDRUM CLUB FOLLOW THE SUN UNDERWATER NUCLAR
ITY KUBRICKINI ATOLLANDESE RIVERROUNDABOUTZI
LLÀ-BASSPACIFIC EXPLAUSSHIVA-MINANDIOTAURISE
LIQUID SUNSPLASHIROSHIMARQUESSOUNDGARDEN HOL
Y WATER ORANJEBOMBASSEXPLUNGING INTO THE RIV
ER VOLGA GANGES AMAZON MOZART HIROSHIRONYMUS
M.A.D. AGAIN MEKING KONG KING MEKONG TUGELA T
UPELO HUANG HO HUANG HOPI HOPISSISSIPPISSUCK
THE MIGHTY RIVER FELA ANIKULAPOCALYPSE NOW K
UTIBERRYFIELDS FOREVER DELIVER THE WORD MWAR
HIROSHIVA DANCEFALLINGAMMADIOS MWATERFALLOUT
SAI BABACOOL & THE GANGES AS ONE OWAH-WAH WA
H-WAH THALATTABOOTSILENCE EXÎLES MARQUISES Y
INNULTRA YANGTZEE! YOURQUELLENNON-STOP WATER
IS THE TRIGGER OF THE WORD HÉROSHIVA DE MARK
IES VAN WATER TAUROTO-FLAMMING IN DIZZEELAND
SGT. PEPPER'S LONELY HEARTS CLUB BANDAMA RIV
ERRÜBBERRATIONAL SPACE BASS SOLO I LOLO! I L
OLO! ONE OWAU TAUA WAU TAUA IVORY HORROR YOU
NUKU HIVA NUKE JUST DO IT RIVIERENAISSANSUCC

IMABUSEASPACE BASSAREUS VASLAVERIVIÈRÂDIONYS
OS POUR SANG DIONYSOS OMÁDIOS WATER WATERMIN
ATOREAU PSYCHOTIC BABY PSYCHOTIC ORANGANESHA
MALE MARQUIS DE SANDOZA LOVE-INTROBIANDERLAN
D HOLLANDER MAGICK MUSHRAUM LET'S HAVELOCK E
LLISTER CROWLITTER HH-BOMBASSUNWHEEL UP YOUR
ARSE OLLANDA ANADOLL SHE-RIDER ECKHARDT DE M
ARKIES VAN WATER SCHIZO-FLOODING HOLLAND THE
LOWLANCÛMSHOOTING HYDRACUNTROLLAND WETTERRES
WETTERRES SHAMANIC DON'T PANIC SPIRIT LANGUAG
E DISORDERRUISSEA HELIOCENTRICHAOSSUCKADELIC
KING MARQUESSINTFLUTTERING SPACE FLOOD HYDRA
ULIC PUMP PUMPINO! POMP POMPINOA-NOA! WATERF
ALLEARY SOULANUS S.C.U.M. SHOOTING UP YOUR AS
S HYDROCEFALLOUT LAUT MELTDOWNWASH URBAN WAT
ERREADY-MADE FOR RÜBBERSCHWEMMING HOLLAND HA
PPENIS ANTI-ARTS PSYCHIATRILOK EUROPEAN CLIN
IC GURTOUR TRILOKOMO LOKOMOHEAVY METALMORPHO
SIS TRY YOUR LUCK GURTUGELA FALLSOUND LEAUNI
VERSAL HYPERCUSSION TABLATTA! TABLATTA! WAH-
UPDATABLA EPILEPSYCHIATRILOK GURTUTU MILES D
AVISNUKE NUKE HIROSHIMAROGOGORUABRAOH I OH I
BISONNÉORANGE ANUSSAU AQUASSUNUS MOONDUSCHAM
ALE MARQUIS WEST SUNTANTRACKLIT FRUITFICKING
RUBBER BANCOCK ORANGE-GROOVE-DRUMMING FUTURE
SHOCK FINNAGASAFFRONICCLONIC ORANGEL FALL OU
T LAUT THE MARQUESSATIRISKCON HARE HARE RAMA
RAMA MAENADS GO WEST NILE YOUNG PSYCHOTIC BA
BYLONELY ARSE CLUB BURNING BURNING BURNING F
REUDFUCKHOLE ESSOLEÎLSDEEE ARSCHMERZBAUBOMBU
ANDEEELIGHT MY FIRE THE PRE-FONQUE DELTAMIRA
MIRA PLAN ONE MANDALLASCÁUX WATERFALLON-PONT
-D'ARC DE TRIOOOOOMPH DE MARKIES VAN WATER W

ATERRAQUASSUNUSSOUSSOLLEAU BOOTSINAR SURYA I
DIGUE PARTY ON PLEISTOCENE SURGERY DISASTERS
FLASH FLOOD INUNVADING DUTCHLAND UNTER ALLES
ÎLES PAYS BASS CLONUCLEAR EROSMUSHROOMBRELLA
EPILOOPIDAURRUSHING MINNEOWAUTAURRA WAUTAURR
A BULLARTOE BULGOE BOOTSYBILLUTSCHI BOOTSHIV
AJEEE CHUNGOOL BELLAS MARQUESAS DE MENDOZA M
AHRATTA! MAHRATTA! OWANJER KNASSAUS TALOS UL
LABOOTSYBILLABYRINTH THE MAZEOPOTAMINOTAURAC
QUA POTABILLABEL MARDUKEDOOMSDAY TRIPTOLEMOS
MÊMMÊMRE MIMMIMRA MARNASS MARQASS MITRASS TH
E ENEUMA ELISH DEEE HAZEOPLOTAMINNEOTOWER WO
W TOWA WOW TOWA LAPSUS LINGAM THE SEA SWEATS
HOLLAND NOA-NOA THE MARQUESSIAMESOPOTAMINOA-
NOA MINOPATRA WAH-WAH WAH-WAH EUPHORY WHORMU
NCHDUSCH ONE OWAU TOWA WAN OWAU TOWA EVERYWH
ERRAKLITAURUS ORANGE UP YOUR ARSE WARHOLLAND
MINDDILETTANT WINDMILITANT EL MARQUESANTHALA
TTABOOTZILLAS MARSHALLAS MARQUESAS MASTURBOO
TSY BASSTONEGO DE MARKIES VAN WATER BURSTING
THROUGH THE DYKES OF REASON MARANATHALATTA M
ARANATHALATTA CALL M BISHMAEL ICKA PRIXODUSC
H DELOBITCH OEVERRHEINFLUSS KRISTEVANUS & AC
QUADAM'S ANALINGUS PLURABIES DE MAAS VAN WAA
L INTERFLUTTING UNTIEL THE ITTEREND EL MARQU
ESCAPE HORNY HORNAMENTAL DISORDER MARQUIS VO
N OOHH BABY MASTERS BATESON & JOHNSON HERREN
KLUTTERREURQUELLWASSIR PSYCHO SUCKSPACE DELT
A BASSHOLLAND FLOOD MIX ANGELS FALLSOUNDAROU
ND METAL CLONE VOODOO-BASS SOLO VISION HEAVY
LO-RIDERS & TIDE-FIT SUNBEAMS WAH-WAH SWITCH
AMANIA JIMI MYSELFABETTSTUHL & DJEMBE DZSCHO
YCE WAH-WAH DISTORTION-VOLUME ONE OWAH WAN O

WAU BEFOAHH... OWAH OWAU THE NAKED VAUDOUCHA
MP BOX-LUNCHAMANIAGARA FALLS AT THE Y-RIVIRO
IN I M FUCKALL I M FUCKALL MAGICK U BELASTEN
MAGICK U BETASTEN LSDEPRIMORDIALSDELPHIDELIC
MARQUESAN'SSI N'SSI CONZETTO SPAZIALE MARQUI
S FANTASTIQUELLETHE MARQUESS ORANG MÉCANIQUE
STONE HAX TO SPACE HAX BUTO BUTO BABY PSYCHO
TIC PSYCHOTIC! WATTEAUX WATTEAUX BASS HORROR
MARQUESUN RÂBIES MEER & BOSCH INTERGALACTICK
A PRICKARKESTRA AT THE DONAUSCHINGEN FETTSTU
LTIKIEFERA NAVENIS THE CLINTRONIC CLITURGY H
-BOMB IN RIVERSE COME LOURDES SKUM BLORDER P
ARLIAMENT PENCKADELIC LEOPARD RIDE KHUMBH ME
LARD MELARD BIKINI SKHUMBH P-FUNGHIROSHIMELA
DRUMMATOLLOGY DE BAPTISMOHEAVY BASS PUMP UPR
IVER WALK THE WATER UNDER THE GG ALL INTROSH
OCKADELICK PUMP UPRIVERREADY-MUTT FOR ALLSDE
CUNSTRUCKADELICKA PRICKABOOTSYBILLASWELLOWLA
NDS DE MARKIES VAN WATER ELLETHE AFTER SHIVA
VENUS IM PELZEELAND VAGINARSCHIUMATERRA FIRM
ATER DOLOROSADOLORASADOLOROSA THALATTHANATOS
THALATTHANATOSSOFF MAKE LAV NOT VAS HWANK HO
HWANK HOLLANDA HWANK HOJOHEHOHOHEHAHOHOLLAND
IN PARADISOTTO IN SUMOHEAVY MARQUIS ORANGE S
UNBORN GOD TO COME DE MARKIES VAN WATER BOMB
ARDING ELECTRIC HOLLADYLAND THE SCRUB WOMAN'
S KICK LIQUID NATION YOU RHEIN THE WORLD ORA
NGE RULETA GRAND MALUM AUREUM GRAND MALUM CI
TREUM OH I OH, GEORGE CLINTONIC EPILEPSY GRA
MMATICAMAY SOAPOCALYSE NOW EL MARQUESSOAPERA
SIERSCHAUM AUM AUM SUN RÂBIOSODOLOOPSIDEDOWN
M-DAY TRIPTISOULMAN MIGROOVE IS MAGROOVE PSY
CHODISCO NAPPA MUNDI HIGH & RISING ORANGÔ GU

INEA HOLANDA WE R. MUTT RROSE-SALIVA CUMREAD
Y-MADE FOR ACTION HEANEYKEN BIERZATZ DIONYSO
S-BOGGUS EL MARQUESAN PIG DANCING THE MOTHER
SCHWEIN CONNECTION ARE YOU UP & DOWN FOR THE
SUNSTROKE ET VOGUE LE NIRVANA ARÂNCIA-ACQUA-
LIMONE ALL THE WAY FROM KINGSTUNT JAMAICAMAY
SUTRANCE EVACUME IVACUUM OVUCOME POLDERGEIST
DE MARKIES VAN WATER CRÂINSCANNILINGUISTICKA
PRICK MARRIOO CHACHACHA MAMAKADA DADA HOOHOO
CHY MACOOCK HOODOO MAE WEST & ALEISTER CROWL
EY THE BEAUTY & THE BEAST SEXSEXSEX WHO'S WH
ORUS? EL MARKASHBACCHUS HOLLADY DIONYSOS DAD
ADANCING AROUNDABOUTERSKIRT NORTH AFRICA WAR
QUIS IN THE MOOD FOR LOVE ONE MANSELMARKIEFE
RRAGE OUTBURST DIKE DIKE BURST HEPATIGRIS BO
EUFRATES CARLOS DE BEASTEIGI MEAT AVARIATION
OOOH BABY DR. TARR & MR. FEATHERS GEORGE CLI
NTON SHAMANDAMANDANUBELY SO GOTCHACHA WEH-
WEH CATCH 22 MEGATONICCLONIC ATTACKAPUT NIHI
LI BRAVO BRAVODA VODA IN THE BIKINI ATOLLAMO
URQUELLEAURANGEL FALLSICK JAMES D. ATWATER T
IME BOMB TESTING TESTING ONE TWO OH I OH, GE
ORGE GAMOWWOWWOW THE DEATH & BIRTH OF THE SU
N HÂPI HÂPI HOPI HOPI ONE OWAHWAH WAN OWAUWA
U DE MARKIES VAN DEN OEVER DE ZEE IS ONS LAN
D TEST TEST ONE TWO WATER WATER HERE COMES E
VERYWHERE THE J. HEALY BAND RIVER OF NO RETU
RN ORANGE KACHINASSAU EL MARRIOOCHACHACHA MA
KAKANANADADA HOHOHOOCHY MAMACOOCH COCK COCK V
OODOO-BOPPEGUNS BASSPACE PUSSY MWEST TO EAST
A-BÖMPSKULLABONEY SULIMONA LISA READY-MUTT F
OR ACTION SLY-MILE & THE FAMILY FOULLAMORE M
ORE EROSMESS SINGING IN THE RAIN MW BOKORPUS

HING MARCASCATARHEINVLOED NARANCASTAR BOJAJA JA NEENEENEE SPERRUNG MOHAVE URINA LOTHIUM J AZZAPPA WHAT'S GONE INTO YOU SUZIE CREAMCAKE & SUSIE ORBACH TO BACH TO BEUYS FETT IS A FE MINIST ISSUCKAMABEUYSSEA DR. MABEUYSSEA RUTK OWSKIWASSERBOMBADELIC NEUROBIOAQUADOLOOPZILL A 95 96 ENCP-FUNKING PISS EVENICE & ADAMSTER DAM'S WATT WATT WATT WAS NOT WAS ADAM'S FIRS T WORTSALAT? OH, HOLANDA SPUTTERING PAST WAS SERMANN & FUNKENSTEIN TEST TEST BIG SHOT HOL LAND NEVADADA ARIZONASSAU OPERATION HOTBOX B USTER-JANGLEBOOKEY POO BOOKEY POO BRITTIDE O PERATION TOTEM & TABU EL MARQUESAN MARCOÏTAL DEATHE MARQUESS VON WATER POOLING THE ORANGE IN HADAISY DAYS APGAR TEST ONE TWO TEST BAKE R ARSE AMANDIONYS.O.S. ONE OWAUTOFELA KUT-QU E-KUTI COITUS IN AXILLA MARQUISE DE PUMP PU MP PEDO YOU KNOW I LOVE YOU FRANZIPPING COÏT US INTRA MAMMAS & PAPPAS & FRENCHIC GENITERR OR ON DUCHAMPOGNON ÉLUSEA ZEN D'ARSE DE TRIO MPHULL AQUÀ CAM AQUÀ CAM AQUÀ CAM FROG YOU O UT PARIS COPROLAGNIOPOLIS GRAPUNQ GRAPUNQ EG G EAU EAU EGG EAU EAU! KOAXKOAXKOAXKOAXPLODI NG FRAPPE DE FROGGE EL MARCASSE-TIDE DE GUER RE UU UU ORANGE UP YOURQUELL DUPETIT TROU-AR SE QUEUERUSH PRETTAPORTER COOK VD MÈRCHIANDE LONGSDWARFF LOA R. SILLIVANNY DEMON DURVILLA IN DR. VON DEN STEINEN MADAME HANDY ANDY QUA TREFAGUES LIBRATOR HEYERDAHL KRUXENSTEIN XUU ZIKILLAA XIZUUKILLUU ALLSDE MARKIES VAN WATE R WATER SURA SURA HOMME LEOPARTAUD FROM HELL AS MARQUESAS DE SANDOZA EL MARQUESANDOZAUBER SPAESI BASSI PAPUA NOAH BIGUINEA IATMOLL L'H

ISTOIRE D'OLANDADA ORANG U-PURITAN THE NEW W
ORLD SUN ORANGE MAGNÉTIQUE MW BOMB DÉBRISSHI
T BARTAUD ALLSDÉLIFRANCE 'N ALLSDUCHAMPIGNUN
S EUNUCLÉAIRES KHMÈR YOU ACQUÀ CAM ACQUÀ CAM
UNUS MUNDAMON BORNEO-AKIN HOVAJAQUA CAM CILL
EBASSUMATRAGUANGEL FALLUCY GRAND MALAYO-POLY
NÄZZEN BOHANNON CALVIN LET'S DOÏT JUPPEE-GAZ
ERAUS HOGGAR BERYLLA BABY THE FALLOUT-CUMSHO
T DR. FOLLAMORURONGELAP-FUNKADELIC P-FANGATA
UFANGAUGUINEA NOA-NOA NOAH-NOAH CHRÉTIENNAGA
IN SCATOLIQUELLOTION NATION EARTH TRAUMARQUE
SAN GG SEBASTIAN ALL-IN STRING BASSES HOME T
O THE SEA (IT BEGINS WHERE THE SEA LEFT OFF)
L'ANUS SOLAIRBORNAGAIN WE TWO ARE DRIFTING H
OLLAND EATING AT THE YSSELMEER WATER WATERST
OFFLOODDIESSEALLES COAST TO COASTELLEAU (I D
ON'T WANT TO GO TO) CHELSEA THE BLOW KUNTRIES
COMING IN FOR THE BIG O THROUGH THE CUNNILIN
GUAPHONE EAU-SHOW-BE-DOOO-BEE MW DRIZZLI GEI
LLOOPISPI GEILLUSPI OLOFAT OMATAT TUTHUP! TU
THUP! TUTHUP! TELECULT POWER THE PEYOTL-KULT
RANSSEXAMANTRA YOURQUELLEPSILLOCYBEAHH BEAHH
CHOKMAH CHOKMAH CHOKMAH ESPENUS DE MILOOP-DE
-LOOPZILLAS MARQUESAS BLOW UP THE BIBBELBATH
BELLANDA NOW H-BOMBILLA DE MARKIES VAN WATER
EL MARQUESSGT. RIOT CHILI PEPPER'S LONELY HE
ART OF DARKNESS ABU ABU ZEQQZEQQ TRUMMA TRUM
MA TRUMMA DRUMM DRUMM DRUMM SHANTIPAPI-FUNKA
TEER OH, GEORGE ZENJUICE YOURSELF AHH... THE
NAME IS BOOTZILLA SILLA ZILLE ZILLU CILLEN Z
ÜLN ZÜLLEN ZÜLN ZULLEN ZULL CZULLEN ZILN SIL
LES ZILLY SILLA SILLS SILLE ZELLA ZULLA MARQ
UISE DE PUMPUSSY DOURQUELLE MARQUIS VON WATE

R WATERRA WONDERFUL WORD DISCOO'D BE LOOK AT
THE SUN JOHNNY RIVERS ROCK M ON THE WATER FI
RE & RAIN PEOPLE GET READY FIAT CAMAY LUXAFU
NKADELUGEOMATRASHOW LEOPARD RIDER EGGHEAD VI
DOÏT DOGGODE MARKIES VAN WODDER HOLGER ZUKAM
AY FLUX ONE OMANGOMORRÂ VENISE DIRTY BOGARDE
ENFINNABEND SEULS HOLANDA TAJ MAHAL ABOUTTER
PRINCE BERNAHARDWARD 6 SUBBERNAROUSALHALLABA
D NASSICK UJJAIN HARDWARHOLLAND DADA ESPAVAT
ARTHOTH THERMONUCLEAR SWEAT UALU UALU FUKIEF
ER HARINGO STARLIAMOUNT NEVERREST POLANDADUB
ELIN BLITZKREEK HYDROTARRAPPEEE-FONG LUNI HE
ARTS CLUB BANDY RIVERRAP KNASSAUNASSAUNASSAU
NA ZOOHARKANYTHONGUE ATOLL ATOLL ONE BUDDATA
BASSIN PORTEAU PRINCE CHARLES MINGUSHING SPA
STORIUS BASELINES ON THE HIGHWAY TO HELLBORG
SPACE WAU WAU WAU ORANGE KLITTAURQUELLE MARQ
UIS HÉROSHIRAKLITTERRATOUR DE TRANCEPHALLOGR
AMMARQUESAN BRAINFALLOUT WAH-WAH WAH-WAH BI
LLASWELLOWLANDS IF 6 WERE 9 PUMP UP & DOWN &
OUT COME SLYCLONE STONEHENGE & THE FAMILY FO
LLATOLLAMOUR THALATTATTOOS THALATTATTOOS TAT
TOOTZILLACONE SUNBURST 6-STRING BASS POWER B
OOTSHRI KRISHNA SUPERSTARKOVSKI MYTHERIALISI
NG WAUH-WAUH-WAUH HADEÈSSEAUDIONYSOSPACE ABA
SSES OPEN UP NILE JUNGAMANDAMAN ROGER WATERS
NOAHH-NOAHH... THE NAME IS BOOTSY BABY PSYCH
OTIC PSYCHOTIC! CALL-KARL VON DEN STEINEN UN
CLE YAMMA YAMMA TATTU-WHITT TATTU-WHITT TATT
U-WHOO-WHOO ROCKY THE HORROR THE HORROR WILL
OWDEAN ANDYWHANK WARHOOLIGANS WAGONTONGUE WA
Y TWINSLOW HOMER SWEET HOMER WATTSPEAKABULLA
UT 2001 ESPACE FLOODDYSSEA ALLSDEFUNKT MAGIC

WASHAMANTRA OMI OMI OMI CAPTAIN AHABACOOK VD EL MARQUISHMAELSTRÖMSTOSS ECCE HOMOBILE DICK APRICK UNCLE JAMADEUS SEX MÀCCHINA BITCH DAUBER WORDWARA THAÏTIKILOTONICCLONIC PFUNNASAGA TIDAL WAKE KING BILLY JEAN KING BILLY LAS WELLAS MARQUESAS KEYS FLORIDANCE MARKISSIMMI MYSALVOBUTT & THE MAR-KEYS MEMPHIS EXPERIENCE SUN RÂDARWINNASSUCK OLANDIZZEELAND BILLABONGO COWWOWWOW THE MILKY WAKE ELECTROBRIAND LOVEMAKING SENSE CALL M HELIOPOLIS FINNEGANCOCK VDE MARKIES VAN WATERHOLLAND ORRITE ORANGE CARAVANNAGRAM CRASHES TO ASHES THE ESPACIFICK BOMBABELLABOMBIKINI TEGRATOLLATTATTOURQUELLE MARQUIS PALEOLITHIUM 66 O TELLY SAVALAS MARQUESAS LES ÎLES LISIBLES WATER NO MORE MORE FADE TO BLACK TABLA RASA PÀROLE-PLAY LAUT ANDRUM WOW TOWWOW WOW TOWWOW WOW TOWWOW NUKE JUST DRUID! ONE HOURQUELLE MARQUIS DE BOMBELLES MARQUISES ALSO SPRACH ZARATHLUSTRAUSS 2001 A SPEECH ODYSSEA I.H.S. INONDATÀ-BLABASSPACE ABYSSPACE BAZZAKAR WAZZAKIR HUSSEIN ANILE BACHWATER REVOLVERRUN ODILONELY REDON MCLOVELY THE WHITE SHAKTI YERBOOTSHIVA MESSINÄSSEA DATAPANIK IN THE YEAR ZEROSSTOSSTRAUSSUCK OR FUCK HOLLAND EJÉKK EJÉKK! YOUR IDOL DILDEODA TOTEM EJEKKOJAKKULLATING CHIRATSHU-MULA-MULÀ-FRAU-LEAURENA LOLOBITHE ROCKITT! ROCKITT! BRIKUNK BRIKUNK BOBBITT FARRELLAS MARQUESAS BOBBITTERRAINCHANT KAISER WILHELM KIEFER EL MARQUESAN MARKOBLENZ WASSERFESTIFALLUS BOBBITT BOBBITT BARON ADOLF KAISER ANSELM SCHIFFER RAX KIEFERRUN IRISH LORD X GINGER È FREUD TRANSFUSION WMWM DIDJERIDUDOK ARCHETYPEEL ARCH

ITEXTOUR TOTEM TOWER & TABU LET'S HAVELOCK A
LLSDIAGRAMMOLOGUESS WAH-WAH WAH-WAH ECHOLATE
XTHALATTABOOTSEASSEASSEA RUBBER BANDROÏDE MA
RKIES VAN WATER (A) SPACE ODDILOONIE ARSE CL
UB MED HOLLAND GUESS WATTER WATTERRAPE UNCUT
PHUNKENSTEENVOORDE BEELDENSTORM IL CONTONIC-
CLONICCLASTIC FURY OUTBRAQUE BE MY BEACH HOL
LAND PSYCHOTIC HOLLAND 1STONE TO THE EGG EGG
ORANGUTANZ PARTY ON PLASTIC LETTERS IN THE S
AND APISS APISS EL MARQUESSCHIZOFREAKY MARQU
ESSCHIZOFREAK BULL-LEAPING ON THE HIGHWAY TO
HELLENISM THE SCREW RIVER HOLLAND BAY JAMAIC
AMAY RIVER WEST SEPIKKA PIG ÈSPASSEPIK DANCE
EL MARQUESSYNCHRO SOUNDAROUNDABOUTZILLASSYST
EM ONE EAUWAUTAU ONE EAUWAUTAUDIO-BOMBARTAUD
ONE EAUWARTAUDDISSEAGULLESPICASSOAKING BILLA
BONGO BUDDHA GINGER & FREDDALAI LAMA QOD WAT
ERHOLES OLÉ OLÉ GUAPAPUA PSYCHO PEEPSHOWER P
-FINKE GORGE CLANTONICCLOON TATTOOBI RIVERTO
NICCLOONAGH MAE MYSELF & I LAFNITZ RIVERALSD
E MARKIES VAN WATER MANUS DEI 25 GRAND MALAB
AMARQUIS WARRIOR RIVERDE MARKIES VAN WA-WAAL
PEDALLAS PETASMANIAGARABBISHMA-MAASSHOLLANDS
CAPE SPACE-BASHEE-MALE RIVERRAUM NASSAU WÄSC
HAMALE MARQUIS ONE MAN GAGANESHOW REFILLIGRA
INS WAX MAGICK FUNK FOR ALL LULU FUKI P-FANG
AMAGÄT DOWN SHAMANASSAU PAPUA NEW GUINNEGANS
SYNCHRO SYSTEM EL MARQUESAN PIG-A-BULL DANCE
STONE AGE TO SPACE AGE PARLIAMENT FUNKADELPH
I PALEO-PSYCHO-POP S.O.S.SCHIZO-SOAP TONIKE
-CLONIKE JUST DO IT PLANET JACKSONIAN EPILEP
SEAS KINGBILLY LASWELLOLLY POP MUSIK JASSPAS
SAGE GINGER & TED NUGENT WEEKEND WARRIORS OH

É OHÉ & LAAKSIDE ONE FANTASTIC VOYAGE PAPOEA NEU GENESIS MATÉRIAL/OAO'JAY CRISS CROSS LEK TURA SUB AQUA THE DEEP RIVER QUARTET SHE'S A RIVER FULL METAL YELLOW JACKETS LIKE A RIVER AZURE MOON BRUCE WOW MAN UP YOUR ARSCHWEINER RHEIN WAAL WAAL WAAL WHAT A MAAS WETTER & WE TTERSNOODDISSEAS MAASSOAP & WAALLOOP WARHOLL AND ASSPASSEAMUS HEANISSEY SLY STONE FROM DE LPHI OBEYAH OBEYAH ECHOLA MÈRWEDE MARKIES VA N WAH-WAH GRAND MAAL & WAAS NOT WAAS MASSA C ONFUSADOLLAND BIG GOES THE BANG FLASH GOES T HE FLOOD! RELAPSUS LINGAM GOPI GOPI HÂPI HÂP I THE BEAUTY FLUID & THE BEASTIE BEUYS OIL O F OLAZ MARQUEZAZZMAJAZZ YSSEL MAASS SEINE DI KE A PONY UNCLE BEN JOHNSON WAX MAGIC JOHNSO N THIS IS WRITING SID & NANCY REAGAN YOU ARE WHAT YOU DESIRE OLLANDA ANADOLLYLINGUALSDE M ARKIES VAN WATERRORATORIOOL MAASWATERRAPSOD Y WAALLSDIGITAALLES ONE OWAUTAURUSSOLOLOBITH ERMAL NUCLEAR SWEATTERSNOOD ONE OWOWDOYOUSAY DEELIZZEELAND BJÖRKHAREN THE WAR IN THE WORD O WHAT A MAASSOPOTAMIA IN WAALSTRÖMLAND KING BILLASWAALLES MARQUISES UNCLE RAMMANAISSANCE THE ETERNILE FLAMMADEUS SEX MACHINE SGT. EPI LIPREAD HOT CHILI PEPPERS WASSALONELY HEARTS CLUB MED EL MARQUESSEX SHOOTERRA FIRMAMA PRO PAGENDER IN HETEROSPECT A RETROSHOCK TAKE IT AWAY BOBBY FISCHER PALEO-PSYCHO-POPPYHEAD VI WATERFALLON-PONT-D'ARC DE TRIOOOOOMPH! QUE T AL USALLABOUT DOKTOR K. TORMINATORTURTLERRIF FICKY LEANDROSS ACROSS THE WATER HILTON JOHN WAYNE BOBBITT BOBBITT MADMAN ACROSS THE WATE R DAVID FOCKNEY RUBBER RINGO STARSE FLOATING

IN A SWIMMING POOL SHE-MOON FOR ART GIRLFUNC
LE JIM ANALLIVERPOOLLULLABY FOR FUNFORALWAYS
FUNDATOMIC DIKE & TUNA TURN YOUR RADIOS UPSU
CK MAAS UNIVERSE EL MARCASTELLA THE WHITE BR
IDE RHINORIDDEN STRESSTANTRASH & DAZZ MISS L
IZZISSALLAZZAPPULL UPRIVERSOAK WATER FLOWING
UNDER HERE'S HERE & HERE'S HOLLAND PUMP PUMP
FUZEBRA WAH-WAH WHO-WHO? EL MARQUESSEX SHOOT
ERRA FIRMAMADEUS EREX MACHINE GUN MÄMÄGÄT UP
EL MARQUESSACRE DU PRINTEMPADELICKAOS STEREO
TYPEE-FUNKING BILLY JEAN KUNG LÖWISE CERROLL
GARNER PROSE-BUDDY DE FRANCO CHAOU ABDELKADE
R MARQUIS VONNAGUAS MAH MAH MAHLAHA KALMAH M
AH MAHLAHA KALMARKIES KUNQUERING THE LOW LO
W LOW RIVERSOECKING HELTER SHELTER IN HOLLAN
DAMAN EPILEPSY WETTIR WETTIR LI OUALAFTOU FI
OUEST KNOL BNAT KOLATLA FIHA KHEIR PSYCHOSEX
UALLSDE MARKIES VAN WATERFALLIFORMAL BEFFING
ERING HOLLABIA PRIAPEI-FONKUDOUCHAMUNDUSCHGE
ILGEIL THE EROS OF UGLINESSAU MANIC-DEPRESEN
ILE PORNAMENTAL RETARDATA BASSLUT ART EAU AR
T EAU ARTICULATION DISORDERWISHANTISOCIALFAB
ETAPHYSICAL JOURNEY THROUGH HADESSOCIATIVE H
OLLANDE MARKIES VAN WATER IN COPULO ESCAPE H
ORNY PORNAMENSTRUAL LIFE-BICYCLE KRAFFT-EBIN
GADELIC BANGOGUINEA PIG EAURANG NÄSSOURCERER
DOBU DOBUBBLING IN MARQUESSEXUALLONG LIFFEEL
THE MOHAVE RIVEREUX FLOWING INTO THE JIMMY D
URHAMMURABISMAH ORCHIPELAGUNA DEMARKIESKIMOH
AVE DOBOOTSYBILL YOURSPRACHFLUSSUCKING IN TO
NGUES GOINGGOING DENGENG-DENGENG BORA BORA K
HABULUBULA KGABUDUBUDU UAL VAL EGBURUBURU KU
NZUKUNZU UMBUBUBURU JATA JATA WUWU OSIRIS-SU

R-MER FOLLABULLROARING OUT LAUT THE ANDROGEN BOMB JUJUJUNODDISSEEING WASSERIJKSWATERSTROO MSTOOT REXKRANKZINNIGENGESTICHT THE BRAINFAL LING OUTVOLLEDIG INSULT XAVIRUS HOLLANDER RI VERRESPONSE TO URINE FROM FEMALES IN HEATWAV E HALLOHEHOJOHEHOYOHEHALLOHOHOJOHEHOYOHEHALL OYOHOJOHEHOHOHEHAHOHO MIJ IS DE WRAKE! DE-BA PTISMONANISMOHEAVY METAL MEER MEER & BOSCH R OCKANJER NAZIEL MANTRADIOACTIVE MODDERMEER & BIESBOSCH ISSCREAMH ISSCREAMH HYDROTRERAPSUP RANAYAMAH MAH MAHATMARQUESAN SEX CYMBALNEOTE RRAPE IM ABENDROTHLUCAN SPA HOUSE DIRTY TALK ING VODUNDUNDRUM UP YOUR ASSID JAZZUIT MOTHE RSHIT SHOWERHOUSINGING LOYOLA GAY IGNAÇION I NONDA MOVE SPUUCHIATRICKA SPASTICKA PRICHAMM AN SPUUCHILLATRIADICK-A-BULLITTERRAPE ORANGE DESSAU MARQUESSCHLEMMERQUASS URTRIPPENWITZEN BUDDHAGOROAR HALLOHEHOJOJOHEHOYOHEHALLOHOHOJ OJOHEHOHOLLAND UNDER WATER WATERATONICCLONIC ATTACKAOS BEAT THE MEAT BUTT THE MUTT GG ALL ADDINSANE INONDEPENDANCE DAY SHE-MAELSTRÖMWE ST YOUNG MANTRAVOLTA L'EAU FROIDE UP YOUR AS SAYAS OOLÉ BULLY DELUGEOMATERRA FIRMATERRA I NONDADATA BASSTEELY DANUBE EL MARSHAMANISMOU SSOLLINILE RODGER WATERS IN DIFFERENT IN DIF FERENT IN DIFFERENT WATERS ENOLA GAIAK GAIAK OLLANDANA MALA WOE IS WE BLUSSGRIEG KINGBILL Y JEAN KINGBILLASWELLES ÎLES MONDO MAGICO LO OK MICKEY'S MONKEY RIVER WALTZ EPILPTIT BOIN G GOING THE BRITES OF SPASSAGE FROM SGT. REA DY HOT CHILI PEPPER'S VALLONELY ARTS PONT-D' ARC TO DUCTOR CIMABUSE FRITZ LANG TIME AGONE ONCE UPOONA RHYME JASSPASSWATTERSNOODDEITIES

EL MARQUASI-BEGINNÉGALA ORANGEOMATERRA FIRMA
MAGIC JABBERFIX SLEEP JUST DO IT! EUNUKE JUS
T DRUIDIA & THE DEEPDEEPSLEEP SEA M MYSELFAB
ET & THE MARQUESAN RIORAMA MAN O'WARROARATO
RIO WHATABOUT WHATABOUT EVERYWHORE CIMMADEUS
JAMABOUEE CRUXIFLUX ICHLE ICHLE EAGLE HOMO D
ER SCHAMANIESMOUSSEA ANIMALLARMÈRZ 6 IMITATO
REN DEEE BAPTISMOUSSEARNOARNOARNO WAY OUTTER
REURQUELLE MARQUIS FLORENCE UP YOUR FANNY NI
GHTINGALE ATOMIC DIKE EAT DIKE MOOKEE MOOKEE
MUPI MUPI BOCKSTUMP BECKSTOMP! BROS.MOND BRO
THERS JOHNSONS WAX MAGIC HEESSALTOES TIEL TH
E END OF TIDES EL MARKISSANNY FANNYFACE STRA
WBERRY HIRSCHFIELDS FOREVERRUN HYDREAMINOFUN
NKLE RAMSKIN I'M IN WATER WATER EVERYBULLY W
ATER THE DESCENTOWER THE DOLLAMOUR & THE DIL
DIOT! WAH-WAH WAH-WAH EVERYBIDDY BULB MCNUTT
PARLIAMENTARY FUNKODISSEA DR. CALLANETIC CAR
L ANDRÉ BAHRROCKY LOOPSTAR THE WHORE THE WHO
RE BAHRROCKWATERBECKUPRIVER YOU ARE KNEEDEEP
IN THE HOLLAND FLOOD MIX UNEASY KING SUNNY A
DAY HOTSY TOTSY MY SINBETWEENUSSYNCHRO REPRI
SE PRESLEY PARK POP LIFE THE LADDER THE LADD
ER MARQUIS VON KEITH HARING BROOD & JEFF KIE
NHOLZER SOS.O.SOS SCHIZO SOAPERATIONAL PROGR
ASSEA THE BOLD & THE BEAUTIFUL & THE BLAUFUN
X WILDEBEEST ONE MANDANANGA ORANGAGA UTANGOG
O WOW MANDALATOYA YONINJAJAJA NEE NEE NEE CU
NTU ZANGMOOHAVE NON MERZY PARTY ON PLASMA EL
MARQUESSOMARQUESSURYASSHOLLANDADA NR. 1 KAMA
KAMA DOG A PONY ALL GOES EAST! BIKINNAKUNN W
AKE ATOLL ATOLL'ORANGE DISASTER WARHORRORATO
RIO PALEOLITHIUM 66 QUE TAL MR. MUTT? MAE WE

STSIDE STORY HOOP UPSIDE YOUR HEAD 66 MÄRKIS
CHER SANDSTONE STORY STORY NITE NITE JASON C
HRISTO SUPERSTAR TO PICASSOCIATE STOP BY STO
P LIVE IN PARIS IKE PRICK & TINA TURM KINGBI
LLY JEAN KINGBILLY DE KOONING DEMIFRISCH WAW
ATERREUR THROUGH THE LEKKING GLASSOAK UNTIEL
ERWAARTSALATTAK EPILEPSYCHO-POPARARA LOE-LI-
AH (WORLD'S MOST TATTOOED LADY) H2O DREAM TO
SLEEP ÄMÄGÄT DOWN DILUVIALL LOVE IS ALLUVIAL
DE MARKIES VAN WATER IN ABODIGITAL RHYMETIME
ZONE GOO GOO GOOBJIBWAH-WAH WAH-WAH SHAMANIA
EVERYWHERE EL TORO SOLONELY HEARTS CLUB GING
ER & MED GORDON GINGER & TEDDY PENDER IS THE
GRASS GINGER & FREDDIE VAN HALEN M OON W AAL
M AAS W ALK I DIKE I TELL UALLABUTTERRANCE Y
OUROBOROCEAN WAH-WAH GUITAR WATT-WATT LIFE I
SN'T LONELY HEARTS CLUB BAND CALL MY FRIDG
E TONY BAEKELAND A REAL MOTHER FOR YA ORANGG
ANGESSOLEILSDE MARKIES VAN WATER COCK ON THE
LUCY ADILDOLF SHITLER W/YOUR RYTHMSTICKA PR
ICK-A-BOO ON WAIKIKIEFER BEACH RAM ON OSIRIS
-SUR-NOSE WAS NOT WASSIR NOSE THE FREEDOM OF
DEFORMATION IS TOO EXPENSIVE FOR YOU! EL MAR
QUESSAUT D'EAU RE MI NA WATRA VODU REMY FA S
OL UP YOUR ARSCH THE WHORES! THE WHORES! SPE
ACH ONE? WE ARE FLOOD... ONE BY ONE HOT MINU
TE BY MINUTE DE MARKIES VAN WATER SPINVADING
HOLLAND ANIMAMA ÎLES PAYS CRUES SGT. PEPPINO
ROTUNNOA-NOA PAPOEASSARAGHINAVEN VIAQUA MARG
OUTTA THANASSIS! THANASSIS! TOTSIKAS MARKASS
EL DOKUMENTAL DISNEYLAND WATERFALLSDE MÄRKIE
S VAN WATER WATER PRECIOUS LIQUIDS EL MARGUT
TALATTA GROOVE O'CLOCK ROCKNROLL SUICIDE SUS

ANA SOLANO U-ALAP YOUR ASS HOLIDAY ON ICE MA
GIC & ILLUSIONS I MICHELANGELO PISTOLETTO HA
PPY TURTLE ZOE LEONARDO WATER #1 WATER #2 VA
GINA #1 GERHARD MERZATZ MERZ LET IT RAIN LET
IT RAIN READY-MADES BELONG TO EVERYONE MARQU
ESAN PIGGS THE PIG BRIX THE BRIX BROTHER NAN
CY RONALD & I THE CODEX BODY HAMMER STAZZEMA
RQUESSERAVEZZA EL MARBLE MARBLE EVERYWHERE M
ARQUIS ALBERIGONAL ORANGE CAR CRASH/YELLOW M
AGIC ORCHESTRA THANKS FOR MY RAIN IT'S RAINI
NG REVOLUTION (BY SPEECH) IT'S RAINING SOLUT
ION RED HOT CHILE PEPPINOARNOA-NOA MOUTHPIEC
E (VIDEO) ECHOLA TERREDE SADE REDE SADE ANSE
LM KIEFERRARIVERRUIN WATERRORCANE LUIS BOURG
EOIS H2OASIS H2OADES LET IT RAIN THE GREAT R
OCKNROLL SWINDLE RED HOTTENTOT CHILI PAPOEAS
S MR. NATURE TAPEFRIK ECCOLA RAISONIPPLE WAS
HED AWAY (BY SPEECH-DEFUNKT) RAIN IS WET SUG
AR HILL GANGES RIVERRAP FLOWING OUT COME MEG
A-MEXICO DE MARCOS VAN WATER RIVERLOCEAN UNU
S MUNDUSCHORDER MELT WELT DOWN! DE MARKIES V
AN WATER WORN BY WARRIORS SPINUNDATA-BASSPLA
SHING THE HOLLANDS O YEMUSALE YEMALE! O YEMU
SALE YEMALE! NAGASUCKINNAGAIN MW TRANCEDANCI
NG IN NAGALAND BURMESOPOTAMOUSSEA-WASHED AWA
H-WAH IN THE SPEECH ABYSS GRUE SAN DINISIO D
IAMOND LILLIPOTANANAVEN GO WEST JUNG MANIA S
CREAMTEST ONE TWO DODOMANIFESTO RAINING REVO
LUTION (BY SPEECH ODDYSSEAS) 20.000 MILES AH
EAD WATER ON WAX MARQUESSUCKAMOTOROTUNNO WAY
OUT LET IT RAIN! RUBBER FANAGAIN COMPACT DUS
K THE RAINING REVOLUTION/PARADE SADE PENIS D
E MILO (PAISLEY ARK) BOOTZILLAMERICHAOS SUMS

UM IT OOPS UPSIDE 1 SUPER ECHO PENISES & EGO
S MWINSPACE THE BOMBORANGE WATER WATER ON FI
LIGRAINS WAX PRINCE WILLIAM BLAKE ALBERT SCH
WEITZER DÄDÄMON SAVONAGRIN WAS NOT WASSIRCON
CISSION PRÉPUSHING MARQUESSEXUALLICE DEEELIT
E EL MARQUÈSPASMODIKE BRAQUE ON THROUGH MARQ
UESAN MARCOCAÏNOMANTRAVOLTA RIVERREDE REDE S
UN RÂISONNY ONE HOURQUELLE COBRATOR MR. GLOW
CARWASH FRITZ LANG THE CATWALK ON THE WILD S
IDE DOWN YOUR HEAD VI VI VI LET IT RAIN MARQ
UESSACRÉATION ICCA PRICCAPUT MORTUUM PHRASER
DISC MANTRA LADY DIANA SLIP WE ARE FLOOD (P-
FLOOD) SUPER ECHOLA MARQUISSEEK THE CREEK FE
LLATIO SOLAIRE FANNY FANNY HILLARYWHORE WASS
IR NOT WASSIR DUKE I WISHAMANDAMAN EPILEPTIC
WORLD UP ÉROTIGRESSO-LSDE MARKIES VAN WATERR
E LAKE ALBERT ELLIS DEEELITE MY FIRELAND RIV
ERRATIONS SEXUELLES ÎLES MARQUISES ORANGE VE
NUSSAU ANANGAGA ORANGAGA PENISTOMOSEAS ANDRO
ÏDE MARKIES VAN WETTERREDE MAMANIMA BE RAISO
NIPPLE HOLANDADA LET IT BE LET IT BE RAIN DE
BAPTISMODERNISMOHEAVY BASSPUDORATA! MARQUESS
OFIA LAZZAROTUNNOA-NOAQUALIKA WATTEAU WATTEA
U EL MARQUESTO MONDO PROIBITO CLIO CLITORIDO
REMY MYSELF & DIAMOND LILITHIUM 6 FREUD ISIS
ISHTARREALITY EUNUQUE D'EAU EUNUQUE D'EAU SE
X LIBRIS EROTICIS BLURGASM INTRA MANUS DIONI
MMISSIO IN VAGINÂM AQUAVANT TOUT AQUANITA EK
BERG PABLO PICABIA ELECTROVA CAPOOLETTI NILI
EL MARCISSIQUELLE MARQUIS MARQUIS EVERYWHIRL
MANUSCRYPTOPSYCHIESKIMORE MORE SGT. PEPPER'S
ODDILOONELY HEARTS/CABARET VOLTAIRE DÉFLORAT
IONILE DADANUBISMARCKIES PORCHIPOOL ATOMIC D

OG EAT DOG HADESTRUDEAU REMY MYSELF & MARQUE
SSATYRS / MARQUESSILÈNES CREATING = REACTING L
ET IT RAIN RAINCHANTING MARQUESSATYRIVER DIO
NYSOS - ZARAGREUSTRAUSS PHALLOPHORIAGARA FALLO
FOLIE NOUROS DE PANAPOLICE! STOP TRIPPIN' GO
GO MW / THE FLOW MOHAMMED DALI APOLLINAIRE 11
EL MARQUESSPACE BACCHUS YOUR PHALLO MAN EL M
ARCASANOVA GUINEA PIG DANCEPHALLOGRAMMARKIES
FLOOD MIX WATTIS WATTIS BOOTSY DOINGDOING ER
EGG EREGG SIGMUND POLKE SIGMAR FREUD ICE - CRE
AM ALLSDÉLUGEOMASSA CONFUSA PEYOTTO È MEZZOA
P - OPERAMSTERDAMNATION EL MARQUESAN MARCOKANE
MY BRAINDANCE PEYOTTO DIX WEIMARQUESAN MARCO
KANE RUNNING ARUNDFUNK DAMPFING RAMSTERDAMPF
UNGHIROSHIMALE MARQUISSTRAUSSUCK AMEN... SME
LL MY FUNGHI THALATTARANTULA MARQUISEAQUA PL
OTABILE MARQUIS LET IT RAIN HOOPSIDE DOWN UN
DER THE SUN H2O A SPACE FLOODDEITY ALLSDIEUN
UKE NUKE JUST DOIN' IT! OWOW BRAVO NEW WORLD
CABARET REVOLTA RIVER SCRYPTOPSYCHISMOUSSEAS
STROLL OVER BEETHOVEN MOZART FOR MOZART'S SA
KE ANIMANUSCRYPTOPSYCHISMOZART EVERYWHERE AP
IS APISCIMARQUÈSAMACORD THE BULLACQUAPISS AP
ISS HISTOIRE D'OSIRIS & FRIED ISIS TRISTRÄNE
N & GRIEVESSOLDEÈSSEAS SPIDER MARQUIS VON OO
HH BABY LOVE = ALLSDSM - 4 - U! PEYOTLOAPISCINEM
ARKIES ONE MANDRILLINGER CITIZEN COKANE MY B
RAIN WELLES ÎLES MARQUISEAS GRANDMASTERMAL T
HE GREAT OHMI OHMI OHMI THE NARRENSCHIFFMACH
ER OMI OMI OMI P - FANKHAUSER WATER WATER EVER
YWHOROSCOOP SPACE YO MOMBASSAQUARIUS! AFRODI
LLINGERMANIC - DEEPRESSADE SADE TRANSSEX PISTO
LLOGY ASTROPSYCHOSCHIZOAFROAQUA! (LET IT RAI

N LET IT RAIN) SPITTORIVER ANONIMOHEAVY BASS
GT. PAPUASS' AUTORITATTOO ONE OWAUTORITRATTO
DE MARKIES VAN WATER CUBE VERSION O. METELLI
ALLABOUT FREDERICOKANE MY BRAIN O. METELLI A
LLABOUT APISSI-BASSITARATHUSSTRAUSSPACE FLOO
DISSEA O. METELLI-FESTA NOTTOURNAVEN SUNNY R
ÂINING MEN HALLÉLUSEAS JUSTINE DOIN IT O. ME
TELLI METELLI ALLABOOTZILLAS MARQUESAS OPOU!
OPOU! OMI MYSELF & FANKHAUSER STOP TRIPPINGO
GO MW/THE FLOWWOW OPOULLAFUCKALL JUNK IN FU
NK PEYOTTENTOT CHILI PEPPER NASSAUCE HALLELU
CY IN THE SKYLIGHT ONE OWAH-WAH (ROLL UP) RO
LL UP UP FOR THE MISERY TOUR (ROLL UP FOR BE
ETHOVEN) FLUTWIG BEETNAVEN/AQUAMADEUS REX PI
STOLS GENTLE GIANTS OF THE SEA PELIKANNIBULL
EPHANTIASEAS TATTOWER INFERNOAH! EPILELIPHAS
LEVIBRATOROTO-BASSMWATER WATERRABORIGINALIAS
DE MARKIES VAN WATER WE ARE SPINNING EL MARQ
UÉSAVAGEOMATERRAP ACIS MARQUÉSA EAU DE COLOG
NE & PERFUMED SOAP EPILAPIS APIS BULLACQUALI
ASTROLL OVER BATESON RAISOUNDFLOOD FREE GALO
OPEE LOOPEE EL MARQUÉSA EAU DE COLONELY HEAR
TS/CABARET REVULTOUR MYSTERRA FIRMARQUESACQU
A POTABULLE TOROSITHALASSA MYSTERRESTREVI FO
UNTHANNATOS WACO JACOPOZZI OPOU! ORANCE NÄSS
AU CAQUACAPHONIE HIFIDEEELITE ECCOLA METHODE
BULLAS MARQUESAS THE ACQUASPIDER MARQUIS VON
O DE COLONELY HIGHWAY TO VENICE PABLORIGINAL
WATTERRES WATTERRES MÁGIC WASHAMANDOLLAS MAR
QUESAS OPOU-FUNKATERROR LET IT RAIN SNOWADAY
S IN SNOWADIZZEELAND PRINCE BERNIE WARRELLAS
WARCASES WORLDWORRELLE MARQUISSINASSAPOLLO E
LEVENTOUX MOONTEAM THE WATERRESTREMBLURQUELL

E MARQUISGEOCEAN FRED HOT VOODOO CHILE O. ME
TELLIPHAS LEVI PLUREBEL PLUIEGG PLUIEGG UNCL
E RAMSTERDOOM AQUAPULCOPULIPSE NOW! TIBER TI
BER BURNING BRIGHT SAINT PETER BLAKE PERRY C
OMO ONE MANDALAS VEGAS MARQUESAN MARCOMOHAVE
NO MERSEY BECKETT WATT WATT PRIMORDIALLES ÎL
ES ÎLES ÎLES MARCHÉSEPIK RIVER WATER WATER E
VERYSHORE ALICE DEE DEE BRIDGEWATER WATER PR
IMONDIALLES MARQUISSEAS PRIMONDIALLSDELIRIUM
TREMLETT ON THE WATERFRONT UDANUBE APU MATAN
GI GIVEN THE WATERFALL & THE ILLUMINATING GA
S EAUX ET GAZ AUTI TE PAPE EL TOROTORELIËF É
PONGEOPOUBULLARTO BULGO GUINEA PIG DANCE FIN
TANNEGANACQUAS LET IT RAINDROPS KEEP FALLING
ON MY HEAD/CAN THE OCEAN KEEP FROM RUNNING T
O THE SHORE? CATCH 220.000 MILES DAVISHNOUKU
HIVA WALTER WALTER BECKETT DONALD FAÄGEN-DAS
HAMALE HOPI HOPIANOAH-NOAH BASSPASSEA GODDIS
SEA WAHN WAHN MANN SHOW HOW ABOUT USW.? (YOU
ARE) A HEAP OF LANGUAGE AQUAMAMAZE WE ARE ON
E/RIGHT ON TIME OMI OMI OMI GODDISSEA HOLLAN
D DÄDÄMON SAVON DOPPELMASKIUMARKIESKIMOA-MOA
SOAPIUMBRILLOA-LOA ONE MANDALASCAUX! DEMIZIN
MANDAMAN EPILEPSTEIN SUN RÂISON RAISUNNY I L
OVE YOPOU ORANGE KARMA CHAMELEON SCIENCEPHAL
LOGRAMMARQUESAN AQUAVATAR ONE MAN CHAUFFE-EA
U/THE WISSENSHIFT SOULTRÄNENREGEN LET IT RAI
N (THE IATMÜLLERIN) ECCE HOMOHEAVY METELLI M
ORE METELLI MORE ECCE HOMOHEAVY METHALES HÈR
AGLITTER GETTING BETTER SHAPE UP DOO-BAPTISM
O. METELLI MORE NIKE JUST DOO-BOP PALEO-PSYC
HO-BOP ANNEXIMEANDER CULPAFRO-BEATLES KUDOO-
BOPPOP-DE SADEMENTIAMATERRABISMAH MAH MAH TH

E CINDERELLA THEORY DOG YOU OUT TVOODOOLOOPZ
ILLA MARANATHAÏTIKEEK-A-BOOTSID & BOOTSINATR
ANCY SINATRASH FINNAKINJECTING Ô DE LAINGCÔM
E ON THE HYPER ASS EGO FETISJ MARKET HAÏTIKI
CKABULLASWELLA-FÓÓÓAMADUSCHGELLGELL MOUSSOUS
SANT MARC GOGONÂVEN CHANNEL NUMBER FIVE CLUB
MEAD FUCK PROFILLACANCÔME CÔME RIO ALORANGEL
O MARQUESANGUINEA MAGIE NOIRE IN THE DIVIDED
SELFATION NATION DESORDORANTI-CRISIS UP YOUR
ASSOUSSOUPLISSOEUR PSYCHOSEXY HAÏTIAN HAIRFO
RCE ET TULA MARQUISUCKAMISSMEARNOFFABSOLLOUD
MEGAWODKAOSSADEÈSSEA WE WANTI-PSYCHIATMÜLTRA
WAVE WACO JACO SPASTORIUS BASSPLATSCH EL MAR
QUISCEANDADANUBEASSYLUM KUM BA YAH KUM KUM B
A YAH MACUMBA WATER VOODOO QUEEN D'VOIDOFUNK
THE WAVES SHE-MALEMONDE MARKIES VAN WATER AL
LSDÉLUGESLECHTSTRIEBBISSEAS UP FROM THE APES
RAINSCANNABISHMA SCHIZOHARCHIPELAGOGO MW/TH
E CIBBERTEXTERMINATOROTO-BASSHOLE REBEL REBE
LS ARE WE RING MY BELL GGÉSUSSUFIBUNACHISSAF
AR ULLA ULLA SOFARRELLASSOFAR-LI-ALLAH TOMBE
R BAP LITHE BOMBER TOUM! THAHALATTASAWOOF! T
HALATTABOOTSILICLOWNSKEAGH ZOURINNERUNG REIN
DEER MY DEAR DO FRIES PULL THAT SHAKE SAI SH
ABABA SHEISSHABAB EL MARQUESATYRISKCONTRANSS
EXUALLUST KITSCH 22001 ÉSPASTICK HEANEYSSUCK
WOW NUDIE PARTY SPLICE-CUBISMARCKIES SKULLAP
SING THE AFFESSESSLITDIKE GRAND MALSTRÖMSTOS
S OFFSLUTDIKE MEGA WADDENZEEPAZZOOPZILLASWEL
LA ÉSPAESSIBASSEA GUINÉEAHH GUINÉEOHH BABY W
ÖLFLIGANGES FÓÓÓAMADOUSCH MOUSSOUSSANT DHIKR
IDDAM DHIKRIDDAMDOURBRAQUELLWASSERMONSOON SE
A YAYA FHIKR FHIKR H2OLANDA A COCKWORK ORGÂN

E NASEAU BRUEGHEL SEA-STORMSTOSS OFFOLLAND E
L MARQUESAN BLACKSPERMWORLD RELISABBATH'S DA
Y FLOOD BREAKING ON THROUGH THE DIKES FROM H
ERE TO LIMPIDITY REASONABULLABITCH DUB HELLE
CTRO-CHIC BURN HARD RIVERRAZORRO HAVOCALYPSE
NOW! FEELUSSEA FEELUSSEA SEAFEELUS SEAFEELUS
SCHUMALE CARNIVAL OPUS NUMBER 9 NUMBER 9 NUM
BER 9 ASCHENBACCHUS COPYING OUT LAUT TRANSSE
XUAL PISSOIRINSCHRIFTEN AUS PARIS DO-IT-YOUR
SELF SWEET SWEET VINCENT THE CLITTERAL HOODD
ISSEY CAPTAIN SAY WATT WATT WATT YO ALFRINNA
KINSEY'S FOAM STAR MARLONELY BRAIN-DOUCHES T
HERAPISS-GAZING IN THE FOUCAUCHONNERIVERMARE
I LOLÉAU! LOLÉAU! ARSE-MADE R. MUTT DERIVE
R DERIVER THE XTCEXUALLICE-CREMENILE MONTANT
WATER WATER NO MORE MORE PARISWETTRICK MEGAW
HOREPOSES LADY DI-PHALLIC LADY DI-PHALLIC LA
DY DI-PHALLIC LADY DIONYSOS MÊMMÊMMÊMMICKING
HINDUTCH SEX DREAM ON THE DAVID HAMILTONICCL
UNIC FLOORSHOW TRUE DEEPARSILLANCIEUX BÀSWEL
L & JOHNSONNY ADÉOS ADÉOS PUNEASY DANCE MAST
ERS & BEN JOHNSUNNY ADÉOS ADÉOS MARANATHALAT
TATTOO-WHITT-TOO-FOAMM MARANATHALATTATTOO-WH
ITT-TOO-FOAMM URMERZBONTEKOE SAGASM WASH NOT
WASHINGTONICCLONIC DÉLUGEOFFROY-SAINT-HILLAR
YWHORE BIKUNISEXUALLATOLL QUEEN JUJULIANA PA
STRANALLADY DIORGASM LA DOLCE VITA MINGUS MI
NGUS MINGUS MINGUS MWATCH TVOODOO-BAPTISTA D
OS SANTOS FRIGGIDEITY MW NILE ARISTOCHÂTTE &
ARISTOCROTTE W/NILOTIC PERSONALITY DISORDER
HOLLAND DADATA BITCH DUBLINEA SERPENTUNNEL L
ET'S HAVELOCKAGAIN WIDE OPEN UPSIDE DOWN & O
UTCOMES OH, GEORGE ORWELL & BEN NONSENSE WAX

HIBITIONIST NINJA TORTURE TEXTERMINATORWELLA SWELLAS MARQUESAS MWATERRE MWATERRA AQUABULL SDÉLUGEOMASSA ICONFUSAPPADELICHAMANTRASH WAT YR WATYR SHE-MALE GOATTACKA BULLSHITTITE RIV ERTALK TALK TALK DE MARKIES VAN WATER EN PRO FILLAGAIN ARSCHIZO-EFFECTIVE SCHEISSOAPHRENI AGARA FALLS 6000 FEET HIGH & RISINGING THE M ARQUESAN ANTHOTHEME IN ORANGALAND HEIDI HEID I HEIDIOLA GAY HEIDI HEIDI HEIDI HOLANDA ASC HIZOÏDIQUELLWASSERFALLOGRAMMAR WATER WATER A FROWHORE EL MARQUESSPEECH-DEFECSTASSEA SPACE BASSOLEÎLES ÎLES MARQUISES EL MARQUÈSPACIS M ARQUÈSA TWIN PIG EXPERRIDANCE ONE MAN RAY ON E MAX ERNST AUTOMATONICCLONIC ECLECTROSEXUAL SEWING MACHINE EL MARCHIPEL MARCHIPEL BISMAR CKIES OMI OMI OMINOTAURQUELLES MATTA MATTA M ATTA DOO-BOPPENHEIM BRETONICCLONIC PEGGY DAN CE EL MARCEL MARQUESSOAPOCALYPSEAS NOWAH OWA H ONE OWAH BEFORE OWAH OWAH WAS NOT WASSURRE ALISMOHEAVY WASSURREALICE DEE DEE ACQUAPSYDE R DADA NR. 1 THERMONUCLEAR SCHMWITT BERLIN A BBAUBONEY MARQUIS DADA COOL PICASS.O.S. HOPI HOPICASSOAP-OPERA BOWWOWWOW TOWA WOW TOWA GO LLY! GOLLY! GO BUDDY HOLLY HOLLY! ECHOLÀ-BAS TIAANSOUL ELECTROSHOCK-MONTAGE DERRIDADA NR. 1 CULTURE CLUB FUCKATRONICCLONIC ORANGAKOQ V IBRATOROCEANDAMAN VIBRATION UNCLE GEORGE MAR TIN HEIDIDGERIDOO-BOP THE MAKING OF SGT. POP PER BEATLEMANIAGARA WALZ THE ABBA ROAD MOVIE DIVERRUN-THROUGH THE LOST LENNON TAPES UNCLE GEORGE MARTIN HEIDI SUN RADIO WESTWOOD ONE T WO ONE TWO MEMI MYSELF & RUBBER SOUL BAND DA DA MERZBOOTLEGGLES ORANGE RECORDS SWINGING P

IG YELLOW DOG AQUANTUM EPILEAPSY THE AQUARRY MEN/RED HOT CHILI PERRY COMO POWER LET IT BE-BOP ORANGE BEETLEJUICE DADAF DE SADE SADE GILBERT & GEORGE MARTIN SGT. PEPPERRY COMOHEAVY METALSDE PARLOPHONE FUNKADELIC LE MARQUIS DE SADELICATE ECCE HOMO DILUDENS LET IT RAIN RADIO TELE MUSIC NIPPONGO PYGMAEUS WEST (NATURAL PORN KILLER) SUN RADIONASSAU NUKU HEIVA O TAHITI TITAUI TAU TAU BOWWOWWOW YIPPEE JESUSPIRORI È FETISHAMALE MARQUISHTARTAUD BODY-HAMMER BLOWOUT HYPERBORIGINAL DREAMTIMEBOMB EL MARQUIZZICALVINNAGANNASSAU THROUGH THE MARQUIZZING-GLASS PROSE ROYCE CARWASHED AWAY BY SPEECH ELECTRAVELLOASSUSPIRORATORIO MORTES MITHRASH MYSELF & PUSSEIDON MCLAUGH THALATTA BULLDANCE WATER WATER EVERYDITE MNVES PRESLEY AGNI B. UNCLE RAMMAN ASSHUR ADADA SEX APIS TOL MERWER MERWER MARQUÈSACRETAN BULLDANCEPHALLOWERREGION ATOMIC BOMBIVALENCEPHALLOWER LOWER DE MER VAN WER TOROTOROTOWER INFERNOAHH ADESSAU TATTAUREAU KUDOMINOTAUREAU ONÈ OWAUT AUREAU ONE OWAUTAUREAU MYTHOS MYSELF & EAU DE COLONIES RIVERBAL TRIPPING STOP TRIPPIN' GOGO MW/THE FLOWWOWWOW SPACE MARIMBASS VIBRAPHONICCLONIC SEIZURE TOROTONY OVERWATER MOTION MUSIC IRON MAIDEN VOYAGE JAZZ ORCHESTRIKE JUDAS PRESLEY AQUA-SKIZZEEFRENIA PRINCE CHARLES MINGUSHING CONTRA BAHHASSA (CONTRA BASSP ACID MARQUÈSA) ONE MANDRILDEODATOROTOTHÈME & TABULL TVOODOO-BOP MCNUTTERRANCE THE CHINASS APPELLEGRINOCEROS ANIMALSDE MARKIES VAN WATER EL MARQUÈSADOMASOCHIZOOVERRAINDANCE EROSIT HALATTABUMBUMBILLA GIRAFAMME POP MUSIC MACHI

NE JAZZ ORCHESTRANGLES TONY VISCONTI / FEDERIC
O FÉLINE FÉLINE PRINCE CHARLES MANGOES PENIS
ES & EGOS IN THE RUBBER SOUL CITY BEATLES BI
G BAND PÄRT 1 BACH TO BACH ARNOAH PÄRTAUD IS
LANDAMANDÄDÄMON SAVONICCLONIC SEASSHORUSSOLO
THE MARQUESSOUNDFLOOD FREE GALOPISPEE HOLAND
IZZEE GULLOOPEE FREEZBEE RIVERS LIBRE AQUA L
IBRA WATER WATER EVERYTHING MASTER BATE'S AE
RATED SPRINGWATER WATERRORSCHACHISSOUL LET I
T RAIN LET IT BMW BEATLAS MARQUESAS WOOO LIT
E IAMMADDEUS SALVATAUREAU RIVERRIER C'EST OP
OU! THE MARQUESSHE-MALE MARQUIS DE SADEÈSSEA
SS THE WHORROAR THE WHORROAR A REAL MOTHERWE
LLES ÎLES FOR YAQUASPIN LENNONDADA BERLINNON
WE ARE FRANTIQUITY DIZZEE GALILEOLESBEE ISSU
CK NEWTON TRAMPETHERMAL RIGOROCK STRAVINCENT
VAN GAUGAUGUIN ONE MANNSEE PROSE-DROPONGORIL
LA PYGMAEUS WEST SPACE DADANUBASS WATER WATE
R EVERYDAY ST. PETER BLAKESIDE FANTASTIC VOY
AGE EL MARQUESSGT. PEPPER SAUCE UNCLE RAMLÖS
ADÖMASÖ K.C./D.C. & THE SUNSHINE BAND WAU WA
U WAU WOWWOWWOW THALATTABASCOBRAHMANIC LAUTB
URST PSICKIATRICKA PRICK! SGT. PEPPER SOURCE
TOROCKNTOROLL SUNTVLOEDWIG AFROBEETHOVEN PLA
Y LAUTBIRSTING SIR JOHN POPE ODDISSEEING THR
OUGH SEE THROUGH YOU ADOLF WÖLFLEIN & THE BR
IDES OF FUNKENSTEIN WE ARE FRANTIQUITY EL MA
RKEY WEST FLORIDADA PERRIER COMOMO THE MUD P
OOL THE BIG PEEL A LIFE ON THE OCEAN WAVE LÀ
-BASS JAN ADER MARQUIS ICONNECTION RHEA-OANN
ES CONCRETE POUR MUD FLOWWOWWOW MIRROR TRAVE
L DHARMA CHAMELEON SPINDARUSHING PAST FUNKAD
ALLAS MARQUESAS FLY LIKE AN EGO URQUELLE FON

QUELLE MARQUIS MADRE DE DIOS PHUKK IT UPUU O URQUELLENNOEN EGGEEPIE-LAND WALRUSSOLO OURSO UND WELLENNON & ONOMATOPEYOTL MUPI MUPI MOBY MOBY DICKA PIGUANALIFF ATOLL SHANTIH SHANTIH SHANTIQUITY ONE HOURQUELLENNOUN & YOYOKO ONO MATOPEYOTTO DIXIE-LAND WATER WATERRESTREVIBR AHMANICCLONIC ICONOMATO PEEE LITE! K.C./BEEG EES LET IT BEEGEES SHAKE YOUR BOOTY DIONYSOS -KIDD FUNKADELIC DO-WOP WAS NOET WASSIR NOSE RINGO SILVER STARSHIP BIG BAND JOHN LENNON-S TOP PRINCE CHARLIE PARKERILLAS MARQUESAS LET IT BEATLE JOHN CAVE & NICK CAGE SLY STONE AG E MAGIC SEX MAGIC WE ARE SHANTIQUITY THE FOU NTAIN MONUMENT WATER WATERFALLUZ DE SOL LEWI TTER WITTER MAGGI SEX MAGGI ONE MANGROOVE RI NGO ALL-STARR MARRIO MERZBOSCHAMOONJOURNEY T O ARNHEMLAND MOBY MOBY DICKA (H) PRIK WAS NO ET WASSIR JOHN POPE ODDISSEEING THROUGH LOOK ING GLASS BABEL/ZIGGURAT MIRROR MIAMI MYSELF & MEANDERING ISLAND COSMICK EGG MAN KAMIKUDO KUMIKADO EL MARQUISGEOMATERNILE GOOSE TALKIN G? NANA LIFFEY-STRAUSS CLOUDING OVER BEETHOV EN MINOTAUROMACHAMELEON JOURNEYING THRUÏDE M ARKIES VAN WATERRALLABYRANCE 1ST KILLOWATTER WATTER AQUA DADAGIO EL MARQUESSEXUALLEGRETTO TEM & TABU ACQUA HOMO LEONARDO DA VINCENTURI O MERZBOOTSEAS NEW RUBBER BIG BAND BÜTTZEECC E HOMO GG ALLINN ON THE MOVE ECCECCECCE HOMO OURSON WELLES MARQUISES OURSOUND FREE OURSON LASWELLES MARQUISES GNUKU HIVA MININANA HÄAG EN-DAQUADAZSUCK KISS MY EGG SUN MOON STARS P A KUA NEW GUINEA MAORI MAORI HOLD ON TIDE LE MARQUISSAUT D'EAU REMYSELF & I ALL ABUNK FOR

TARARAT! CALL M THE BIG POOLYGLOTTONY BACH-T
O-BUCK TOMTOM CLUB FUCK CARLOS FREGTMAN SHAM
AN MUSIC FOR DEEP ENCHANTMENT GRAND PAPPY DU
PLENTY MOMMY WHERE'S DADDY BABALONGLEGGLES S
PACID JAZZOETRY RIVERRANSOME KUTIBERRY FIELD
S FOREVER NAME-SHADING HOLLAND MILK IS A QUE
ER ARRANGEMENT WRITING THROUGH DE MARKIES VA
N WATER EVER A-COMING EVER A-GOING IRISH GIP
SY MEETING OF THE WATERS SEA GIPSY H2O CINEM
A SEA OF DREAMS EL MARQUESAN GRAMMÈRDESTRUCT
ION ABOREDGEONILE WATERRORATORIOOLLANDAMAN KR
IEG THE FUNK BISONS IS BISONS PLAY POPEYE AN
TIPOP HOLLAND FUNKIEFERALLSDELITTERRA TOUCHE
ATERRESTREAMADEUS MOUSSARTAUDIOMUTT MARQUÈSA
TANTANGO GUINEANDERTELLING THE TALE OF WATER
HOLELAND BÉLA TARRKOVSKI & I NO CORRIDA! HOL
LAND STARFUCKING DE MARKIES VAN WATER IN ECH
OLAND BOOHOORU! BOOHOORU! LADONILE MARQUIS T
RAMPÈRE BLINDNÄSS TREVISION & DEEPILEPSYCHOC
EAN IN DARKNÄSSPACE BAZZAKARMARKIESLAND SGT.
PEPPER'S ODILONELY REDONNY SIDE UP OSMUNDUSC
HAMALE ANUS OSMUNDUS ONE OWAU MADNÄSS SILENC
E WATER FIRE BLITZCREEK LEFONQUE ONE MANTRAM
P ONE MANTRAMPLADONITELLO ALLABOUT LONELY ON
ELY LADONI KNOW! NO DERRIDA DADA-MERIKA DA
DA-FRIKA ET TU BUNGALOW BILL HEALY SELASSEAS
BLACKBIRD PIGGIES DANCE JANETALIA JACKSONIAN
EPICCLIPSYNTHÈSEIZURE IN THE KUDONATELLONELY
HEARTSSCHLAGG SOUNDGARDEN SUPER UNKNOWN LENN
ON-STOP/DON'T STOP THE MUSIC DIONYSOS KID CHA
RLEMAGNE LENNON DA VINCI DREAM LANGUAGE ONE?
WOLF THE GANGES RAMMADDEUS MOZZY & IZZY STAR
ISSY SOUL MATTHEW MARKIES LUKE & JOHN LENNON

IF YOU DO IT DO IT NOW! ÈREVERRAIN RAIN RAIN RAMSTERDAMADAM TO INFININETIES! ONE OWAU MAR ANATHALATTAHITI HINDUSCHAMPOOLAVICOLLANDADADAD A DEE DADADA JOHN LEMON KURTZ KOBANA SGT. PE PPINOA-ROTUNNOA PANTHALATTA X-RHEI THE MARQU ESSERENADE SADE SADE LIZZY IZZY SOLLUBULL WO OO LITE AMADEUS AQUADADAGIOTTOTEM I M THE EG O MAN SHAMMAN 69 BEST BEFORE SEE TOPPOP! VIV AT BACCHUS LEBE! SO LET BACCHUS E'EN CALL! I NN INN! INN INN! URQUALLE MARQUIS IN NIAGARA WALZHAMMER-DISSEAZZEELAND AQUATSCHAMALE MARQ UIS AQUASSELYING ABUTTERRANCE KILLOWWETTER W ETTERRANCEPHALLOCRÈME AQUALMARQUEST FOR POWE R AQUALITIDES TO GLORY EL MARQUELLWASSER AQU ALMING ALL ABUTTERRANCE KILLOWWATT WATT WATT ROTTERDAM IN HELL AMSTERDOOMNOCEAN JUNKADELA CQUALONELY HEARTSSCHLAGER IN THE STRAVINCENT URIO VAN GOGHADFATTWAZZAG WAZZAG! WAZZAG! EV ERYONE NATION UNDER A GROOVE! ÈDEN ÈDEN ÈDEN ADÂMEVENEZIAGARA FALLSETTHOTHÈMES WAZZAGG WA ZZAGG WAZZAGGOMANIAGURU FALLSUCKA PIGGIGG PI GGIGGY POPPOP POPPOPPY POPEYEGGEGG EGGEGG! U RQUELLASTICITIES OF WATER A'DAMÉVENEZIA'DAMÉ VENEZIA'DAMÉVENEZIATMÜLTRANSGRESSION RÉCITIE S OF AQUASPEECH GEOWATERRAMMARQUESS AQUAPUNN ING IN GEONESEASH GRAVE O'CLOCKWORK ORANGE N UMINOUSSAU EGO-CONSIOUXIE IN THE MARQUESSPAC E ABYSS ALPHABUTTERRANCE KILOWATTPOWER META- WORDSELLIT SELLIT! EGGO HOME PRIMAORI WATERR ED HOTTENTHOTH VOODOO CHILI PEPPUASS REBURST ING OUT LAUT COMES THE EGG EGGO EGGOGO MW/T HE FLOWFLITTERRATURHINE METAMORFAUSSEAS EL M ARQUESAN MARCOHERANCE KILOWATTERRANCE WATTER

RANCE CAPUT NILINEA SERPENTINAVEN CLIO CLITO ROTORISE SUNNY HALOVE YOURBAN KUMSQUATTERRAI NDANCESQUADDER MARQUISSA'RE A'RE A'REALITEEE METAMORFOXY WATERBABIES FLUTTING IN LAKE PER RIO KHARMA COMOLION KING ELVISHNUKU HIVACQUA VÉLAVALLANCE TEST ONE TWO MORE MENS MORE WOR DWASHUPSTREAMADEUS H-BOMBECKEN TO BECKEN ONE OWAUFBAUWOWWOW ONE OWAUFEINANDERRIDAZS SPACE BASSINASSAPPELLEGRINOUSEROES WHO GOT THE SPA CE BASS THALATTABOY? THE MUD POOLABULLY BAAL ABILLYBOOTSY'S RUBBER BANDY WARHOLLANDESCAPE BLITZ ON MY MINDKRIEG MATTER MATTERHORN ARRA NGEMENTAL BRECKERDOWN LADABOOONG VLADABOONG ASMATTERHORNY HORNAMENTAL BRECKERDOWN BROTHE RS OOOOOJIBWATERREXSTREAMADEUS PARRY COMOZAR T THE PSYCHÂMELÉON EL MARCASMATTERREBEL REBE L BOWIE BROTHERS HORNS & MOZARTY SMASHFLUTES MIWOK MYSELF & MOHAWK GRAND RIVERREBELLAS MA RQUESAS JOHAN SEABEASTION BACH TO THE BRICKO LUTION BRIQQIQUE BRIQQIQUE! ROBERT FRASERRUN AWAY SGT. BUBBILKO'S LOLONELY HERZATZAUBERFL OODDISSEE THROUGH YOU HOPI HOPI ZUNI ZUNI MY MYTHOMORFOSSILES ÎLES MAREXQUISES CUM FUNKEY WEST THE BOMBISONNENUNTERGANGES HOLY WATERRE ON THE MAPPA MAPPA MAPPA MUNDRIAAN STEPPE BY STEPPE THE BISONNENSYSTEM BISONS IS BISONS I S BISONS OOOOOCEANIAGARABORIGIPEL & OOOOOMAH A SECRET SOCIETIES PAWNEE PAWNEE PAWNEE EVOC ATION ORANGE/LADY SUN UNCLE JAMES FRAZERRUNA WAY ALOONIETSCHIZZEREADY-MADE FOR FLOODING A BORIDGERIDOO-BOPPEGUNS BASSPACIDGERIDOO-BE-B OPPOP-DIDGERIDOOOOOCEANIAQUASSPACE BULLAQUAB BALLASSPACIDGERIDO IT DO-IT-YOURSELF-BEWEGUN

G DIDGERIDOURBARRAQUELLASWELLAS MARQUEUSSEAS
DIDGERIDEAU REMY MYSELFATION & AÏGEAU AÏGEAU
TRANSTIGRESSING WATERRUIN PISS PSICKIATRICKA
PRICKA PRICK DANCES & MOREROSMESSIAMESSOAPOT
AMIAGARA FALLSLUTTERRANCE KALEIDOSCOPPERRY E
SKICOMO & AÏGEAU MW/THE GLOWGLITTERRATURTLE
S WE ARE WATER WE A'RE A'RE A'RE WAH-WAH WAH
-WAH EVERMORE WAH-WAH SPIRIT ANCESTOROARATOR
IO MORTES BLITZKREEK THE FONQUE THE REALM OF
A RAIN QUEEN THE MENOMINITOROARATORIOOOOO CA
LL MMMMM THE BIG PEUL AQUA-FRIKA TOTEM ET TA
BOUEEEK-KEEE TIWI ARE TEWA TEWA WINNEBAGO CHI
PPEWATERRE ARANDADA HORDE MARKIES VAN WATTHA
LATTABOUEEEKKEEE HOMOHEAVY METALSDE MARQUESS
AMOA-MOA EVERMOA BULLKLEY RIVERURQUELLÉVI-ST
RAUSS MARQUESAN JOURNEY TO URNHEIMMATTERLAND
JFKLEE PEUL KLEE JOSEPH KLEE POOL KLEEFMAN M
ARCASSIOUX KLEE KLANGING TO THE ASSOCIETY IA
TMÜLTRANSGREASE IS THE WORD IS THE MOTION OR
ANGE NAUSEA FREI FLOW FEMMISSEMENTAL ILLNÄSS
AUT D'EAU DIDGERIDDLES & BASSOLORALLIES HÂPI
HÂPI HOPI HOPICASSOAPI-FUNKARAFA AKINNAGANSE
AWAKE WIDEAWELT THE OOOOOCEAN THE ABEUYSSHE-
MÂBOUEASSEALLSDE MARKIES VAN WATERRACOTTAURU
S CLITORUS STIMULATOR UPRIVERDUREGEN EL MARK
ASR EL YAHUDSON JARRY COMOCEAN ABORIGINAL MA
STER DUB BAGDAD DADA BASS SPERMINAL NUCLARAM
EL BOMBBOMB & CHOCOLAT MARQUIS WAH-WAH-WAH N
EZ-NEZ-NEZ DMVW THE SPACE BAS-BALALAIKA IN T
HE KALVIN KLINIK WASH & GOD TELEVANGELLY SYP
HILAS FREAK OUT FIRE & RAINWATER WATER EVERY
WHIRLPOOLAFUCKALLES ÎLINXUCK OR JAMBISTA! TR
ANSMITTELEUROPA DANUBE MW POP MUSIK JASS THE

ACQUATOMBOMB MAR-KEYS MEMPHIS EXAPPERIENCE T
HE LEAU COUNTRIES BASIE BASIE AFRICAN SUNRIS
E STEP RIGHT UP SUN KING SUNNY ADÉONYSOS CAL
L-CARL ANDRÉ RAM ON WOUNDED NIETZSCHE! LÀ-BA
SSÀ-FEU-LEAU THE CLINTON CLINICCLONIC ATTICC
A PRICKAOS AQUA-PHALLOILANDICAQUAPHONICCLONI
C BIONYSIAMESOPOTTO È MEZZOPOTAMIACCHAOS ZAR
ATHUSTALKERRUNWAHWAH MÄRKISCHER SANDBLAST IM
AGE BREAKING MARKIES CROSSTALKING IN TUBES TR
ILOKOLLIDEMOTIFFOLLY GURU BAHASA TUTU TRANSS
HIMMALLAYYA MARKAS BESAR WOLFGANGES DRUMADEU
S RIVERRANJ MEIN RAAHAT MINOO PURSHOTTAMTAMB
URUNDIONYS.O.S. MOTHERS FUNEST DOUBLE BASS D
RUMMING THE BOMBARTAUD ESPATIALICE D1 D2 D3-
DE MARKIES VAN WATER & AIR BAHHASSADE BEELDE
NSTORMFLOODGATE 2001999 ÈSPACE BASSOTERICKAC
QUAPRIAPUSSYKANT INDIAN TONICCLONIC ARSCHWEP
ILEPSY LET IT SCHWEPPES THE AFTER SHIVA EPIL
ÈSSIA! EPILÈSSIA! FLUTTOURISMOHEAVY NO REMER
SY BECK MARQUESAN BULL-SACRIFICE IN SPAESI B
ASSIOUXIE WATERWORLDWAR LÀ-BASSULEAU MON ONC
LE JAM BOMBUMMING HOLLAND WASCHING THE GUILT
IGNITZSCHING THE BOMBUANDIONIC HEAVY RIDE HI
IS YOUR HI HAT CHINESE LEOPARD RIDER ECKHARD
T LET IT FLOWLANDS ANOTHER BEHEMOTHER FUREUR
SPYROBASSIAMESOPOTAMOUSSAMPLIFUNNDRUMMEGANSE
AWAKE UP LOOSE BOOTY OH GEORGE PERRÈC PERRÈC
LEEKEE COMOLEON CLINTON & HUGO BALL HAILEY S
EELLASSIE-MAELSTRÖMSEXPLAUSSION SPASSIBASSMO
RE PROESCHIZOCEAN TABLATTABLAVATSKY-WATER EL
MARQUESAN SKY OPENER H2O'CLOCKWORK ORANGANES
HAMANUS DEVI DEVI SING-SINGALONG ONE OOH, OOW
OWAUTAUROTATTOURROCK ARHÔNE THE CLOCKWORREKK

WORREKK! SQUEEZE THE FRUIT (WALTER ORANGE) A
RHÔNE ARHÔNE ARHÔNE THE WORRELL WORRELL PLAY
LOUD DON'T FLASH YOUR IVORYWHORE HOLLANDSTAND
ING 2000 STONE IN ONE SOCK WATTIME WATTIME W
ATTIME IZEUT? OOHH,OOWW OOHH,LO! ONE OWAUDIO
VISUALSDE MARKIES VAN WATER EL MARCOULE MARQ
UISDELUGÉOMATERRA INCOGNITABLATTABLATTABLATT
ABOOTSITARRISE USTAD ABDUL HALIM JAFFER KHAN
ORAGGA ARAABIS ZIGGURAT STARDUSTORTION DELAY
LAMA DELAI LAI DREAMTIME MEKKAMA WATTIME IZU
TRASH THE MARQUESSPEED METAL BASSCHÖPFUNG TE
XTOBJECT-BOX LYNCHMEATAPHOBIAGARA WALZHAMMER
DISNEYTZSCHE WATERFALLUS UP YOURQUELLE CUL L
A FRANCE EN ATTENDANT LE GODE EL MARQUESACRÉ
TANTRIC BULLY-DANCING U.S.A. AMERICA EATS IT
S JUNK EUFRIED-TIGREASE IS THE WORDURHEIN EP
ILESSIVA EPILESSIVA THE MAREXQUISSOAPOCALYPS
YNTHESEA-SHORES NAUMANTRAVOLTA RIVERRUNDFUNKA
DELIC SHETHERMALE DIOS DEL SOULTRANSVESTRITO
N BOMBIZARROTATING IN DELPHILOSODOMY VAS NOT
VAS LAV NOT WAR DANCING IN THE SUN SUN RÂ WE
ARE IN THE FUTURE WATT WATT-A-MACEO PARKERIL
LA MARQUISE D'ORANGEADE SADE SATO SATO DAFKA
P DE SADELICK SUCKADURUTTI DANCE II HILARY O
NE MANN TWO RIVERS FINDING THE SEA MARCUS MI
LLERRELLAS MARQUESAS DE MENDOZAPP! STRANGE F
RUIT SOLAR BLUE 'N BOOGIE UNDER THE BRIDGEWA
TER SUNSET & BLUE UNTIL THE RAIN COMES DON W
AHWAH CHERRY THE MAN W/THE HORNY HORNAMENTA
L DIZZIGGILLOOPSUCUNDURUTTI COLUMN SPACE JAZ
Z RÈVERIVERIES MILES DAVISHNUKU HIVA EL MARQ
UESSHHHA PEACEFUL HOPI HOPI HÂPI HÂPI IF ONL
Y THIS BASS COULD TALK TRISTANLEY MARQUISOLD

E & BOOTSILLY PUTTO FLUTTING ON WATERRE WATE
RRE FANNIETTY-GROTTY SIX I NEED 7 LYNCHES OR
MORE BOBBITT BOBBITT 66 FIGURES ONE HOUR GRA
NDMOTHERFUNK RAILROADMOVIES THE ALPHABETT SH
A MAN THE TELEPHANT MANTRAMPÈRE UBULLABYRINTH
MANIÈRAZORRINE EAU DE COLONELY HIGHWAY TO HE
LLBORG BLUE VENUS IMPULSADER MARQUIS VON OOO
H HOTEL DE SADE SADE TV GORILLA IN SPACE BAS
SOAP POP-OPERABIESPACE BASSIAMAZE TWIN SPEAK
ABULL OR TWINTY NEON PEAKS ACROSS THE ELEVEN
TOUX MOUNTAIN KAMA KAMAH KAMAHL CHÛTERRA FIR
MATER DOLOROSADOLORENA BOBBITCH DUB THE CALL
-IN TV-EXORCIRCUMFISSIONISTS PLAYING THE ELE
PHANT SONG REGIMENTAL VERSION GROOVE O'CLOCK
BULL BEEF BANG UP JURASSICK ARSE BABY PSYCO
TIC BABY BUTTUH-BUTTOH HENRY THE HORSE! MIRO
MIRO ON THE WALL ALL MARQUESSENTIALL FIRE FI
RE AGNIETZSCHAMMALETHE COSMOSIS THE FALLOGOS
ICKA PRIKKAOSIRI-SUR-MÈR DIONYSOS ANTHROPORR
AISTES VYPERTEXTOURQUELLEVIATHANIC DON'T PANI
CCACQUA SPACE FLOODDISSEAS RAISONABOMINNABEL
MARQUINTA ESSENTIAMATERRA FIRMARQUESS HOM HO
M UNIUS LIBRILLOLITERRA INCOGNUTTERRORANGANE
SHAMANISMOUSSEAS GUESS WHATER WHATER SPACE B
ASELITZKRIEGGEGG KRIEGGEGG ALL WRITING = PIG
SHIT THERMAFRO EUNUCLEAR SOUNDSETBACHANILES
ÎLES MARQUI SES S.O.S. SCHIZO SOAPOCALYPSO NO
AHH... TEMPORAL GLOBE EPILEPSY PARTIAL SEASHO
RE DISORDER JAMELA ANDERS ZORN MEGA VATTEN D
ITHYRAMBASSADOR GG ALLEN POE-FONG DITHYRAMBÖ
SEXUALSD. TOKLAS LAURA ESCHER HOMO PRINCE CH
ARLIE PARKERILLAS MARQUESAS KEYS IN CYBERFLO
OD MIX ERNST KRETSCHMER OLANDIZZY DELUGILLES

PIE-FUNK RUBBER LÖWELLAS MARQUESAS KEYS LOMB
ROSODOMYSELF & I ATOMIC DOGGIN' AROUNDABOUTZ
EBRAHMAPUTRASHAMALE OLÉ OLÉ PAPUA-PSYCHOPATH
OLL PATHOLLANDMARKIES THE THE MIND BOMB GG-S
TRING BASS & TROUBLE SLY & THE RIVERROBBIE C
UBE LANGUAGE BARRIER WATER BURNING LIKE LOVE
JAMES BLOOD ULMER STAHLVERSION MARKIES VAN
WATERRA HANGAKOGNITANITA GINSBERG RIDING THE
GOLDFINGER GILBERT & GEORGE LIFFEY SKIN SUFF
OCATION SCULPTURE SM 69 G&GG & THE MURDER JU
NKIES THE GILLGILL-MAN BONEY MW MEGAWATT SAD
O RIVER MASO RIVER BARBARELLA BAEKELAND HOTT
AH HOTTAH FLESH GORDON GINGER & FRED HOLLAND
WHAT'S THIS ALL ABOOTSY? BIKINNERSTATE ATOLL
-TALE-TRAIL ARE YOU RHEIN MONSTER VENUS MUNC
HDUSCH HYDRAFLASHBACCHUS PHYTO-HEÂLY-EAUTOBR
ONZANT THE DEEPSLEEPILEPSYCHOSEAS POP-OPERA-
APERTABULLA RASSAVONARAFA TRISTRAMPÈRE UBU &
SÉOULDE! OB YOU PO WE ARE NILE RYTHM & RHEIN
RYTHM & RHEIN WAS NOT WASSIR NOSEA JAZZID RA
INFALLSDILUVIALL WATER WATERRAINTELLECTROSHO
CKING OLLANDA ANADOLL TO BE AMPLIFIRE FIRE E
L MARSHALLSDE MARKIES VAN WATER PEAVY-FUNKAD.
ELIVRANCE BIKINI ATOLLUS ALLABOUT DR. ATOLLA
MOUR UP YOUR ARSCHIROCADE SADE BAPTISMORUROA
QUAQUAQUAQUOI LSDEBILLABONGOES THE BUTTON IN
THE TIBETHAÏTIBERIACQUARIAN VAUDOUCHAMPOOING
HILLYSÉA T.A.Z.MANIAN P.I.L.GRIMAGE TUTUPELO
LO DE RAMPAZOID DISORDER 5333 DOURBARRAQUE D
ULL ODDE SEE PALEOPARDUSCHAMMALE MARQUISSTRA
USSUCK OR FUNQLE D'EAU QUE D'EAU ICKA PYGMEE
MYSELF & ZEUS CHTHONIOS BAEKELAND SCUM LOURD
ES CRUE DELA GROT CALL MADADAME UNCLE PEEPIN

G TOMTOM MIXAVIRA HOLLANDER MARQUIS VON OOHH
HENRY AAHH RICHARD! SPACE BASS.O.STINATO WAT
ER GUSHING FROM THE ROCKNROLL OPERETTE ROCKN
ROLL OPERETTE ROCKNROLL OPERETTE KÖRPERSPRAA
KWASSERFALLAUT MARQUESUNSNAKESKINSKIWASSERWI
RBEL MARDUKE FLAMMENMEER & VORSTENBOSCH ORAN
GE NOUSSOUSSOULÉOU MIND GAMMADIONYSOSSMATOSS
SCHWAPPAP SCHWAPPAP! KÖRPER KÖRPER EVERYWHER
E TRANCE TRAVELLEAU TRANSITARRIDE DE MARKIES
VAN WATERBUFFELLINIGERRAGUAGUAGUAAAAAWK! FEE
FAW FUMATRIX! BULLWHIPPING THE WORD-ASH ZULL
ING ZULPING ZUNGING THE LÂMÉ-CHANT ST.REMY M
AW MUM MYSELF & I OH I ONDA DUNBARREL DUNDUN
DRUM DOINGDOING DENGENG-DENGENG ERUNK ERUNK!
ERUNK ERUNK! EGGA PIGMEESELF & I M THE EGG M
AN THE TAALLATTATTHOOTEMTANZ MCMURDO SOUND &
FISSION RIVERRESPONGE ON NUCLEAR POWER STATI
ONTOSTATION SGT. PEPPEEPING ATOUMTOUM GG ALAD
DINFLAME CLIT CLUB FUCKALL-DSCHUNGOOL BELLAS
WELLE VINNYL ANILE BACHWAH-WAH SPACE BASRÀ W
INTIBERLIN DADALAI LAMA MAA MAAA ROMA HAAGEN
DER MARQUIS VON OH OH! 8 1/2 PAPUASSARAGUINE
AS ECOFUNKING ON THE BEACHES OF BABYLON Z000
ÈSPACE OBBEASSITY MASOPONTAMOUSSOUNDFREE HOA
NG HO HOANG HO HOPI-FANGOGONÂVENUDE FINNAGUA
S WAGNER & RIMBARTAUDELAIRE RAINVERTING WATE
RVALUES IN AUTONGUE DADA FEST ORANG LAUT COM
E LORD JIMI SUN RÂDIONYSOSTAYEN WORLDCHANTIC
RASH ORANG-OETANIC DON'T PANIC SPACEAU-DELÀ-B
ASSISM & X-RAINFALLSDEMENTAL DIZZY SEAS THIS
SIDE UPSIDE DOWN & OUT KHUMB MELARD MELARD T
IKILOTONICCLONIC RAPISCINEMARQUIS SQUEEZE TH
E FREUD ADAM & EVERYWHORE! ONE MANDALASKAMAR

QUESAZZMAT.A.Z.Z TOPPOPEUROPERA QUE TALMUTTE
RRA INCOGNITA EKBERG SUN RÂ IN THE BEGINNING
ATOLL-TALE-TRAÎLES MARQUISES WATERRA WATERRA
EAUDIONYSOS THE MARKISS OF DEATH MOHEAVY MET
ALPHYSICS FUSE MEGAGA HOLLAND TRILOKILOTON B
OMBAY GURUBY KUBISM TRIKILOTONGUESS WETT THA
LASSALIVA! THALASSALIVA! TIKITARLIAMENT PHUN
KADELIC ON THE VOODOO WINTI-NET THALASSODOMY
IN BLUE DUTCHLAND UNTER ALLES WATERREUROPAPU
A NEW GUNNASKULL EUNOCTURNAL EMISSIONARREN P
YR-DANCING WATERMARKIES ELECTRIC MUDSHARKFIN
NAPOOL SHARKCALLING JAMS JAWS 3-DMVW THIS IS
NOT TV CREEP INTO THE VAGINA OF A FEMALE WHA
LE ALIVE HÂPI HÂPI HOPI HOPI MADADAM CALAMIT
Y PSYCHOPOMPING SHIPPSHOPPING THROUGH THE TR
ITSCH TRATSCH POLKE DUSCHKABINEN SAMPLING BA
CK TO THE BURNING FOUNTAIN MUSST MUSST GULA-
GULA TRISAN-TRISAN THE LUCIFERSAL AQUAGROOVE
RAINSANE BRAINDROP-OUT MEDULLA OBLONGADI BLO
NGADA UBUNGABUNGA DE DIFFI DIFFI BEGADUNG ME
GADUNG FATA MORGANA! FATA MORGANA! THE ROYAL
RIVEROTOMANIAGARAPPLAUS FALLSUCK SUCIO SÜSSE
R SUKHETA ORANGE BAY OF WRECKS KETTLE DELLEN
POTTEN OLD WIVES LOS MOLLES BUCK HEAPHY DUNG
QUAT BUSH ENCOUNTER HOTTAH HOTTAH GOD'S MAMA
ASTROLABA KISKITTO BERNARD ABALEMMA EMMA EMB
A EMME EEM EMS EMA ELBE LABE LIPPE LUABALA L
INGE RIO BUSHKILL TONGELREEP HOTTAH TOTTEN G
LACIER TONGUE LOW BUSH LOWER LIBBY-BIESBOS T
HE LICKING RIVER KIZI CUZNA LIKA TONGO TUNGA
TUNGHI TUNGIN HO TONGUE TUNNA TUMA KIZI LIKA
KISKITTO AKITIBI KITTAKITTAOOLOO ALABEMMA EM
MA EMBA EMME EEM EMS EMA FAD GROSS FORSS OLD

ALTE ELDE AULD AUDE CHENIL WOMAN OLD WIVES G
ROTE POTTEN VOLLENHOVER LOWER LICKING CUNNIN
GHAM LYNGUA CUYUNI LUNNA CANNING LINNHE BERN
HARD FINGER LAKES MANU MANU STIKINE LUIKITIL
A UKYKIT AKITIBI WILHELMINA OLD SUKPAI ECKER
OMO ECHO COCKBURN HART HANCOCK KOCHER KOCA C
OXIM COOK KLOK CROOK KOKWOK SNAKE LAKE UTOKO
K KOYUKUK KUKPOWRUK SUCK SAUK SUKLI SUGGI SU
KPAI SÜSSER ZUGER SUCIO SUKHETA SUKHONA INZU
SA SUKHAIN SUCKER HART BRINGS DEEP GORGOS TH
E DEEPS LIKATI SUKHAYA TUNGUSKA FELLA FJÄLLA
HÖFN FELOELASI VAL NISHLIKA KISHORN COW HEAD
AVALIK SEMLIKI SUCUNDURI TATLAWITSUK KUSKOKW
IM WILHELMINA RIVER ORANJE NASSAU NOSSOB NAS
SER BHERI BERAU BERIH GAIL JULIANA JULIANA N
ICKERIE BASHKAUS FAGUS VAGAY VAIGAI FAGÎRA V
AHIRIÀ SAGINAW VAGGATEM FANE FAHI VAHSE FONN
O FENNY KUN KOTT ISKUT COTHI IRKUT KOTTO HAR
I SCHEUR MOESI SPLEET BREEWIJD JULIANA WAMBA
LUWUMBU WOMBUNDERRY CANYAPUNDY SWAMP BURRELL
BURRO BURITI CUTTABURRO ROTTOCK PRÜM ROTT FO
UL GORE SALI VAAL RANCE GUNZA FOYLE GORYN SA
ALE SALIKE SALITO GUNNERUS HELLEGAT KRABBERS
GAT REPULSE BAY ESTOMIZA BRAKMAN FOMICH WABA
SH AWASH WASHAGO THE WASH SOPE MOUSSA FOAM S
AN BERNARD LAKE DE SADE LAKE SUPERIOR BAZA U
LLA BAZIK TUELLA SEVILLA TANZILLA UNADILLA U
MATILLA SALADILLO CASTILLA DOMINICA MARCHESA
WARREGO SADO RIVER SAN BERNARD MASO RIVER GR
EAT SLAVE BEG OBEY BOOTHIA LEFF BOTLEK LICKI
NG TEES BAFFIN KNOCKA BEATON VECHT BATTLE LI
GEN KAFFER MCSWYNES PORKÖTLUSTADIR BERNARD L
EOPOLD FREDERICK EBREHARTZ JULIA KOUROU KHAR

I GOOTFRIEDA PETRE LIBBY-BIESBOS MOND OPEN D
HRINO NIPISI NIPISSO NIPISSL NIPISSIS URIBAN
TE URARICAA CAUBURI CACAOUI FEZA DRAC GIER D
UNG MUCO BUNGA FANGO MESTA CHIESE BOGGAL POO
POO QUABOAG GODBOUT BEERATO DUNAREA DHIARRHI
ZOS EATSUK BERVIE BEAVER ORANGE NOSE NASS NI
SA NESS NERA N'ZO NOSOB NAZAS NUNEZ NAZLU NE
STE NAZYM NAZKO NO'OZ NEUSE NECHE NEISSE NIS
SAN NYSIOS NUECES NASSER NISAVA NISSER NESTO
RE SAGANASH BLUENOSE NEUSIEDLER MOOSENOSE NE
SHAMINY NASI DELLEN KETTLE POTTEN MONO MOGAM
I MARIMARI MARIAGER BEATRIX WILLISMIEN ARMGA
T ARZ CUE AAR ASA CUL AÂSI ACUA CUAO ASCO AS
ID CONN CONA COCO KUKU ANIUK ASHIE AARE HAAR
E KONNE ASSEAN CULLIN AARHUS CONWAY ARSENO C
UIUNI ACIGOL CUEMARI KUKUKUS CONECUH CULLAUN
ASSEGAAI KONNEVESI ASSEKEIFAF ASSISIBOINE BL
ACKCAVE TUNNEL BACKSTAIRS PASSAGE OCEAN HOLE
CAVADONNA CALABONNA JARDINES DE LA REINE GAR
DINERS BAY NULDERNAUW RANSELGAT HOLSPRUIT RE
ITDIEP BEATRIX HOLTEMME HOLLVIKEN VIC FOG VI
G FOXE VICO FUIK VAKH FAXE FEKKE FINKE OFIKI
FUCHUN FOGLIA VAKHSH FICUZZA FAGNANO FUQUENE
AVIEKSTE DRANGAVIK SKALDERVIK CUITO TERGO SH
OVEL OB HINDSVIK RAMAPO RAMSDIEP HINDSMARSCH
GAIL GAIL WAU WAU GILL GILL TITOMA TITALUK T
ITICACA TSITSIKAMA TITTABAWASSEE JULIANA TUA
MADRE BEATRIX ORANJE BOVEN AARE AARE RAMA RA
MA IJ KUM IJ KUM MAHAKAM KARAKOEM PUTAYAMO K
ALAMURRA PONGUNNAK MOORNANYA POOLOWANNA UMZU
HMLAVA RUAMAHANGA KALLKOOPAH BRAHMAPUTRA PON
GIPUTARI RIBAGORZANA BOOLABOOLKAH MOOSEMENGU
NTICKA PRICKASSHO HOLLAND READING EPILEPSY F

OAMGLAS DE PURRAA PURRAA THIS IS THE ANTLOPH
OBIA DIPILUNAS LABIAGUAS SALIVULVA LAVIFAUNA
1STONE TO THE EGGYPSEAMAMMALLÀ-MUNDIOENYSOSS
MATOSS HELLOO HOORAY HORRUS BLUE TURK GUTTER
RAMCAT VS ELECTRIC EGYPT CALL M HELIOPOLIS M
NELVIS MNEMVIS ATOEMIC DOGGODBOUTZILLÀ-BASSP
LATSCHAMANIC ZAPPEN ABBAHHASSADE SADE! HYDRO
CÉFALLEAUGRAMMARQUESSPLASJAHWAHWAH ESPACÉAFI
C OCEANIC FEELING POPUA NEW GENUINE EPILEPSI
E WATER ON THE BRAIN HOLANDA SLOUT UPSUCK TH
E TALKING. DRAUM-KONNA SPEAKING NORSKFROST IN
THE SKY THELUJILLA THELUJILLA! THE MARQUESAN
N-LEIKR LA MÈRKI-STÖNG OLLANDAY-ANADOLLY PAR
TONIC DON'T CLONIC SEESHORE WHAT WHAT'S THE M
ATA HARIVERRENDIONÄSSEA WATER RESAMPLING THE
SOLAR GANGRÂ WASSUR TERRE NOT WASSUR MERRE S
KÖMMSKÖMM VÖMMVÖMM IKUNNLEIKILLINDILLINGER B
OB DILLINGER RAZORRUNNING ARUNDFUNK THE BRAI
N BLOB! BLOB! BLOB! DILLINGINGER & FREDDA ST
AIRWAY TO HIFI EURODISIAC DYLANGINGER & FRED
BONE WOUNDED KNEE NUKU SIVA STEIFFELLINILE T
OWAH-WAH PEDALLAS MARQUESAS TEA FOR THE ZIMM
ERMAN HURRICAN ANDREW SOUND REJECTING TEENAG
E MUTANT NIETZSCHE À-FEU-L'EAU FILLICRÂNES W
AKAN TANKAWAKAN TANKA WAKA/JAWAKA HOT RATS C
HIRATS SPANKING IN FROGGOGH! FROGGOGH! WAH-V
OLUME TUTU IRON COBRA BASS DRUM SOLO DANCE C
ONFORM TO THE RHYTHM LSDOO-BLOPZILLASWELL CO
CKWORKSINGALONG THE MWATCHTOWER TOWER TO WAR
TO WAR MAHRATTA! MAHRATTA! SLADE MASTER O RH
YTHM THE BLONDIE BOOTSY & THE BEASTIE BASSES
MEGA HERZOG RIVERREMIX AQUAPELLA FLESHBACCHU
S FELLINI INTERVIEW GEORGE CLINTON BUTT TO B

UTT RESUSCITATION OF WALKING ON ICE NEAR MÜN
CHEN-PARIS FRIED EISNER FRIED ISEAS SCREAM T
EST ONE MARQUESSAMBURU SUNSET HYDROMISOGEN H
ERACLINTON AQUA BLOB FIAT FLUXAFONKIN' SLITZ
KRIEG WORDWIDE OPEN UP VENUS IM PELZFRÜHSTUC
CO KOSMETIKAMIKAZE! CRUE SEINE DANIS DANIS T
HE PARISSEX-MACHINE PUNCH REACTION IN X-STYL
E SUBSTANZ PARTY ON PLASTIC SOUL SURGERY DIS
ASTERS MAUNNAR AP MERS APOPA WATER WATER EVE
RYWHORMONO BIKINI SCATOLLOGY GG-SPOTPOURRIRE
MWEST ORGANZA MASQUEROS GODE MARKIES CRUE SA
DE DANUS DANUS LET IT RAIN LET IT RAIN ORANG
E CARLOS HALOMARQUESAN RIFFERRARISTHOTALLOS-
MATERRA PUTANAVEN OECHAHIS OECHAHIS! POPM PO
PM! M PEOPLE RENAISSANCE BOMB-MUTT HARD TV T
RANSZENSEXUALLIES GILBERT THE BOTTLE & GEORG
E THE GLASS THE MAKING WAY FOR MORAL WORKS I
N THE MODERN WORLD FOREVER RUBBING REASON DO
WN YOUR EARDRUM WATT EAU WATT EAU GILLES DEL
UCIA ENTRE DOS AGUAS LE CAMARQUIS TAURUSTIQU
E! THELONIEST MONKABOUT WALKABOUT SGT. GERMA
IN-ENLIL FIXERCY-POISSEAVOODOO JIZZ DEAD HOT
PENIS VIANDE SADE LISADE LISADE ZEN-POP-OPER
APOCALYPSOAPOCALYPSOAPSODOMY NOW! RAINHARD T
HE VIXEN GG&GG-SPOUT ALLADDINFLAME TWIN SPEA
K EXPERIENCE WORLD IRRIGATION DEMONATION UT?
HO! RAINFINITY-NETSEXPLOSHIVA MINIKINI AQUAT
OLL ATOLL ATOLLAND DADATABLASTING EROTIKON-T
IKINI ATOLL EL MARQUESSAIS NUCLÉAIRES SCUMMI
LINGUSHING AQUATONGUESS VATTENFALLUCY IN THE
SKY ÉCUMMILLINGAMES MURURORSCHACH TESTING ON
E OWAH WAN OWAU BEFORE OWAH OWAH TOWAW TOWAW
THERMO NUCLEAR SPYROLFOAM INNER CIRCLE MUSIC

MACHINE WALK ON WATERMARQUESSANTATTAK LEAU L
ITERRA HANGACOGNITA EL MARQUESSACRÉOLE MARQU
IS WATER WATER EVERYWORD'S A BEAT OF MY HEAR
T THELONIOUS M INK DE DEVILLES MARQUISES EAU
TELLUS-MATRAS ALLASWELL GODBOUTCHIRATTLE & R
OLL MESOPOTAMIË TVC15 SHAKE ZIGURATTLE & ROL
L OPERATELSLANGEL DUSTEIFFELAS COCK TV TOWER
CLAUDIA KUTIKIEFFERRUNNITT RUNNITT! TÖGREASS
U-FRIPP ÄASSCREAMENT THE HIGH PRESTIGER TIGE
R U-FRIPPITT FRIPP ITT ECHOLA BULLE MARQUIS S
PONGILLACQUA SPOUTTERRABULLBULL-ALL-ALL-IN G
ERMANIC-DEPRESSION ECHOLA-HÖLLANDÉPRESSALIVE
HIGH-HEALING TELLUS-MATERMOHEAVY METELLUS-MA
TERRASHAMANTRAVOLT 22001 ESPUSSY OBBEASTIALI
TTER TABULLASZILLASSHE-MAELSTROMSTOSS OFF GE
T GET OFF! TRISTANTIS VERBIZEUT KALLAXO-FLAM
MING THE ORANJE NASSER RIVERMAAA MAA MA MABU
SE! HOPV HOM OC HOPV HOM OCULO MOTORROTROTTI
NG NARNULFGANG JAMADEUS RAIONARDO THE VINCIN
EMATERRA FIRMATERRA RIFFIRMATERRA RIFFIRTUAL
ICE-KÜBELKA FILMT ARNO ARNOA ARNOA-NOA ARNOY
A-NOYA ARNOAHHH... ARNOLF WÖLFLIREONARDO ÜBE
RZEIGNUNGEN YOUR PORTRAIT 66 FLORIDANCE TAKE
M TO THE GUIDO RENISSANSUCKSTEAM CHAPEL PSYC
HEMICHELORANGELO ACQUAPELLAGOASISTINA ALL-ST
ARKOVSKIWASSERBOMBACCHUSTRA CYBERFLOODING TH
E RIVERRENAISSANSSOURCES WÂWTÂW WÂWTÂW OVARY
WHOREBEL REBEL THE BIG H AMORPHINNATURA & LS
DIEU AFROESEAQUA EPILYPSILON IN MALAYSIAN PA
LE FIRE GRAND MAL ATTICKA PRICKA WAN OWAH ON
E OWAU BEFOAH HAW AURÂH CLINTONIC-CLONIC CLO
WNESQUELLINTON AQUASIA JONESON AFRICAN SPACE
KRAFT-EBBING EBBANG (THE) ESSENTIAL EPILEPSY

GORGY PORGY & HEAVY BASSAGARBATA! BASSAGARBA
TA! ANDAMAN TRUNK ROAD EPILEPSUCKADELIC MARQ
UESSPLATSCHAMANTRA WORDCOME NEPALEPTICKA PRE
ACHER KÂLI KHOLO KUDA BAILA KALI KHOLAZALA K
UDA BAIZALA LET IT BE-BOPP-FUNQUE D'EAU FUNQ
UE D'EAU KUDOO-BOP GUNNAFARA PO-FONQUE ALL-S
TARNOA ARNOA-NOA THE KUBO KUBE DD ALICE D-STR
IPETITIAN LSDTRIPPÛTTITIAN CRUEMASSENFOTOSSM
ATOSS EL MAR EGGITADADADA DEE DADADA FLASHLE
ITMOTIFFOLLITERRATATATA TEE TATATA OMBROPHOB
IAGARA FALLAS MARQUESASQUATSCHAMALAKUTIKIEFE
RRUIN SITUTU MÄRQUISCHER SANDYMOUNT NEVERRES
T METAHOEROBOROSE-BUDDAZEBRAZO DE MARCASA DE
ORANGUTANGOGOGUINEANDERLAND MARQUESSAN MACRO
-MAGNON EL MARCUIT CRUESAMTHALESMOON DIOS DE
L SOUL RED HOT BUTTERED SOL NIGERRAINS NO WA
KE! AKWAABA ORANGES PHALLUS C LA MARQUISEA D
'OSIBISOTTO IN SUB-WOOFING IN THE WATERBULLR
ING BAYREUTHIKAQUABASS ORANGES PHALLUS C SUN
BURST TROUBLE HOLLAND LIE DOWN (A MODERN LOV
E SONG) KRAKAKAKATORA-TORA FLOWING FREE FORE
VER IN MY LIFE ONE OWAH ONE OWAUTOREADOUR TH
E MARQUESSIAMACEO PARKERILLA SAXIS MUNDI MUS
ICK MACCHINAVEN OPIATMULTRA NAVENDRIX CALL M
HELIOOOOMPH DELAMARQUISE D'O TOTEMKORPOOZI G
UN HONEY MA BAKER CORPORELLADELICH GLAUBEATR
ITONICCLONIC HOLANDAMAN EPILEPUSSY POWER ONE
MAN SHOW NO MERCY EL MARKISS THISSEPULTURA S
EX PISTATOLL FREE SPEECH FOR THE DUMB EL MAR
QUÈSPUMARKIESPUMAH-MAH WAH-WAH PAROLE OVER B
EETHOVEN! BUTT TO WATERRORANGE WARRATIONAL V
ASLAVALANCHE OCEANDER CULPAPUASS SCHIZOHARLE
QUINNAKUTI VASLAVATAR NIJINSKY WARDANCING IN

HOTEL DE HOLLANDE AQUANTA AQUA! VANN OWAH VA
NN OWAU DE MARKIES VANNSINNAGUNA WATERFALLOU
T ANALLEVIUS LEMNIUS ONE MAN CHAUVETTSTOOL S
TURM & DRECK NASSAU DAY SHORTY GEORGE THE MA
RQUESSEA-BREEZIN' IN THE LOW COUNTRIES BASIE
BASIE WAAN OWAH WAAN OWAH PO-FANGATAUFTAUF W
AI WAI WAI EAU VAI VAI VAI EPILEPSEA-EAGLE H
OMO CUM & SEA HOLLAND LSDIABLE DE MERZAUBERS
PLASHHH! EL MARQUESSEA-WALL OF VOODOO COMING
DOWN COMING DOWN COMING DOWN SPERMAJISS SPER
MATISS SPERMAFISSUCK WAUTAU WAUTAU WAUTAUROM
AJIZZMOHEAVY BASIE = MC2 SPASSEE BASIE ORCHEST
RAUSS & BLUE NILE HEFTI ORANGEMENTS E = MC2001
THE CYBERFLOOD STEP RIGHT UP! TNTIME FOR THE
TVÄRLDSHAVE TRAMPAZOID MARQUESSPUNGILLA MARQ
UÈSADE PUMPAPUA ON THE WAY TO POLYNASSAU THE
MARQUIS DE PUMP PUMPEDO DE MARKIES VANN PUMP
PUMPEDO PADREFILLIO SPEEDOFALLSUCKADELICKAOS
UPRIVERBALLASWELLE KUDO CD.LTD. INFANT SPERM
O COME TO THE WATERS AND THE WILD BLAUB BLAU
B BLAUB YELLO YELLO SHARK MOZART REQUINAM JU
N PEACE HYDREUGEN BLEULER UP JURASSIC MARCAS
CADEMENTIA PRAEGO HOLLAND PABLOPHILIGRAINS W
AKAN TANKA TYPEE AFROBIOAQUASCHIZOARSCHÖPFUN
GHIROSEASHORE ORANG SCHIZOPHRENIASSOUL NIGER
-CONGOGO DUTCH LÜTTERRAPE TOURING AMSTERDAMP
& ROTTERDUMP WATERROTTERRAPE USEMI USEMI QUA
NTA ACQUANTA ACQUANTA ACQUA EL MARQUINTA ESS
ENTIAMATERRA FURMARQUESS FONKIN' W/HEAVY SE
A SEA-ROCKIT ROCKIT JAZZMARAZZ DE MARIE MARI
E HOLD ON TIGHT THE BIG BLEULER UP YOUR ARSC
HAFFENBURG CLUB FUCK HOLZLIMLOM LIM TIMBO LI
MPOPO HOPI HOPI TAAL ATOMIC DOG ATOMIC DOG A

TOMIC DOGGODZILLÀ-BASSPLASH! HOOYERRUN DMC E
SCHER WALK DIS WAY SGT. PEPPERTUAL MOTION WA
TERFALL I HAV! I HAV! NO MERZILLÀ-BASSPLATCH
QUANTA ACQUANTA ACQUANTA ACQUANTA ACQUA EL M
ARCASCADE SADE SADE MEGA WHORE PAUSEAS & PRI
APUSSEIZURES! THE TRAPEZOID ILLUSION (IS JUS
T YOUR HAPPINESS) MWC ESCHER HOMOTION KRAEPE
DOLLING TO THE SPEESCHER-KRAFFTWERK-EBBINGO-
BANGLADUSZEXTRÄAVESTIDES TO GLORY GLORY HALL
ÉLUCY IN THE SKY W/DIAMOND LILLITSCHAMALE O
RAGE HARD SJÖMANIC FRIED SEISCREAMOSIRICE-CR
IME TIME THIS IS NOT TV SPEECHEEZZEE BOOZZEE
HEINZEIKEN BEER PEER PEEP BEE BE LOW FREAQUE
NCY HIGH CAMPLITUDE THOTHE IBISMARQUIS DANUB
ISMARQUESS TUBE-FEEDING OPUN UPON THE CREATI
VE WORLD OF HAIRIVERBIGENERATIVE SPEECH PROD
UCTION OH I OH I GOT LIFE BROTHER WORD UP YO
UR ASSOCIATION NUCLEAR SCHIZOPHASIA SPEECH &
SAMPLADELIC SOUND FEATURES SLY STONE STORY S
TORY NITE NITE! TRANSLETTER FREAK OUTPUT WAT
ERBUFFER IN NON-WORD WRITING DIRECT-ROOT-REA
DING ALEXIA IN WUNDERLAND BEI NACHT NACHT PR
ÄGNANZ STATE-OF-SHOCK-SOUND-SHADOW-ROCKING G
G ELLEINFANT SPERM TARGET WORD RECOÏTUS ECHO
PRAXISTRANSFORMATION TAKE METRAUX THE ODDITO
ROY MUMMORY SPANK TEST ONE TWO PHONAME-TO-GR
AFOAM FONNINAME-TO-GRAMMOFOAMA UNCLE JAMES B
LACKBERRY WHITESNAKE LET IT BE-BOPP-FONQUE D
'EAU QUE D'EAU EL MARQUESAN NORTH SEA-PIG DA
NCEFALLOGRAMMOPHONABONES ACQUASYSTEM LET THE
RE BE BLOOD ORANGE SUNSET & BLUE BRIDGEWATER
AMSTERRAM ROTTERRAP VANNSINNSUCK ACQUETTABOO
TSY BABY MARKIES HYDROPICKA PRICK THE HÂPI H

ÂPI HOOKAH HOOKAH THE MARQUIS VON WATER WATE
R-PIPE-FONK-N IN NAGALAND THE BEASTIE PEPPER
S THE BEAUTY PEPPERS & THE BEASTIE BEATLES W
ADE IN THE WATER HERBIE ALPERT & TIJANA BRAS
S DE MERDE MARKIES VAN WATER TONICCLONIC FOR
THE POTAPHOBIC MAKING SENSE UNIQUEUNUKE TEST
ING ONE TWO OWAH MORUROARNOA-ARNOA MICHELANG
EL FALLIC FLASHBACCHUS UNDER WAH-WAH WAH-WAH
EL MARQUESANTA MARIA MADDALENA DEI PAZZIBBER
SPACE-BASSPLASHING HIROSHIMABUE ARNOA-NOA RE
D HOT CHILLLES ÎLES MARQUISES WOWWOWWOW TOWW
OWWOW ONE MANDRILDOURQUELLWASSIRACUSE LORECC
HIONYSOSMOUSSEZ! MOUSSEZ! DUCHAMPOOS HEALEUS
EAS EAU SAUVAGE HYDRA-STARLIAMENT DUTRONCADE
LIC BLUE VELVET VAN GOGH EARZATZ OCEANOCEANO
HOLLAND EARZADKINEMARKIES VAN GOGH BUSTING M
ARQUIS DE ZADKINEMARKINOSTRADAME BUSTING NOS
TRA DADA FOUNTAIN WATERRUNNING LIQUID SUNSHI
NNAGAGA INUNDATABLASTING THE EPILABYRINTHINA
GE FLUIDS LO! ZONDLESSSS HEARING SUNDLOSSSS
S HOERING AROUNDABOUTSIAMESOPOTAMINIATOUR AB
OLLOCKS JIBBERHODOO JABBERDEAFUNKT SYBILLÀ-F
OU-L'EAU TIME UPRIFF RAFF HYDROJEAN GENIE KR
IEGGILLING DRIFFT-UBBAHN FREI GALOP KALL-KAR
L SAUKJUNK FRIET ECCOLA MARQUISE DODO REMY M
YSELF & I OH HO I BELIEVE IN GOD WE TRUSS ME
YERDAHL EROTIKON-TIKI EXPEDITION HOITY-TOITY
HAITI-TAHITI DER TOR HEYERDAHL & THE RED HOT
CHILI CON-TIKITSCHIFFER NOAH-NOAH NOAHH-NOAH
H HIGGERLADY PIGGERLADY HIGHIGHIGHIGHIGHEYER
DOLLDRUMSTIKI BUMBUMBASSALT DUNDUNDRUMSUCKAD
ELINQUENT TIKI FULWOOD THE HYPERUCOLOSSALT N
ARRENSCHIFFICKON TIKINNECTION TRANCEFALLOGRA

MMARQUEUSAN PROTEST-BEWEGUNG HEIDI HEIDI HEIDI HOLLAND UNDER WATERRA MYSTERRA INUNDADA WATT EAU GILLES ÎLES DELUGES OH I ATOMIC PORC OH GEORGE GERSHWINATRASH BOOTSY-TRAPSODOMY IN BLUE RAINONDATA-BASSPLASHES NETHERWORLD UP RIVERDAMPFUNGHI LSDIONYSOSSIFICATION OF AQUA-TUNGUES SATANIC DON'T PANIC HEIDI HEIDI HEID IONYSOSMOND BROTHERS JOHNSONNY WATERRESADE CALCUTTABOOTSY P-FUNK ALLSDIONYSOSTÉABLAST! QUANTA ACQUANTA ACQUANTA ACQUANTA ACQUANTA ACQUA MWOLFGANGES AMMADUSCHLAMMADUSCHORDER MARQUIS VONAFLESH WASSER EAU DE SOURSEARSE METEMPSYCHO POPERA WAS NOT WASSERGEANT RED HOT CHILI PEPPERS AQUAQUAQUAFONKING IN SUNSET MARQUIS HOTEL POOL BLOODSUGARSEXMAGIKWATERFUCKMILKSPERM GRIS-GRIS MONDO TOPLESS MONDO TABLASS WAN AWA AWAA AWAAA! MA'AMA MA'AMA MA'AMARQUESANTA ACQUANTA ACQUA MARE AGITATTOO LOS MARQUESES LAS MARQUESAS AMOR FATUHUKU TAHUATA HATUTU INTERTONGUE MUTISMUS APHONIA 666 GRAND MALÀ-VÖXTRA-TERRASSADE MARKIESSSAINT MICHAEL ORANGE JORDAN RIVER UNCLE SLAM DOCTOR DUNKENSTEIN H2OOP AMOR FATU HIVA ECCE OMOA P-DUNK MIND TOUR VAS NOT VASLAVERIO MWATERRANCEDANCER UNDERSTANDING BUSHMAN ROCK ARTAUDISSEY LIFE IN THE BUSH OF GEORGE AHHOY AHHOY! YAYOI YAYOI! 1000 BOATSHOWABOUT EL MARKUSAMARKUSAMARKUSAMA SIGMARKUSAMA POOLKA DOT BIKINI ATOLL ATOLL THIS IS THE ENDLESS LOVE-IN FESTIVAL DE MARRAKECH VAN WATERRA-AQUARIUM LES ÎLES MARSCHÉDELLACQUA-TERROARIUM DE MARKIES VAN SIGILLATA REFILLIGRAINS WAXA/JAWAXA HOT CHIRATS RICHAST NIXON ORGY FASHION SHOWWOWWOW WO

WWOWWOW EVERYWHORRY WHORRY DR. DIONAISHIMARU INFINITY-NETSEXPLOSION FLOWWOWWOW SHOWWOWWOW MARCUSAMAMARCUSAMAMARCUS-NECKER-NECKER DRUMP OOL MARCUS WAKE MARSHALL ISLANDFALL CHAIN RE ACTION IN LIMITED POOL (LE KUDOEÎLES) SIGMAR KUSAMARKUSAMARKUSAMA POOLKA DOT HEPPINGER TÖ NISSTEINER ROGASKA-QUELL HEILWASSERBOMBIZENS UAL EXCURSION TAFANASAFARI MARQUESAS UNCLE S AMOA WE WANT SAMOA! EL MARQUESS AGUA DE MANA NTIAL GASIFICADA CONSUMIR PREFEREMENTA ANTES EL FIN DEL MUNDO REMY MYSELF & I NOSTRA DADA BASS ODYSSEA UP YOUR ASSALMA YA SALAMA SOLAN ASSAU VERSUCE WARHOLLAND SKUDO CD.LTD. GULFY WARHOLE IN ONE HOUR BEFORE THE FALLIC FESTIV ALLIC FISTIVAL DE MARRAKECHIRATTLE & ROLL OV ER BEETHOVEN OVERTURES ALEX IN WUNDERLAND HA PPENING ANTI-ARTS ZOBI ZOBI ZOBIZANTI SERENA DE SADE! GOINGOING DENGENG-DENGENG BORA BORA UAL UAL TABLA MOTOWN TAMTAMLA MOTANE UNCLE G EORGE ALLINTUNE UP FOR THE AFRO/ASIAN ECLIPS E TABLA MORGANA! TABLA MORGANA! TABLASSA! TA BLASSA! DRUÏDESSADE MARKIES AQUA BOOGIE MAGI C KNOT WRITING THE MEDICINE MANTRA POPEYE-OP ERABIOSODOMY MYSELF & EGOLATEXTERMINATORO IN HEAVY WATER PRODUCTION PROCESS AWREEETUS AWR IGHTUS DE BAPTISMODERNISMOHAVE EPILEPSY FADE TO BLACKOUT MALAY MISTRAL WEEKS ASTRAL WAKES THE MARQUESSODANAND SADONAND SODONAND SADANA ND NAIMPALLIPULL UPRIGHT UP TABLATTABLACRIMA BUNDUSZAMAN GO AHEAD IN THE RAIN DIEUNUCHAMA N WATERRAINDANCEFALLOGOS MINGUSHING IN WONDE RLAND TELECOMING & COMING DIONYS.O.S. TELEPH ONICCLONIC EPILEPSYBILLÀ-BASSES PSYGOTHIC BA

BY PSYGOTHIC O'JAY.S. BACHADELICK SUCK SUNCU
NT FUNQUELLWASSERBOMBA INDIAN RIVER OCEAN SP
RAY GRAPEFRUIT LOLOVE TO JUJU-I MAGUS U BELA
STEN MAGUS U BETASTEN NORTH SEA-PIGNORANGE N
ASSAU YOLLANDA ANADOLLY RAINCOGNITO FELA KUT
IKIEFERRALISDE MARKIES VAN WATERRRAZORROTORO
BOCOPPER ESKIMOHAVEAU-DÈLA SHAMALE SOLO ZAPP
ZUNAMIS JUJUPITERRA-AQUARINNENRAUM YOUR PORT
RAIT IN THE AQUARIUM & PEOPLE LOOKING (AT) T
HE AQUARIUM DON'T DOÏT KUDOLORES DEL RIONYSOS
HIHI-HELLBORG IN SPACE BASSINASSUNAMIS BOOTS
Y BABY! MARC-MARIE MARCUS-MARKIE MARCUESS-MA
RKIES LE MARQUIS DE BOMBELLES ÎLES MARQUISES
MARANATHALATTABOOTSY'S RUBBER BANDA TAURAPPA
PUA NEW GUINNILUCY WAKATOLLATTACK & RIVERBAL
TERRORCANE SUN RÂIN MW CUM SUICIDE SPACE BAS
SONANCE IN HADESCHGEL ECHOLALIQUELL COPRORAL
EAU DE PARFOAMSTERDAMPF ORANGE JUSTEAM DAFFU
SION DE SADE MWASSACHER MOUSSOAPOCHISMASSEAS
DE MARKIES VAN GOGHOST-DANCE FIREWORSHIPPING
LSDUCHAMPOOLLICKAPRICKA WOMANDA LEARY FLOWWO
W MEGAWATTERRAQUA-TERRAQUA-TERRARIUMBRILLO G
ULF WHORE ONDE DE BOUCHE BABY DOLL SUCK OR F
UCK WHORROLLAND SCOUP DO IT ROCKY RAMBODRILL
ARSE WHORROLLAND TABLATTACITURNING UP PRINCE
WILLIAM BOOTZILAÉU TRANSGRESSYLVANIAGARABIES
BIES MEER & BOSCHAUMMANIZEUTRISTANTIS VERBIS
SHOT UP UP UP TRANSFRIGGARO FRIGGARO FRIGGAR
O TRANSFLUIDIPUSHEMALE JET DO RE MIA PSIQIAT
RIGGER TRIGGER BURNING BRITTITT BRITTITT GIL
BERT THE GEORGEOUS & GEORGINE THE GILL-MAN F
ATA MORGANYMADE FOR FONKIN' IKKAPRIKKAMARQUE
SAN SPASMWOOG BASSEAULEAU-DÈLAFRIKKAEROSPACE

BASSEINE EAGLEPREAGLE MARQUISLES MARQUISEASS
ST. KUDO REMYSELF & AHH THE MARQUESSO-LSDE
LUGÉOMATERRA-AQUARINNENRAUMSCHIFFERREUS ANAL
LIFFELLINILE TOWAH-TOWAH PEDALLASSHE-MOLLY J
IMPUNSEAS AQUA HOMO UNCLE YAK TAPPITANZ-PART
Y TO THE PEOPLES VITELLOISES MARQUIS CHANT M
ARQUIS DANCE VUURQUELLWASSER EAUDIEU EAUDIEU
ESPACE BASSIMILATAURO DIONYSOS-SHIVATICANNIB
ALLA BALLABIALLSDE MARQUÈSCALADE SADE RAMPAZ
OID DOURBARRAQUE DULL ODDYSSEA ANADOLLOBRIGI
DA DADALAILAI LAMA COOL DOWN YOU ARE IN YOUR
ELEMENT AMA'AMA'AMA MA'AMARQUESSTRAVINSKY TH
E FLOOD FLOSSILLABOOTSEA RAINSANE IN THE MAR
QUESAN AQUASYSTEM ONE HOUR OUR DILDOPO CHRIS
TOTEM MARIA DEVI DIVA DEVO CHRISTOSS OFF THE
RECORD BROTHER WATER RESISTER THE MARQUIS OF
OOHH BABY LE COUP D'O LET'S GO! LET'S TANGOR
ILLAST BUDDHAGORAST. REMY FAFAFA HOMOTOROTO-
BASSST. REMEDY ELLE MARQUIS DE BOMBOLLOX UNU
KING THE ALPHABET MANTRANSFORMATION IN SPACE
IN MOTION LIQUID INONDATION THOTHALES WATERN
ITY RIVERMWANK OCEAN BLUE MARQUÈSCADE SADEPR
ESSION IN THE CLINTON CLINIQUE DUSCHREFLEX E
PILEPSY & GEL INTENSIF HYDRATANT HYDRA SÉRUM
BRILLEAUDIOTHERMO NUCLEARASILLÀ-BASSPACE BAS
SAUT D'EAU YOURQUELL'AN-SHE-MILLES ÎLES MARQ
UISES MAHU! MAHU! MAHU! UA TU TE HAKAIKI! ON
E OWAH-OWAH ONE OWAUTONOMIC EPILEPSEE MWATCH
OUT MAJI MAJI MAGICKITSCHLAMMANIC RAINDANCÉP
HALLOA LOA DEEE LITHIUM 6 KARAFFAËLLEAU FUNK
ADELLACQUA ST. MICHELORANGEL FALLS/F-ENCOUNT
ER LEONARDO DADA DOOM PATROL SOME BEUYS KISS
& DONATELLO TRILOK GURTURTUES NINJA HERACLIN

TON AQUA BLOB WATERRITOROARATORIUM OFFRETLES
S BASSOLLOW SAINT PETER BLAKE ALBERT EINSTEI
N WAN OWAU DRY ORANGE ARSCHWEPPESCHHHEISSICK
NASSAU THE BALD & THE BEAUTY PEPPER'S ODILLO
ONELY ARSE CLUB BAND REDONE AQUAMADEUS REX M
ACCHINASSAU EGO ASS WHIPPING WARHOLLANDADA G
RAPUNK GRAPUNK GRAPUNK! BACCHOUCHORUS SHAM R
AGE OUTBURST DE MARKIES VAN WATER PALEONARDO
REMYSELF & AÏGEAU AÏGEAU DRIZZLI GALLOOPISPI
-FUNKAOS MAGIC NOT WRITING SGT. PAPOEASSEPIK
KAPRIKKAOSSUR-MÈR HOPI HOPI HOPI COYOTE TRIE
S TO STEEL THE SUN KUNZUKUNZU WER-WER OWER-O
WER EREG-EREG KUNDRUKUNDRU! LA GÉODE MARKIES
VAN WATER BURNING UP I M ON FIRE OVER YOU HO
LLAND ONE HOWABOUT UT? HO! FROM OM OM THE CR
EATIVE WORLD OF GEORGE CLINTON COMES THE FRE
AK OUT COMES KUDO YOUR IDOL BITCH DICK QUEEN
EMMA DEÈSSEX MACHINE GUN MAAAH MAAH MAH EMMA
NOÈL NÈGRASSEE SUN RÂINCORPORALISDE MARQUESS
OAP-OPERAQUANTA ACQUA SUN RÂINDUROTAUREAU ON
E OWAUTAUREAU WAUTAUREAUDIONIETZSCHEVALL-STA
R CAVEGLI DEEE ZENNAKIN THE HORSES! THE HORS
ES! MARQUESCAPE HOPE VEHINE PO-SHU-MISHUMALE
BUTTERRAINDANCE SAMOAMOA WAUTAUA-TAUA HOLLA
ND ARSEGAPING ON THE HIGHWAY TO HELL WAU MAR
QUESSATANGAROARNOARNOARNO 666 AQUA IN BUCCAT
APULTING HOPI THE HULA MARQUISEAMALE MARQUIS
RIVERRES MWOLFGANG AMADEUS RIGHT AS RAIN ORA
NGE SLUICE OLLANDA ANADOLLOBRIGIDANUBEAH OBE
AH OBEAH! PAPUALU UALU UALUAQUAOUAUH! BACH T
O PUNA PUNA VAITAI VAITAI EVERYWAH-WAH PEDAL
LAS MARQUESAS WELCOME TO HELLUCINATING HOLLA
ND DELTA-WELLE MARKASI KASIMIYAQUALIASDE MAR

KIES VAN WATER HALLUSEABRÈFICCUTTING THE BAS
S COUNTRIES HÂPI HÂPI AFROSCHIZODIÄQUATORIAL
AFREAK OUT COMES DARTONIN DARTAUDISSEASCUM S
CUM SCUM SPIRITO PARACLINTON DUB DUBLOB DUBL
OBLIN VERSION ECHOLA BULLETHÉATRE DELA CRUEA
UTÉ ARTAULLARTAUDIONYSOS-JEZAGREUS SUPERSTAR
SISTORRESPONTANZZENMENTAL DIZZINEMARQUIS VON
OO, AWFUCK JACCULLOTTOP RIVIÉRES JISSUZY JISS
KRIM SUPERVIXEN LISANTONIN LISARTAUD RIVERRU
INVADO QUEENSLAND GILBERT THE RIVER & QUEBEC
GEORGE THE LAKE EL MARQUESAN IMAGE DESTRUCTI
ON MÈRDA MÈRDA MÈRDA G & G ONE MANZINO'S SHI
T MANIA LA MÈRDE BEELDENSTURMANGRIFFES MARQU
ESAN PSYCHOPATHIC RAGE OUTBURST SÜNDFLUTTERI
NG THE WORD RAPILEPSY BRAINCESSANT TALK TALK
TALK WET WET WET EXCITO-MOTRICELECTRIC DISCH
ARGE LSDELIERZATZIBBERSPACE BASS-LINEA SERPE
NTINA FOAMADISORDER SCUMADISORDER WE ARE ÉCU
MMING & CUMMING FUCKAOSMOUSSHAMPOOLEPSY LUCI
OLEOPARDO FIRE-FLY W/MYTH CUT-UP YOUR ASS &
QUEL-TELLY SOFALLUCY PSYCHO SOLLERS ANALLAZY
SGTELLY EVANGELLY POPPERS DUBBING DUBBING BE
RT KAEMPFERTS KRITICKA PRICKALL-GIRL JUNGFRE
UD AMANDALIDA LEARY NOSTRA DADDY DIRLA DARLA
WORD UPRIVERVE PARKERILLAS MARQUESASSMATASSM
ANIAGARA FALLSDE MARKIES VAN WATER WATERFALL
OUTPOURING OUTCOME WATER THE OUTLEAU TRAMPÈR
E UBULLOTAUROMAGIC VAGUEBONDA BEGGARATOSS OF
FRETT AMOR FATTWATT WATT ECLECTRIC DISCHARGI
NG UR-BASS-SITARLIAMENT WATSON WATSON EVERYW
HERE WANT TO TA-TA YOU BABY MEGA WATT SUNN
Y I LOVE YOU MOFANG BABONE OBSERVE IN MIRROR
TATTHOTHALLES RECALLICKING SHANTIH SHANTIH S

HANTIH MAGIC WHAT MAGIC SPACEMAKER RAPSODADA PALEOPARDUSCHAMALE MARQUISS ICE AGE ART BABY TAN SPERM & CREATIVE GEL REMYSELF POLLUCY IN THE SKY ORANGE ONASSIS NGELAKKA MOGUL INTO T HE CRUYFF SGT. PAPUASS H-BOMBUANDIONIETZSCHI ZOSSMATOSS HOOKAH HOOKAH POP ANALECTROLLYSIS STRAWBURRY MANSFIELD FOREVER BLOCKLOBSTER BI TCH DUBB THE BEST OF BUDDHA LOVIN' SPOONFULL WASH & GOTT MONDRIAAN OPERATION SEA LÖWEAL L ÖWEAL SHAMPULL THE STOP JUST DO IT DO IT WHO 'S AFRAID OF VIRGINIA WÖLFLI & THE TIJUNA BR ASS? THE LONELY BULL (EL TORO SOLOLORENA BOB BITCH) ROGER RAPPITCHIVAGELLY JUNKKOOL PEPPE RTUALSD WATERS' SUNSETSTRIP RADIO-KAOS WELCO ME TO THE MACHINE BLACK BIDDY BOOB MCNUTT TT MATICK MOTOROTOTEM POOLABILLY OCEAN LOVE REA LLY HERZATZUCK URSOUND WELL... CITIZZEN COCK KANE MY BRAIN RAM IT! JAM IT! UP YER POOP CH UTE UPRIVERBALLASCAUX GRANDMURDERFONK' REELR IDE HARD WATERRILOK GURTUBE SYNTFLOD DÉCHARG E CLINTUNE UP LASSIE & GENTLEMEN THE HINDUST RIAL SOUNDVLOED ONE O WAUDIOVISHNUALSDÉBRUIT SEXUELLE MARQUIS DE SADHU SADHU SADHU! WOLFG ANGGA & FRED ICE-CREAMADUSCHGELLY SAVALAS MA RCAUXASSMATASS TRANCE PARTY ON PLASTICCE OMO BANDA TAURAPPMATAPP SIEGFRIEDRICH NUTZSCHALL TECHNUKE NUKE NUKING ON IVENS' DOOR THALES A LL THALES ALL ORAGA NOISEA POOLLUCY IN THE S KIES POOLLANDA ANADOLLOP ABYSSPRACHÉOLÉOPISS EA 6000 MILES DAVISHNUKING WATERBABIES WATCH ING TELLY O TELLY MWATCH TV EPILEPSY THE OPT ICAL DISC NR. 66 FLORANGEL FALLSTRAUSSLCK ON E MAN JUICE 20JAHRHUNDERTWASSER BEEP SHOW IN

THE SPACE MUTANT AGE OF REASON POUSSANIC DON
T PANIC! AGUANACO-FURRY FREAK OUT POOLKAMARQ
UIS ÉTANGOGO DE TAMPTAMPAN ALL ARHÔNE ARHÔNE
MAE WEST INDIES ILLAS MARQUESAS LIGHT/RELIGH
T MY FIRE URANIUM 238 PLUTONIUM 239 DISCO HA
DESSAUDIONYS.O.S. CATCHAMALE 22001953 PLUTON
IUMBRELLA MARQUISEACQUALIBIDOUCHATTERRES WAH
-WAH THERMONUCLEAR REACTOR/CREATOR REACTOROT
OROTO-BASSOLILOQUY NOSTRAUSS DADA MARCOULE J
ETTSTULLÀBULL MWATCHAMALE WAH UP! URRIVERBUM
BABILLA NATOUR ABULLIREBULLEAPPOOL DE MEUSEL
LE MARQUESSAÔNE NATION DÉBORDE MARKIES VAN W
ATER TZARATOSSATHOT GIANT POOL BULLES LES AL
PILLES ÎLES MARCHÉSEAQUA LUMINUKING KAISERRO
AR WILHELM KIEFERRHEIN MA MA MA MA MARQUOISN
É NÉ NÉ MA MA MARNÉ NÉ NÉ ANTENNAVENLOLO EDI
POCALYPSE REX! AQUA LOOMINUKING UNCLE JAMADU
SCH LOVEGANG MOZILLA MARQUISE LET'S DRUÏD BA
BY DRUÏDIPOUSSING THE ACQUATACLASHAMANUS DEI
EI I M ON FIRE WALKING IN ICE WATER WATER EV
ERYWHORRAPERAQUETT RAQUETT! ROCKET TO RIDE H
AVELOOK LSDEPRIMORDIAL MWMARQUEUESS OOOO FIR
E TAKE METHRUÏDE MARKIES VAN WATER MEKKA WAT
TIME IZEUT ONE NUCLEAR GORILLA FOUNTAINHEADF
UCKING NOSTRADAMOCLES NOSTA BABA BABA COOL D
OWN NOOKIE NOOKIE HIVARC DE TRIOOOMPH! OURQU
ELLEONARDO COHENDRIXARD NIXONDATING PSYCHOPU
LCOHENDRIXONDATING WATERGATECRUSHOCKITAMY MY
SELF & I OH DONNA OH I OH OH GIB MIR HONEGG
ER CUYUNIMOHAVE SAMOA LINGUA? URODISNEY-DEEP
LANDALLSD.E.V.O.C.E.A.N. MA MA MA JAJAJA NEZ
NEZ NEZ JUST DO ITTEREN MWMWAN OWAU ONE OWAU
VUURQUELLE MONDE MARKIES VAN WATER DUTCHA WA

NNA GO DUTCHA WANNA GO DUTCH? KAMA KAMAH KAM
AHLSTROOMNETSAVE THE OCEANS OF THE WORLD/THE
ELEPHANTHIASINGASONGALONG MWORDCHANTE MAREXT
ASEA SLY & THE FAMILY DUNBAR-KAY'S BOOGALEAU
INSTANT EPILEPSY EL MARQUESAN MARCOSMIC SLOP
ZILLÀ-BASSPLASHAMPOOL HYDRA-FLUXBECK CASCADA
TABOOTSYBILLASWELLE MARQUIS O FEEL DE LEAU-D
ELA SOULTRA WAVE S.O.S. SCHIZO SOAPOPERAPSOD
Y IN BLUE NILE WATERRACOTTABUTT SUCKSEAWATER
MARQUÈSTEE LOUDER & LOUDER ALPHABELLA STARFO
AM HYDROXY ACID JAZZ & SKIN FLUIDIPEAUDIONYS
OSSATOSS OFFF... IATMOLECULES ÎLES MARQUISES
TIKICKA PRICK TIKILL KILLES ÎLES SEE SEA LO!
UA-POUA-POUA-POU-TUTU-FONK & I. FATU HIVALLY
DOMOAH-MOAH HÉRACLITTLE RICHARD HYDRAPUMPING
IN WATTSTAX WATTSTAX SHAFTER THE RAIN LET IT
RAIN THAÏTIKINI TOSSATOLLASWELL TRISTAN KENT
ON & IZEUT CLINTON FLUTTING ON WATER WATER A
LL THE TIME! ÀFFEU-LOLO FIDEL CASTOR DEÈSSEX
MACHINE PULLOMA PRICKASSUP AÏGEAUÏSTE! AÏGEA
UÏSTE! BABYLON BY BASS TV BUDDADA BASSACRE T
FS/MUCK OR S/FWUCK/7 ORANGE/27 GOLDGELB EVOL
UTION ORANGE/ELECTRIC NATION LET'S CRUYFF YO
EL REBEL REBEL MARDUKE JORDANNUKE MARKASR EL
HUDSON CHERCHEZ LA FOAMM GRAPUNK GRAPUNK GRA
PUNK THOTTANIC DON'T PANICKA PRIK ONE HORRORA
NÎM JIMJAM PAIK ROGER RABBITT RABBITT! KLAUS
WUNDERLICH HAMMOND POPS POP-LIFE POP PRO-LIF
E BABOON COINVOX ONE MANTOVANNY SOUND TRANSM
ISSION DISCO LOOP ONDE DE CHOC TV HIGHWAY TO
HELLBORG TRANSVERSE TYPEE ORDER-DISORDER PHA
SE TRANSITION DIFFERENT IN DIFFERENT IN DIFF
ERENT WATERS HIPHOPPERING SLUTSLITTERING CHI

TCHATTERING EVERYWHERE (THE) ORANGE NASSOULS
UCKING JERKADELTA PLAN MARYLIN MOONSUNNY FEU
RER WALK W/MUCK HADESPACE BASS/MSTERDAMPF E
L MARQUESSAY SUNNY EN ENFÈRNILE WATERRESTREA
M O CONSIOUXNESS ERECCLAMMY MYSALVETO & AÏGE
AUDIONÄSSUPER ECHO & THE IDIPUSHING EARLY ST
ONE AGE SEXUAL MAGIC NOT MAGIC MARQUATSCHIUM
ARRIO MERDE PIGLOBIA HELL HELL HELNO ROTABLA
TTABLASTING HELNO BISON BISON BURNING BRIGHT
TAJ MAHALTA MAREA MAREA HOLD ON TIGHT FIAT F
UCK CALVINNEGANEESE WAXWORK ORANGE OEVERRAGI
NG TABLOODYSSEA GAGANESHANTIH SHANTIH SHANTI
H ICHAOSMOZARTAUDIO MIONYSSAU HAPPI HAPPI HÂ
PI HÂPI API API 7132 M ECHOLA BOMBE MASOGÈNE
SUCK H-BOMB MOTTERRAINCHANTING UNINDENTIFIED
RADIO EVANGELIST DE MARKIES VAN WATER TV TRI
MMING SUN RÂ BOMBOOLLA RADIO MARQUIZEUS MADB
ACHOS SOLSETRONIC UNCLE RAMSTERDAMES IN THE
TABALLABULLBULL-ALL ALLSINASSAUNAVEN ÇRITUAL
BEFORE THE FALLOUT! WAS NOT WASSIRRATIONAL P
ROGRESSEAWÀTERREPETITIVE RAINVERTING ALL THE
TIME OUTFLOW BBCNN WORRELLASERVERSES HONEY I
N THE HORNY HORN MISZILLANIOUS TONKABOUT TAL
KABOUT POP-POP-POP-MUSIK JASS TILL THE END O
F THE WORLD-PERFORMANCE-METAPHYSICAL-TELEPAT
HIC-ACTIVITY IN THE ELECTRONIC CIRCUIT DO NO
T ATTEMPT TO ADJUST YOUR RADIO VIDEO AUM AUM
HEK WOL AK LUB MOR MA! MAGIC WASHUPRIVERBUMB
ABEL-MARDUDEK-DÜRER DE MARKIES VAN WATER EUN
UKING HILVERSUM HOLLAND TV TOWER TOWER WORLD
FMW LONG WAVE RADIONYSOS TV-TRÖNNING BUBBELL
ONELY MEGA HERZ CLUB MEDDIESSEA JATA JATA WU
WU WUWU ONE OWAH-OWAH GLASS TOWER TOWER WATE

R WATER ONE OWAH ONE OWAU TO WAH TO WAR ALLS
DEMOLITERRATOUR POOLABULLY BIKINI ATOLL BOMB
ABEL-MARDUDOK TOWA TOWA EVERYWHERE BRAVOCEAN
IC BUMBABILVERBUMBUMBABEL MARDUDOKUDUCK COCK
VDUDOK ORGYTEXT EL MARDUKOCK VOODOO JUJUNUKE
DUDOK DOK EUNUCH NUCH KUDO COCK EXPLOSION HI
LVERPOLIS DUB PERVERSION THE BOMBABEL MARDUI
KERRUN LSDE ZONNE-ANUSSUCK-REFLEX TNTV TOWER
ERSTÖRROTATTOTEMPLE TOWA TOWA NUKU NUKU HIVA
HIVA ECCE HOMO SWEAT HOMO MARQUESUN RÂDIOS D
EL SOL NUKE NUKE NUKE HILVERSUM 1 MARKELOPIK
KAPRIQUESAN PRYTHMSTICK UP YOUR ERECTRAUM HO
LLAND WAVE SHOCK WAVE HANCOCK VAUDOUDUKE DOU
DUKE LIGHTNING FLASH SOUNDABOUTTERRORSCHAMAL
E DE MARKIES VAN WATER PUNVADING FIRELAND TH
ALATTA! THALATTABOOTSITARLIAMENT-FANNIGAUGUI
NEA PEPPER'S BULLONELY HEARTS FOREVER! THE S
PLASH ORANGES IN WATER HILVERSUMANTRA ORANGU
TANTRUMMING EL MARQUESSOAP PADSINK IN FUNKAM
UDDY WARHOLLANDUDOK TOWA TOWATER TOWATERRE E
L MARQUESSO-LSDIEUNUKE NUKE MUTTSHARKFUNNAFA
RA! YO EL REQUIN DUDOKEANUS COCK VDIEUDOOKEE
SUCK HEILWASSERFAHLSTRÖMFLUT AFRIQUENCY POWE
R POWER TRANSPERANTO MODULOCEAN AWRIDDLES A
WRATTLES TATTOMIC DOUCHAMPADOK TOWER TOWER E
VERYWALKABUTTERED SOUL IN PARIS MWATCH TV BU
DDHA & THE CHOCOLATE BOX PÀROLES PÀROLES PÀR
OLES PLAY LAUTSPEAKING IN SPIELTONGUESS WHO
WHO DUDOC DUDOC! PROFESSOR BAFFIAANSELM TEAS
ER & THE TILLERMANTRA DUNDUNDRUMMING THE RAI
NFALLING OUT LOUD YA HONZA YA HONZA ZAPPATIS
TA MOON UNIT FRANK VINCENT VAN VLIET & GEORG
E DUKE DUKE ON VAUCLUSE À-VAU-L'EAUCLUSE HUA

NG HO! HUANG HO! MELLOW YELLOW RIVERRAIN HAR
D DE FOUCHON NUCLARAMEL BOMBBOMB & CHOCOSLUT
EL MARQUESAN MARCOHENDRIXONIC FELLINI HEAVEN
THIS IS NOT TVAUDOU JIGGABOOLAPULL UPRIVER N
ILE DUBBING NEUROSIS THE WORD AS LAW SHE-GOA
THE BOMB MUSIC IS MY TAUROPLANE GREILES ÎLES
MARCUS ÉCLAIRWATERREVIVALLAS MARQUESAS WE WA
NT BOOTSUZIE QUATROCE & THE BANSHEES HOME SH
EES HOME FROM SEA DRUMPING THE DRAUMPOT SCUM
LAUDESSY THOTTHALES! THOTTHALES! DRINK M DRI
NK MEANDER CULPAPUASS ICKA PRICKISSOCOMES MU
TING THE MAGIC OF WATER GRAFUNK GRAFUNK GRAF
UNK EL MARKISSOPHOROS KOJAKULOCEAN MARQUESSU
CK OR ESP/FUNKUDOGGABILL ATOMTOM BREATH VARI
ATIONSUNK IN WAH-WAH THE MARQUESSYMPHONINNEG
ANS WACCOUSTIC DAMPFINESS WAKELECTRIC MANTRA
WATERBOY WATERBOY LET IT RAIN LET IT RAIN! D
EFUNKEGANS WACCÈS MANIAQUELLWASSER QUESSEXTA
LER FONT VELLATIO AQUAQUI PURROUSPORNER KISS
INGER PASSUGGEROLSTEINER SPRUDEL SPRUDEL OBE
Y YOUR FÜRST BISMARCK LA BULLÉTHE MARQUESSK
ULLABYRANTING WASSIR NOT WASSIR PSYCHOSEXY J
AMES LAST VOODOO PARTY ON PLASMATTICCA HONEY
JESUS WHAT'S PUTSCHNITT PUTSCHNITT DOIN'? SH
IVASO-MOTOREAUTO DADA VISHNU MADMAN ACROSS A
MERICA ADOLF WÖLFLIREMISSOUL-SUFFISCIENCE IN
THE DECIBEL MARDUKEDOOMSDAY-TRIPPITT RIVERRA
GE WETBAND CUT THE WAKE! WRAP-WAURITONIC RAP
E-ROARICLONIC AURIGHTON BUBRECKER BROSMOSERS
JOHNSON CURB DATA LUST KICK IT TO THE CURBIE
CANGAQOCK TV DINNER & 33 1/3 SPIRAL TURNTABL
ATTABLÀ-BAS-BULLALLLAKA-LAKA FIRE FIRE NIGHT
NIGHT MWORLD PACIFIC MUSICANAI DUTTALOS ANGE

LES ÎLES ÎLES SUN MYUNGLE MONSOON RÂ & THE L
OVE UNLIMITED ARCHESTROKE EAULÀ-BASSPACE BLO
ODISSEA KICKA PRICK IT TO THE CURBIE CANCOCK
IT UP PRINCE BERNARD EDWARDS OPEN UP BURN HA
RD MAIN TITLE BLOW UP 1:35 READY OR NOT HOLL
AND THE HERBIE HANGACOCK SOUNDSYSTEM SPEEDBA
LLASWELL MEET AGAIN BOOTZILLATRON CARTERRY T
HE MUNCH JONES HELLBORG JONAS HELLKORG VOCOD
ER MARQUIS VON OH OH LOUIS LOUIS JOHNSONNY R
OCKIT JENKINS KOOL BELLASWELLEQUEINT DUKE DU
KE JOBE JOBE MARCUS MILLERRELLAS MARQUESAS L
ES ÎLES FLOOTTATTOOTTANTES HÂPI HÂPI HOPI HO
PI DON'T FAKE THE FUNK PRINCE CHARLES MINGUS
DIONEERING IN SPILLITTERALL AMSTERDAMPTINÄSS
MEDITATION ON A PAIR OF WIRE-CUTTERS LIVE IN
AMSTERDAM SUCCUMMIKG TO THE INTERGALACTIC FO
NKATIVITY SPACE THE BASIE STEP BY STEP RIGHT
UP AFRIQUE LET THE MUSIC PLAY THE BASSTOSSAT
UTUPELOLO BATABATABLA-BASSPACE BASSPASTORIUS
BASSOLO LIVE FUZZ BOX VOODOO BUGG LIGHT BODY
COBHAMMER EARTH BEAT QUADRANT 4 SPASTORIUS B
ASSTÖRUNG EXPLOSION WAVE IN WATER PLANE EART
H AUTODRIVE SPACE FACTOR STREAM FUNCTION FUT
URE SHOCK EXITATION EL MARQUESSSINTFLUTSCHAM
AGIC ORANTZHABERSPACE BASHEFER WEBIYYO! WEBI
YYO! TORRENTAURRANTING RAIN OR THE ROOB MARE
MARE RAMA RAMA SJÖSPRACHAMANTRASSA RIVERRIGO
RABOOTY MOIST O' ALL DE MARKIES VAN WATER WA
TER INANIMUTE BEING BILLABUMPIN' IN THE ARSE
OF REASON WAU WAU WAU FULLAGAINSTANT WIQA DR
OP OUTCOME THE ORANGE MARSUMATRASSA U-TANGERI
NE DUNDUNDREAMMACHINE MW NAZZAMAN AN-NIL PRO
FILIGRAINS WAQ'AQUA IN LINGUA FRANCULA QUOIQ

UOIQUOIQUOIQUOIQUOIQUOI NO VASELINE PRINCE T
RISTAN TZAURA BERNARD MEGA MERZ IBEX HEAD VI
SPACE BEUYSS/KLAVIER OXYGEN ARP ODYSSEA 2600
STRING BASSPACE BASS MEMORY MOOG MMMMOOOWWWW
HYDROGEN HANGAKOK RAINBATH ON FIRE IKONOBLAS
T WAR MASCHINE AQUA DUBBITT DUBBITT! UNCUT J
UNK READY OR NOT THE BUMBABEL MARDUDOK DISCO
TOWER INFERNO HOLLAND DADAQUATIC RAPOLLOCOCK
CITY DIONISIA EUNUKE EUNUKE NIKE JUST BOBBIT
T FARRELLAS MARQUESAS BONEY MWACO JACO SPACE
TAURUS BASSPLATSCHALL & PERCUSSION INTRO CON
TINUUM FREEDOM DOLPHIN DANCE SMOKE ON THE WA
TER WACO JACOPULAPSUS LINGUESS WAU VOYEUR WA
LKABOUT W/MEANDER CULPAPUASSARATOSSATOUT BO
OTSINISTERRA INCOGNITABOOTSY COLLINSTANT KAR
MADELIC PSI-FUNQUE LETHE BAUBOMBOOTSY PEPPER
S & THE BEASTIE BLONDIES UPLIFT MOJO PARTY O
N PLASMAGIK LETTERS FMWAKA/JAWAKA/WAKARIAGAR
A FALLSUCUNDURINE SUKHETA! SUKHONA! SUKHAYA!
BIZARREPRISE WHOREA WEST WAH-WAH WAH-WAH EVE
RYWAH THE CHRYSTAL WATERS 100$ PURE LOVE BAC
K IN BLACK AC/BEEGEES ANGUS YOUNG MEN ARE WE
NOT MEN? SONG FOR BARRY GIBBONS DUSTY HILLAR
Y CLINTON QUASI JOHNSON WALK ON THE WATERRES
FIREDANCE CLEARWATER REVIVALDIONYSOS THE RIV
ERRUNDFUNKBILDERSTORM ALLSDIGITHALES WASH NO
T WASH & GODDOGZILLÀ-BASSPACE BASSEISMIC SHO
CKWAVES BOOTSYBILLASWELLAS MARQUESAS UPRIVER
RUNDFUNKFREQUENZILLABLES ÎLES PAYS BÀSSOSSPA
ESI BASSCHIZO-BASSPASSIBASSI SPASSIBASSPEEDM
ETALSDIGITALSDIGITALSDIGITAL 00:00:00:08 STR
ING BASSPACE BASSAREUSSOLO DIONÄXOS UNDERWAT
ER MARQUESSOUNDEXPLOCEAN: AEROS SPACE BASSES

FROM THE DEPTH OF THE WORLD... DIONYSOSVLOED ISSEA THALESDIQUETHALES PAYS BOSCH JINNADELI CONOSPASTICK FURY OUTBRAQUE BASSPATIALICE DI GENITALSDIGENITAL GEORGE PLANKTONICCLONICCLASSIC TUBE IMAGE BREAKING LET IT SCHWEPPES HOLLANTIS EL MARQUESUN RÂDIO-KAOS TVIDEO-CLIPS UCKLICKZAPP KNEE YOUR TOUR-HOSTESS (NOT) KNEE DEEP THROAT WENDY WINTERS LSDANS LES VILLES ÎLES ÎLES TÉLÉSPLANKTONICCLONICCLASSIC FUR RIRE FREAK OUTBRAQUE YAPPUPA HOW DID YOU KNOW W'D LIKE TV? PSYCHOANALLIZZY MICHAEL JACKSONIAN POLLOCK THE WATERBULLABASSARTAUDDISSEA BULLGOGO MW/HUGO KUTKA KUTKA ROTA GOTA ROTA GOTA ANUS MUNDUSCHAMPULLABULLABASSPACE BASSO LOOP-DE-LOOPILEPTICKA PRICKA-BOOTSYBILL ECCE HOMONOTYPEE-FANGAUGUINEA JU-JUNGK-TONGK-TONGK SPACE BASS I ANUS MOONDANCE WAN OWAH ONE OWAUTOXICOMANIC HELIOGABULLOTAURAPAPUA NEW BEGUINEA ARTOLE MOMOHEAVY META-FISSION THOTHALES ECLIPSUCK PAPUASSHOLANDA SPIDERWEIB VACHE NOT VACHE HYPER ASS EGO MARSCH CONFONK LSDEEP WAH QUANTA ACQUANTA ACQUANTA ACQUANTA ACQUA BALL-OUT RONGELAP-FUNKADELIC JAMES MARSHALLAS MARQUESAS REFILLAGUNES ISLANDAMANDAMANTRA WAU WAU WAU VAGINNANANA WHACKAPHONE ADOLFLI WOLFGANGES AMADISORDER WORDSURFING ON ÈRAC LUTTORAL HOODDISSEAS TELLER MORE TELLER MORE WRONGELAPSUS CALAMITY MILES DAVISHNUCLEAR DU CHAMPIGNON FLOATING IN THE HERBIE HANFORD GREEN RIVERRUIN NUKEY POONA POONA RAIN KING EL VISHNUKEY HIVA 200 MW NRU-REACTOR/CREATOR TO THE TEST ONE TWO TEST BAKER BIKILLKILL ALL WHOATOLL ATOLL RAIN IN THE MAKING KNANINJA! K

NANINJA! M W EARTH DEFECTSTOSSEAS JANGALA JA
NGALAWATER DREAMING DE MARKIES VANNSINNATRAN
S WHACKAPHONE WAU SCUNT SEA ATHHHING HOLANDA
SCAN I SCUM THE MARQUESSAIS NUCLEAIRES YO EL
RAIN MEGALOSPERMHEAD VI TEST TEST ONE OWAUTO
SUCK VAGINAVEL FLOWING UPHILLARYWHORE FELLAR
E FELLARE BILBOQUET & BAUBOCUNT THE WILLENDO
RF TO POWER KOGI KOGI HOPI HOPILEPTICKAPRICK
APOONA POONABOMBOOTSY QUEUNUKEY NUKEY RAIN K
ING SUNNY ADEÈSSADE SADE MARKIES VAN WATER H
YMEN... SMELL MY FANGER STARTAUDOUFINNAFARAI
REBIRTHMARKIESKIMOHEAVY JUNCLE JAMPERE UBUTT
FONKING ARES EAU NASSAU WATT AQUA PITTI PITTI
FLOOD 666 LSDEVILLES ÎLES MARQUISES TATTUTTO
SCORREVERSION TATTUTTO È CONNESSOAP-POPERAQU
A WATCH OUT/TOUCH MONKEY BULL-OUT HOLLAND WA
H-WAH WHO SAYS... URBAN EROS (NOT) ANOTHER W
ORLDWAR (WE ARE) PORN TO BE ALIVE MARQUESSHA
NTI-OEDIPE THROATTACKA DELASUCK APPRESSURE G
ILLGILL LES DELEUGES EBBIGGY EBBANGADELICKAO
S SHANTI OEDEEP THE DEEP WATT THE WATT PSYCH
IATMÜLTRANCEXTATIC ORANGE POP GOD FUNKADELPHI
NNATRON JAHWAKE URMYTHE MARQUESSAGOGO MW/TH
E FLOWLANDS NIJINJAHWAH-WAH MINOTURTLERRIFIC
KAPRICK SPASMATTERRA FIRMAGIC WAS NOT WASMAT
THEKKAPRICKAQUADOOLOOPZILLAS MARQUES.A.S. WA
RLORDS/NUCLEAR ATTACK WAS NOT WASSERBOMBUAND
IONYSAN MARQUESSUCHAWOMAN (WALTER ORANGE) FU
RA DEL BASS EL MARQUESPACE BASSÀBYSS SUPER M
WARQUEST FOR POWWOWWOW H H (O) MAON MUAAAKK!
PRINZHORNY HORNAMENTAL DISEASSEAS WASSIRROUN
DABUTTING THE MARQUISES ISLANCEFALLOGRAMMARQ
UESAN SPIDERTEXT IN CIBBERSPACE FLOODDISSEIZ

URES WATT EAU WATT EAU LSDELEUGES GILLES ÎLE
S MARQUISES BECK TO BECK/OLANDADA THISCO LIT
TLE PIGGY POPPOP JOHN SINGER SARGENT PEPPER'
S LOONEY ARTS CLUB BANTARCTIC BISMAH ARCHIFU
NK THE BLUE BEUYS IS COMING ON EB EB EB ORAN
GUTANGERINE DREAMADEUS MOUSSARTAUDIONASSAVON
UNI CURA LET IT BGG ALL-INTROSHOCK GIBB IT A
WAY GIBB IT AWAY GIBB IT AWAY NOWAH OWAH OWA
H-WAH PARTY ON PLASTIC ONOYOTE BAND ONE HOUR
BEFORE OUR HOURQUELLENNON-STOPABOUTSUCKADELO
RANGADELIC FALLSUCK MUDDY WATERS LET IT BB K
ING! SMASHWATTERRA FIRMASOAPOCALYPSODOMY MIS
SELF & GEORGE EEUYS YOYOTE BABYLON BY BEUYSM
ARCKIES ARCHIPELAGOGO MW/THE FLOWLOWLOW DR.
MABEUYSSEA H2OYOTE LES PAYS BOSCH DE MARKIES
VAN WATER WEE WEE WEE ALL THE WAY HOMER BERM
UDA PIG DANCEFALLACQUA OOGAGAGA BOOGANESHAMA
NIAGARA FALLSPERMADELICK HOG POWER TO THE PE
OPLE WE'RE ALL WATER ACQUASMATTERRA INONDATA
BEUYSSPUSSEAS BASSAGO WEST SHOW YOUR WOMB AV
ATAR AVATAR EVERYWHERE ESPASMATTACKADELLACQU
ASMAT WE ARE ONE OWAH-WAHJEH WAN OWAU-WAUJAH
JUJU FANNYKINBOTE PRINCE CHARLES KINBOOTSY C
OLLINNEGANS MOTORPSYCHO SPASMAT BAHASA INDON
ESIAMESE PNIN PIKABOO-DE-LOOPZILLATRONICCLON
IC SPASSMABASSOULTRA WAKE HUGOGO MW/THE FLOW
WAU WAU CHACHAPINNACULA SNOLLAND RHYTHM & MA
RQUIS NEW PORN MONKEY ARNOAH-NOAH & THE SUBR
OVNICKS WATER UGH UGH GET WET CHI BOEM FRIPP
MAGRIPP ENOAH-ENOAH WIND ON WATER TAKING TIG
ER TIGER MOUNTAIN GARI GARI AKU AKU MOTHER M
OTHER MOTHER'S FANNAKINBOTE'S MAGIC CARPET R
IDE 1 TO 7 FIRE TO RAIN LET IT RAIN DE MARKI

ES VAN WATER IN AQUASMATTERRA FIRMARQUESAN V
OODOO-BOPPIGEON BASSPACE ODDYSSEE HOLLAND BO
NZO DOG DOO DAH-DAH HUGO MW/THE BALLROOMBLI
TZKRIEGGMANTRA NON-STOP TRIPPIN' GOO GOO GOO
JIBWATER WATER EVERYWIND & ALL'N ALLSDEE-LIT
E MY FIREFLY SCHWITTERSNOOD NR. NINE NR. NIN
E NR. NINETY FIVE FIVE FIVE AVATARLIAMENT FU
NKADELPHILIGRAINS WAXIS MUNDIZZLI MWELT ANTI
-OOOOEDIPPEE-FONQUELLE MARQUIS I'M THE ONE D
E MAZE VAN WAR'E AR'E AR'E EL MARQUESSARO WI
WA-WA WA-WA NIGERIAGARA FALLSPASMOUSSEAS ACQ
UALATTABOOTSUCK HEIDIONYSOS GILBERT DELEUGES
& OH, GEORGE CLITTONICCLONIC BONZODOMY MISSA
LVATION ARMY MYSELF & AÏGEAU AÏGEAU & THE BU
NNYMANTRA SUZANNE FELLINI HEAVEN UP HERE'S H
ERE & HERE'S THE WA-WATERRIBLE WATER HORSE T
O HORSE BACK TO BACK PALIO-PSYCHO-POP MARQUE
SIENNAVEN THE BIG H HUGO BEUYSS FOR MEN HOLL
AND LOONEY BROODARSE CLUB BONZO DOG DOO DADA
HUGO BALL MEN'S WEAR ESPISSPASMATTERHORNY HO
RNAMENTAL MARQUESSTILLIVE! THIS LITTLE PIG T
RANCEFALLOGRAMMARQUESSUCKING OLLANDA ANADOLL
ON MUTTMOUNT MATERPORN BACH TO BECK THE PUMP
BARRY TO BARRY WATT WATT WATT MEET THE FREAK
S ARNO UP YOUR BROEDARSE DE MARKIES VAN WATE
R UNDER THE BRIDGE THE DEEPILEPSYCHO-POP ERA
MOJUBA! TORTUGA! WAN MANDAMAN VIBRATORTUGAGA
NINJAHWEH-WEH MOJUBASS! TORTUGABB! WATERLAND
PSYCHIATRIPPOLIPOOL THEKADELICKOUT CUMMUMMUM
APOCATHEK NOW! EB EB EB AM AM AM AM SWEET AM
THE SOLAR ANUS LSDIVINE MARQUIS MARQUISTADOR
FUCKUS LYNNE COCK IQ SUITE FOR THREE ORANGES
WEINER WORKSTUDDISSUCK JAZZICA STOCKHAUSER U

NCLE JAMINENCE GRIZZLI WAS NOT WASSIR KARL P
SYCHO POPPER'S ARSE CLUB BUTT DULLIONASSEAUD
OMY WATER WATERLOO EB EB EBBA DR. FUNK EINST
EIN D/T FABULA NARRATURQUELLES ÎLES MARQUISE
S 8-KLOSSOWSCHIZO WATERACLITUS THE WARRIOR B
ASSOLVING THE EGGOGO MW/THE WATERLEAU FOLLY
LINGUALL'N ALLES MOTS ET LES CHOCS I AM AM A
M FUCKALL UPPSALA YOUR ARSEASEA PINEL-FONQUE
SERA SERATOSSTREAK MW VENUS ENLARGER GGERART
O DE NERVALLIN GOGOYA MW/THE MIMMICKERY MOM
MOCKERY KUNG FOO-BULLFIGHTING OH, GEORGES S
TONE & SLY BATAILLE ORANG UTANGERINE DREAMLI
FE MUTOSS OFFLOODDEEPILEAPOCULIPSE NOWOOFUNK
ANTI-KRISTEVACUUMSHOT/MOUNT MATTERPORN/COSTA
DEL SOLLERS GIBB M SCUM BROADARSE MARQUIS BO
X OFFICK OPEN UPPSALATTABOOOH AAAHARE HARE R
AMA RAMARQUESSATYRISKCON BOWWOWWOW SCUMMUMMU
M VOODOO-DAH KUDOO-BOPPITANZ WAH NOT WAHARAP
WAHARAP EL MAR Y SOL LEWETTER & WETTERSNUTTE
RRAINDANCE TRUMPETTERRAINCHANT BLOW JOPLIN B
LOW HOLLAND DSM-4 YOU! ATOMIC PORC EPICCA PR
ICK LULUBA TAWAWA IMAGEOMASSA ICONFUSAPSUDAN
UBE MW VOSTOKADELIC GAGANESHARHIN CLINTONICC
LOSSOWSKIZOAPERRATIC SIR NASSAU IN SLEEPDRUM
MING IN ESPACE EBBISSAU ONE OWAUTO SHAMPOOLL
AND WIWA-WIWA WIWA-WIWA EVERYWIWA-WIWA WE SH
ELL NOT DE MARKIES VAN WATER GRAND MALTHUS A
TTACK WE'RE ALL WATER WATER EVERYWHERE ECHOL
A MERKAZ VANE VASER ORANGE NOSEE N'ZODADALAI
LAMARQUESS BUSH BUSH DELA MORE MORE CUNTDOWN
HOLLAND MALE QUESITE MALE PERDITE DADANU BE-
BOP-A-LUALLU UALLU UALLULAMA LA VIE LÎLAS MA
RQUESAS ALLSDEMENTIATMULTRA SUPRAECOXIS MUND

IES ILLA MARQUISEAQUARSEAQUALLSDIONYSOS OMAQ
UADIOS DIGNE TAUREAU LET THERE BE WAH BACONN
AFAUN BULLHEAD 666 MWASTER DUBLIN LITHIOPOLI
S/N.Y. CITY DIONYSIAMESOAPOCALYPSUCK NOWLOWL
KÔMOS O YE BECKHAE STRAWBURRY MANSFIELD FORE
VER LET IT WAH! HAIR BETT PISS PISS SARAPISS
SARAPISS AQUASAR-AQUAPISS GIBB PISSACHANCE U
R-MÈRRATIONAL EAGLE PREACH THALATTABOOTSYBIL
LOOTSCHIZOFRENIAGARA FALLSUCKABASS TVD SPLIT
BEAVER-SHOTTENTONGUESS WATTICKA PRICKKICK PR
ICKKICK ELEPHANT BILL HEALY SEALASSIE CRAINM
AKING WORDSMOG IN METAMORPHINNATROT WOKABUTT
ERRA FIRMAGICK FLUTTES FW CAPUT HEALY HARE H
ARE GAMA GAMA SKIP ANDY WIPP STREAMSTOSS OFF
CUNTSUCKNASSEAU SPIDI DUBRO SILAN BORDERLINE
PSYCHO POP URINE TESTING ONE TWO WATTAMESSOA
P ORANGE OOPS UPPAPUARSEASS ARSCHLONGA EVITA
BREVISTEST TEST VOICES VOICES VOICES TRISTAN
TALIZING TONY BECKALAND SHE-MALE PENCKUNTRIE
S LUSCIOUS LYNNISSOLDEEP IN LSDEEPILEPSYCHOD
ISCOACQUATOMIC BUMSPARADIES INDEEP-THROAT-SI
NGING DE MARKIES VAN WATER ON THE HIGHWAY TO
HELLEUSIS DUNG HO HOLANDA FLAT & LOW DUNG HO
HOLANDA FAT & SLOW! EL MARKIESKIMOHEAVY HORN
-BERING SEA-MALE O GOTTLY BULL COME HITHER D
IONYSOS-KIDDIPUSHAMANIATMOLTRANCEFALLEAUDION
YSSUCKADELPHINATRAUM BULLABASSARAWAKAOSIRISU
RMERZATZIBBERFLOODISSEA-MALE MARQUIS UNDISCO
PULATE LAUT BIG BANGALAWATER WATER UPPER NIL
E BARI WHITE THE BLUE NILE HEATWAVE AMATHONG
O! AMATHONGO! SPACE BASSOLOMON SEASMATERMALE
SOLLEAU DE COOLLONELY URSEASMATTERHORNY HORN
AMENTAL CLUB MEDICEAS DOG EAT DOGGOTTLY BALL

HUGOGO POMP MW/THE FLOW LSDETOILETHE CULLIN
AGASUK WAKASSARAPISSING DOWN PISSING DOWN PI
SSING DOWN PLAY THE FLOOD HOLLAND SIEG HEIDI
FELLASSIE IN THE SKY MW/DIAMOND LILLET IT B
E LET IT BE YOURQUELLENAIACQUA HIPPOPOTABILE
MARQUIS LET IT RAIN LSDELASOULTRA WAVE OCEAN
HIGH & RISING THE MARQUESSYNDRUM O DOWN UNDE
R TRANSSEXODUSCHAMPEEKABUTT P-NILE FELLA KUT
SILICONSKEAGH HOSPITAALLSDIGITHALES ÎLES MAR
QUISES EVERYWHERE WAXOMAMADEUS SEX VAGINAVEN
FWAXOMAMARQUESSAI EBBATHONGA EBBATHONGA THON
GA WAUTAUA WAUTAUA EVERYWHORMONEY EVERYWHERE
MYSKINNAKOOL WAKILEPSY ATOMIC BOY GEORGE CLI
NTON WOOFGANG UFOAMAZONE MOUZZARSE RIVERRÖNT
GEN SPASSID EVENEZIATMOLLY & AM AM AMSTERDAM
'S ORANGE WARQUESSEX-THOTHEMISMOUSSILICLOWNE
SHALAMARQUESAN PRICKA PRICK DANCE IN THE YEA
R O THE PIG AQUAWATT-WATTACKING WHIRLWIND IN
FOLLYNESIAMASOPUSSOPOTAMIA TAIPHONE BRENDA B
E HANDAMAN MWANKALLSDECOLORILLA ALLURELLWASSE
RBOMBIOTEXPLOSIVE ESPERMICOBRA SPEED METAL M
ETAL UALLABOUT WOWWOW WOWWOW THE DUTCH ACT U
P YOUR BREEDAARS TELEFONICLONES WANKASKATALO
GY APSUPER EGOGO MW/THE MANIATMÜLTRAPSODOMY
IN BLUE BLUE ECLECTIC BLUE VOLPINASE KISSING
THE ORANGE ENDOGEAN GENIE ECLECTICKA PREACHA
MANTRAVESSTARDÔME DUNDUNDRUMATOLLOOPILOOP BA
RNETT NAUMANIA & BRUCE NEWMANTRA WHATCHA LAC
AN ET TUTU H-ERA KLITTERRA INONDADATABOOTSYB
ILLA-BASSOAPASAURIC OH, I! WWFW WWOW MMWM WF
FW WOOW MWWM WFWF WOWO MWMW WFFF WOOO MWWW F
FFF OOOO WWWWAH-WAH CALLANCÛMSHOT DIORGASMUS
NIKI LAUDA SAINT PHALLESDELTA PLAN LOVE LTDE

MARKIES VAN WATER ORANG UTAN TITEL BRANDT NE
W SPARLIAMENT PIG BACCHUS NIKI JUST DO IT FL
OATY FEU FIGHTER AQUARISTOCRAZY HOLLANDA COW
COME TRUE EL MARQUESADOMASORIGINAL STONE PHA
LLUS BONING YOUR MOTHERTHONGA THONGA WARA WA
RA EVERYWARA ATYPICAL SHE-MAL ATTACKAOTICKAS
KADE SADE MARKIESKIMOHAVE NO MERCI BOCCACE 7
0 TOBBY OR NOT TOBBY DAMMIT SAY BUBA PUPA BU
BASSOLIWARA WARA MERI MERI HOLD ON TIGER TIG
ER ONE M/MCDILDONALD LAING VAUDUSCHBURGER FL
OATING IN ECO-TERROR GROENPISSEAS WOW TOWA W
OW TOWA O PISANG ORANGE DEPRESSEAS O SCUMMUM
MUM BACARDI ORANGENSAFTER THE RAIN FLOAT/FLO
AT ON HOLANDA THE TV BUDDHA & THE SPACE BEUY
S TONGA MIMI SAMOA HOLANDICA MARQUESUN RAMAD
ANUBE MW ZERO ZEROTEE'ACHAMANIAGARA'MAAH RA'
MAAH DE MARKIZAAHH... THE NAME IS BOOTSY'S R
UBBER FETTISJ'MAMAAHALIA JACKSONIAN SHEEPILE
PSI-FLUT GEORGEOMASSA CUNTOFUSION ROCK AND A
LSO WATER AND WATER TAKE IT TO THE BRIDGE EL
MARKISKOESJ'MAMAAH MA AH MA AH DJAZZAPPABASS W
AH-WAH EAU MINERALE MARQUIS WATER WATERMARQU
ESST. MARTIN IN THE STRAWBERRY FIELDS FOREVE
RRUIN EL MARKISSINGER SARGEANT POP THE ROYAL
SCAMPARI ORANGE PRESSADE SADE MARKIESSUCK HE
ILWASSIR PSYCHOSIS SEXY MAGICK RAM LIQUID AR
OMARQUIS WOOVERLAPPING EREXORCIS/M WARASSHOL
AQUAROMARQUESSGT. CIBBER'S RUBBER CLUB FETIS
J BANDAMANDADATA BASSPACE BASSOLILOQUI AVATA
R AQUAVATAR SPAQUAVATAR ESPAQUAVATAR MARQUES
PAQUAVATARKOVSCHIZOPHRENIAGARA FALLSDOMENICO
TAKE M TO YOUR BACKWOODS NOWWOWWOW EB EB EBB
A PJORN AGAIN JOHNSON & JOHNSON MENTAL FLUSS

FOR THE GLOBEEHIVE OH, GEORGE BATAILLES ÎLES MARQUISSES HUBRISSETH BAHRTAUDOLLAMOURQUELLE BOMB MUTTERREUROPAPUA NEW GUINEA PIGGY POPPE NHEIMAT TANZIBBERFLUTWAKE HAPI HAPI HAPI GEI L IS DE NILE BABYLON BY BEUYS HERE'S LACAN E T JUJU ET TUTUBA OR NOT TUBABYLONELY ARSE CL UB WHORES AFRAID OF ADOLF WOLFLI? WAH WAH EV ERYWHORE ONAONEY CUMBELL SUBMITTERRAINFALL-O UT IN THE LANDMARKIES HOTEL LAS VEGAS ONE OW AUTO DA FETISHAMALSDOO-JOPLINES M MYSELF & B OBBY FARRELL AWAY SO CLOSE OPUSSEA ULTIMUMMY MUMMY MATAHORN HARIKLIT STONE FOR STEAM AORT AQUAVATARKOVSCHIFOAMADEUS IMAGINING THE HOLL OWLANDS MAKE LAVATORY NOT WAR/MAKE SHOWER NO T LOVE NAVEEN MARKISHORE SEAGULL CIRCUS WASH NOT WAXAMPLE SOME O DIS NOT DAT MARQUESAN PI G BROTHER'S WATCHING JUJU KIDD-CHARLEROI RIM BAUDELAIRBORN TO BE WILDE MARKIES VAN WATERR A FURMAMA COOL DOWN APEPSILEPTICKA GODOTTO È MOUSSEAU SHOCCOCA/COLATTHE FUCK BUTTONICCLOW NESQUELLEOPARDOUCHAMAN MW/SNAKE WAKE HOPILE PSY Z001 ESPACE ODDHISATTVA MAGICHANT DELA T ERRATIONALITY PRINZHORNAMENTAL DIZZLIN'ZOPOC ALYPSODOMY IN BLUE MOVIE EN RROSE C'EST LA V IE EN RROSE BUTTER DIKE YOUT HOLLAND THE MAR QUIS TO WATER NOW ULYSSES TO MWAH! UFOAMARQU ESAN SHE-MAIL ADRESSUCK OR FLUT WATER OOOH B ABY BABY IZITSOA WILD WORD LANCÛMMING CÛMMIN G CÛMMING OOOH BABY POÈME PARFUMAFRENIC WOK AWANKING RONALD LANCÔMING CÔMING CÔMING LACA NCÔME OH YEH BACCHAE WET WET WET PORN BY THE RIVER VYPERVERSION KUDOMAHU MAHUGOGO MWESTEE LY DANUBISSAY PEG DANCE ALLES MARQUISES GAUG

AUGUIN MW/THE WATERFALL ACQUANALLSDELO WAXC
ESS MAKE VASLAV NOT WARHOL AMERICUNT MUMIA W
HATTISSAY SCHIZODELIC GRAND FUCK MALTHUSSATO
UTTERREURRAPE WE'RE ALL WETT/WETT/WETT MWAKE
LOVELACE NOT WARSENILE MARQUESAN DENYS DENYS
DOCTOR WU WU WU HEALY DAN BODHISATTVA CULTUR
E HAITIAN DIVORCEE-MAIL MADDRESS-MEKKAOS FRE
SH WATER WATERFALLSUCK OR MALFUNKSHUN MARQUE
ZE ETHERIDGE ESPASTICKAPRICKABULLÀBASSPACE B
ASSARATOSSTRAUSSAUGGADELICUNTIFICKATION NATI
ON UNCLE JAM ALL MUMIA ABOOTSY JAMAL WILLIAM
TABU-JAM-ALL-STAR MUMMIAM TABOOTSY JAMALLINS
SHAMMANTRABU-JAMALIAGARAFALLS U M MUMIACCHUS
ABU-JAMALCOLM X! AM AM AM AMERICAMPOMANICK S
RAAT PRICKING FLOODWETT MACDONOR'S NEVER GOI
NG BACKAGAIN (H)NAHM (H)NAHM HOLANDA (F)KOW!
MAH MAH MAH THAI YUP! BLACQUAVATARLIAMENT H-
BOMBADELIC MILES OH MILES DADAVISHNUKUDOMAHU
GOGO BALLSDE MARKIES VAN WATER WATERPOWERSPI
NVADING THE LAWLANDS LAWREETEE LAWRITEEE MAR
QUESRANANTONGOGO MW/THE FLAW WAN OWAH ONE OW
AUTOLEASE VAN DE WATER OH LORDURE LET IT BMW
WETSOUBITCHIMALES BIKINIKI LAUDATOLL ATOLL A
TOLLIFE 'N PERSPECTIVES OA! PAPUA NEW GENUIN
E CROSSOVER COMEBACK THRU THE GATES OF THE B
IG FRUIT ORANGE UP YOURBAN DANCEAFAULLEAUGRA
MMARSEANILE SQUADIEUNUKE NUKE AQUA-BOMBUANDI
EUNUKU NUKU HIVAGINAVEN IATMILLERIN SHEALY D
AN'UP YOUR ARSCHUBERT MARQUIS MILLER P-FUNKI
N' FOR JAMAICAMAY SOAPSULA MARQUISEAMAMALE M
ARQUIS MILLERRELLA MARQUISERENGETI-REX MACHI
NE SMASHANTI-OEDIPEE-FONKUNG SPACE BASWAN HI
GH DAMSTERDAM IN NORTH SEA DELTA FLOOD-CUNTR

OLLAND CLUB MWET WAR W/THE SEA HOW LOW! HOW
LOW! GRANDMOTHER'S AIRPIG BE MY SUNSHINE WAT
A WATA JUWU JUWU NOW HEAR THIS DE MARKIES VA
N WATER TRAVELING LIKE EGYPSY RAIN C/CHAMAN/
BASS SMOKIN' TO THE BIG M HANSON CALVIN ACQU
AQUAPIA JOHN STONI SEX MAGIC FRUIT ZIMBOMB Z
IMBOMB ZIMBOMB EREKTA-BOOTSYBILLASWELLENNON-
STOPABOUTSUCK EJACQUES LANCÂME TO THE WATERS
AND THE WILD SULA SINAS DRUP SULA LEMON DRUP
YOYOMAHA OMAHA KUMBH MELADRUMMATOLLUCID JUNC
LE JAMRIT YUNCLE YAMUNABOMBINGGO BANGGA YOUR
QUELLE MARQUIS DE SADHUCHAMP BECK TO PUNA PU
NABUMBING THE ORANGELLANDS OMAHA OMAHA KUMBH
MELA MARQUISEAQUALLOOP PUN-A-BOMB HOLANDA CA
NALFICKADELUSIVE SUCKERZEEPILEPSEE LAND EREC
CLAMPASWOMP ICKAPIK MEER EL MARSHAMALE MARQU
IS RUN DEEP LINDA MCCOURTNY LOVELACE THE MAR
CASTANEDDADA'S HERE'S THERE & THERE'S ZOHARL
IAMENTAL FUNKADELISQUESCENCE LIQUID SUNSHINE
SHINE SHINE THE LIGHT ON M WAHJEH! BJÖRP ECH
ON VOULEZ-VOUS-FIGHTING OH, GEORGE CLINTON P
LAY THE BEUYS ORANGE NASSEAU DO RE MIWOKABOU
T MYSELFUCKADELUGE & I KNOWHOWABUTTERMOST O
HOLLAND HOWABUTTOSS OFFLUTWATTWA NOET WATTWA
TERRAQUAVATARLIAMENT P-FUNKADELISQUESCENTURY
GRAND MALLAHABADDISSEY I I I AMRITTEN ON WAH
-WAH EREVERYWHERABOUTZILLAS MARQUEUS.A.S. NE
W H-BOMB DE MARKIES VAN WATER ALLSDIEUNUKING
WATERRATIONALITY WAH WAH WAHITI DUSCHAMPEE-F
ANGOGO MW/TELLY BLOOM & MOLLY SAVALAS THE W
ISHWATER-BLONDIE & THE ESPUSSY BEUYS MARQUES
SCRUMTESTING FOR THE GRAND TRUNK ROAD-MOVEAB
LE FEASTING YAMMUPI YAMMUPI LES ÎLES SODOMAH

A KUMBH KUMBH MELA MARQUISE DE PUMP PUMP WED
O PUMP PUMPAPUA NEW GIMMY DURHAM TLUNH TLUNH
DATSIMABUSEAMALE SOLO GIMMY GIMMY DURHAM YOH
OHEYHEYEYHEYHAHYEYEYHAHHEH YOHOHEYHEYEYHEYHA
HYEYEYHAHHEH GLOBAL WARMING YOU FALLAWATRA C
UTTABURRA KITTAOOLOO GLOBE EPILEPSEA-LEVELLA
TIONALITY REMEMBER HOLLAND, MY LAND BY THE S
EA HOPI HOPI LIPPI LIPPILEPTICKATHIANAL TABO
OTZEELAND 5333 EL MARQUEZANDVOORT, TO THE SE
A VENUSSUICILLA IM PELZEELAND YOURHINE RIVER
REVANGEL FALLS TIDE IS HIGH I/AM MOVING ON S
LYSTONE THRACEY BIKILLING STARWINDAMAN ATOLL
OWLAND MW/SPACE BASSALT BLACK UHUROROA FIAT
FLUXUSSUCK BONG POW ARGHILEH NO-MO! BIOFRUIT .
EPILIPOSOMPLE SAME O DAS SOMPLE SAME O DIT M
ARQUESAN WARRIORGASMASSMWAH-WAH BECK TO FRON
TOTEMPORAL SEAZURISE RISE RISE DEEPOOLAPSU G
OGO WESTO'EAST TRANSITION FROM ORANGE TO YEL
LOW LOLOLANDADA LO-LI-ZEI! STARRIBASSI STARR
IBASSI MW PALAEOPATH TO GLORY QUE THALES MOR
E THALES MORE THE LOVE FLUIDIPUSSY REXPRISCI
LLA PRESLEY KILOTONICCLONIC ATTICKAPRICKABOM
BOOTSEAMALE MARKIKI DE CUNTPARNASSAU PAPUAQU
A NEW GYNE BURN OUTER SPACE BASS BETWEEN THE
DEVIL & THE DEEP BLUE SEA MWARANATHA! MWARAN
ATHALATTABURIGINILE DRUMTIDE=HIGH/I/M MOVING
ON VAS NOT VASLAVAGE STARWASHAMMANIA PSI-FUN
K LETHE BOMBOOTSY COLLINSTANT KARMADELIC TRA
VELLEAU WAVE JOJOBIMMING IN TESTICLE HEAT FL
UX IATMÜLLAS MARQUESAS HEAVY WATER REACTOREA
UMACHINAVEN WAS NOT WASSERMANN TESTING ONE T
WO VAS NOT VASLAVERY SOUL/ANUS WARHOLLANDICA
MAY SOAP-OPERABIOSODOMANIAGARA FALLSDSMWAH-W

AH IV STOP LACAN HERE'S LACAN AT YOU KIDDIPU
SSY REXPENSIVE POMP POMPUSSHE-MALTAMIRA MIRA
OMEGA ORANGE YOHOHEYHEYEYHEYHAHYEYEYHAHHEH Y
OHOHEYHEYEYHEYHAHYEYEYHAHHEH! DE BAPTISMODER
NISMONO BIKINI ATOLL PENUS IN FURGINIAQUADOL
F WÖLFLI DE MARCUS VAN LÜPERTZ STEPPENWOLFIN
G OUT IN AGUADELOUP-DE-LOUPZILLA BABY WATERW
ORLD UP SHE-MALE CHAUVINIST PIG DANCE JEZEUS
MÁDBACHOS URINE TESTING ONE TWO ONE OWAH WAN
OWAU R. MUDD-BONE PORN TO PERFORM PARKERILLA
S MARQUEUSSEAS TILLALALA TILLALALA O BE O BE
O BEATRICKA PRICK LSDEFUNKT THERMOHAVE EUNUC
LEAR SCHWITTERSBACH WAS NOT WASSIR PSYCHO SE
XY LAWRENCE ALMA-TADEMARQUESAN GRAND MALMARK
IES-TADEMARKIES COME BACK TO THE FIVE & DIME
JIMMY DURHAM, JIMMY DURHAM CLUB MEDDADA TRIT
ONICCLONICCLINIQUELLE MARQUISTABOUEEEKKEEE H
2001 ÈSPACE DRUIDDYSSEAS THE CATACLITURGENCY
FIRE FIREWATER WATER FREE FREE MARQUESPASSOC
IATIVE CINEMARQUIS VON STROHEIMATTERRA PUNON
DATA GREED IS THE WORD IS THE MOTION HAPI HA
PILOOP-DE-LOOPOCALYPSE NOWHORREURQUELLWASSER
KOLONILE KURZ SCHWITTERSBACHAMANTRA FLUTWAKE
YO EL RHEIN GIVE HOLLAND THE BOOTSY THAMES F
ROM THE BLACK HOLE WE A'RE A'RE A'RE BLOOD S
CHWITTERS & TEARS TO MELTMERZ THE FRUIT IS H
ERE IGLEAU IGLEAU ARSCHIUMARIO MERZDOWN PSYC
HE FUNFARE WAX NOT WAX APPOGIATTICALYPSOGNOA
H-NOAH THE FRUIT IS VERY BEAUTIFUL MERZBAUBO
OTSITTA IRREALE MARQUIS MARQUIS MOTORCYCLE P
HANTOMMAHAWK WAX & RUBBER BAND RIVERRETURN U
P YOURRADIONYSOS PAPUASPUMANTI-CHRIST SAI AB
BA I/M BJÖRKAGAIN EL MARQUESCOFFIER BRENDANU

BEAH OBEAH CHOKMAH MR. FLOETWIGGLES APSU APS
U APSOUS-LEAUTTERROAR ANTE CHRIST DE MARKIES
VAN WATER HYPE/HOPI NEUROTOROMACHIE FOLLI/FI
LLIGRAPES SEA WAKABOUTANKAOS IN FIUMERZBAUBO
NACI PROGRESSION WE ARE NOT PROPERLY FRUIT O
RANGE FEBONASSAU BUMPER TO BUMPERMEABILE ONE
OWAU WANDADA OWAHWAH MASOCHAMALE ONE OWAUROR
APE WE WANT WATER ARSCHWERES WASSERPENT IN W
ATERRA FIRMOTHERMALE HOLLAND & THE SEA WHO M
ADE WHO AQUAJACUZZIPPMAFRIPPADELIC MARQUESSP
ANISH COASTLE MAGIC WASH LEAU BUTTOM M MYSEL
F & ENO NOTHING WAHNSINSIDE ONE OWAU I WISHA
MANUKU PISA LAS MARQUESASSODADA TURN BLUE PE
GGY POP WELLE WELLE WELLE DE MARKIES VAN MOR
RISON MADAME GEORGE CLINTON DIAL M FOR WATER
WAJAGGA WAJAGGA PUSSY AQUA SEX OOGAGA BOOGAG
ALORE SCREAM PRETTY PEGGY SCREAM & DIE RATIO
NAL WORLD ORDURE ONE OWAUTOPORNY PORNAMENTAL
DISORDER IN THE PARIS CABINEMATHÈQUE THE MAR
QUIS & I NO SHOCK CORRIDOR! PORNO WAY OUTTER
REUR WATTELEPATHICKUM ALLSDEBILITIS SOULANUS
MUNDUSCH SCUMBRAILLEAU FINNATRIP WAGNUS DEIL
IRIUM BUDDHA DUBBHI ORANGE UP YOUR ART HOLAN
DA HUANG HOY FIN DEL MUNDOUCHE FARE DE MARKI
ES VAN WATER DELIVER THE WORTSALAUD IN WARTA
UDISSEAS DELUGEOMISCHMASHING THE WORD-UP FOR
THE DOWN STROKE VAGINA WÖLFLI ENEMA ELISH DE
E DEE UNDER THE BRIDGEWATER NON-SENSE UNIQUE
LLWASSER WASHING WELLEZZEEPILEPTICKUM KUM KU
M DANCE DANCE DANCE DEUS DEUS DEUS VAS NOT V
ASLAVALANCHEFALLOGRAMMARQUESAN FOAMFUCKALL C
ARL JUNKUNTARSEAS ECHOLALITTERRAPTURINE HARE
HARE KARISMAH MAH MAH ONE MANDALLAS JR MUTTE

RATONICCLINIQUELLEAU DE CUCCHI FONTANA EBBRA
HMANIATMÜLLAS MARQUESAS YOU ARE LOOKING KUDO
ICKA PRICKASSOAPOCALYPTICKA PRICKASSOULTRA W
AVE TSUNNAHMI MYSELF & QUEUDEAU QUEUDEAU BAS
S AQUA FUNK SCUM CUNT AQUANALFICKAPRICKAPUSS
Y VAUDOUCHAMPERE UBUNGABUNGA SAY BABBOT POUS
S'SUKHAYA EPILEOPARTAUDIOZZILLA PUDISTAS WAH
-WAH KLAPPLAUSSING TAFKAP THE ARTISTS FORMER
LY KNOWN AS PRINZHORN MEGA-MISHMASH DE MARKI
ES VAN WATER GOD IN DAMLAND PRINZHORNY BASTA
RDOM ORANGEN GESCHMACK BECAUSE WATER AIN'T W
ET ENOUGH BARBARA SUCKFÜLL AGNES RICHTER MAR
IE LIEB ON THE ELEPHANTONIN FARTAUDDYSSEY EL
MWARQUESSEXTC ORANGES & LEMOONSOON YAYACQUAH
WAU WAU NUGA NUGA NUGANESHAMANNEQUIN FLY LIK
E A HUGO BALLA-BASSPACE BASSLASH 'N BURN RUB
BER BANDAMANDADA SAY ABBABA COOL WATER WATE
RRORANGE ENEMARQUIS UP YOUR ARSE HOLANDA THE
WATERWORKS P/FUNKADELTA PLANCOMESHOT DO-IT-Y
OURSELF DIFFUSION YOURANIUM SLUTTERRAINWHORE
THE VELVET CUNTERGRUNT ZOMBISMARCKLITTERATON
DUSCHORDER RAISONABORIGINIL CAESARATOSSATHOT
ACQUANNOENSINGING TYPHONICLONE WAXWORK ORANG
E OWAU STRÖMSTUSSAUDISSEAS TILLALALA THE END
O THE WORD IN SURGE O WATER LOW LOW LOW DOWN
NOUN-STOPPOPERABIES NEPTUNUCLEAR PHUSIS AQUA
MENTAL GEILLNESS LOA-LOA HOW LOA-LOA LICHTHE
IM TESTING ONE TWO ONE OWAH-WAH MARKIESKIMOH
EAVY THERMAL WORD POWER DUNG HO DUNG HOLANDA
LIQUIDIPOUSSY REXWATERSTAAT PSYCHOBATHING IN
NON-SCHIZODELIC FROGGFOAMM NOZZLE UP OLLANDA
ANADOLL EPILIPPING IN THE NAZZLE WATER WATER
JU-JUNGADELIC ENEMA LOVER LUBBING UP FOR THE

ANIMA ORGIES OLLA OLLA EL MAR DE PERSONASSAU
LET IT SADE STOP LACAN OIDIPRIAPOUSSEA REXTC
RIVERBETTWETTING HOLLANDICA LAVAGE LADY ENEM
A LSDI HOLDING THE WATER WATER EVERYWHERE CA
LL M THE BIG E ORANJA NOUZZLE EPILEPTICKAPRI
CKASSTICKANOZZLE OZPORN UULUA UULUA MW ENEMA
MUNDI AQUAMADEUS REX VACCHINA EL MARQUESRANA
NTONGOGO MW/SLY & THE FAMILY STONE FREE FRE
SH WATER & ORANGE SUNSHINE EXPLOSION MAGICKI
TSCHLAMMALE ARSCHIUMASOUVERAINDANCE CLUB BAN
D HERE COMES THE WATER MBAQANGA! MBAQANGA! M
BAQANGA! APSULAPSUS CALAMITY DELA NABU SHAMA
NUS DEI ONE OWOH-OWOH PARIS TO THE SEA APU A
PU MATANGILLGILLGAGAMESHMOSH DELEUGEOMATERRA
INONDATABLA-BASSPACEO PARKER VAI TAI VAI TAI
VAILALA PALEO-PSYCHO-POPOPOV MARQUESSLYCLOWN
& THE DOLL FAMILY STONE AGE LAS MARQUESAS DE
MARKIES VAN WATERATON-SCHIZ-O-RAMA RAMARQUIS
BIJACKULATING WORDPOWER IN THE BRANDT NEW WO
RLD ORDERRUIN DELTABUTTERING THE NARRENSCHIF
FER HEY MEN... SMELL MY FINGERTIP VISION ESP
USSIEG BASEMENT 5 SILICUNT CHIPPENDALLAS KOR
PER KULTURE KRASCH LOS DADALAMOS TESTING WAH
N TUTU RUBBLEDEHOPPLE UVOODOUFINNALOUP AQUAD
OLFLI WOLFGANGANESHAMALE SIR NOSE DOUFEEDDAF
UNK ORANGE UP YOUR ARSCHISMARQUESAN LITERATO
URE KUNDADA WASSERWITCHING DE MARKIES VAN WA
TER MAKING CONVERSACE ANALLOUNSINGING MAGICK
WASSIR NOSE D'VOIDOUFFUNNABASS WAGOGOSPEL GG
ALLEISTER CROWLIN' MYSOUFI & ION DE BEAUMONT
MW/MAH MAH MAHOLIA JACKSONIAN EPILEPSY FROM
HERE TO UNREASON ART FOR ARTAUD'S SAKE GGÉSU
ALL-IN EPILIPPO LIPPI APOLLOOPPEE HOLADY DIO

NYSOS RIVERSUS APOLLIZEITGEIL ONE MANTRAVEST Y RAPAPUA ERARARA TYPHONICCLONIC CAMILLE MARQUIS HURRICANE PARTY SMWASHING EAU M AQUA FROM H TO O TO BECKOBASSEAU DECORPUSSY PRIAPEORUM ANAL LITHIUM PLUIEIREBEL GOTS FO GOET HOER MUTTER EARTHAUD ARTAURAHUMARA! ARTAURAHUMARA! CIPPERFECSTASEA BEFFANGOGODE MARKIES VAN WATER SGT. PABLOLONELY HEARSEA CLUB BANDAMAN TRAVOLTABOOTSY'S RUBBER SOUL HÂPI HÂPICASSOD OMEGA ORANGEOMATA HARI FANNY STASI NIPPLE ARSE ENFINN SLEUTS! THE GREAT MOTHER'S MILK ARRANGEMENT TELL M TONY TELL M TONY TELL M TONY TELL M WHY-HY THE MARQUESATANTALIZING TONY BAEKELAND SHE-MALATTACKASSOLO H-BOMBILIC DESLIMPLODING TELL M WHY-HY WHORRICUNT PARTY ON PLASTICCAPUT NULLY IN SOLARKOVSKIAN MINOTRANCE OWREETI OWRITEE HOLLAND HIDING IN THE HELLO FOAM TELOS MORE TELOS MORE COME HITHER DIONYSOS MARQUESSOAP & FOAMADEUSCH LSDIVINTRAUM HORSEMEN HAÏTIKILOTON TNT.S. THE ELIOT MY SKINTRUMA WAKILEPSY 6000 WATTERRESTREAMSTÖSSO SATYRICONSCIOUSNASSEAS AMOURPHINNATRIX ART AUDDOUFILS! UMBRILLOPIUMBRILLO LO! SLAVE NEW WORLD FUNKIN' W/HEAVY SEA MW DREAMTIMMERING THE TIME BOMBASIE BASIE NASSAU DAY 999 NASTY NASTY (LIVE) MW-JUJU YVES SUCK LAURENCE WEINIE SHORTY GEORGE OPIUMBRILLEAUTOMATIC FOR THE PEOPLE INTERWET HOLLANDA SULARIZONASSAU EL MARQUESSU DAMLASILLA MARQUISEAQUANÜSSINNÄSSE A-PORNAGRIN AP AP APSU BASKINI ATOLLANDA SUL ARIVER AP AP APSUGIBI AWAY NO ONE MAN SHOW NO MERCY WIDE OPEN (WALTER ORANGE SCUMMODORE) EB EB EB HOLANDA KAROCKEYING INTO MANIC-

DEPRESSIVE DUB SHOW GLOLO! GLOLO! GLOLO! WAT
TER TO THE MOUTH & IGO IGO IGO, TRANCEAGRESS
ING RIVERRAPE, CRAZILLAZY PSYCHOMÖTORHEADFUN
K WAR / FADE TO BLACK ONE OWOMANOWARRIOR CUNT /
FUCK / SCUMBACCHUS THE MARQUESSUBVERSIVAÏSMOUS
SEA-MALE FRIPP-FAKING THE FUNKERILLA IN MENT
AL BOOTSPITAAL I M THE EGGY POP MUSICKA PSYC
HIATRICHAOSSYBILLASWELLA FOAMADEUS MOZART FR
EE MACEO WATABOOTSY & THE BEAST OF NO NATION
EGYPT 80 ! MARQUESAN AUTO DA FAKE SPITTERWEIB
TESTING MAYHENDI JOBBEASSEAS AM AM AM TABOOT
TOMAN VIBRATION LA-BASSU GÜCIBBERALL LIVELY-
UP-YOURSELF-BEWEGUNG BIKINOA-NOATOLLACQUANUS
SOLAIRBORN DELASOULTRA WAVE OCEAN HIGH & 3 F
OOT RISING I / M FUCKALLSDIVINE HORSEMEN / DEVIL
'S RIVER THE MARQUESCAPE DUTCH MANUS DEE DEE
LITE M FIRE FIRE ARNOAH ARNOAH MANICK STREET
66 BASS CULTURE MARCHI MARCHI EVERYWHERE LET
'S FANGO & VANISH ALL IS COPPER MARQUESKIMMO
OH, GEORGE CLINTON KWESI JOHNSON & JOHNSON'S
WAX T.C. MAGICK NUKU HIVA BLEU MEGALOMANYSOS
AVÉ EVA MUTANS GENUM WET WORLD'S NR. 1 LUBEA
H LUBEAH AP AP APEIRON MAIDEN SUN & STEELY D
ANUBEAH BEAH ORANGE MAREMELODY MÖTORIKE LEAU
RÂNGEL MOUZART TO PRAGUESS WAH! MEKA MIXA BÉ
BÉ PSYCHOTIC BÉBÉ PSYCHOTIC WHAT OVID WHAT O
VID WHAT OVID MARQUESAPUNNARELL ROUND & ROUN
D & ROUND THE NEW WORRELLA FOAMADUSCHORDER A
ÏGEAUDIO-NOZZLING INTO THE BLACK HOLLAND DIO
NINE NINE NINE ST. VITAS DUNCE DUNCE DUNCE U
NDER THE PEARL HARBOR VITAE HOLANDA SPILLITT
OO GENTILLES ÎLES MARQUISES PICATZOHARMALINE
THORA-THORAZINEMAH MAH MAH I MINERVA U MINER

VA DO IT AGANNAKIN FUNJAW THE SNOW GRIZZLI-B
EUYS DRIZZLE-PISS RAIN-IN-THE-FACE MEDECINE-
MAN P DE FONQUELLE MARQUISTABOOTSYBILLASWEL
LAS MWARQUEUSEAS NGURURU JUGGU! NGURURU JUGG
U! NGURURU JUGGU! DE MARKIES VANNATCHEZ RAIN
CHARMADELISCHAMANISCHOCKADELICAQUAPHONIAGARA
SINNÄSSEAPPLE IN VACHINANUSSAUS SPEAK-A-BOOK
LEAULITRANCEFALLUSSHEE SHEE SHEE! ASSAYE ASS
AYE BABALLOON THE MARQUESSYMBULLOOPALYPSE NO
W! IGG WHAT IGG EGGBIRTH HUMPERDINCKY TOY MY
BOY MIGHTY MIGHTY LIVE SOUND LEAURANCE MYSEL
FABETTWEINER & THE CHIMPUNSCHOCK SILHOUETTAT
TOOING HOLANDA ANADOLORES HAYES HADESRÂP THE
THE ÈSPEACE ABYSSACRIFIZZION IN PROGRESSOLE
AUTTE MEE WEE FEE TRANSHIBERNIAN TÜSPUTABOOT
SY UPSIDE ONE OWAH-WAH WAN OWAU-WAU LO! BEHO
LD THE INSTRUMONGOLIATMÛLLASKAOS M MYSELFABY
SS & I UNPACKING MY LOBSTERY LOVERLUCKY BLOM
STERBÖHM MELOMAPPA MUNDEEP RIVERRUNAROUNDABO
UT THE MARQUESSYLLABLES ÎLES MARQUISES FIKUP
FOR FLESH NEALY EL MUNDO NOV, ZOLE FLEN! ORA
NGE LUNASSAU/PURPLE ASTROLANDA ANADOLORES HA
ZE UP HOOG & HOAR HUNT HYDROPHOBE SPONGAZILL
A DE MARKIES VAN WATER TABULA RAZOR LIVIT OR
KIKIT ROY WITTGENSTEIN WARHOLLANDY WARHOL FI
GHTS FOR LIFE (MARCUS TAKING STAND) WAS NOET
WASSERSKIDOO-BOOBBULLY MCNUTTERATON HEREWHIP
PITT! HEREWHIPPITT! OPUSSY POWAWA OVARYWHOER
LETITGOGO MW/DE MARKIES VAN WATER VASLAVERY
SOULANÜS DIVERRUÏNCARNOUGHTING IZNAVIKNEK NU
NAVAKPAK ANAKTOEVAK OUELLE OUELLE OUELLE KOO
MBANA DUNMANUS WHITEMUD LAC QUI PARLE/SPRAGU
E WATER ONAPING CUMALLO KOOZATA CHIRGUA RAPI

RRA HOLLAND DREAM MW LETIT BE FUNSHINAGH LAK
ETALK LO BEBALD BISAACLES HAZE NAZZAUSING IN
ORANGALAND HOWWOWWOW DO YOU DUCHAMP R. BUTT?
SHEIZUNGENLAUT MERZUSHAMMENBAU RIVERSPEECHOÏ
STE! SPEECHOÏSTE! HOLZBACK CAVETOWN REMEDIOS
WASSIRKULATIONSPUMPING PUMPING YOURHINOCEROT
ICH NILE-MARQUIS FLOATING THROUGH THE VALLEY
O FOLLIE ZUCKZUCKZUCKADOLL DADAMANDA LEARYON
ASSOWWOW OH HENRY UH RONALD AH RICHARD WATER
WATERGUTTERRORSCHACHAMALE TESTING TESTING ON
E OWAHALLAS MARQUESAS I/M DILAUDID JIMJAMMIN
G THE AQUARISTOCUNT EL MARQUESSOULIVAGINAVEN
I MOHAVE THE RITE TO KNOW! HÂPI HÂPI HOPI HO
PI EJAKYLL & HITE REPORTING ALLABUTTER HOLAN
DAMERICA LANCÔMESHOT-BRAINED & DIORGASSMEARY
ONAONEY CUMBELL SOUBMITTELL WIWA-WIWA WIWA-W
IWA SARO-WIWATER WATER HOLLAND PUDENDADA & E
JACKZUNI HYSTERY ORANGAËTAN DEVILLEAPING THE
MARQUESSILK-ROUTINE IN ONAZZAUBERHEINFLUSS A
QUANUS IN FURCULLINE BARBINTROBIANDY KAOSCAR
PANIZZABBERSPUSSY BASSPERMAFREUDISSEAS KISSI
MWEE! KISSIMWEE! SPUITTERWAUB & ZIBBERSPOUSE
DE MARKIEZIN VAN VEERE ZEI GOD ONE MANDALLAS
WELLA FOAMMSBÖWÖTÄÄZÄÄUU PÖGIFFBÖWÖRÖTÄÄZÄÄU
U PÖGIFFUNKADELIC COSMIC SLOPILEPSEA SPAESSI
BASSI ORANGE NETTO TELL M MORE TELL M MORBUS
LUNATICUS ART EAU ART EAU ART EAU ICHOR STRA
VINNAGAGANESHAMALIAGARA FALLSDE MARKIES VANN
SINNASSOAPOCALAPSUS LINGUAGUAGUAE KWIIEE KWI
IEE 'T LEAU 'T LEAU 'T LEAU ORANGERIATRICK-A
-NAZIOSENILE TESTING TESTING ONE ONE TWO TRI
NITY UPSTART REPARTIMENTO AZERO WATER EVERYW
HERE EGOGO MW/THE FLOWLANDSLIDE ONE MAN CHO

W-CHOW, IQUDO IQUDÖPPELOEUTIGREASY LICKING S
UNDAY MORNING GLORY GLORY LSDE ZEE... PALEO-
PSYCHO-SCHIZO-POP MW/RED HOT REICHILIAMENT-
FROMMADELIC PEPPER'S LEAUNIETZSCHILI HIRSCHF
ELT CLUB BANDAMANTRASH WE WANTARCTICKABILLA!
HOLANDA HEFFERYWHORA ET LABORA DE MARKIES VA
N WATER POLY-PSYCHOTIC FLUX MUNDI AQUALITATE
QUAQUAQUA SHE-MEL PRO SEMPERO ARSCHIZOMOODDI
SSAY WAH ARDH-KHUMBHA KHUMBHA MELA ARTAUDH-K
HUMBHA KHUMBHA MELAKE ALOONIE KILOTUNE HIMAL
ADEUS SHEX-WOLFGANGGALAXY MEKKA-MACCHINA CIP
PERGO ET CIPPERAGO POGO MW/THE FLASHING THE
HOCHEHOCHE RUN DEEPEROSPASSEANBLASS BERUFENS
TEALY DADANUBASSPUSSUCK HAIL, FOREVER HAIL O
SEA LENI BE YOUR LOVER JAJAJA NEIN NEIN NEIN
NR/9 NR/9 NR/9 P-FENG SHUI WATERBUCKHORNY HO
RNSTOMPITUDE WAVE FALLOCITY RADIONYSOSSMATOS
S RASSPÛTASS JASSMATASS SAVE THE OCEANS/OCEA
NS OF FANTASY/ROCKITT FARRELLAS MARQUESASSMA
JISS NASSPASSAGE BASSKUDBALL JUST DO IT DO I
T WATCH IN A NAME TELEFUNKWELLEQUEINT DUKE D
UKE JOBE-BOPPITT BE-BOPPITT NUCLEARWATERREVI
VALDIONASA BOOTSUZICLONOCLASSWOLL STOP THE R
AIN BOOTSUZI QUATRONICE (NIETZSCHE) QUE DICE
BONEY MWACO JACO SPASTAURUS DUB MARCUS SAY F
LY LIKE AN IGLOO! MARCUS 6:49 MARCUS 4:39 MA
RCUS 1:10 SPLATCH 4:45 MARCUS MILLER UNFUNKY
UFONKIN' FOR JAMMEKKA 4:40 BOBBING BOBBING T
AKE IT AWAY BOB SPYRMECCE HOMONOVAGUINEA PIG
TANZ SLYCLONE DUNDUNDRUMBAR & THE ROBBIE CUB
E CARL LEWIS LEWIS JOHNSON WAX MAGIC WALTAMI
RA MIRA ONDA WALTA WALTA BRECKER BRASS SPACE
BRASS AMPLIFIRE STATE-OF-THE-ARSE BILDERSTUR

M TRANSMITTEREUROPA THE BLUE DANUBE / RITUAL FIRE DANCE MARQUESAN MARKOJAK PASTAUROTA BEUYSS ARCHESSTHRUST BAGHDADUDOK CIVIC CENTORO WAR IS COMING PLATINUM JAZZ RIVER NIGER H2OVERTURE DELIVER THE WORD! PARTY ON SPLANET SPLURGERY DISASTAURUS WASSIR NOET WASSIR DUKE WILD DOG ATOMIK KUDOK ATOMIK KUDOK ATOMIK KUDOK TOWER ALL OVER THE WORLD MAN BEBUQUINTETSUOMI BODY HAMMER MELTING OLD HUMANISM BY ELECTRIC SOUND THE WMWM DUDOKKODRILDEODATOWAR TOWAR O BABBILLY ROTOCOBHAMMER AEROSPACE BASS DRUM-RIFFEUER MARQUESAN MARCOZY POWELLASERMALE NEUKÖLN VIVA LAS VEVEGAS TAKE IT AWAY BOBBILLY OCEAN VOODOO SPELL N.Y. JIMMOCCA BOBBING HAMAR TAKE IT TO THE SKY RONNY ROCKET ROCKITT ROCKITT JENKINS FIRE EXIT ONLY 3O/S OVER TOKYO DISCO TOWER TOWER INFERNO WMWM FACTOR WALTEVERE MARCHETTIBER WASSERMUSIK FWMW FEUERWERKSMUSIK THE FIRE-BIRD & WATER WATER IVORYHORNBILLY COBHAMMONDIALIASMATER IVORYHORN BELLY JONAS WAILBORG COBHAMMERING THE BASS MATERTAAL WATERTOOL OWAU TRILOKOMO LOKOMO JONASSPACE BANJONASSPACE BANJONASSHELLBORG BARRETT BARRETT NESBITT NESBITTABLATTABLATTABLATTA ONE MAN SHOBAROCKIT NASAPOLLO BLOW-UP 0:50 ELECTRIC MUDMOUNT EVEREST WETTBAND WATTLAND SPACE BOSSA NOVA GUINEA SPANK-A-LEE LAND PALM GREASE IS THE WORD KOJAK BRELCREAM LES MARQUISES POKA'AQUA DIGITALDIGITALSDIGITALLES SANDROGYN MORESCHIMMÈRE NAVE MEDEA CANELOS CASTRATTATTONEDA 20.000 MILES RUNS THE VOODOO DOWN THE FUNKY SEA / FUNKY DEW ST. BRIGGITT BRIGGITT LA GOCCIA D'ACQUA ALSDIGITALOSDEFUNKT

LAUTSPEAKABULLA CAMARGUESS WHO LOVES YA BABY
PUSSESSION BY SLITTANY FINNTRILOQUIZZICKA BA
SA SANGIANGEL DUST LAPURA ILLAMINA LAPURA IL
LAMINA ALPONGURA LAPURA ILLAMINA LAPURA ILLA
MINA WE SEE / WE'RE ON A MONKABOUT NEURO POP A
MEGO-AMEGO WALDOUCHAMANTRACK BOMBIENARY WADI
KEEP IT ON ICE PAPA PUA PUA WAWA (KIVA KIVA)
UPHILL RIVER FLOW LOGOS-LEGOS AFRICAN SUNLIG
HT-MOONLIGHT-BEWEGUNG PAPUA GENESIS NOA NOAX
ACA NOAXACA NOAXACAMEGO-AMEGO ASTRAL MARX TE
LONIOUS ABOREALIST WAWA WAWATIERRA DEL FUEGO
TAAORA TAAORA THE PAPUAN TRAIL UPHILLOGOS-LE
GOSPEL IN BOCCA D'INFERNOA ANOAXACA ANOAXACA
NASUMO BAZIRO TITICACANOA NOAXACACA TIDAL MA
GMA MAGMATER MATER ADAGIO ADIO LA MÈR-PERROS
KUDOSHAMAN BREATHING MOONBONE NEW ARNHEMLAND
ABOSTRALIA SANAMU SWAHEALY ONE OWO TO, TO, T
O, TO, O PI, PI, PI, PI-FONQUELLWASSERBOMBUA
NDI-FRUIT MAGIC WASHLOVE NOT HOERHUNT HOW DO
YOU DOO-BOP DADADA D DADADAVIS TUTULALIAN LU
LUNAEZ? MARQUESAMOA-MOA PAPUA NOA NOA GUINEA
MWASHRAUMBRILLEAU LO! TÜSPÜTNIXON MW/VOGULK
OPF LUNAWALKING WAN MAN MASOGERM WANDAMAN EP
ILEPSYBILLY JEAN KUNG FOR A DAY GALAGALA BI
NYA BUNINGA NGALI EPILIBIDOUCHAMPOOL-DE-LOOP
ILEPSYBILLÀBASSARATOSSTOSSONDERSPRACHAMANTRA
SHAMALE MARQUIS CHANT MARQUIS DANCE SPIRIT-S
LANGUAGEOWATERRE WATERRE NGARAUAN UDJA KUNDU
BAI BUNINGA MELINTHI PHILIPAGRUNT GLASS SONG
S FROM THE LIQUID DAYS VIVA ROXY MUSIC PYJA
MARAMARQUIS KIEFERRANELLE AGUA MINERAL NATUR
AL SIN GAS! EL MARQUESSOMNAMBULLOOP-DE-POOLL
ANDA ANADOLLOPITRANS RIVERSLEEP-SPEECHAMANIA

EAU DE CULLONELY HEARTS CLUB BAND HERE COMES
THE WAH-WAH KALLKOOPAH RUAMAHANGA POOLOWANNA
KALAMURRA KALAMURRA! KARAKOEM KARAKOEM! MUSI
C FROM THE BULLRING ANGELITO FALLSDEELITE ON
E OWAUTOREADOUR RANDFUNK RUNDFANK FEELACRÂNE
TROPHÉE TREPANÉ, ORNÉ DE DÉFENSES DE SANGLIE
R, NOUKA HIVA, MARQUISES, UA TUKI-E! UA TUKI
-E! UA TUKI-E! PORNOMENTAL TATTÖWIERUNGADELI
C MASS CULT URHINE AUTOMATOPEE ONOMATOPISS H
OLLAND WAITING FOR BOGGODDOT PSYCHOPATERNOSF
ERATUR IN ÈSPACE BASSILIKERK VOC M WIC M SHE
LL OILLANDA IRRAGAL IRRAKAL! CRONUS SIPPAR R
APPIS GREAT FLOOD LETHIOPOLIS DE MARKIES VAN
WATER ORANGE RIVER TO NASSER LAKE AAA-FREAK-
OUTTERRA INCOGNITABOOLLAND DON CHERRY IATUMU
LTI-CULTI SHE-PRICK RIVER SOCIETIES CRIVIÈRE
S ÉCRIVIÈRES CHIERIVIÈRES SUNSET WARQUIS DOI
NDOIN BODY ARTAUD IN LEOPARD SKY MW/DIAMOND
LILLEESQUIDDEEPOUSSING KALAMARQUIS INTO COCT
OPUSSY IGLOOPUTA! DADANILE SPOERRIVER WAHWAH
KING HULA SOULLEASSOUP UPSIDE YOUR HEADYSSAY
TAR & FETT URSE DOUR-BEUZ FROM BRASYLUM IN M
EERZATZIBBERSPEACE MARQUIS O BATH RECONSIDER
ING TREATMENT O EPILEPARS FATALE ABERRATION!
APOCALISSÉLAVY VARIATION ON AN IMPROVISATION
FOR A COMPOSITION OF AN IMPRESSION ZOOM THEM
A SINTFLUT IKONIK MEMORY SPIN BRAINSKANDINSK
Y DATA BITCH DUB NOT KNEE DEEP (THE) COCHONN
ERIVER EL MARCASA DE BANHOLLAND THROAT-SINGS
INGING KHEMS/KHAMS KRITIKKA PIG RATIO SHOW T
URN IT UP PINGO PONGO PYGMAEUS WEST MYSELFLO
ODDISSEISMOGRIFFITTI & MARQUESAN PIG DANCE P
ARTY ON PLASTIC ZIEGFELD HAIR FOLLICLES ÎLES

MARQUISES PIG DANCE / RUU CHANT SCHWEINFLUSS C
OCHOUNDFLOODFREEE PRIGGY POP - PIG KILLER ELEC
TRIC SHOCHONNERIRE SHUI - DE MARKIES VAN WATER
BRAINSCANNIBULLONELY PIG SPEECH 1984 A SPACE
YENISSEY RIVER NATION IATMÜLLITANT SÉPIKKA P
IG OLLANDA ANADOLL MUPI MUPI WAS NOT WASSERG
EANT RED HOTTENTOT CHILI PEPPERS LOONIE MEGA
HERZ CLUB FUCK MARQUESSATYRIASSEAS PRIAPUSSY
ENVY SUN MOON RIVER CITY PALEO - PSYCHO - POP MU
SIK JASSMATASMANIC DON'T PANICCAQUA KING BILL
Y COBHAMMERQUASSNAKESKINNIBULL RESISTANZ PAR
TY SAGARBATA SAGARBATA! SAGARBATABLATTA SAGA
RBATABLATTA! FUNDER MARQUIS VON H2O VOLTAGE
RIVERMUTTSHARKFUNNATRIX BUFFALLUS BELLIPSE D
E MARKIES VAN WATER WAHNARBEITING IN THE LAN
D WHERE THE GREEN ANTS DREAM ONE MANFÄLLES Î
LES ÎLES THE NOTFALL ONANNY UFONNY EL MARQUE
SANDENISTEIRESIAMALE THE MARQUESSCHIZOFREAKY
MARQUESSCHIZOFREAK BULL - LEAPING ON THE HIGHW
AY TO HELLENISM INSTANT KARMARKIES VAN WATER
SKIZOPHRENIA SIMPLEXAFONKING WILLIAM BEUYS C
OLLINS COK! MÄ! COK! MÄ! ART TOYON AGUAGUAGA
TALKING IN CIRCLES ÎLES MARQUISES YER AMMESI
HOLLANDER MARQUISLE MARQUIS DE HADES HADESCE
NDING INTO THE NETHERLANDS ORANGE NASSAUP - OP
ERA APERTABLATTA ST. VITUS DANCE SÉMÉLE SOLO
HERACLASH BACHILLES ÎLES MONDOPPELGANGESTURE
THE OWAH OWAH GLASS TOWA TOWA TAKE - OVER & AB
ORIGINILE SIBERIAGARA VALSZ P.I.L.EO - PSYCHO -
POP MICROPHILIA MARQUESAN WORDSCHMERZ EPILEP
TISCHER DÄMSTERDÄMMERZUSTAND - UPRIVERSUCK ORF
LUSS KUDOMITILLA CATACOMBOMB ORFLUSSODOMUTT
ILLA ALLABOOTSY THE NEVERLANDS WATER WATER IV

ORYWHORE MIRROR UP TO NATURE HOLLAND RAINDEA
D EL MARCASCATALEPTIK TRANCES IN THE NUDE DE
R FL. HOLLANDER MARQUIS VON OMO SEPIK EPIK R
IVERRAGING UP YOUR ARSE DESCENT VAN GOGH INT
ATTUTU THE NETHERWORD UP YOUREA LYRE OLLANDA
ANADOLL TÀLTOS ALLABUTCHU BUTCHU GRAND MALTA
IC PRIME MYTHIKKA DRUM PEOPLES MARQUISES HID
EOUS MUTANT DE MARKIES VAN WATER BISONSTEAMI
NG THE LOWLOW CUNTRASH P-JUNK FRUIT MAGIC EL
MARRIO MERZEELAND 53 ORFLEUSS ONE NATION UND
ER A GROOVE ALL ALL ALL AROUND THE NETHERWOR
LD LA HOLLANDEPRESSADE SADE ÖRGI TELL ALLARA
KYROARRATORIONYSOS ORANGE NISAN-SAMAN BORORO
TATATTOO YOU BABY TOMSK PHALLI BELLY BOMSK T
ABURROTATATTOO BABY AQUA BOOGIE TATTOO MAN C
OWWOWWOW YIPPEE YAH YIPPEE WEH HOGGGG HOLLAN
D ASSYLOOMING UP CREASTIFF MARCASTRATOTEMPOO
LE MARQUIS IN THE GEILLAXY OF DREAMTHAI YOUR
PORTRAIT GEISHEOL SURCHING THE LOWER LAPP RE
GION SHAMAN DUB FREUDLESS BASS MIXAVIERABIES
BOSCH MEER EN BOSCH DRINK REMY DRINK REMY MY
SELF & NOSTRA DAM DAM AMSTERDÄMMERING ROTTER
DÄMMERING HALLEZ-LUJJAFFRIED-ICECRÄMLÖSAGARB
ATATATA TEE TATATABLATTA UNCLE RAMLUCY IN TH
E SKY EPOCHALIPSZ WAU DO IT! DO IT! UNCLE RA
M OF YAMOESSOKRO UNCLE YAM OF RAMASSOEKROKOD
RILLOLO TEST TUBE SPEECH DEFUNKING PRINCE BE
RNARD FEATURING MANUS DEIBANGO GUINASSAU GAU
GUINASSEAS ELECTRIC AFRICA SVIN! SVIN! SVIN!
BRAVODISSIAK MARQUESTIONMARKIES VAN WATER ST
EMMUTILATING YOURSPRUNG ROMININA HÄAGEN-DASZ
EXTRÄAVESTIDES TO GLORY GLORY HALLELUCIAH TH
E INTERTONGALAXIC ICKA PRICKASTROPICAL TROPI

CORCHESTRAUSS THUNDER THUNDER ALL THROUGH TH
E NITE ZAMZAM ZEUS DO IT DO IT MAGICKITSCHLA
MMAN ATOMIUMARKIES VAN WETTERRES SOUNDWAXING
SHAMMOONS & JAZZSTARS DEIKHARA-DE KRISHNAVEN
'ARE 'ARE RAMAER RAMAER MWASHANTIKRISHNA BOM
BO-DE MARKIES VAN WATER SPERMMUTTILLATING TH
E HEFFERLANDS DOWN DOWN TO THE BONE CALVINTE
RLUDE RABIOSODOMINANADOLLAND TALK DIRTY MAMA
FUNKARÁINNBÖW SOUNDVLOED & NUCLEAR VISION EL
MARQUIS CHANTE MARE UNDAEMOONNER DEUSSENDING
THROUGH THE NETHERLENS AGRIOPÉNOSE LÀ-BASSPA
CE STATIONTOSTATION WASSER NOT WASSERGEANT P
EPPER'S & CAPTAIN BEEFHEARTS CLUB BAND ON TH
E RUN QUENITAL QUENITAL T'ALMA ALLARA KYROAR
ABOUT THE LICKING TUNGUS IN TRANSINDENTELLES
MARQUISES FLY LIKE AN EGO HOLLAND EGG WHAT E
GG? SGT. BRAINDEAD SHAMAN BONING HOT JELLY P
EPPERS DOWN THE RIVERREVERIVER MARKUSUPERMAN
DADADDLES I M THE EGG MANTRAVOLTALASSAGARBAT
ABLATTA I M THE MAKBULLTOWAH-WAH-WAH TSUNAMI
S SAGARBOOTSY BABY LÀ-BASSPAESI BASS IMIA TRE
E IN SPACE MAZE IN MOTION THE OPERABIOSOAPER
A HOG HOG NIDHOGGLANDER LOLOBITTING THE SCHI
MMANIC KOASTRÜMMER ICH WHAT ICH MARQUEZZAMAN
-ANNILLOTION FLOWING BACK TO THE LOLOWAR REG
ION HOLLAND MATER DOLOROSA SPACE WAZZA WAZZA
EVERYWHERE WORDWOKKING AROUNDABOUT UREINDEER
TUNGUSHAMENNER S/PERMING KRANKHEITSPROJECTIL
E MARQUIS DE HADESSAINT PHALLES ÎLES ÎLES MA
RQUISES NETHERMAL REGIONDAWAY TO NUCLEAR THE
RMAL SCHEITTERING SEVEN SOULSALSAGARBATABLET
TERRE MADAME CALAMITY WORLDWANKING ON THE EL
ECTRIC CHAIR OF LSD-ESSODOMINATION SUCK ORPH

IC RAMHEAD VI SUCKRIFFISSIALL FIRE FIRE DOMI
TILLA THE FLOOD HOLLAND KRISHNAMÈRDE MARKIES
VAN WATER NUKING KLONE WATERWAVING IATMULTIT
IDES NINGIZZIDA! NINGIZZIDA! GILLGAGAMESHRAU
M YOURQUELLIFFIATHANICK LASER LOVE AFTER THE
FIRE FIRE APSUPER EGGOLATEXTUALLITTER RUBBER
BAND MAN BOOTSY BABY DELTA DAM DAM PROJECTIN
G COSMIK AXISTER SPERMASOIDE MARKIESSEREVERI
VERREY HYDROLIPPING CÖRPSER CÖRPSER EVERYWHE
RE YO EL REVERRIE YO EL RIVERREY PRIAPRIVATE
SYMBULLIMANIA SUDANESE EPILEPSY PSYCHOMENTAL
SOUNDNESS ARBEITSTHERAPEEE-LITE DUCHAMPUNNIS
MOUS SUN RÂDIOLOGY THE MARQUESSAMOYED JIMITA
TIO CHRISTRIX MARQUESAN MARKOORIVERREVERSION
DUBBING DUBBING SJÖSEF BEUYS MIELVILLES ÎLES
MARQUISES JIMMY GG ALLOADDINNAGASUCK BOBBITT
BOBBITTERRAINDANCING ON THE BEACHES OF REASO
N HORNHOLING HOLLAND LID ALL MARSHY UPJOMP &
PUMPING REFILTHY RICHARD NIXY GIRLS GIRLS GI
RLS FANNY THE FALL-STAR PUSSEPUSSEPIK RIVERS
ODOLLAND WELL WELL WELL LECK EN WIEL BUSSLOO
BITTEREN ZOTTERDAMMERZODEN BOXMEER & SAMBEEK
ONE MAN DRIEL UP YOUR OSS ON THE BUSSLOOBITC
HES IN THE BIKINI OATOLLKAMMER OASSALTBUMMEL
LEKKE HOMOOKERKDRIEL RAMDUNKSCHZVUREN FEESSE
N TO FEESSEN HORN TO HORNHOLY WATER THE VERY
WATER INDEEP THE DEEPSLEEPSEA-MARQUESSCRIPTA
SSKY-OPENER OPEN UP SGT. GINGER & FREUD ARSE
STAIRCASE TO HEAVEN PYRAMINOFETIZULU-PSYCHOA
NANABIOAQUA-BETHALATTADOLOOP PRINCE BERNARD E
DWARDS JIMMY DOESMOND TURTLE JIMMY GG ALL-IN
GET IT ON GEORGE CLINTON FAMILY SERIES WAZ N
OT WAZZAGMUND FREUD ELEUSIS WAZZAG WAZZAGMUN

D FREUDDIS SEAS 2002 ESPACE SODOMY S.O.S. SCH
IZO SOAPOCALYPSE WOWWOWTOW WOWWOWTOW LAS AGU
AS DE NOVELES ÎLES MARQUESAS PARTY ON PLEIST
OCENE HOPIFONKT PALEOLITHIUM 66 PRE-HAIRISTO
FURRY FROG OUT COME THE FROGS THE 2ND COMING
OUT COME THE FREAKS ÜLGAN ÜLGAN! AIHAI AIHAI
INE! EL MAR-KEYS ANGEL DUST 4:49 GINGER MIST
& FRED RAIN LES ÎLES CLOWNS MUSIC-HALLUCINAT
ION ALLEGROVEAU'CLOCKCLOCKCLOCK TELEVANGELLY
SYPHILAS FREAK OUT FIRE & RAIN CHATTANOOGA C
HOO-CHOO BANG HO BANG HO HUBUNGAN SEX MAJJIC
UNCLE DJEMBÉLANDADA BASS NUKLARINUTT BULANCÔ
MING IN RIVERSALJU YANG TERUNAWAKE! BOM OM O
M ATOM TOM TOM GG ALL-INSANI BAHASA PLAY LAU
TANDRUMMING ACID MARQUÈSAMUDDERA ALEPHILEPSY
NOW! MEMOIRÀ-BOIREMÊMORY ÈSPUSS OPUSSY ONE M
ANDRILLINGER & FREUD ICE-CUBISMARCK ORCHIPEL
AGUNA-GUNA PARTY ON NÉO-PLASTIC CALL CARL AN
DRE WATER WATER EVERYWHIRLPOOLAFUCKALLES ÎLI
NXUCK OR JAMBISTA WIDEAWIK-MUNKAN TRIBALLA B
ALLA! OW OH LO! MARQUESAN EXOMATOSEAS KUDOO-
BOPGODAZIPPAPUASSPACE-ABASSY-OIBONO ORANGE U
NUSSAU MUNDUSCHAMALE MARQUISSODOMITILLA MARQ
UISE DOO-BOPGODAZILLAMARQUISE DOO-BAPTISMOUS
S SPLATCH! SALMA YA SALAMARQUESSALSAMARQUESS
YA SALAMARQUISEASSALSA YA SALAMA MAA MAAA BO
SPHOSFOREUS FLUÖRPHEUS ESPONGILLATING HADESS
AU OW HO MARQUESAN MARKOJAK DEUSSAINT REMYSE
LFFLUSSING THE PROTO-TURKO-IRANO-MONGOL SING
ALONG THE HIGHWAY TO HOLLAND EGG EGG EGG MAR
QUESSENTIALL FIRE FIRELANDFALLING ONE OWAH-W
AH PEDALLAS MARQUESAS PRINS BERNADEBT SUBIRI
AGARA FALLSUCRICEAN FALLING LEOPOLD FUCKER L

EVINUS LEMNIUS NINJAH HÄABER-MASZ UNCLE GEOR
GE MADURO RIVER TETSUMI KUBRICK BILLASCAÙX B
ASS MARIMBAUD BASS-LINES UNCLE RIMBAUDDISSEA
S & JIMBAUDELIRIUM TRANSMANCHURIAGARA FALLIN
G CHUKCHEE BERRY WATT WATT LITTLE RICHARD NI
XON ELVISHNUKU HIVA KOLONIL KURZEIT GINGER È
FREUD GINGER É FREDDY FELLILI MARLENE BRANDO
O-BOP GUMMI OMI GOTT IST THOTHALATTABOOTSY D
ADDY COOLLINS SLY TWOMTWOMBLY & THE FAMILY S
TONE FELA KUTIKIEFER BOOTSIOUXIE & THE RUBBE
R BANSHEES EL MARQUESSACHER MAASZOUK WARCHIL
D KOLONEL KURZ SCHWITT ONE OWAH WAN OWAU BEF
ORE OWAH OWAUTOMASOPEEE-FONQUELLWASSERBOMBER
SHIROSHIMALE HEINOLA GAY NOT MUCH TODAY TODA
Y HHH2001 APISS! APISS! ABYSS ABYS S PACE ODDI
ESSEE THE BONZO BEUYS & ZEUS CLINTON FALLING
LET IT RAIN! EL MARQUEZZUYDER ZEEMALE HERRE
N·KLITTERRA FIRMASSA CONFUSADOMAASSHOLLAND FA
LLING IN THE YEAR OF THE PIG DANCE EL MARQUI
SSICKA PIG ORANGE NÄSSOW NÄSSOWWOWWOW ONE MA
N SHOW WADDI WADDIZZILLAND FALLING WAH-WAH-T
EIRESIAMESOAPOPOTAMMUS THE TA-TA BULLEO-PSYC
HO-PATHE MACHINE HORNIMAN O' HORNIWAR EL MAR
QUEZZYKLOTHYMANIAGARABISHMARQUESSLAM DENKABL
AUF ANGELSEA FALZHAMMER FALLING THE THOTHÈME
THE WA-WA-FALLUS THE THOTHALLES ICONSTAND-IN
BRANCUSI-MAMALE FALLING INTO THE HOLE LAND H
OLE LAND THE WAAL O LIFE BEFFERRINGSOME ON T
HE AQUASPOUSEABYSSIMABUSEAS HUANG HO HUANG H
O! MAE MYSELF JINGER & JANGO FREDWARDS TRIST
REAM & FLUSSOLDE PERMANENT SAMPLADELIC DRUMD
EUTUNG CALL-KARL MAY MYSELF & I M FUNKALÀU I
M FUNKALÀU-BASSPAESI BASSIMETRY SUNARTICULLO

OSE SOUNDFLUTTING THE AXIS OF THE WORLD DOWN
THE AINU AINUS AINUSSAU BLUE/WEIB/YELLOW LOW
SUBMARINOCEROS SIHR PSEUDO SEXY ÇRITUALIASDE
MARQUESS SKÈ-LETTONIC-SKÈ-LECCLONIC FAKIRIST
IK FEATS SLY STONE STARRY NACHT ERLICKKICK L
ICKKICK WORLD PILLAR FMWM DUCHAMPADUDOK! HEM
ELLAYYAK WOKKABOUT THE PERRIERRIVERRISE OF M
YTHICO-EARTHE MARQUIS OF OOHH2OOHH STARKOVSK
IWASSER CROSSMOLEGGICAL AXISINASSISTER HOLE-
FLYING UP UP CENTERRAQUASS SUCKRIFISSION QUÉ
TAL QUÉ TAL DE MARKIES VAN WATERWARS & PSEUD
OO-BOP VUURTRANCES THE LOW CUNT COSMIK EREGG
ION CHUCKCHEESE PUSSEASSION BREKKROINK! BREK
KROINK! COK MÄ SOLLYRE PILLAR OLLANDA ANADOL
L OPEN IATMÜLTRANSMISSION UNIVERSALT WATERDA
MDAM EJECTING DANI DANI BONDEGEZOUZOU! ORAN
G UTENGRIVERCONSTRIKEN ORANGE NASE DE MÄRKÜT
VAN WAHH-WAHH... TSUNAMIS MARQUESSINARTICULLO
OSE SOUNDFLATTING THE LOLOLO LSDEPRESSURHINE
NOSE EROSE MARKIES-BAKKIKOS DIORIONNYSOS DOM
UZ-DOMUZ DOMUZIK-JASS! DUMUZI-TAMMUZ NINGIZZ
IDADA NINGIZZIDADA! DUMUZIK TAMTAMMUZIK-JASS
! POP!-DUMUZI-TAMTAMTAMMUZIK JASSPACE BASSIN
ASSAU! DOBBOBBOB DOBBOBBOB WATER THE DESCENT
APOCALYPSODOÏTILLA ALLABOOTSYBILLA-MARQUISE
DO-DOBBOBBOB EGGIPSY POOLLUXORPHEUS & MARCAS
TOROTO ROCK TWIN SPEAKABULL EXPARROTOMENTHAL
ES EXPERIENCE PARAPSEUDOMITILLA CUR DEUS HOM
O? ECCE HOMOTOROTO-BASSPACE STATIONTOSTATION
ORANGE NASA KUDOMITELLA WHERE IN HELL IS THE
BIRD? WHERE IS THE BIRD? MANU KUA OPEA KEHEA
MATUKU MW POKA'AQUA PSYCHO-POTABILE SPIRIT L
ANGUAGE DISORDER-ABERRANT SHAMANISM-SUDA

NESE MOOD SYNDROMES-WIND SPIRIT RAGE OUTBU
RST-SEA DYAK AGORAPHOBIA-NUBA NEUROSIS &
NUBA PSYCHOSIS-INSOMNIA & SOULTRAVEL-OCE
ANIC FEELING-PAPUASSES UP HOLLAND WORLDCEN
TAUR SIMMELAYA TO STEELY DANUBEATRIXITA-TA Y
OU BABY LOVE TO LOVE YOUR IMAGOGO MUNDIONASS
AU WATER WATER EVERYBODY AUTO DADA FEEL FALL
FOAM LES ÎLLITERARY SPIDERWEB CRACKING AC/TC
ARNOAH-NOAH DILU DILU ALLU ALLU! AKKUDOMITIL
LASER DANCES OPEN UP/THE DRECK APOTHEK OF RE
ASON HERE & WAU ONE HORROARATORIO MASTERY OV
ER FIRE & MYTHICAL ANIMAL ANIMATION UTCHA UT
CHA UTCHAMAN BOUTCHAMAN ABOUTCHA COLLINS & Y
URYAK GAGARHINNERRANTING GLAMMANIC NEVERRANT
ING PISS LADY SUN EVALLUTION ORANGE GREASE L
IGHTNING! HOLANDAMAN EPILEPTICS RAZORRANTING
PAST AMSTERDADADAM & EVEVENICE ESKIMORE EPIL
EPSEAS HOLANDALLAS MARQUESAS MANCHURIAGAROAR
EINDEER TUNGUSHING PAST EVENEZUELA FEMMÈR FO
LLE MARQUIS ANGEL WALZAUBERFANGO FANGOPI GOP
I HOPI HOPI-FUNKATRUX SGT. UNCLE PEPPER TAMT
AM ANDAMAN VIBRATION FINNAFRIPP SARAWAKE/NOR
TH BRITISH BORNEO PSYCHOPATHELLO ALLABOOTSEE
WACO JACO SPASSTÖRUNG & SPAYS BASSKUDOMITILL
À-BASSPAYS BASS PLAY THE BASSÖHKO DE MARKIES
VAN WATER VERSUS WATERWARHOLLANDLUBBERS BELO
W BELOW FREAQUENCY HIGH CAMPLITHOTHE DEATHAD
ES SPACE BASAVAMEDHADHARMARQUESSPACE ABASSY-
OYUNAVELLÀ-BASSPACE BAS-TUT-KAN-KISI ORANG U
TANGARA MARQUESAN MARKOYAIK KARAINBÖW VERSUS
PRINCE WILLIAM BEURYAT SPACE BASSAGANI BÖOTS
Y MARQUESANTABLATTABOOTSEAS MARQUESANTABOOTZ
ILLAS MARQUESAS SVIN! BARI ME SOUL HOLLAND M

ATER LOLLIROCHARSE LOLITERRA FIRMATER DOLLOR OCKARSE WOTTO WOTTO UNDERWATER GROTTO È MEZZ OPÛTAMOUSSOUND FREE YOUR ASS & YOUR MIND WIL L FOLLOW THE LIEDER TUNG HO TUNG HO! HUIT ET 2000 ! DE MARKIES VAN WATERRE PIG DANCING DOW N THE HOLE LANDS UN DOS-GEEPIELAND MUSIC WHA T'S A TELEPHONE BILL? MEMMEMMEMOTIONILE CHAO SSAGARBATA SAGARBATA! LASCOMARQUISES HANA HA U HAU HOLLAND PATU HOPE HAKA NOHO TITOI PUTA KEOS KEOS EVERYWHORE GRAPONQ GRAPONQ ATOMIKE BAUM AUM AUM AUM SOUNDEXPLOSSIFFOSSILES BOMM ING AROUNDABOUT HOLLAND LOWA LOLOWA LOLOWAWA TER CHTHONIC-TYPHONIC-PYTHONIC-CYCLONIC BIKI NI APOLL APOLLO WATERRAPOLLOGOS SWAMPWORKING THE LOW LOW UNDER HYPNASSAU PLAY LAAT MEER & VORSTENBOSCH SGT. GINGER & FRED HOT CHOCOLAT E EVERYONE'S A WEINER BABY BOOTSY'S NEW RUBB ER BALL THROWN INTO THE AMERICAN FALLS NIAGA RA FALLS BOOTSY'S NEW RUBBER BALL THROWN INT O THE CANADIAN FALLS NIAGARA FALLS SPACE BAS SSARATHUSTRAUSSPACE BOOTSIMABUSEA-MALE PRINC E WILLIAM BUTTSEAS THE TACITURN IT UP BURN R UBBER BURN IT UP PRINCE BERNIE WORRELLAS MAR QUESAS P-VONK ALL-STARLIAMENT ELECTRUNKADELI CATE BEEFHEARTS CLUB RUBBER BAND WANNA BETSY BABY VERY BOOTSIFULL SINDEEP THOTHALATTATTOO THOTHALATTATTOO ZIBBERSPACE ODD-MAN-OUT COME SAY, THERE'S THE RUBBER BAND MAN THE BEAUTY & THE BASSPACE ODDISSAY OUT LAUT UNCLE JAMEL A BAYMATCH ANDERSONNOFFABEACH DEFUNKADOLPHIN NATRASH GINGER & GEORGE GORDON LORD BYRONICC LONIC GILBERT & FRED AUSTÈRIA BOOTSY'S NEW R UBBER BALL-STARLIAMENT-DUNKADALLAS MARQUESAS

BRATATATALATTATABOOTSIMABUSEA-MALE MARQUIS I
CONTROVERSUS BRAT! BRATATATATA! BRATATATATAL
ATTHAITIBETANZ PARTY ON PLASTIC SURGERY DISA
STERS WÂWWÂWTÂW WÂWWÂWTÂW EVERYWHORE SPACE B
AZZAKARMATAHARIFEUNIXON UP YOUR ASSES YOUR P
ORTRAIT MARKIESKIMONO BIKINI ATOLL BUMBA BIL
LASWELLES ÎLES MARQUISEAS KENNEDY VYPERSPACE
BASS MISSILE TEST CENTAURAZORBLADE RUNNER WA
UWAUTAU WAUWAUTAURABILLASWILLIAM BUTTSEAS SP
OUTTER SPASSAGE THROUGH THE RED SEA WATER WA
TER MOST FOUL UPRIVERBUMBABBELLASWORRELL WOR
RELL TO THE RIVERBUM CARO FACTUM EST! I M FU
NKALL I M FUNKALL BOOMERANGUTANTRUMMING INST
ANT LIVESPERMSMASHFLUSSWAVES AHH... TSUNAMIS
MARQUESSAWAN BABIZAPPAPUAFURIKA NO CULLORADI
O MOHEAVY WATERGATECRÊCHEYENNE BRANDÖPPELLIP
SE NOW I M FUNKÄLLA I M FUNKÄLLÀ-BASSARASTOS
STHRAVESTETSUMIZU BAU WAU WAUTAUA WAUTAUA WA
WWAWWAWSHA WAWWAWSHAMANDRILLA MARQUISSEAMALE
MARQUIS DE MENDOZA QUE TAL QUE TAL OMM SWEA
T OMM DE MARKIES VAN WATER BURNING INTO AER
OSSPACE WARHEAD VI MARKIEZENFABRIEK FRACTOR
Y ZONESEX NIHILOLITA I MW THELUJI THELUJI IN
THE SKY THERMINAL NUCLEAR SWEATTELLITE ZWETT
ELSTREAM PORNOA-NOA PORNOAH-NOAH PORNOAHH-NO
AHH! ARARATTLES & AEROSSNAKES GEILGOTHA HAVE
PORNOAHH DADANUBIAN NOTT & GLIDDONAUAH-NAUAH
GILLGILLGOTTA HAVELOCK UP YOUR ALICE DEFUNKT
BANANGA-ORANGA NASAFRODISNEY WELTCUMLAND SID
& NANCY SINATRASH YOU ARE WHAT YOU DESIRE TH
ESE BOOTS ARE MADE FOR FUNASLUT! AFRODIZEESU
RGINGER & FREUD EREKTO-ABSOLUT VODKAOS ON TH
E HIGHWAY TO HELL ELL EL MARRIO MERZBAU WOWW

OW H2OR EUROLAGNIATMÜLTIMEDIAGRAMMARQUATSCHL
AMMALLES ÎLES MARQUISES FLOTTATING IN MINDWI
ND 6000 MILES TUTU MWIMBISHMA ORCHIPELAGOGOG
UINEA PEPPER DADALAI LAMAE WEST SHANTEDILUVI
ALL GOES WEST! HOPPYOYO HAPPYAYA HIPPYIYI LU
BALIBA FUKI LOWATERRA FIRMANIAKAAL MARKIESKI
MOHAVE HEAD DOWN BY THE LASER RIVER THAIGRIS
-GRIS EUPHRAT ICE-CREAM IS A REALITY YOUR PS
YCHIC HAIRSTYLE HYPERINEALL SPONGILLA IN THE
GARDEN OF ÄTÄTURKKITSCH DELUTEATEA VANGAGOGH
ORANGAKOQWORKING THE BODDILY WATERFLOW OUTPÛ
TASSEAS EJAQUWAYQUWAYQUWAYSEA UNCLE JAMBUBBE
L MON FREEÈRE! WATT WATT WATT WAN OWAH BEFOR
E OWAU OWAH WAN OWAH BEFORE OWAU OWAHALLACON
OVENAVENA CAVAORTAORTAORTAORCANE ORCRANIAL P
UMPING AMERICANAL LIVER BLURRAPPOOL HOW IS T
HE CUNNUS CUNNUSS CUNNUSSAU ORANGE NAZZAUBER
DACHES PISS SGT. BRIGGIT BARDÄXÄDOT & MADAMS
TERDAMŜ RETURN TO GENDER CROSSING WOMAN EMPT
YING BOWL OF WATER WATER EVERYWHERE FIRE FIR
E IN THE FUNK PAGLIA-PSYCHO-POPO FAECES TO F
AECES DE MARKIES VAN WATERRANSSEXUAL SGT. PE
PPUASS NEW GUINEAHOOLA HOOPI HOOPI PLAY LAUT
COME THE TLINGIT DOWN PINUPSCOT THUMBASSONOR
OUS RIVER TRIBES FLOATING ON WATER WATER BUR
NING BRIGHT IN HYPERBOLICSYLLABICSESQUEDALYM
ISTIC ERZATZ HAZE! THE BODY CLOCKWORK ORANGE
CHART KALEIDUSCHKOPFANGO DZUNGLES GO DZUNGLE
S WORK DAT BODY WORK DAT BODY BRICKENBECKING
BASS ECHOVERB SPEED LOOP SAMPLIFIRE RISE REL
EASING VOCOD SITAR CONGA GLITZ STARS RAIN SN
APS PAIN SLAP SPLASH SPLATTER HAPPI AZTEC DE
VIL ZONES HOO! UUT? HOPV UOM OC HOPV UOM OC?

WASWAS NOT WASWAS TIKITOI KAUKAU NUBÂA SUN R
ÂA & ORCHESTRASBURUNDIONYSANDENISTABUMBUMBAB
ILLAKE ALBERT PORNOGRAVITY WORKING IN WARHOL
LAND HELIO HAIKU HOOP DE MICHAEL VAN WILLIAM
COLLINSSATYRNASSAPOLLOAFRICABINETWORK DAT BU
DDHA WORK DAT BUDDHA IGG WHAT IGG? MARQUASIM
ODOMY MISSCHEDELPHICK & I TEXTC-MALE URANFA
NKING IN YOURSPRUNGANGAQUATIC SUNKULTUR LSDE
MONSTRUORUMBRILLEAU SOAPOCAPPELLIPSUCK WAU W
AU WAU KNOUMHOTPOULAFUCKALL-KARL ANDREJ STAR
KOVSKY SLANCÔME POÊMEGALYPSEAS NAUMAN CHANGE
L & ENGEL FALLSIAMESOPOTAMIATMÜLTRANSWORKING
CHINESE LEOPARD RITTICA-DODDICHRIST SUPPERST
ARLAMENTAL URFUNKADELIQUID SUNSHINE BANDADAM
ANTRACKING DE MARKIES VAN WATER WRITUALISING
THE NETHERWORLDS SGT. PAPUA NEU WORDMUSICKAW
AH-KAWAH THE MARQUESSYMPHOPERAPSODY IN RED Y
ELLOW & BLUE HERMAFRODIKES & SPERMATHODAMS E
CCE HOMO PIGMAEUS WEST ELLENFANT SAUVAGEOWAT
T WATT KNOUMHOTPOULLABAILEY JEAN KUNG AMALA
DOLF WÖLFLYNN ON THE BEUYSABOUT MÙNDISCO-KID
DIPUSSY REX MACHINE TAKE IT TO THE BRIDGEWAT
ER HOLLABIA MAJORACLE ORANGE JUS PRIMAE NOCT
IS ATOMIC HOG EAT HOG EAT HOG! BRIAN HEINO &
THE BARRY GIBBONZO VOODOO DADA RUBBER BANDA
MANDOLINEN UND GITARREN LET'S RAISE HAVELOCK
ELLICE FROM DALLAS MARQUESAS H.P.-FUCK THE B
UTTON THE CLINTON CLITORIS THE MARQUESANZABA
ANZABA NZABA ZABA ZABALANCÔME CÔME CÔME Ô DE
TELLIOT HELIGON OCEANDAMAN DETOURGENT HELIOC
ALM AQUAVITAL THE ABERRATIONILE BOMBOOTSYBIL
LA HOLLANDE MARKIES VAN WATER ELECTROSHOCKIN
G BLUE BLUE ELECTRIC BLUE ONE OWAH WAN OWAUT

OPSY-TURVY PAPUA NEUROPATHI SEXUALIS GUINNEE
ABEAT SIMONE SIMONE DE BOVARYWHORE MARQUESSA
PPHONÄSSEXAU HOLANDIKE COW COW KAWA KAWA YOU
RZUSTANDAMAN VIBRATORATIO THIS IS ONLY THE B
IKINI A'DAM ANFANGADELICK CULEAU LAMOUR SOUS
LÉMASQUELLES ÎLES MARQUISES LEAU BUTT TAMTAM
MIWI MYSOUL & HOLLAND URINARY PEOPLE TEST TE
ST TO THE TESTIS DE MARKIES VAN WATER ÉSPACE
VOODOOSSEA ONE OH, I OWAUTOEROTICKA PRICKADE
LICKA PREACHAMAN VOODOO-EROS/AFRICAN ABORIGI
NES & SEX HORMONES IN THE MACHINE AGE ONE MA
NTRANANGA-ORANGAGANASSAU THEY CALL M DOG GEO
RGE CLINTON & THE FAMILY DISCOGLOSSIDANUADADA
TANGALOP! TEPOANIM! IMMILUTAQ! TARABILLA! DE
DANNUBIAN NUTT MW.T MW ALPHASLOPPHETHALASSAD
E BITHGANGREL BAHAGOLTAUN CLOCNAGEILTACHTUNG
ORANGE ORDER MARQUIS VONNEGROT WATT WATT ANU
S MONSDUSCHKOPFUNKATERROR OH, NOZZLE DE FRIG
GAROTOROTEAUTOPSEAS BINNAKINSEYS ALFRED HITE
THE KLITTOURGUINEA BANDAMANTRA WORDWITT TO W
HO-WHO! WORDWITT TO WAH-WAH! MUTT IN HOLLAND
WAHSINNÄSSEAS & TERRATIONALITY DIES INTEGRAT
IVE PSYCHOSILLA ECHOLA HOLLANDE REDEPERSONAL
ISATIE STONE AGE AT ONSET DELUGILLES DELA TO
URETTHE BOMB THE BOMB 3-DSM-III-DELUGIONIL 3
-DISORDERRUN GRANDAMANDIOS TYPEE 200/203 ÉSP
ACE EROSSITY SUPREMATURE DÉJACULOCEAN TRISTR
AMP & AROUSALT AUTOSITE & PARASITE MINDBLOWI
NG LEAUGUSHING DIGUERILLEROTICKA PRICHLEAU D
E MARKIES VAN WATER COLLAPSING HOLLANDIKE VE
NUS IMPULSE CONTROL DISORDER W/INTERPERSONA
L VAGINISMUS RIVIERLINGHUAPHONASLITT LEEGHWA
TERHOOFD WATERSHITDOWN & OUT COMES HOLLAND D

E MARKIES VAN WATER W/WRITING DISORDER D-I-
S-O-R-D-E-R LASCALVINNACAN ARE WE NOT MEN ON
THE MOON? CISHE-MOLL MONDSHINE-SONATA EAUPUS
SEA NR. TUTU AQUADADAGIO S.O.S. TENUTA-ATTICC
A GRAND MALLEGRETTO-ATTACCA PRESTO AGUAGITAT
TO WHITT TO HOLLAND SCATULLUS MARKISSES MARQ
UESSEXUAL OFFINNAFFENCE LET'S HAVELOCK ELLIS
COOPER IN WONDERLAND OH I OH, KING GEORGE OR
ANGEL-OETANGEL FALLSUNNY ADIEUNUCHAMALE PRIN
CE CHARLIE BIRDFEATHER & THE AFRICAN CITY BE
ATS BAND SLOW BOAT TO CHINA, MWATER & REASON
SPACE AGE AT S/ONSET SPRAGGFLUSS MORPHINE AD
DICTION IN CHIMPANZEES JIMPUSHEMALEL MARQUES
AN MARCOÏTUS IN ANOMALIECTROSHOCKING THE FLO
OD IN THE PALMER/MASS/HOSPITAL FOR EPILEPTIC
S WATT OVID WATT OVID (SHOWERMAN, G, TRANS.)
HEROÏDES & AMORES AGUA DULCE AGLJA SALADA NEP
TUNICCLONIQUELLEAURÉAL YO YO EL RE HEINOLA G
AY HEY CAPELLO LO! SHIROSHE-MAILES ÎLES MARQ
UISES COMING INTO BEING THERE THE WORD ATOLL
ATOLL ONE ORAH BEAFOA HOW ORAH ORANGEL FALLS
3212 FEET HIGH & RISING SUNMASSEA MUMMY MUMM
Y WHAT'S THE AQUARIAN ALPHAPHONE THE HELMHOL
TZ CHESSBOARD THE MAGICAL MYSTERY MUSEUM THE
ZÖLLNER-HARING ILLUSION THE PLANET OCEAN WOR
LD THE MOSSO ERGOGRAPH THE ANSCHLUSS STROBOS
COPE THE JOE SPOOK ECTOPLASM KIT THE TOPLESS
WITCHES SABBATH THE NOAA HURRICANE CENTER TH
E KIRLIAN SPIRIT PHOTOGRAPHY THE BISSKY ELEC
TRODIANOSCOPY THE RANSCHBURG MÊMORY DRUM THE
TARKOVSKY PHENOMENA THE HADRONIC STATE IN EL
ECTRON-PROTON INTERACTIONS AT HERA MOMMY MOM
MY EVERYWHORE OBEATA VIRGOGO BEATI PUSSIDENT

ES ECHOLA MARQUISE VON OO-SHO-BE-DOO-BEE-BOP
EBB EBB EBB SAY BABATAVIA TESTING ONE TWO MA
X IS MAKING WAX GRAND MALBLASSERTWARTSALAT E
L MARQUESAN SCHIZOPHRENIFORMAL BEHAVIOUR INT
ERMITTENT EXPLOSIVE DISORDER VIVANGEL FALLS
WASWAS NOT WASWAS TIKITOI KAUKAU NUBAA STRAS
BURUNDI SANDANISTABUMBUMBABILLAKE ALBERT POR
NOGRAVITY WORKING IN WARHOLLAND DE MICHAEL V
AN WILLIAM SATYRNASAPOLLAPOLAFRICAFRICAFRICA
BINETWORK DAT BUDDHA WORK DAT BUODHA POWERIN
FERNOGRAPHICKAPRICKALL EDIPO REDIPO RETURNIL
E RAPPATISSERHINE THE DEEP WATERS! TESTING O
NE TWO BLACK PEARL HARBOUR FOR THE FRENCH DE
AD MADAME OVIRI OVIRI OVIRIWHORE CALL MEE SW
AHELIUM NEON PSYCHOANALLASER MARKUSUKUMA MBI
LIKINIMO ATOLL BOMBABUKASIMILE SOLO EL MARKI
ES VAN WATTURTLERRIFFONQUE IN MONO BIKINO AT
OLLIPS FROM PRAMSTERDAM CHUNGWAWA MWASSIMILE
MFUNGWATER BWAWANAWAKE-DEVIL REFILLYNOTT KIM
BUNGA CLARKES ELECTRIX HOLLADYLAND MAE MYSEL
F & I WANAWAKE BWAWANAMAKE-MICKEY'S MONKEY'S
MOUSSEPIKKA PRICKAPUTSCH NILI MICKEY LOVE NO
T WAH-WAH OLLA NAVEN FAI ORGASM NÄSSOWWOOW MI
GALIKO VOODOO CHILE BERING SEA DISKIMOHAVE N
O MERZ! YUK KUK SUX THE KUK RIVER ICE-RUN JE
SUSKRUSENSTERN SUPERSTARQÈQ TARQÈQQÈQ QÈQQÈQ
GRAND MALTAMIRACLE ART FOR ART TAYLOR'S SAKE
PSYCHO POPTOPHONICCLONIC-SEISHARON STONE & T
HE FAMILY SLY SLUT SLICK SLIVER SLITHER & SL
IPPERY WHEN WATT WATT! THE EVER COPULATING O
NE MANGAKOQQOQ QOQQOQ IGLOTZ TV IGLOTZILLA P
AY-TVAUDOOBOP-MCNUTT BUDDHARMARQUESSOUNDWAKE
UUME SWEAT UUME SOM ROM HAAGEN MOONSISTER SU

NBROTHERHOOD DISCO CRISCOVERY MIR MIR SPUTLI
GHT ONE OWAUTOTONICCLOWN THE BURLESQUOONEEDE
EPTHROAT UNCLE JAMBISHMARQUESS IN IJSFABRIEK
SHAMROCK FEAR DEATH BY WATERRAP SOFTLY, TILL
I END MY SONGALONG LONG TIDE AGOGOGO UNCLE S
HAMROCK PUNDAUN SCHAMRÂDARRÊGAL TWIT TWIT TW
IT COCO RICO COCO RICO ONE MANLOGOGO BUNG BL
AGO BUNG BLAGO JUNGLE JIF JUJU TONTONTONNERR
EURQUELLES ÎLES ÎLES EPILEAPSILLA BOMBÈCILES
BEATLES ÈLECTRONICCLONIQUES EL MARQUESSPLIFF
INTANNEGUINEANDER MARQUIS VONNYVAXENDENTALES
PSYCHO POP JUMP & UPSUCKFELD SELASSIMILES PRA
NCING NIGERIDOO IDOO-BOPPENOSEA BASS EL MARC
OJONES EVAGUAGUA CULOLO PHALLEO-PSYCHO-POPEY
E & OLIVIA NEWTONICCLINICAL OIL OF OLAZZEDIN
E ALAÏALATOYA JACKSONIAN EPILEPSILASSY FANNY
GOES TO HOLLYWOOD HOTT BUTTERED SOLARIS PRAN
CING NIGERIDOO DELTAQUASPLANE KUNA KUNA BACK
TO POONA POONAH POONAHH FRIED ISCUMBAGHWAN O
RANGE SUNNYASSIN CINÉASSINASS & SONNASSASSIN
ASSAU POONAGRAFFITTIT POONAGRABBITTIT FLYBAG
HWAN NATION KUNA BACK TO KUNA LINGUS KUNA TU
NGUS WATER WATER IVORY GHOST MINNITORO MIRIB
OKKO O LOLO TORO I LOLO I LOLO! PLAY BONNY J
UJU PLAY BUNNY JOJO I JOJO! ABASSI SPAESI MA
NA OBASSI JUJUSU CRISIS ARANGA SODA POP OUT!
BOOTSYBILLASWELLESDEFUNKADELICTRONICCLONIC R
IVERBETTSY & THE ALPHABEAST THE BEAUTY & THE
BASS I SUPPACE BASTIAANSEEE-LITE ETCHE OHOMO
GANESHAMAAN MEGANESHAMALE MARQUIS SPERMANENT
DEFUNKADELICT RUBBER DICKA PRICKANESHAPENISD
O-BOP ORANGE NÄZZAUBERPOP ROCKY RORSCHACH SP
ACE BASEMENT 5 BOOTSILICON CHIPCHOP THERMONU

CLEAR SCHWITTERS SPACE BASSEEMILES AHEAD ONE
MAN RAY CHARLES MINGUS SHEIMATTERHORNY HORNF
IELDS FOREVER OLÉ OLÉ GUAPAPUASPACE BASSESS
EEKRIEG THE FONQUE D'EAU QUE D'EAU EL MARQUE
SSOTARRIZAUBERROBERRIA ONE MAN CHAUVET APOLL
O 11 BORDERLINE CAVEMAN BEBOOTSIMALE MARQUIS
WUNDERSEA-MILLY JACKSONIAN EPILEPTICKA PRICK
NANCY THESE BOOTS ARE MADE FOR TRUNKIN' SPAB
BUZZIN' ELEPHANT WALKAQUABOOTZILLA DURY MARQ
UESAN TEACH-IN/GINGER & FRED DANCE CLINIC/SP
AESSIBASSI SPAESSIBASSI FEEL THE FIRE HOLLAN
D DADATA BASSY BILLINE BASSOLOWER REGION ERE
KTA-BOOTSIEGFRIED NOTZSCHALLSDSM-III-DE MARK
IES VAN WATER DUCHAMPUTATING HOLLAND SUCKERK
RANK OPUSSIBASSI TRANSMUTTATION MUTTATIS MUT
TANDIS BOOTSEESPRACHAMANIA BOETZEE COLLINS C
OETZEE DICTIONANTRA WILLIAM COLLINS SONS & C
OBRASS DOUM-DOUM BALAFONY GONGOMAMA KAMEN ON
YA JUSU CHRIST ORANGE SODA POP! THERE YOU GO
EAULAND DILDOKUDOO-BOP MEAT NATION SKATING O
N BLACK ICE I JUDGE THE FUNK QUILTY! QUILTY!
LO! . . . OLÉ OLÉ AGUAPALEO-PSYCHO-POP HECTOR P
OLEO-PSYCHO-POP-METAMORFOSIS THALATTABOOTSTE
ELY DANUBBER BAND H2O'CLOCK THE MINOTRUNK WE
LCOME THE WATERFOOL ADAMAORIVER IN ALMERE EL
MAREXWATERSTOOT EL MARKUZBECKISTAND-IN DR. M
ABUZBECKISTAN CALL MEE ÂPHELIUM AGUAPEEGEEQU
ANEE JIMMICKY MOUZBECKISTUNT TÜSPUTABOUTSY A
LTER EAGLE EAGLE RIVER A WORK OF TWO PARTS F
OR ONE SPACE BASSEEBEBING FEATURING BERNIE W
ORRELL A TURBULENCE INDUCED IN A BODY OF WAT
ER/LUCHT YOU ARE BERNIFAL ONE WAHNTHEMATIKKA
PRICKAPUTSCH BUTO BUTO BABY YOUR ARE BOOTSIF

UL AQUATA-KOEM AQUATA-KOEM AFROASIAQ (EL) BU
XU BANGAKOK HALALA HE-HE-HE HALALA HE-HE-HE!
I M FLESH & BLOOD I M FIRE & AIR SODA POP! S
UPERGROOVALISTICPROSEAFUNKSTICAEQUESALINOVER
ACEOALUMINOSOCUPREYOVITRIOLIC SPAGUYANA AQUA
BOOGIE KING GEORGE WATERFALL EL MARCASCADE S
ADE ONE NATION TIDAL WAKE MEGANESHA MIX GENO
SHA WÖLFLI MILES DEEE TUTU SILLA IMILLA REVO
LTA RIVERBIPOLAR ICEKIMOONBROTHER WATERMARQU
ESUNSISTER HYDROOMYSOGYN BOMBERANG UTANNIK U
TOPPIK UFOBBIK UFALLIK WORDWHIPPING THE KELV
IN WAVE MOTION IN SPACE IN MOTION! BLOP BLOP
LIST OFF HOLLAND URSOUNDWAVEFRONTAAL DUTCHER
IDOO-BLOPITY BLOPITY BLIP BLIP ONDES DE CHOC
TREATMENTAAL DUSCHORDER DOLL UP YOUR KUNDT A
NGEL DUST TUBES OLLANDA ANADOLL UNTERWASSERS
CHALLTECHNICALVIN EXPLOCEAN WAVE WAHN WAHN R
UBBERALL WAHN OMAHAO OMAHAO GEORGE CLINTON &
THE NUCLEAR FAMILY SIZE PLANTERS CHEESE-BOUL
ES-BOULES FLESHING OUT LIVING NAMES & NAMING
IN FINATRUNK WIK MONKAN TRUPPER BAND SGT. PA
PUA NEU GUINNEPAL WORD-WARA MAKE LOLO NOT WA
WA PAEPAE-FONQUELLE MARQUIS DE NADA ALL AROU
ND THE WORLD PVANKUDOLLY MFUNGWARBABY NUKUDO
HIVAQUA VAIPO WATERFALL-STARLIAMOUNT PYRONAS
SAU RUMPAZOID MARQUESAN MEAT PLANET O KLITTA
URAVESIFALL SPACE BASSOLOMONSOON RADIOACTIVE
FALL OUT LAUT MEGOVATTENCEFALLOGRAMMARQUESS
UPERGROOVALISTICPROSEAFUNKSTICAEQUESALINOVER
ACEOALUMINOSOCUPREYOVITRIOLIC SPAGUYANA AQUA
BOOGIE KING GEORGE WATERFALL GIB MIR HONIG / H
ONEY IS FLOWING LES ÎLES JARRELLAS MARQUESAS
WISHANTIPSYCHOPOTAMIA PSIQIATREATISE TRISTAN

GETZ OUT IZOOT SIMS! THE BIKINI ATOLL BUMBAB
ILLABONGO BUD POWELL WELL JOHNNY SITAR WATSO
N WATSON PRINCE WILLIAM COWPER HUGO WÖLFLI B
OB DYLAN THOMAS LOVELL BEDDOES GINGER & FRED
DIE & THE RED HOT RODS ONE MANGAN SHOW CLARE
WATER WATER RUBBERRUN LOWELL WELL EL MARQUES
SPARAGMOSSPHEREPRISE WE WANT BOOTSY THE DITH
YRAMBIENCEFALLOGRAMMARQUESAN PIG DANCE PARTY
ON PLASMATIC TUNGUSIC ORGANIC DELUCY SYNDROM
MW/PSYCHODISCOCYCLOSCHIZOTIC FEATURES MARCU
S MILLER HYDROGENESIS 1:1 TRANSMUTTAALMUDDER
MARQUIS VON OO-SHE-BE-DO-BEE-LITE SCHUMANTRA
UTCHA UTCHA UTCHA UROPHILIAS MARQUESASQUATCH
AWWRITE BOULES-BOULES DECYBERSPACING THROUGH
THE ELVIS MIRROR MIRROR TOMSK TATARS & BOMSK
BABARS! SENZA TITOLOLO FEAT SLY STONE FREE T
HE BIRD OF PARADICE-KHUBHIKKHUDOLLAING DEMIL
KRAEPPULLING UP THE ORANGAKUTANGERINE SUNSHI
NE SKYWAY OVER HOLLAND UNTER ALLES KAPUTZ NI
LI SELAVY EN PRROSE SELAVY SOYÉZ-MYSTÉRIEUSE
S ENTRA TATTUPAPAU NEU GUINEAGUA DURAGUA FIN
AGUA VIVAGINAGUA DE MARANA LIVIA FIRE IN THE
HEART MAQCCHIKUY BELASTEN MAQCCHIKUY BETASTE
N OTELLATTAATA-VAHINE TELLATTAATATTOO-VAHINE
RHEINDEER TONGUS MANCHEW SHAMANIC DON'T PANIC
PSYCHOCEANAL PALEOPARDÖPPELGANGES WAWWAWSHAM
ANESS NONTRANSSEXUAL TYPEYOTLOLO TYPEE FUNKI
NG IN FLIGHT OF IDEAS WAS GIBT'S NEUES, PUSS
Y? THE HYPERILLA NEOLEAUJAZZ PSYCHOMOTÖRHEAD
FUCKSTREAMMACHINE LEMMY BE YOUR LOVER TÜSPÜT
NIKE ENOS MUNDUS OLA WAWA MISEE HERBIE HANGA
KOCK FAKING FUTURE SHOCK TELEVIZYON EPILEPSY
AGUA DE MARQUESTRELLA DE MARKIESTRELLA DE MA

RQUESTRELLA DE MARKIES VAN WATERREMOTOROTARY
CLUB FUCK NIPPONNASSAU DON'T TRY TO CATCH A R
IVER LET IT RAIN & TEARS END OF THE WORLD AP
HRODITE'S CHILD IT'S RAINING MEN GG & GINGER
& FREDGAR ALLEN POE-FUNGIMAMA BEBOPAFONGADIS
COPALYPSODOMY & MY SHADOW 1.2. TEST ONE NAT
ION EL MARQUESAN SHAMMANNERIST WAHNSINUSOÏDA
L WAVE POWER TO THE PEOPLES HAPPI HAPPI LOOP
I LOOPI UNCLE YAM YAM ACID JAZZ RADIO EDIT T
ÜSPÜTNIXON! FENJAL AVANT-GARDE BAIN MOUSSANT
FEN HE! FEN HE! FENJALSDE AQUAVANT-GARDE MAR
KIES VAN WATER BAIN MOUSSANTHALATTABOOTSYBIL
LABONGO BUD POWELLAS MARQUESAS EUNUKE JUST D
O IT NACHASDIONYSOS EUNOOKIE NOOKIE PALEO-PS
YCHOMOTOR AGITATION NATION GINGER & FREDVARD
MUNCH SCREEMTEST TEST UVOGULKOPF MOONWALKING
ON AISCREMA SOLAR ECLIPSINC TAKE ONE TEKHA T
EKHA SHARA MATZKAALA TO STRESSBURYAT ZEN DAN
IS THE DARE DEVIL M DIRTY DSCHUNGEL M DEEP S
EA DRILLING DRACULAYAMIWI MIWI DRACULÄMÄGÄTT
OBARDOT HELLZAPOPPING IN PEPPERLAND HOLANDAG
UA DE NARANJABONOSA DOLOROSADOLOROSA PSYCHOK
ELLER KELLER FASTER PUSSYCAT KILL KILL HOLAN
DAGUA DE MARQUESSUCCESS DE SADE THE DEEP-SEA
RAIN! RAIN! RAIN! LET IT RAIN WOWWOWTOW WAUW
AUTAULIPANG SHAMALES & CRAZY HORSES AHH... T
SUNAMIS BONDING IATMOLECULES DEVIL CRAB & TI
GERFEET KÖRPERFIELDS ARSCHIFFERRUIN FOREFFER
HALLUZ DE LUNATION THE WATERFALLUZ DE SOLWAR
ATELSNAKEREIAPOPEIA ONE OWAUTAULIPANGILLA TU
NGUS MANCHUKCHEE BLOOD SUGAR WAX MAJIC ASTRO
BOSCOPPER DUSKIMOHAVE WAWWAWSHA WAWWAWSHAMAN
US DEPRESSURHINE TONGARSOAK HAILEY THE MAR-K

EYS MEMPHIS EXPERIENCE MEXÀGO MÜXE SHAMIX TH
E RUBY LASER RIVER ICE-KÜBEL MARDUCKSOAPWORK
DAT BOUDIN BOUDIN THE DUTCH TREAT CIMABOOTSY
BILLÀ-BASSPACE ODDIESSILLA BACCHUS WHINE OWA
AAH WHINE OWAAAH ARNO ARNOAH-NOAH WE ARE NO?
TSUNÀHMIS SCHMIDT H2O'CLOCKWISE ORANGE UP YO
UR POP ARSE WARHOLLAND DOWN YOUR HOLZER BOX-
POP VENUS IMPULZ ROCKY POP THE HORROR THE HO
RROR POP SPACE ROCKY POP THE HORROR POP SOAP
POPERA POP SOUPPOPERA ZZ TOPPOP SODA-POP SOD
OMY POP-UP DEMENTIA PRAECOX PRE-POP THE FRED
FLINTSTONE FUNGHI FACTORY! PALEO PSYCHO POP-
OUT COMES NERVALLUCY IN THE SKY ON THE FLENT
ROP ORGAN IN THE NETHERLANDS REFORMATED CHUR
CH IN LOENEN A.D. VECHT HARD COGNITIVE SLOWI
NG MIMMIMBO JIMJIMBO L'EAURANGE GILBERT BÉCA
UD & GEORGE SPLANKTONIKKLONIC AQUAKIRIVIER K
LITTERRUN OLÉ! O'CANGACEIRO AGUA DE MARKASIH
ALL-IN PRIMORDIAL KAOS KAKI WAIKIKIEFER BEAC
H I LOLOBANG I LOLOBANG ECHOLA MÈR FOLLAMOUR
JERUK MANIS DEI EI I THE BULLAWARRATIONILE M
ARQUIS FOLLABULLROARING IN SPACE BAHASA BURU
NGA BARANGA TANGELOP TEPOANIM TARABILLA IMIL
LUTAQ! BATTEAU BATTEAU IVREAWHOREAKLITTORO Y
AYOI YAYOI! EL MARKUSAMADEUS SEX MACCHINAVEN
MONUMENTAL RADIOAKTIVER ABFALLING DOWN FALLI
NG DOWN FALLING DOWN IAMATTERASUMOHAVE METAL
SEX MACHINE KAMI KAMI KAMI ON YA KAMAY RIVER
WATER WATER COMING ALL OVERYWHORE OLA WAWA M
ISEE-FUNKT MARKISSIMMEEE-LITE LOOE LOOE KING
ORANGE JAMBORIGINILE MWÊ-MÊMMOMO-MAKING JAME
S MARSHALL IS. ATOMBOMBEN & HERE COMES THE W
ATER WATER EL MARQUESAN MARCO IS. CHRISTO SU

PERSTARNOA DIZZYGOTHIC DELUGILLESPIE-FONG-AL
L-STARNOAH-NOAH HAPPAH-HAPPAH! ÇMARTELLO TAJ
TAJ MAHALLABOOTZILLATOLLAND HIGHWAY HOTELLER
PLAY BUNDA PLAY COMMENDO BUNDA THE BULLETTRI
STOSS & GRIFFESSOLDES FLOATING ON WATER WATE
R & LÊMON LAVALAS MARQUESASQUATCH HOOPAH HOO
PAH HOOPAH ESSO-LSDONAUQUELLÊMONGOLIAN ASTRA
LSCHLANGEL FALLSUCK OR FAKE THE KAEMPFERT TO
UCH PLAY ESKIMO COMPUTERGAMES HOLLAND DEFUNK
T-ALL-STARLIAMUNDWASSERMOON JOURNEY TO IXTLA
NTIS BUTUH BUTUH BABY UUME SWIT UUME WATRA F
ODOE WINTIBERLIN DE MARKIES VAN WATRA MAMARK
IES VAN WATRA PAPATOMIC ABOMAGAMARQUÉSAFRAN
TIC ASTROFLASHING DISCHARGE AHH... TSUNAMIAM
IAMIAMI MYSELFABLASTHMAKUMBUMBABY HOLLAND L
ISTEN UP JUST LIKE A DOG EAT DOG EAT DOG (WH
O LOVES YA LOLLY) ICCA PIG ASS EAU OLLANDADA
HIMMALAY-OUT LAUT DANGER DEEP WATER DE MARKI
ES VAN RIVER WATER CASCÄTÄTÜRK DAMNATION ASW
AN OWAH ASWAN OWAU BABARADADA WASH YOUR FACE
S SALT FROSTING RAZZAZA LAKE VAN WATER ANUBBI
SMARCKIES VAN KILOWATT SALTSOAKING BRAINCHAR
MING HOLLAND TABOOED O GOODLY BULL! O GOODLY
BULL! MWATER YOUR AXO-MAMA POTATO-MOTHER RAM
ANGA MAN VIBRATION JAHWEH THALAPSUS! THALAPS
US! CUMAE CUMAE HOLLAND PERGOLUCY IN THE SKY
SEXTETSUMIZUWALALA MARQUISEAMARKIES VAN WITT
AR WITTARKOVSKIWATER HURRY UP BEN HURRY UP J
OHNSON BIG BENBEN-WAWA HEIDIPUPUSSY DON'T YOU
TOUCH THE QUEEN OF TAHITI THE KING OF CAMBOD
IA TIDESUMIZU KUDO HAPPENING SOUS-LA-CRUE WA
ITING REVELATION IN THE RAIN OF HEREDITY-CHR
OMOSOMEBUDDA WATERMARK SPITZEAS TURN THIS MO

THRA OUT NILE BASSING BOOTSY WAN HORRORA BAB
Y DOLLAMOUR MYSELF & I OOH I BABY BURNING UP
ZAVATTABASCOBRAT! SPRACHILLE ZAVATTENFALL YO
YO EL MAR CELLOLO MARCEAUX WAZZA WAZZAVATTAB
ASCOBRATATATATA! BASS SOLIKUDO SAXUM DRUGS &
ROCKNROLL ESPUMAE WEST LAPIS LAPIS APIS APIS
SPACHÉOLÉ OPUSSY 3002 LE MARQUIS DE BOMBELLE
S POPPYS SGT. PAPUASS' BAND ON THE RUN BABBY
COOL DADA NUBA BABBY COOL WAZ NOT WAZTEC THA
ITIGRIS-GRIS EUPHRATEASE MAGIC WATER O BEOWU
LFLI HOLLAND DADA ADAD EL MARKISHTAR SHAMASH
AMALE UNCLE RAMMAN ANUSKUDO AAH YA SHIH TEMT
EM! RAINMAKING IN OURMANIA POPM POPMLTSIC SWE
ET MUSIC FRIPP OFF HOLLAND GOGO LYNCH TWIN S
PEAKSEXPERIENCES DR. JAKAL & MR. HIDE JAZZ T
HE RIPPER JAZZWATAZZ WATAZZ JAZZAUBERFLUTWAK
E & TELEFANNATRIXIASIS JASS MUSIK SWEET MUSI
K AND I SAID JAZZ O JAZZ! RIVERRANG DOO BEAT
THE MEAT RICHARD SCHIZOOFILIA EVERYWHERE MIC
KEYS MONKEYS MOOSE ON THE LOOSELY IN THE SKY
LIGHT ONE OWAH ONE OWAHWAH METEMPSYCHOTERIP
PERY PARROTTERY & PAROLLERY THIS IS WHAT YOU
IS MATERIA PRIMATERIA PRIMATERIA PRIMARQUESS
WORDS WHICH CAN HEAR WATER REBEL REBEL SCHNA
BBEL SCHNABBEL UFOAMERICA & AFRO DOLLARS HYE
S ATTES! HYES ATTES! MARQUESAN PIGNITION YAM
FLUG PIGLOOLITALATTABOO-BOBGODZAPP THALLIS M
WATER WAWAKAN TANKA GEOCEANOMATER WATT! ETER
NILE GEOWATER SGT. PAPUASS' CHILI POPPERS VI
TTELLOISES/VITTELLOONIES RAINMAKING IN EBBIS
SINASSAU POPM POPMW POMPMWATER TO WATER MUDH
ONEY MOTORAPSYCHO BLACKSNAKE SEXUALITY IN WO
RLD CINEMA VOLUME 1 ONE OWAUTO ASSASSINOPHIL

IA YOU UP DO IT FOR VAN GOGH! ZAPPORINUL URQ
UELLEPHANTIASIAMESOPLOTAMINIATERRES D'ARNHEM
MATTERRES D'ARNHEIMAT BE-BOPAZOWIE GET OUT O
F WORRELLAND LASWELLAND WARHOLLAND BE-BOPADO
LLY FARTON DR. FURBURGER LSDEFORMATTERRES WA
TERHOLE-LANDSCOPE ATOM MIX RIFFARTUAL REALIT
TER SUB RAWHOLANDICAOS WHOLLAND HOWLLAND WOR
RELLAS MARQUESEAS HOLI-HOLIPHANTIJJAZZ WATER
WATER EVERYWHORRANT HOOKAHH HOOKAHH! MARQUES
SPIRAL JETTY DODO BROKEN CIRCLE (BREAKING TH
E DIKE) ONE MANGROVE MEANDERING ISLAND YOURQ
UELLE MÄRREXQUISSIT IRRATIOOOOOOMPHALLUS GET
GET ON UP YOUR ASS NINJAH HÄAGEN-DASZEXTRASH
BOOTZILLAH, LIBYA SPACE BASSATYRS & BOOTSILÈ
NES GO WEST MAENAD BOOTSILANUSTRATUMTUM TITA
NIC DON'T PANIC HERACLITONIC-TIPHONIC SPASSAB
AZIOS & RAPEIRON PRESENT HINDU WARHOLES THRA
CE THE LIONDATION OF NAXAU ZOROASTRAL BODY M
AGIC STARRAPRIAPIS B/FUNK MPS TO THE MPSYCHO
MAASSOSSCHISM MARQUESAN MARKOBLENZKRIEG MARK
AISER WILHELM SCHIEFFER & BULLBÖHR FACTORY Z
ONES POPMPS TO THE MPSMEGATOM MIX GLAMMURDER
MARQUIS VON OOHH BABY POWERSPINBOOTSY ROTATI
NG EPILEPSY DE MARKIES VAN WATERRILOQULTS/THE
MARQUESS OF WATERRA MARIQUESS EINFLUSS ONE N
ATION WATERTIONYSOS FATS KUDOMINO LIVE AT MO
NTREUX PHAT! SKUDOMINOAHH... KUDOMINOVA GUINE
AHH... MARQUIS GRAS IN NEW ORLEANS PASSING T
HRUÏDE MARKIES VAN WATERRES STONE FREEZE GYP
SY EYES CUBES OW! DIG, OW! HUH! YEAH! TV TRA
NSSYLVANIAGARA FALLSSS TO THE MMM JAZZING TH
E RIVER H-BAMBOULA MARQUISEASSTARSHINE CAMAR
QUESSUTRA STAY WHERE YOU IS THE SPAZTHEK DEV

IL ZONES TSUNAMIS JUPITER ALLINES W/MARS FE
E-LIN' SWEET FEE-LIN' OO, AW! ACQUA NOUN MUT
ABILE MARCASTRATOTEM KUTIGREASER & GREASER M
AGUS U BELASTEN MAGUS U BETASTEN MASCASTIGOG
O CRAZZEE MARCASSIUS KLEE MARCASPIUS CLAY MW
RADIX-MADE ACQUATACLYSMOUSSEAS MARCASTANEDAD
A COULE MARQUIS RABIODOLOOP RE-BOOP BAPTIZOF
RENIAGARABIODOLOOP RE-BOO-DOP RABIDUSCHAMALE
ESPUMAE WEST MYSELF & I SCABIESMARCKIES MARQ
UESAN SCABIES MEER & BOSCHAMAN BACCHABUNDUSC
H THALATTABUMBUM BAPTISMARQUESS MAMILLA MARQ
UISE GOODMORNING ANGEL DUSTARSHINE JUSTINE D
O IT HARE HARE REMY REMY SLY & THE FAMILY DU
NBAR JORDANNUKE BASSTARBACH LET THE SUNSHINE
INN SGT. PAPUASS' LOVELY OCEAN FRED & THAMES
TOYS HOME SWEET GEORGIA CLINTON ECCE HOMO LU
TINS À-VAU-LEAUCLUSE LOOKING VAUCLUSE ARHÔNE
ARHÔNE ARHÔNE AIGEAU WORLD PERFECT UP YOU'RE A
RSE GIBSY MIR HONIGGER DOBRA DOBRA TELLITTA!
TELLITTA! WARRTARR WARRTARR BEBUBRECKER BROT
HERS BACK IN BLACK VENUS IN REVERSE LASERRUN
SPERMÈRE NÀHM JAM PEAK TVIDEO ECLIPSEE YOU T
HE MARQUIS DE BOMBELLES FILLICRÂNES LIQUID N
ATION VAUDOUVILLENEUVE-SAINT GEORGE CLINTONI
CCLOWNIC MONOPRICK JOHN THOMAS DOLBYSTEREO H
IGH-HAILE-SHELASSHEMALE H/H BOMB LOVE DOLL S
UCK YOU CAN DRUÏD AQUA HOMO WATERING WATERIN
G EVERYWHERE SATTAMASSA GANABYSSINIA NIRVANI
C VULVANIC GALGANIC ZAPPANIC KUMBUMMING ARHÔ
NE AIGEAU INTOTO THE SCHIZZAUFRENATICK EPPIZ
ONE BRATTHATTHATHATHALATTABULA RASALVATION H
OLLAND THE CHIRHOSHIMALAYYA MW SPIRIT-SPEECH
ING TO THE NATION ONE MAN TSHO SAY NO-MO VOL

CANIC DON'T PANIC BRATATATATA BAHASA POP TELA
GAVISION EPILEPSY MAADAH MAADAHH MAADAHHH PL
AY LAUT KULZUM RE EL MARKGREIVISHNUKE NUKE S
ULA SULAH SULAHH THE HYDROGEN GIRAFFURRY SPE
ED FREAKS AÀRROKKING BEYOND THE VALLEY OF TH
E DOLLS BULDO-BOP BANG! WAU TOA WAU TOA MARQ
UESSEX JUNIOR AQUA BÔGI WAKEE FALLS HOMME SV
ET HOMME SPLYASHES TO SPLYASHES OGAWAKAN TAN
KAWA VADADAPAT VALNAVEN TELLUSMANTRANZEETNAY
AWATER DE MARKIES VANAWATER THE RYEKAOS BOOT
SIBILLAH BILLAHMUJIZAZZ YAUSA YAUSA YAUSA MA
RCASTAWAY ALLONE LA MÈRMENNILLE MARQUIS ARTE
MIS ZOO EL MARCHICHIBU O MIAI FUROTO CHACHA
BASEA JAPANASSAU BOOTSHEILA & HENRY THE HORS
E KITZINGER'S IMMERSION FOR PSYCHOTIC ADULTS
BRATATATATAKARAWAWA HOT SPRINGS MARQUESSITZB
ATHE MARQUESAN SPELLEGRINO CHINOTTO JACUZZIZ
OFRENIAGARY GLITTERRHEIN! NO ADMITTANCE WORK
IN PROGRESS AGUAGUAGUAGAIUMBUQUIN LETHIOPIRA
DIONYSOS NEBUCHADNASSAU & MR. MUMMUTT IN THE
HOODOOLOOPHOLE OF REASON DO-JIGGER & ROLL OV
ER VODADA VALLUS POPLAVA MARKISNI KAPUT NILI
ÇMARQUEST FOR WAVE POWER MPOWER THE MAGIC CI
RCLE CRY ME A RIVERFUN IN ECHOPOOLCO ONE ORA
NGAKOKWORK ORANGAKOQWALK ONE OREGAN ZILLA SR
AMANA GILLGILL TYPEEKKEEE CHERIOKEY WEST SY
NDRUM TRAVOLTA TRANCE SYNTROM THE FUCK BUTTO
NICCLOCCLONIC WURMHOLE VAUDOUCHAMPOLL NA BPE
IST SCROTAL SKIN DEEP DRUMSTAGNÉANT WASSERMA
N & FUNKENSTEIN TESTOYSTERONE TWO TEST SPAES
I BASSI LOW LEND CHASERS COBRA SKIN TRASHERS
& ZEBRA BONE SMASHERS DRUM BEATERS RYTHM CHE
ATERS BOOTSY MARCASPER FLUSHLEITHREASKENNEDY

SPAESILICLOWN CENTAUR WAVE-ULLATAURRA HOLLAN
D MARQUESAN POLL DUBH VERSION POLL DICK JACK
SONIAN SHAMPOLLLOCOCK EPILEPSY ÁIRAINFALLAUT
JACKSON POLLOCH BUN GABHA GABHA ALPHABETA SH
APE UP PICASSOAPOTAMIA PSIQIA ROCKY POLL HOR
ROR MAGEIA U BELASTEN MAGEIA U BETASTEN ATOM
IC DOG EAT DOG EAT DOG D-DAY AFTERNOON MW OM
ADIOS TESTOYSTERONE TWO HERAKLITHYRAMBAUD BA
TTEAU BATTEAU IVREAWHORE AQUATERNITÄT ICARUS
SAND OF THE MARKIES VANSELMARKIES VANSELMWAT
ERRES RESURREXIT EXIT MAIKIEFER SANDBLAST JA
SON CHRIST SUPERSTAR MARKAISER & BÖHRER BRIC
KINI ATOLL FRACTORY ZONE SYSTEMS GO MWAUTAUA
URROCKY WAORROAR OIDIPAUS REXCLAMATIONMARKIE
S SOLLO ASSA ROCKY THE KUBISMUSHRAUMFILM ZEI
SS-IKONOGRAFEINNATOLL WAVE 3-DIONYSOS STEREO
SPACEVISION & FANTASOUND UNCLE BOOTRIECHIS M
ARCHI JAMBUDVIPER EL MARCUS MILLERRELLAS MAR
QUESAS PSYTHON COLUBER CONSTRICTOROTO BASSNA
KE RATTLE & ROLLANDADA MOLURUS BIVITTATTOO D
E MARKIES VAN WATER IN THE SABRA PSYCHIATRIC
HOSPITAL BEIRUT WEST GO WEST MAENUTT ANOEREX
WATERSTOOT TIBETANIC DON'T PANIC UPASTHALATTA
MAH MAH MAH EL MARQUESSATTVA VA VA DON DAM B
OEN PAPOEASS LONELY ARSCH CLUB MIX PABLUTION
PRICASSO KAMARQUESSCHAMELION SPEAKING PAYU B
ASSPACE TRANSKRITTLES ONE MANDALAS MARQUESAS
FRACTORY ZONE NATION UP YOUR AZZIDINE ALAIAH
H... MANDALAI LAMARQUESAN MARCO APOLLO 12 SN
AP 27 ZARASOETRA & KAMATHUSTRA IN SPACE IN M
OTION NARQUESAN NARCOSIMA VON BÜLLOW COUNTRI
ES TRISTANTRA & ISUTRA FLOWING ON WATER WATE
R BURNING BRITE H2OLEAUGRAMMARQUESSÈLASSÈLAV

Y KNIFE IN THE WATER HALLUCIO FONTANA IN THE
SKY STREET 69 MASS CULTURE ARTIST AT WORK DU
B ORANGE MACONNIQUE MOHEAVY MERCY BOKOR SACR
ÉOLES MARQUISES APOCALÜPERTZ NOWÖLFLI ! TRAVE
LLOA HALLUCIOLE MARRASSADE MARKIES VAN WATER
RES ERZULIBA! ERZILUBA! TELL MY HORSE AGUAGO
U'TA-ROYOTATING IN MARQUESSAUT D'EAU BORD DE
L'EAU BOUT MWORLDE MARKIES VAN WETTERRES JEL
L'O JELL'O MARRIO ANAGOYA ANAYOGAOSMOSEAS BI
OCROMPRIAPENSIBILLA HOLLAUNDR. DRÉMITOURGENT
GRAND BIBILIKINI ATOLLAND APSULA MARQUISEA Y
OURQUELLETHE BOMB UPPOSEIDONAU WELT DIZZEELA
ND MAJI MAJI MAJI WATER SOAP & MAGIC SINGSIN
GSINGALONG MISIS HURRICANE SPUME FOREVER PIG
DANCING ACROSS THE PACIFIC WEITER WEITER EVE
RYONE NATION MATERNILE WATERLINE IN SPACE IN
MOTION BURO BURO OEOE OEOE MANGGASIENG MANGG
ASIENG SEBURUBURU TOMLULUR PUUROROHUUOUPA AB
UME! IT'S A FAMILY AFFAIR TIAMATMÜLTRA TIAMA
TAPSUPRA DIQUETALIS AMADEUSTORTION ECHOUPOLA
NSKIWASSER LAHMU LAHAMU MARQUICKSAND PRIMORD
IAL MWAVE FRONT PSYCHI-HATRY RIDE OMAGHICA O
MAGHICA! HH CHINESE LEOPARD RIDE BOLD IN ONE
WIPP DAZ LEMON RADIO MICROLUX VORTEX ULTRA B
RILLO FRISCH CAMAY CLASSICK SEXTON GEORGETTE
& THE IDIOT ITS A FAMILY AFFAIRY-TALE THAITI
GREAS & EUPHRATHALASSODOMY SUN MOON STARS MO
ONDUSCHAMPULL UP MACEOPOTAMIAMADEUSCH DIMSTI
RDAM TAMSTERTHAMES CIAU FEDERICO! VENISEA VE
NISEA EL MARRIDDEN TO THE SEA MABEUYSSEA SGT.
BRIGGITTS 3-D-DAY SPACE IMBASS GRÉINE GOCCIA
GOCCIA GOCCIA OCEAN FRED TARLIAMENT JUNKADEL
IC PEPSICHIHATRY RIDE UP O BACCHAE BY DIRCE'

S STREAM! WAN OWAH EL MARQUESSURYATOMBOMB LI
THIUM 6 SOME COW FONQUE TSURINAMISS BOB HOPI
PI STRIPTOLEMESS YOURQUELLEFONQUE SUCH A MES
S ON MY DRESSOLAR SPYRMWHELLEFONQUE SPINNINJ
AROUNDABOUT THE WORD IN ONE DAY-TRIPTOLEMOUS
O TELEUSIS SAVALLAS MARQUESASSMAJASS EL-HAYA
T LASERPENTAGRAMMARQUÈSCAPE FROM ALCATRASHES
TELLEUSEAS TELLEUSEAS SOAPHALLUS ONE AUMOS O
NE AUMOSEROTIKKAPUT MUNDIONYSOS ONE OWOMANDA
ICCA PIGG IAMADEUS IAMAMIADEUS IAMAKLÀ-BAS H
OLLAND IAMADAY-TRIPTOLEMASBUTABABIA MIMRABIE
RABISRABISMARCKIES MIMMIMRA MÊMMÊMRE H2OPIRI
A MIA S.PIRAL KLITTANIC DON'T PANIC! MRIOMAR
OOO MARS DERMADUST SOUL BRELCREAM SEA SUN SE
X FLASH FORWARD PRROSÉVASLAVY MANIJINSKI LOR
D DIONÄXOS FROM THE LAND DOWN UNDER A GROOVE
HIGH WATER MARKIES LOW WATER MARKIES SAENADS
MATYRS MYTARS TYRAMS KILL! KILL! WATT WATT W
ATT? HORN BUSH RIDE BACK TO KUNA KUNAPIPI AR
NHEMLAND UNCLE GEORGE BOPPACRUX BASSPACE WAT
ERREUROPAPOEA NEW GUINEANDERTHALES MARQUISES
DOO-BAPTISMARQUESSANDOZ DAY-TRIPLE WASHING J
OHN 15:3 IMAGINE ALL THE PEOPLE YOHIMBEABOOT
SY AHHEAD LSDE BAPTISMOHEAVY WATERREURQUELLE
FONQUE PEYOTLSDE MARKIES VAN WATERRES D'ARNH
EMMER OUT COME THE BIG D TOPI TOPI HOPI HOPI
APOCALIPSY WOW! AQUÂMESOPOTABILE WAUTAU WAUT
AUROMAQUILLAGE ECHOLABIARINTHE PUSSYFAKE OCE
AN PULL UP TO PUSH BUTTON HOLE EL MARCASH FL
OW FLOW KONX OMPÀX KONX OMPÀX KONX OMPÀX IAM
AMARKIES VANDAMAN EPILEPSY NOW! SPACE MARQUE
SANZABASS/FONQUE DO-IT-YOURSELFANA MANGANO T
RISTANQUILTY & LOLIZZOLDA SEEING THROUGH SEE

THROUGH YOU GOO-GOO-GOO-JOOB MAJIC SPACE BAS
S SITARKOVSKIUMARQUESSOLO KUSCHO! KUSCHO! PU
MP UP THE VOODOO ZOMBY WOOF! SOMETHING IN TH
E WATER RUBBISHMA RUBBISHMA ORCHIPEELAGOGO I
LOLO I LOLO SCEICCO BIANCOBRABISHMARQUESSAMO
A SAMOA! TO THE RIVER SPACE BASEMENT 5 FLY L
IKE AN IGLULIK LE MARQUIS DELOBJIBWATER YO E
L REY SOL TORORATORTUGA DE MARQUÈSPUMAGUA SA
LADA DREAM TIME BOMB RIMINI ATOLL DADAI LAMA
DALLASKA ICE-JAMSTERDAM DRAUM LANGUAGUAGUAGE
S COMING TO GET YOU TTV-2 SCHNEIDER ATOMIUMA
RQUIS FADE TO BLACKOUT SONUFOBITCH DOCTOR DU
B ATOMIC BUMI BEGITU ATOLL SGT. BRIGGIT BAND
OT AKUÏSTE! AKUÏSTE! IAMA PUNCUSHION BITCHAM
AN DUBBITT DUBBITT RAMA RAMA HARE HARE EPILE
PASHAMALE MARQUESSINE QUA NONGOL BABELANDA B
EBUBUKKINEMA 2001 A SPACE IDIOSYNCRASY AVOID
THE JUNK ROPPOPPONGI WAKARIA (WHAT'S UP?) EL
LE MARQUISRI LANKARMARKIES FRAGILE LIQUIDEEP
YOKO ONO WATERCLOCKWORRÈK WORRÈK EUNUKU VIVA
LAS VEGAS MARKIES MEMPHIS EXPERIENCE COBHAMM
ONDOO-BOBBILLASWELL MEET AGAIN POP-UP FOR DA
TABASSES STOMP! WERE UNLISTED NY. RIVERSOUND
WAVESMASHAMPÈRE UBULUPALAKUALTAMIRA MIRA OND
A WALTER BRECKER BRASS INTERTONGALAXIC ORKAS
TRATOLLÀ-BASSPACE UNDERGROUND CONTROL SALTWO
RKING IN THE HYDROGEN JUKEBOX MATO GROSSODOM
Y MYSELF & EPSTEIN ONDA BEACH SPOETNIKE JUST
BOBBITCH ECHOLÀ-BASSOLORENA ACCELERAZIONE AZ
IONE CUT! THE IKOONSOAPLASTIK FEUERRORSCHACH
TEST ONE TWO NESBITT! BARRETT! BARRETT! NESB
ITT! EL MARQUESSPACE BASSOLOMON MEGA WATPI-F
UNK AQUA BOUGAIN VILLET STRAITSPACE COÏTUS I

N CANOE ONEOWO ONE OWO-OWO NONOA-NONOA THE C
ANOë/COFFINNAQUIS WAKEA UNTERWELT DOWN ORANG
NIASSAU NONOA-NONOA POSSO? POSSO? OWO-OWO OW
OH-OWOH OWOHH-OWOHH... POSSO-SEA-DYAK VOLCAN
IC CAVE BURIAL/MARQUESAN CHRISTOVAL RUÏNCARN
ATION/ATOMIUMMARQUESAN SKULL PRESSURFONK POS
SO? POSSO? THE SHARK IS GONNA GET USW. NONOA
HH-NONOAPATRA CANOOKE NOOKE MARAE WAKEA TORA
TORRES STRAIT DOWN TO BEING FROM MÈR ISLAND G
RAND MALAY ARCHIPELAGOGO UNDERWORLDE MARKIES
SEA-BURIALL-STARSE HERE COMES THE SUN FIRE E
XIT ONLY MARQUESSUNSETTING OUT TO SEA BATTÀK
BATTÀK! SEAS HOME SEAS HOME POLYNESIAMESOPOT
AMIABEIG-BANGHOLOLO UNDER ARRASTA-PE-FONK AQ
UELEMUNDO ENCANTANDO AFRODIONYSIAC TAMTAMBOR
INAGE ILINXING LE MARQUISS INTO THE ISLAND A
FTERWORLD BIKINI MULATATOLL ILINXUCK OR FONQ
UE HOLI HOLI LANDFALL EL MARIO CARNAVALAS MA
RQUESAS (1 IATMULATATTOO!) WATCH TV TVIE TVO
L TVET TVIDA TVENI TVORM TVOIL TVIVI TVEIN T
VIZZE TVERDE TVENTA TVOLTA TVOLGA TVIZELA TV
IRGIN TVERNON TVENEZA TVENOGE TVENAMO TVILAI
NE TVEIVATN TVICHADA TVIBORAS TVOLTOURNO WAY
OUT COMES HYDRONYMUS BOSCH EL MARQUESSUSPIRO
DE COBRA VERDE MARKIES VAN WATERZATZAUBERFLO
OD BIRD-TOTEM PENIS TV & TABLOOB BLOOB BLOOB
JIBWAY OUT COMES HIROSHIMA BOSCH SPOTLIGHT O
N DEEE LITE WOOO LITE SHE-MALAY MAGIC MANTRA
SPEECH SURROGAT POWERWORD-UP CARROLL OVER BE
ETHOVEN WORD REFORMATION BLICK BLANGUAGE BRE
AKDOWN SPASSIVE BASSNAKE DWELLING IN SPACE P
ATHOLLOGY TITOI PUTA KEO! MARQUESSATURN UP J
OHN LEMON SKULL-DEFECT EGO ALIEN II ECCOLA T

OURRETTE DE BABEL THE HOLLANDSCAPE KIEFER AN
D KIEFER ALL THE TIME SKYNILE VISTA WELTMERZ
BAUBOROBOEDOEK BARRAQUE DAIBOETSOE VAN KARAK
OERA UP YOUR ASSOEAN-DAMMARQUESSUEZ PRANCING
NIAGARA EUROPAPUA NEW GUINEA ONE NATION IN T
HE MAKING FLIPPY FLOPPY MORESCHIMMIRRU MIRRU
ONDA WATER UNTERWASSERSCHALLTECHNUKE JUST DU
BBITT BOOTZILLACON CHIP CHOP UP THE WORD! SY
NTEXTOURRETTHE BUMBABULLE MARQUIS DE BOMBELL
ES INSANI BAHHASA MUDERABISMARCK SEAWATERMAR
KIZES UNIVERSALJU YANG TURUN EL MARQUASINASS
AU CHIP CHOP UP SPEECH & REASON WOOZZOOBERLU
BANG HO! ONE OWO WAN OWO-OWO BEFORE OUR OWWO
-OWWO-OWWO HIGH FREAQUENCEFALLOGRAMMARQUESSE
XY HOLLATLANTIS LUCY IN THE SKY WITH DIAMOND
LILIPÛTE AQUAFALLSDEEP-FUNK-ALL AT SEA IN CL
EAR BLUE WATER BATTAKK! BATTAKK! SUPER EGOLA
LITTERRAPTURE THOTALIBISEXUALICE KOLATONGA S
AMOA TEST ONE ONE TWO TWO SLY & THE FLAMMILY
STONE AGE LO-BITH-AHH! RYTHM KILLERS FIRE! U
RSOUND WELLES MARQUISES FLOATING IN WÂWWÂWTÂ
W WÂWWÂWTÂW SKUDO YOU SILLA DEVIL OUT THELON
IOUS MINK DEVILLE MARQUISRI RAMA RAMA KRISHN
A THE SHEIK VS. TIGERFEET SINGHALONGH RUBBER
BAND MANDRIL SUNSETBACKFLIPPITT FLIPPITT HIF
IROSHIMARQUESS PRANZHORNY HONIGGER SALSOUL 3
001 SPEECH-IN BUSH DOCTOR DRÉ-EBING SEXSHOOT
ER DOLORES DAY & ALICE DEE DEE BOMBORANGE MA
XIMUMISNESSAU ECHOLALIAGARA FALLS NEVER NEVE
R LANDS NEOLOJAZZMWA-WA NILOJISSMWAH-WAH I M
BUCCALL I M BUCCALL MASTER WASTER WORDSOLLID
MIME MYSELF & QUE D'EAU QUE D'EAU WATERWAR
IS COMING MAR-KEYS ANGEL DUSTADRIL BRILLO SC

EICCO BIANCOBRAMALE MARQUISSHAKTIBERNINILE M
ARQUIS TAKE IT AWAY BOB FARRELL AWAY AWAY EC
H! ECH! ECH! 'OMMACHINE MW MISNAMING THE WOR
LD ARSCHIZORROTACQUADOLLOP OSMOSIS PHASE ONE
ROCKITT BOBBY WORRELL MARCUS MILLER MAGIC OU
T OF CONTROL SPAVAPARLIAMENTALSDE MARKIES VA
N WATERRESTIALSDE MARKIESSPAVATARLIAMENTLSDE
MWOH CULT VOODOO SHOP WE WANT BOOTSILICON CH
IP HOLLAND THE PROSTESTANT EXPERIENCE ICONOK
LISMAREFILLICCLONEOCLASH TFSHOCK OR S/FUCK M
FACTOR ONE DA DOO RON RON LAING RAMA RAMA LA
MA DING DONG PRABHUPADA KRISHNA CONSCIOUSNES
S BROTHER JULIUS CULT THE MEHERBABA MOVEMENT
THE MYSTICAL MAZE DIVINE LIGHT MISSION SAINT
S ALIVE CROSSING ABBA ROAD RIVER DEEP/MOUNTA
IN HIGH PALEOLITHIUMBRILLO MARQUESSOAP PADSU
CK OR HOLE-LAND ORANG-UTAN-TITEL BANG-UTOT A
TTACKK! PNEUMARQUESAN WORDGEISER SPOUTCOMING
THAT-SHIH-FANG-THANG ROTA-GOTA ROTA-GOTA TOO
RTA-GWANNANG NATZI-VIZ! THE CLINTON CLINIQUE
VAN GOGH PRIVAT KRANKENHAUS VERBODEN VOOR TO
URISTEN MAREMYSELF & I SOULÉOU SOUS-LEAU WOR
DPLAY LAUTPUT MONDO PAZZO I, A VIRGIN TEENAG
E PARTY GIRLS I LOVE BLUE GREASE MONKEYS THE
RIVER MEN AQUASEX MAGIC PSYCHOMONTAGE WILD D
ALLAS HONG SEX FREAKS TATTOO ANGEL ON FIRE J
OHNNY MINOTAUR I, MARQUIS DE SADE THE LUSTFU
L TURK GEORGE WHO? EAUZOOMMOOMMIASMARQUESSO
LSDSMARQUESSM-III FOLLOW THE RIVIERRUINVADO
BOPGODZIPPAPUASTRAL SOLIKUDO I.M. FORETELLUS
ALLABOUT MICHELLE MA-BELLONE BUTO BUTO BABY!
TABLABSUS! TABLABSUS! STABLAXAMENTUMTUM STAB
AT WATER MUTTIERZATZ OCEAN BRATATATATA MIRA

NDO BRECKER BROS. HUH! OOH! VENUS HIGHWAY HO
TELLATTATAU COÏTUS IN ANONIMITY GOO-JOOB-A-L
ULA GET IT ON GO WESTMAHH. . . ONE MAN JUICE A
ROUND WAITING FOR THE SUN RIDE THE LIZARD KI
NG HOME AMANDA WAS HERE JESUS IS THE DOOR GR
AZIE JIM IS GOD LOVE BABSY COME BACK JIM ONE
AURINGONSÄDE VESISADE SADELLA MÈREX MARKIISI
DE SADE HAPPI HAPPI-FONQUE D'EAU FONQUE D'EA
U ARE SPAESI BETSY MCBOOBBITCH MOO-COW? MARK
AISERSPECK ECK ECK! DISCOPALYPSE NOW! PIG UP
YOUR ARSE HOGLAND BUTA BUTA BABI DOMUZIK JAS
SPRACH THE GRAPEGG GRAPEGG MAN QUBI QUBI ULT
RA WAVE WHAT OVID ORANGE NÄXOS? RYTHMSTEXT O
NE TWO TEXT ONE TWO CLINTON IN VOODOO-LAND P
TAH PTAH PTAH PTAH! I M THE WORD EGG I M THE
GRAPEGG MAN VOODOO ANADOLL OLLANDA PRIAPUSSY
TO PUSSY HYDROCÉLESTIAL URROBOROSION I M THE
YGGDRASILLAMAN WASSERFLAXING IN HELIKONTRAVE
STY DE MOOG VAN WOOG SYNTFLAUSSING PLANET DR
UM SPIRO SPERO NILE MEDIUM EST HYPERGO ET HY
PERAGO FIAT FLUX MUNDIONYSEXIT ONLY HARDH KU
MBHA MELAR HARDWARHOLLAND APSULAR DISKIMMONO
BIKINI ATOLL BUMBUMBASSWASTIKI BUMBUMTIKI BU
MBUMBASSWASTIKI TABOOTSILLA-TIKIEFERRUN AMAD
EUS SEX WOLFGANGGANGA MAI KI JAI! THE HOLY-H
OLY WATER EVERYWHORRUS GAUGAUMUKH 12770 FEET
HIGH & RISING VULTOURQUELLE MARQUIS DE SADHU
& L'HISTOIRE DHOBIS MAHU MAHU MAHEO MAHEO! W
ASHTIKA KUMBHA BUMBUMMELA LO-LAR-KA SHASHTIK
ANGOTRILOK GURTUTU GANGOTRICKLING DOWN TRICK
LING DOWN TRICKLING DOWN GUTTA GUTTA GUTTA C
AVAT LAPIDEM 6000 MILES GURTUTU DAVISHNUKU S
IVA SPACEODDIZZEELAND TALOS MATER SGT. BRIDG

ITTIT BURNING BRIDE ALLAHABADABOUT THE HOLI-
HOLIKA LAND ACROSS TELLUS WATER ALLAHABAD HA
RDWARHOLLAND THE MELAS MARQUESAS SHIMALAYA H
IMAVATTEN ONUS MOUNT KAILAS MARQUESAS MARQUE
SAN MARCOBRAHMARQUESAN SHIMALAMALAYYA SOLO D
E MARKIES VAN WATER ONE MANDALAS MARQUESAS T
RANS-SHIMALAYYA WASSIR WASSIR EDMONDUSCH HIL
ARYWHORE BOL GANGA MAI KI JAI! BOL GANGA MAI
KI JAI! MÊMMÊMMERU MUMMUMMERA MUMMUTTMOUNT M
ERU MERU! WASHTIKA BUMBUMBILLALABABASHRAM UN
CLE RAM CAT SNOWWOWWWOW LEOPFERD D.I.O.NYSOS
GO TO THE RIVER ADOLFGANGES WÖLFLIGANGES GAU
GAUMUKHIMUKHI WAN MANASAROWAR HOLLAND BILOWA
BILOWA WASHTIKINIBOMB WASHTIKINIBOMB-BOMB GH
OST IN THE INVISIBLE BIKINI PLAY LAAT! UNCLE
GEORGE DUKE COUNT BASIE & THE MARQUIS OF OOH
BABY E=MC2= LOW COUNTIES SPACE BASIE NILE HE
FTIKI BUMB ARRANGEMENTS & DE MARKIES VAN WAT
ER ITTITTICHAOTIC AUM AUM AUM-COMING WOLKENP
UMPEN-KUXKUXHEIMAT TONNERSCHALL & DONNERSCHLA
GG EL MARQUESSAGARBATATATA! SKIN I'M INK DIS
COPATHIA SEXUALLIESSEA-MARQUESSPEECHAMALE WA
SSIR NOT WASSIR BACKING UP YOURQUELLE MARQUI
SSCHIZOUL FRACTORY ZONES PLAY LAUT BILDUNG H
O DUNG HO WOMB WUNDERS ATOMICK DOGMATICK DOG
SPEAKING AMESLANCANIAN OHM OHM OHM DOUBLE-OH
-OH TOP DOG MUSIC JASSTARRGANG FATWA MORGANA
FATWA MORGANA DALAI LAI DRUMTIDE LO LOW LEAU
FIST OR FUCK HOLLAND VIVA REXY MARQUATSCH ON
DA ASS EGO MARKET ET VOGUE LE NIRVANAVIRE! W
ASSER NOT WASSERGEANT PEPPER'S BILKO UP YOUR
AZZAGHAYAH AZZAGHAYAH! MARQUESAN HOMBOG-ACTI
ON UNCLE GEORGE KLIMTONTON LSDEFACING COCKWO

RK ORGANE NASSOUR MJOY YOURSELF MPOWER MPOWE
R WAN OWA ONE OWA-WAFRIQUE OUT LAUT THE WILD
EBEESTIE BEUYS! PHAT! PHATATATATA! TATATATA!
BRATAT BRATAT! FAFAFAFAFA! EPHATATATA! EPHAP
HAPHATA! JAJAJAJAJA NEE NEE NEE NEE NEE FETT
WATT WATTER WATTEVERYWHERE WATER WATER IVORY
TOWER TATTOO TONY PEP RUE SAINT DENISE MCCAN
NIBAL TATTOO MAN DIRECT DISC PHASE A: TATTOO
MAN 3-M MUSIC NIKKEI (225) JUST DO IT BECKAB
OO! EUROLAGNIAGARA FALZHAMMER SONG DONAUWELL
EN (LOVE AND HAMMOND) THE MARQUESSEE SEE RID
ER MARQUIS VON OH MEIN PAPALEO PSEUDO PHUNKY
DISCO POPS SHAFT LET IT ALL OUT LAWRENCE RAI
NER SPACE JUDDISSEY ICKA PRICKABULLROARSCHAC
H TEST ONE TWO PSINOTHER THEROPSIN NOPSITHER
NEPHTTHOMAOTH NEPHHIOMAOTTH MARAKHHAKTTHA DE
RAARAIAPAOU ZSARSASARTOUD KOUKIAMIUMIAI INFR
AGMENTAL MRIODOMARCHÉSEACQUAROGOGORUABRAO OO
O! MINE IS THE SUNLIGHT INFRA RAGE MARQUISGE
-AROGOGO ASK THALEISTER CROWWOWWOW HURRIKLIT
& HERRACANE POU POU POU-FONKIN' IN IATMÜLTRA
STEREO SPEEDWAKE IATMÜLESCULES ÎLES MARQUISE
S PERRIER ORANGE UP YOUR RIVERRECTUMTUM CLUB
FUCK ALPHAHYDROXY MUSICKAWATER WATER TWIST &
SPRITE LET IT ALL SPOUTCOMING WIPERRIER CITR
ONICCLONIC ATTRACKING DE MARKIES VAN WATER T
EST TESTING ONE TWO TEST TESTING THE MARQUES
SOINS SOLAIRES THALATTAHITIKINNAKRIEG GEORGE
CLINTRODUCING DER MÜDE TODD & EVA BROWNING'S
FREAKSHOW DO YA BEUYSWELL JOHNSTONE HH-BOMBU
ANDIORANGAGANUS MOONDUSCHAMANIC-DEPARRESSIEU
PSYCHOTIC BABY FARRELL AWAY MATAHARIVERTUOSO
DOMISSELFAYE WEST DUNDUNAWAY HOP YOYO'MAMA T

A-LAY ALLABOUT THE KLONUS MÚNDUCHAMPISSOIRIN
SCRIPT TIGERFEET R. MUTT IN HEAVEN TRITONI
KKLEUNIK TONICCYCLOHNIC MARKISSKO DIL DE DOO
N THE POP QUEENS WATTEAU WATTEAU GILLES DELU
GES ULYSSEN UP HOLLAND SCHIZOEMEOMARKIES VAN
WATER RIVERBALISING THE NIGHT AWAY AWAY POP-
UP THE VAUDOUDOUFI DR. MEGA MERZ SPOCK SPOCK
LOA LOA SOUND & VIZIR JEAN GINGER & FREDDOLF
BRITLER CUNTSPEECHING IN ZIBBERSPASTICKABALL
AKE COMOHEAVY WATERRORGANZA MARE MARE RAMA R
AMA ARE JUJU W/M MADAME LA CAMARQUE? WÂWWÂW
WÂWWÂW STRUNG PACE BASSATONGUERRIEROTICKAWÂWW
ÂWTÂW WÂWTÂW IN THE BECOMING THERE WAS THERE
THE WORLD ATOLL'ORANGE RULETA! THE BOMBIONYS
OSSMATOSSTRÖMSTOSS OFFUNKADELPHILEAU! PHILEA
U! BECOMING & COMING REFILLOSODOUFI MYSOULTR
ANCE & GILLETHE COOL WAVE DELEUGES HARE HARE
RAMA RAMARE MARE BRUNOAH-NOAH BRUNOA-NOA WEL
COME TO THE MARQUESAN KINDERGARTEN O DELIVRA
NCE THE RIVERBETTELHEIMAT WORD UP IN THE AIR
& DOWN YOYOTE UBAHROCCOCOYOTE EL YOYOLOYA GA
IAK GAIAK PETER PETER BURNING BRIGHT BLAKESI
DE ONE FANTASTIC VOYAGE OWAU FRIEDRICH NIETZ
SCHE LASWELL TO POWER TRUNGPACE BASSOLILOQUI
STABOOTSY MISSUFFOCATING & I OH I M THE #ONE
TELLY SYPHILIS ON THE ROAD TO NAUMANDSLAND P
OPM POPM AP AP AP MOTOR BOYS MOTOR YELLPATAQ
UI BULLPATAQUI FALLPATAQUI HELLPATAQUI DOLLP
ATAQUI GULLPATAQUI ZILLPATAQUI JALLPATAQUI T
HE NÀHM-DROPPING THE BOMB TRANSPLANTHALATTAB
ULA RASADOLOROSADOLOROSA THE GAP BANDAMAN VI
BE EL MARQUÈSTEELY DANNATT ALL OVER THE WORL
D MAN FANTASCIENZAUBERDÄXÄDOTTENTOD TUBE SNA

KE TRANSYLVANIA BOOGIE WOOGIE KING WILLIAM B
URRO INTO THE BOOTSWANA SKULLINS & GORGES CL
IPPERTON FRACTURE ZONES BAU XAU XAU EUROPAPU
AFRIKAMERIKAUSTRALIAMERIKAFRIKAWA AHH... TSUN
AMIZUZAMZAM CHALLENGER DEEP THROAT DE MARKIE
S VAN WATERMARKIES VAN WATER WATER KEEP IT G
REASY SUNRISE REDEEMER NO BABY SNAKES FOR CA
LVIN CLOWNUS DEMONDUSCH DE MARKIES DE WASA V
ERSUS DE MARKIES DE WATA JAH JAH JAH JAH JAH
NOH NOH NOH NOH NOH MALAY IS MY LADY MI OH M
I GOATTIKKAOSTARATHUSTRADIONYS.O.S. TO THE W
ORD DR. DREFFT-EBBINGO GUINEA CARL GOSSIP JU
NK SAVE OUR SEMEN CLINTRODUCING GINGER FLYNN
& FRED WESLEY JAMAMACEO PERKEO W/MANDERILLA
NEW MOON FREAK Y'ALL ONE OWAUTODAFUNK AIR ME
NGARAS LUTUT HOLLAND OPEN AIR BAHHASA CALIFO
RNIA CALLING DR. LOVE PILU LAUT EPILEPAS UFO
ODOO FELA FELLINILE-MAGICKABOOOH I AMMI AMMI
THE SLIME & THE PURPLE LAGUNAWAN NATION UNDE
R THE CHERRY MOON THALATTATATA TEE TATATA IN
FRAGMENTAL ILLNESSESSITY UP FOR THE DOWN STR
OKE HOLLAND JAFFA ORANGES/JAFFA LEMONS BIG M
ACNETIC BANGAQOCKING IN JAMSTERDAMSTERDOOM S
PIRSIGGA PRIGG MASTER HAGGARD SHE-MILES AHEA
D DAVO IN DISGEISER FOAMPIN' THE SPACE BASUI
N MADWETMAX ERNST MW/PRINZHORNY HORNAMENTAL
DISORDER ON THE PIGGY COCKENHEIMATTERHORN MU
TTMOUNT VENUS IN REVERSE SOMMERSOLLING MW CA
LL M MINNEAPOLIS DIRTY MIND GAMES MINNEATORA
TORA WAS NOET WASSIR PALEO BORDERLINE PSYCHO
SEXY JAZZ JOHNSON'S WAX MAGIC SHOCKADELICA E
ROTIC DOG BIZARRE LOVE TRIANGLE ZOO MUSIC GI
RL PSYCHOTIC BABY LOVERMAN HOOLICOOL DOWN YO

U ARE IN YOUR ELEMENT SPACE BASIC MILES AHEA
D EAUM EAUM EAUM SUN MOON ARSE LAGERFETTSTOO
L & THE WILDEBEESTIE BASS AUMW AUMW AUMW THE
BOLD & THE BEAUTY OIL ON CANVAS & THE PORN T
O BE WILDEBEASTIE BEUYSMARCKIES ARCHIPOOLABU
LLY COBHAMMONOWATER NILE GINGER RODGERS & FR
EUD FEELIN' BITCHY SHE-MILLIE DE VILLES ÎLES
MARQUISES DATA BEACH DUB KALVIN KLOON EL MAR
QUESCROISEDITZKRIEG RIVIERAZIMARQLTESAN UNCLE
JAMBASSADE DE SADE DAFKAPITONIK-KLONIK SCHIZ
OPHRENIA AT HOME SWEET HOME DELUGIONAL THINK
Y-TOY-BAUSWASH LSDEMENTIA PRAECOX ON THE LOO
SE THE THE CASPERMARQUESSOLAR DUSK THROUGH L
ASERRUBBER RIVERRAP WATER & WATER ALL THE TI
DES UNCLE JAMMERTÀLOS IN HAMSTERDAMMOND ORGA
N SOUNDFLOÖDLAND SHOW YOUR WUNDERLICH HOLLAN
D HAMMONDRIAANSEESIEK HAMMONDSCHEINSONASSAUS
MANUS MUNDUSCHAMALE MARQUIS WOR(L)D-CLINIQUE
SHE-MILLIE JACKSON POLLOCOMOTOWN PUPA PUPA A
WRIGHT PSYCHOTIC BABY THE DIRRITANTI WALKING
THE BEACHES OF BESTIALITY HOPI HOPI B-52 PLA
NET COULEURWATER REVIVAL NIKE JUST WASH & GA
UGUIN EL MARSOULAS MARQUESAS RUE SAINT DENIS
E MCCANNIBAL TABBOO MAN SEE SEE RIDER MARQUI
S VON O LA LA LA MARQUISE D'O LA LA LA! T.C.
MATIC ARNOA-NOA ARNOAH-NOAH BYE BYE TILL THE
NEXT TIDE WILLIE WILLIE DE DEVILLES ÎLES TAB
OOTSYBILLESBOSWELL AMSTERDARMATRADING M MISS
ILVANA MANGOGO & I THE ORANGE MAN LIONDATING
THE ANUS ROERMONDUSCH NAVENLOLOBITHERMAL MOE
ZELLA MEUZILLA WAALLSDIEPILEPSY NAP DE LA MA
RKIES HIGH & RISING RIVIERREGEN ALL OVER THE
WORLD MAN SUMMANUS MÚNDUSCH UNCLE JAMSTERRAP

RIAPEE-VING SOUFISTOCRAT DEBUNKING IMITETSUM
I CHRISTI DA YA BAEZ WELL ADAME LA MERGUÈZE?
WATER WATERRESTRIS AFLOAT AFLOOD RIVIERRE VA
OLO VASSOLLINILE BASSIN SALE EAU DIEAUNYSIAQ
UELLWASHING TEOREMARQUESAN SEXPENSIVE DISCHO
RDER EXTRA-X-STRAP-ON-MW HOLANDA SANA M DOMI
NA DEPRIMORDIAL M IS FOR MURDER HADESPUMOHAV
ELOCK UP HOLANDATURA BASE WIE BIST DU, WEIB?
DE MARKIES VAN WATERRA DEFUNKTUS SUMMARQUESS
GRAND MALMAMA TADEMATERRA INONDATATTACK TATT
ACK WORLD PERFECT ARUIND & ARUIND & ARUIND A
ÏGEUA AÏGEAU DEMADISCO MUTO! AHH... THE NAME
IS... A FRUSTRATING MESS LIMITADZIO CHRISTIX
UP YOUR ASSCHENBACCHUS DIRTY BOGARDE MARKIES
VAN WATER TRANSSCRIBBLING THE MAPPAPUA NEW M
UNDI MISSISSIPPISSINGING E-S-P (VOCAL REPRIS
E) JÖSEUPHRATLESS BASS UP TIGREASSYBILLABOOT
SY BACCHABUNDUSCHAMALES TRANSEGOCENTRIFUSING
FIRE W/RAINSTANT KHARMARQUIS LET IT RAIN LE
T IT BMW IN THE RAINTEROCEANIC DON'T PANIC! T
RANSEGOCENTRIFUSING SOMMERSOLSUR ORANGES MW/
VENUS CYPRUS CITRUS THE BOMBMCNUTT. MW.T. BY
NATURE EL MARSCHIZO BEYOND THE CALL OOOH REA
SON MW MAD & FOLLY BUCKETED POWERSPINSERTING
TUBES FROM H TO OOOH BABY SPACE & FRUIT TRAN
SVERSALITY ON THE RUE SAINT DEMIS ROUSSOS WE
SHALL DANCE VIVAT BACH M BACH DEMINOAH-DEMIN
OAH KAMKASEKAM KAM KASEKAM EL MARKIRISALAS M
ARQUESAS BEAUTY MAGIC THERMOHAVE NO NUCLEARW
ATER REVIVAL UO-POU-FUNKEDALIBIDOUCHANT WARA
I SWITWARA I KLIAQUATSCHLAMM! YOUYOU CAN BRI
NG MY BULLOOPING THE HIGHWAY HOTELECTROMARQU
ESSEPIK-WAGHI DIVIDE MARKIES VAN WATER RIVIE

RROUSS.O.S. SCHIZO SOAPILEPSIS PLAY BUNYI PLAY JUJUNCLE JAMJAM' LOBANG JOBONG! WAZZA WAZZA WAZZA TRISTANGANYIKA & IZOOT ALLURES FLOWING ON ORANGE LOVE JUICE EVERYWHERE YOYO'MAMALAY SGT. PAPUARSE APOLLONELY HEARTS CLUB RUBBER FETISHTARLIAMENT FUNKABALLA THE ACQUANUS MOONDUSCHGEL PULL UP TO THE BURN OUT UNCLE ZAMZAM NOT WAZWAZ EIN ZWEI DRY ORANGE AQUA NON MUTABILE FIRE FIREFALLUNA SEA SEA RIGHT NOW BABY PSYCHOTICKA LYNCHMEATAPHORIAGARA FALLUUNA SEA SEA LET THE BLOOD RUN FREE FREE CALL MW HELIOGABALLUS UP YOUR HOLL HOLM HOLT HOLLE HOLDA HOLOS HOLBACH HOLBERG HOLAPPA HOLLEMAN HOLSTEIN HOLTZMANN HOLLANDUS HOLLERITH HOLDSWORTH THE HOLI-HOLI PARTY OH, HOLANDA A NOA-ANOA OOOH BABY THE SEXUALLY ABERRATED WOMAN AS SHE IS HEINO WARHOL SPATTING THE HERA CLITURGY W/HEIMWEH-WEH IN CARNAVAL DE RIO RICHARD HOL RICHARD NIXON RICHARD ASSMANN GOO GOO GOO JOOBBERWAQQUAH IN URRANGELAND NAZ-TEE MAYYEN FRITZ OUT LANG 2000 METROPPOLICE NOW! MAMMANIC PAPPANIC! THE FLYING SAUCERS ARE REAL GILLA GILLA SAY YES ONE OWAUDRY LITTLE RIVER KAWA KAMA KAMAHL KAMAHLER SUNRISE SUNSET SUNRISE SUNSET OLD MAN RIVER DE MARKIES VANZETTI BROTHER TO BROTHER CAPUT VANNELLI THE RIVER MUST FLOW ONE OWAUDIORGASMUSSOLLINILE FLOWING FREEPPERBAHN MR. HUMBOGGLES MR. GUDWIGGLES KUMBUMBABBLE KUMBOMBUBBLE DADDY LA MAMAI COOL DOWN! LE JET BAKER MAAAH MAAH MAH BAKER PLAY LAUT KULZUM RETURN TO MIMMIMPE MÊMMÊMPE MÊMMÊMRE MIMMIMRA TATATATATTOO & TABUH OH (FOAMME FOAMME WATTIS YOUR NAHM?) WRITT

EN IN WATER WATER AVERYWHERE HEIDIPAUS TT-RE
X AVERYWHEREWÖLFLI DROOPY DROOPY SCREWY SQUE
RRELLE THE BREAST MANTRA BALLROOMBLITZEEWOLF
KHADAFFY DUCK IN HOLLYWOOD AFREAKOUT LAUT VA
UDUSCHAMANTRASHAMALE TRANSRATIONAL MARQUESSA
I BABA COOL DOWN & CUMMING CALVIN CLOWN TORT
URE DE MARKIES VANNY WETTART YOUR STARWAY TO
LOVE HARE HARE RAMA RAMARKIESCAPADE SADE DAF
KAP DE SADE MARKIESCAPADE M IS THE FUNKAOSST
RAUSSPACE IDIOSSEY ANUS MUNDUSCH & BODYMILKY
WASH & GORE VIDAL SASSOON MINOTORA-TORA SCHI
ZOHARLEQUINTETSUMINOTORA-TORA KUDOGGODDEITTY
ENCEFALSTAFKAPTAIN BEEFHEARTS CLUB BANDAMA R
IVERRED HOTTENTHOT CHILI PEPPERS LONELY HEAR
TS CLUB MAGIC NOT MAGIC BANDERILLONELY HEART
S CLUB BANDOUILLES BOLLYWOODBEEZMARCKIES ARC
HIPELAGOGO MW/THE BLOW UP YOUR ARSEA HAPPY-
GO-ROUSTABOUTROPHADONAUTTY ORANGEL FALLSCHIZ
ONESSAU WATER WATER OVARY WAR BUT NOT A BOMB
TO DROP! HÂPI HÂPITAMTAM BABI PALEO PSYCHO P
OPPENHAMMER ATOMIC HOG DANCE POP SABINE POPP
AEA SPILT SPERM EATERS POP PENIS ENVIE POP S
IHR PSYCHO SEXY POP CHELSEA GIRLS, GIRLS, GI
RLS, POP MERRE WRECKABRIDGE POPPINGAWIER MAR
KIESTRA POP TONY BAEKKELENKIT POP PETER BLAK
E VOLTAGE POP CATCH 220 VOLTA RIVER POP M PO
P MUSIK POP COCK VD POP POP POP FLAMMANTIA M
OENIA MUNDI THOROUGH FLOOD THOROUGH FIRE I D
O WANDER WANDER EVERYWHERE H2OMOHEAVY DILUDA
NCE MAX ERNST HORN WATER TREATMENT IN RIVERB
EDLAM CIBBERSPACE WASH & GOYA THE MAD MANTRA
WILD RAIN GILLETHE (SPACE) ODDILLUGE ALLSDÉL
UGILLES DELA TOURRED KUNDADA HOT RIVERRUSH T

RANQUILLIZARTAUDIONYSOS NEVERRUNFONKIN' IN T
HE HADESPIRAL HADESPASSABYSSIN' HADIZZEELAND
HADIZZIE GILLGILLESPIE-FUNKADELUGEOLANDA ALS
DELA SOULTRASHAMANTRAMALE MARQUESSALPÊTRIÈRE
CIBBERRUN ALLESDÉLUVI THIS IS THE ENDELUVI I
GOTTA BE MW VAN GOGH DER SAMANN PRÊT-A-PHYSI
QUE STACHELSCHWEINDANCING W/UNCLE RAMLOIS-S
CHURIMINI DER SCHLAMMANUZKEY WEST ALL IS THE
DELUVI & DELOVE EL MARQUÈSDILUVI CRESCENDOLO
BITALLSDOLOBITOMY MISSELFABUTT ACCÈSDOLIBRE
ALL ES DOLOVIE PROVENÇOUL EL MARQUÉSCRIPTURA
TURA EL MARQUESGLATTERDAVO SHE-MILLIE JACKSO
NIAN ANTILEPSIS WAN OWAH ONE MANTONIN SHOW M
OZARTAUD YOU CANT FAKE A GOOD TIME HOLLAND O
RANGIA FIGARAFA DADANUBIAN NATSCHIBINITSCHIB
IKINI ATOLLACCI BACCI UP YOUR ARSCHLABA PUMF
ANGOGO GUINEANDERTAILLES ÎLES ÎLES RIVERRUNZ
I-FUNZI HINKITY HONKY THELONIOUS MONKIESCHLU
MBASSABULLY PLUMBA-STRUMPI-FONKUDO I. M. FUC
KALLSDE MARKIESKIMOHEAVY MARQUESQUIROLL OVER
BEETHOVEN RIPPLE RIPPLE ESPAZI BASSHAMANDRIL
DO-BOPTISMOZARGEANT PEEP SHOWER MAGIC WASH &
GOGO À GOGO GAGANESHAMMARQUÉSIMIDEUS MOUSSAR
T WATERRA LIZAH-ZAH WATERRA FIRMAH-MAH ALLSD
ELUXOLLAND MULTIPURPOSE GREASE IS THE WORDFU
NK TIDES MONSTER & SUPER CREEPELIN S.O.S. SC
HIZO SOPOTAMIA PSIQIA TRIP BUDO BUDO BABY TH
E MARQUESSAFRAN-DANCE COUNT BASIC MILES AHEA
D LITTE MELONAE MAENAD WESTORSEMEN DIONYSOLA
R HADESPUMARKIES VAN WATERRAIN RAIN LET IT R
AIN ESPATZ BASIMENTAL ILLNECESSESSAU LETHE B
LOOD RUN FREI LIQUID ZENSCHEIT DUCHAMP DIBILI
SI OLABI-BIDAY WARM WATER FOR WENDY CUMMAH S

LUTRA PUMPING CHOCOLATE MARQUIS PORN AGAIN A
NTI-CHRISTIES & SODOBIDAY-TRIPPIN' STOP TRIP
PPIN' GOGO BMW/THE THE SIX MORE MILES AHEAD
HARD ON FOR LOVE BIG-JESUS-TRASH-CAN & DIONY
SOLDA RIVER DEEP MOUNTAIN HIGH HEY YOU'SOUSS
OU N'DOURBAN DANCE SQUAD MANIAGARA FALLSDILU
TIONILE SPLYASHEBOOTSYNDRUMBONING OLLANDA AN
ADOLL KABALLA BALLA GET WET CHI BOEM JUST WA
ITING FOR THE FLOODS UNUS MUTTMUNDUSCHAMPOOL
LAND EAUWAU-MAULOOPZILLÀ-BASS PARADISE MOUNT
EVERIVERENCE S.O.S. SCHIZO SOPOSITOROTORA-TO
RA WASH & POGO GIMMEE PIGGY PUMP PUMP PEDODO
HADÈSORDRECKAOSMOSIS HADESSUS LA TOURRETTE D
E BABULLY MAKE OR MAR NITSCHIBINITSCHIBIKINI
ATOLLOGOGRAMMAR SHAMADEUS WÖLFLI GAUNGGANYAN
GES MARKIZZAT THE LIMIT? MAKE OR MARQUESS MA
Y THE FLOOD MAY BEAR M FAR FARAJ AWWAY AWWAY
HINKITY HONKY MONK TOY-SHOCK THE MONKEY READ
& REREAD WIND & REWIND PLAY & REPLAY THE ATO
MIC DUK-DUK MYSTERIES MAKE LOVE OR MARCHESEA
DAYAK-DAYAK SPELL NEW IRELAND VERSUS NEW ENG
LAND YOUR SKULL IS MY KÄLLABASSHAMANTOVANILE
BLOB BLOB BLOBJIBWAH-WAH THE MUTTELLOCEAN OF
THE WOR(L)D IGLOBALLA BALLA MAMMASSATALIK ES
KAIMONITAUREAU BLAUBLIN BLAUBLIN BLAUBLIN EL
MARQUESAN PIGGY-WAKE WASH & GOD DE MARKIES V
AN WATERBULLOOPING ON THE HIGHWAY TO HADES T
EUFELLATING GOD'S MONKEY WHO GOT THE HADESPA
ZI BASSPACE BASSATANTRANSITIONAL NUCLARINET?
MUTTELLÈCHEZ LA PHLEGMME! DIONYSOSSYNOID IMI
TETSUO II CHRISTI BODY HAMMER GENDER CRUSHIN
G HOLLAND THE SLOUTTERRATIONAL SLITTICCASH F
LOWLANDICAS SINGING PRICK HOUSE WOMEN HOLLAN

DA ANALHOLD SCATAPULLING THE WORD INTO ZEROT
TIC MISSERY NORTH SEASEA-LISTENING DUTCHEASY
DOLORES DEL RIONYSOS HOPI HO HOPI HOLLAND TH
E IRON MAN TETSUO KUDO BUGIS WUGIS WARTANZIN
G CEASE RAIN CEASE RAIN! JASPERRUNG JOHNSONI
AN EPILEPSY I/M THE SLIME & THE PURPLE LAGOO
N SEPERMA & SUPERMA MAAA MAA MALAY MAGIC & W
ENDY WINTERS THE DELIGHTFUL WIMMY WOUNDERS-K
NEE YOUR TOUR-HOSTESS SPACE KRAFFT-EBBING KA
NGURUBYE BYE BANG LICHT MY FIRE 137/DISCO HE
AVEN YOU ARE WELCOME TO WATERFOOD I M THE WA
LRUS ANDY GIBBONS HEINO HINTJES CUMMODORE HE
AD 666 ONE OWAU MAN SHOWER LES NÎLES MARQUIS
ES FLUIDOFIUMEUSI USEMI GORILLA GORILLA BERI
NGEL USEMI USEMI JESUZY SCREENCHEESE USEMI U
SEMI VENUS IM PELZAPOPPING AP WHOLONELY HEAR
TS CLUB BAND THE FABULOUS FURRY FREAK OUT EC
HOÏSTE! ECHOÏSTE! TALITTLE TALITTLE! DOO-LIT
TLE MARQUESAN PIXIES DANCEFALLOGRAMMARQUESAN
PIGGRIEGG PIGGRIEGG I AM THE PIG MAN POWER T
O THE HALF&HALF RIVER PEOPLE DISOTTO IN SUMO
DE NARANJA NASSAUS BEATROCE BEATROCE ECCOLAC
RIMARQUISEMEN FLUSSING OUT COMES MOONFACE TH
E MAZZATORRENTEVEREVERRAUNWARAZORRUNDFUNKATH
ARSEAMAMMALE KUMBUMMING IN THE KINTERCHORTEN
OF DEEE-LAUT THESE BRIDES ARE MADE FOR SULKI
NG UNDISCONYSOS KIDDEÈSSE TOTEM (A MACHINE G
UN) & TABOOTSY BECK TO BECK IN BIDAY W/DE M
ARKIES VAN WATER ÉSPUSSY BASSATANTRACKING TH
E WET WET HOLLAND IN THE NETHERWORLDS THOTHE
MES & TABUQUEEN THE HYDROGEN BÖHM ÖHM ÖHM TI
BETANTRASHAMANIATMULLAS MARQUESAS JUNCLE JAM
FAN (HOT) CHILI PEPPER'S LONELY HEARTS ARE M

ADE FOR ASSHOLES ACQUA SAN MINERALE FRIZZANT
E S. GIORGIO OURMONEY BECK IN THE DAY TRIPPI
TT! TRIPPITT! THE BEST O BOOTSY ONE MANTOWER
INONDATABLÀ-BASSUNDRAUM TURKISTANLEY CLARTER
& BOOTSIBILLY COBBALZHAMMER I/M J.S. BECK SQ
UIDIPUSH REXTRAIT DE LEAU WEINIE WEINIE HOLD
ON TIDE YELLOW MELLOW GOLDEN SHE HE E-MAIL D
ITHYRAMBONNEFANTIASIAMAAS TWIN SPANK MEGAGAN
ESHAMALE LE MARQUIS WEST YOUNG MAN LIFFYRAMB
AUD DJESUS CRISIS SUPERFREAK BIZONNESTUDIONY
SOLEÎLES ÎLES MARQUISEAS JUNGLEDREAMS SITTIN
G ON A TIMEBOMB DE MARKIES VAN WATER NONJA T
URTLE IN THE KINDERCARDIN OF LSDELIGHT PAPUA
PSYCHO PUMPING COAST TO COUSTEAU H2OKUSAY WA
VE OFF KANGAWAH-WAH! THE OPEN BOATZILLAWARRA
MERCURY FOUNTAIN WOLLONGGONGADELIC PALEO PSY
CHO ROTORO MW MUSICLAND TO THE DONAUWELLEN (
LOVE AND HAMMOND) SHAFT LET IT ALL OUT LAUT!
WATER WATERBULLABILLABONGO BUTT PLUG MUGG PU
SH WALTER WALTER BECKER TO BECKER MY WATERLO
O DOWN IN THE BOTTOMTOM CLUB MEDLEY HAPPAH H
APPAH TEATEAMATI PO TE KITEATEA WAH-WAH TERR
ATYPEE H2OPII FUNKEY WEST UNCLE GEORGE BEN J
OHNSONTRA ZWILLINGERIONEISSAU DEUPHRATEX ZWE
IDEUTIGRIS TWIN PEEKABAUHAUSSCHLAMMMÈRDE INT
O THE MELVILLE FRACTURE ZONE MONOO TYPEE TYP
EE & THE DOLLY HOOLAH HOOLAH HOLLAND MY SUCK
ERKIND PACIFIC WARHAMMER FANTASY ROLE PLAYME
AT SPACIFICKY LEANDROSS ACROSS THE WAH WAH W
AH DE MARKIES VAN WATER & THE SPACE MUTANT A
PES OF REASON IN THE HEFFERRUSH TRANQUILLISA
TRANSPENISSYLFANNY FANNY BATHING IN SUSPENSI
ON OF DISBELIEF (DASENDEDAS20JAHRHUNDERTS) P

RIMARILY CRUXSTARING DISTURBANCE [OUT] COMES
CARLO BOND MEAT FREAK AQUABIONYSOS DUCHAMPOO
NA POONA BACH TO BACH ONE NATION DR. GOLDFIN
GERTRIPVISION & THE PEAU-FONKIMONO BIESKINIL
MACHINE TEL-EL-ARMANA-DE-AKASA DE BANHOH I O
H IBEUTZE BILLAH LASWELLE JET D'O SOLE MIONY
SOS WATER WATERREURQUELLE MARQUIS HYDROCÉPHA
STRALE DWELLANGCÔMING IN THE PSYCHOTHÈQUE OF
REASON UNCLE JAMSTERDAMPOOL PLAYING GOLF WAR
IN ACQUAPOLKA DOT BIKINI ATOLL NUNDRESS ARS
ULA WHATER WHATEVER WHATEVERYWHORE TRANSANTAR
CTICH SCHIZOGENESIS OR TRANSITION FROM ORANG
E TO YELLEMONOWWOWWOW DR. FUNKENSTEAMMACHINA
VELLI KEMEH ON YAH WARHOLLAND EL MARAMANDA L
EARIS CADAVREXQUIS IN THE ORANGE ROOM 5333 M
AH MAH MAH Z.O.Z. SCHIZO SOPOTAMMUZ ALL ABOU
T KING LAR-LAR GLEIRIS I.M. KING BENGGAWAN B
ANG TUKANG BENGKONGO WEST JIN & JUNG I M DEL
EIRISEI I M KUNG FU & CO WATER WATER GILLES
DELUGES EVERYWHERE BUDDISMOHEAVY METAL DRUMB
IBLICALVINIST EGG DANCE I M THE PIG MAN PORG
ILLAPOOLABOOTSYLLABOSCHAMAZONASSAU ÉSPACE GO
DDISSUCK OR FLUT HOLLAND WATCHING TV TRÄININ
G MISS OMNIVERSE U.O.M. MYSELF & BERLIN DADA
CLUB FUCK ROMA HAKA HAKA API API NERAKAOS GI
LA BABI BUTTUH BUTTOH BABY PSYCHOTIC SHE-MIL
LENNEON SEE-MILLENNOEN SEA-MILLENNONE PRINCE
RAMARQUESAN RAM JAM ON THE FREEWAY TO FELLIN
OLOGY MILES AHEAD 6000 FEET ABOVINE HUMANITY
HUMILITY HUMIDITY HHH-BOMB IN RIVERSE UPSIDE
DOWN UNDER THE BOARDWALK OUT KUMBUMMIN THE F
REAKAFREAKAFREAK OUT KUMBUMMING EL MARKIZIL-
KOEMBOEM DE MARKISALE MEER & BOSCH DE MARKWA

SSHE-MAELSTRÖOOMPH! KROMOSPHÈRRAPRISE WE WAN
T ROCKY THE HOROWITZ HEINOLA GAY-GAY ALLIN H
ENRY KISSINGER THE HOBBY-HORSE LET'S STICK-A
-PRICK HAUSSCHLAMMADEUSCH MOZZIE MOZZIE PABL
O PIKASSEL DOCUMENTAL ILLNOZZLING GO WASTE C
ALL CARL JUNG MAN CARL LEWIS CARROLL OVERRUN
RONNY LAING NANCY & ISAAC HADES GET OFF YOUR
ASS & DJEMBÉ DJEMBÉA DJEMBÉATRIX NOTRE DOUM-
DOUM TAKE YOUR DEAD ASS HOME BALLA BALLAFONT
ÜRED GONGOMARQUESS ALL-STAR TRANZAPPUALLEBEN
SLAUFBILD LAS MARKIZAS GELAR-LAR ORANGE BENG
SAWAN AURA WAN AURA ONE OWAH YELLOW ORANGE R
ED ORANGE YELLOW RIVERRENNAVEN MILES AHEAD F
AROE AWWAYYA FAROE AWWAYYA ONE BULL TOTAAL A
QUALLIBRIUM TANK UP YOUR ARSCHLAMM DUNKADELI
KKA PRIKKABEINURQUELLE MARQUIS DELOCEAN BOMM
ZWETT BOMM MANASKALLITONICCLONIC WATERMERKIS
DURODAMNATION DE MARKIES VANKUNNLEIKILLINGUS
! KUNCLE JAMAD WANTS YOU JURI JIRI YURI YOURI
JORGA JOERI ALEKSEYEVICH GAGARHINOCEROS MARQ
UESSATELLITTERRATOUR GO VOSTOKADELIC HOLLAND
FAROE FAROE OUT WORD UPSIDE DOWN NEVERMIND T
HE LITHIUM HERE'S THE MARQUESAN SEX JOKI JOK
I EREVERREXCORCANE PO-SHU MISHUMALE PAUPAU N
EW HEKE WAUTAU'A WAUTAU'A WAUTEATEA WAUTEATE
A ENA O TE TO'E TE KAI 'O TE HAKAIKI! TITTOI
PÛTA KEOTUS IN ANOA-NOA THAÏTI WAH WAH WAH W
AH WAH OBAY WAH WAH WAH WAH WAH O BAY PAS TO
MBÉ BAY DAY BAY OH MAN JAH EE! BAY DAY BAY D
AY OH MAN JAH EE! TRISTAZMANIANILE WATERMARK
GREIVISSALT SONGALINGALONG W/MFINNATRUX PAL
EO POPPOSEIDON PSYCHOTIC PSYCHOTIC HÂPI HÂPI
HOPI HOPI DE MARKIES VAN GOD VADERLAND & ORA

NJE IN THE BUFFALO SKIN SANCTUARY ALINGUALON
G THE ARIZONA HIGHWAY TO HÖLDERLIN HELIOCALM
ACQUAVITAL THE BLUE WRITER FIBONASSAU 2102 A
SPACEODDITY MEGAMERZBAHHASAY NOMOHAVE NO MER
ZATZ MELODY OOPS UPSHUT YOUR ASS NEZ NEZ NEZ
BABBITT BABBITT NIKKEI (225) JUST DO IT LSDE
E DEE 25 MEGAMORPHOSIS OVIDEOCLIPPITT CLIPPI
TT LSDIEUNUKE NUKE MOHAMMOND ALICE DEE DEE B
RIDGEWATER WATER TRANSSEXUAL HORSE LOVERMANI
A & MEGAPHYSICAL PASSAGE THROUGH A ZEBRA CLU
B FUCK MEDLEY WHERE'S THE BIRD-O-PARADISE?
WAH-WAH-WAH-BULLÀBASSPACE BAHASA LAKE GEORGE
RIVERRUISSEAU HERBIE ALPERT SCHWEITZER SPRIC
HT ZU UNS HOLLAND SPACE BASHKAUS RIVER BITCH
DUB P-FINKE FLOOD FLATS DROWNING RIVERRUBBER
& LATEXTOWER MAGMAGIC JOHN LENNON VOLCANIC D
ON'T PANIC PLANET O WORLD OCEAN FLOOR SHOWER
NINOTAUROTHALISMANIAGARACQUA JESUS CHRIST SU
PERSTARLIAMENT FUNKADELIC MISCH MISCH PSYCHO
SIS SUN RÂPE SNAKE LOVER UP YOUR ASSONANCY P
UNGEN HERE COMES HENRY PORTRAIT OF A C:ALVIN
UNDERSEA WORKHORSE (NOT JUST) KNEE-DEEP THRO
AT WATERGATE 2000 PORNEOCEANOAGRAPHY IN GEOR
GE WE TRUSS KUNGADOLF WACH-SCHLAF REGULOCEAN
PPP-FUNKADOLPHINNEON FLOODWAKE VON BEETNAVEN
A SPERMANENT DEFUNKADELICT ORANGANESHAU ON K
INTERNUTT M.W. MARQUESANDOZAUBERFLOODILONELY
TONGA BLOW-HOLE FLY RIVER FLY SPACE BASSEPIK
DANCE DANCE DANCE CONNEGUNA WAGHI RIVERREBUS
QU'APPELLE MARQUIS OH LOODIEPSLEEP SEA SEA S
EA! QUE SERA SERATHUSTRAUSSUCKER DADANUBA MA
RKASSERINDIIONYSOS DUBBERREVERSION DUB MARCU
S SAY EI EI EI UWEILA UWEILA UWEILA SUDANUBE

WALZHAMMER DIZZIE GILLESPELUGES LET'S HAVELO
CK ONCE MORE MORE BOBBITCHAMANUS DEI THALATT
ATTOO-WHOOO-WHOOO WASH NOT DIGITELLQUEL MALL
OY BLOMB VODUFONKT VODUNDUNDRUM CLUB BANDAMA
N DILUVER THE WORTSALATTATTOO-WHOOO-WHOOO BL
ACKWATER BLACK SEAMARKIESPACEO DESSAGAGA BRO
NZING NIGER ASTROTHERMAL SUDANUCLEAR BLACK S
PERMRAINFALL OUT LAUT AGUAJAJAJA PISSADANUBA
DEWANNEE NEE NEE POOLLUCY IN THE SKY NÄRRESC
APE FISTFUOCOBRA VERDE MARKIEZINASA TABUDDHA
HAMMERKUS NUBA HIVA NUBACQUA HIVACQUA MARQUE
SSUN RABUHTUH BUHTUH BILLION DOLLAR WAR BABI
ES MAKIN' BABIES SPEAKING IN THAI WAI THAI W
AI THAI FLOWING ON WAHWAH WAHWAH MAGIULINGER
& FEDERICOBRAVOODOOPER TOM MUKI MIX RIMINI A
TOLL ATOLL GEORGE KINGKONG & THE DOLL FAMILY
SNAKES TONE SIZE BULLES-BULLES TABLATTABLAST
ING INTO THE SULAR SYSTEM 66 MEGAPLANKTON SY
MSYAHHWATT? NEVER MIND THE BOLLOONIES TABBLE
MUNDZUCKER JACKSON BOLLOCKS HERE'S HENRY THE
KISSINGER PORTRAIT OF A SERIAL SULU SEA-FREA
K ROTOFUNKING IN COSMONAUT SEA-SPAESI BASULU
FUKAI FUKAI MW MASTER O WATERS AGOUE'TA-ROYO
EL REY AGUAGOUE'TA-ROYOYOTATING IN COPYRIGHT
CONTROLGATECRUSHING LEMON CRUSH ORANGE NASSA
U GOGONAVEN MADAME CILLA & THE DEEPDEEPSLEEP
WOEDOO LOVE SORCERY ELA ERZULIE GO CANZO RON
ALD LAINGLEGBABA RUMMAGAIN VA LOCO LOCO VALA
DIONYSOS LOCOMO LOCOMO! LE MARQUESSAUT D'EAU
HIM GO DREAM TO MAMA TELL MY HORSE ZORA NILE
HURSTON MAMMAMMAMBO LE MARQU'EST-CE QUE C'ES
T UNE FUNKADÉLICE? DAFEAUDILDONATION ALL-FUN
FRANSUÇEUSES S TO THE M! BRATATATATA BAHASAD

OMASSA CONFUSADOMASSA CONFUSADOMASSODOMY MYS
ELF & THE ORANGE UP YOU HOLZER ALL THE HOLES
IN YOU ALL READY-MADE IN HOLLAND MASTER O WA
TERS AGUAGUAGUAGOUE'TA-ROYOYOYOTATING IN THE
JACKSONIAN EPILEPSY BURN CENTRE/37 DISCO HE
AVEN EL MARKITSCHIFFERRUN TREVITE TREVITE QU
E TAJ MAHAL ABITCH VIRGIN MEGA WHORES MAGICA
SEXUALIS & RIVER NAVON DRIFTWOOD EAT IT SHIT
WELL ECHOLA BOMBA HIDROGUENAVEN UNGAIAK UGAI
AK MWRITE M WRITE MW RITE PALEOSCHIZOPHRENIC
SPEECH TIMEZONE THE NR. 7 WATERFALL DILUSION
STUPOROSOULSTREAMING INTERTONGUE INTERLANGUE
THE MARQUESAN MACHINERY HARDROCKLOBSTER UP Y
OUR ASSAMESOPOTAMUZZAN URSEAS! DUTCH UNCLE M
EAT ADAM & YVES SAINT KLEIN CALVIN CLINTON E
ASTWATTPECKER P-FINKITIR MIND TOURE KUNDABUL
LY BILLABEL MARDOOKEE THE BIG D & THE DUKE-D
UKE MYSTERIES NANCY MITFORD & I JUDGE THE JU
DGE RIVERRANNAHHH... TSUNAMIS QUILTY QUILTY!
LO! MARQUIS DE SADESFREUD EI EI EI EISCREAMA
SULAR SNYPERREALITY TELLUCY ALLABOOTLES DECO
NSTORTION NEVER MIND THE POLLOCKS HERE'S THE
EJACKULOCEAN POOLLOOK THE DEEPILOOP ZEELANDM
ARKIES THE NIGHT DANCER THE WATER BULL SEA C
HANGE & THE FLAME! PABLOLLOCK ICKA PRICKASSO
AP JACKSON DE POLLOCK UP YOUR ARSES WARHOLLA
DYLAND ÉGOUTTEZ ÉGOUTTEZ MWATCH TV-8 OLDMOBI
LES AILES MARQUISESSSSSS MARQUESAN MARCO AP
OLLOCK 11 MEETS THE SHE-WOLFGANGGHAGHARAINHA
RD DE FLUSS MARKIES GIVING SUCK HOLLAND GIVI
NG HEAD SHAMPOO HORN TV GLOTZER NEUKÖLN HIVA
ONE OWLA BUFO OWL OWLA ONE OWLA BUFO OWL OWL
A FELLAGRAINS WAXIS MUNDI LETHE MARQUIS OF O

OOOOOOOOO TOTEMIC BUMBARIVIERAPTUREVE RIVERRH
EINHARD DE SHAMPOLLOCK HORN FLEISCH & AFROMA
SO SACHERTORTURE WATER WATER AARFORIVERRUINA
ARSKUMBUMINICASCADO VANK YOUR FAMM ROKKUR'NR
OLLER THE DEEP PURPLE ERZOTZ HAZE & SMUCK ON
THE WATER MARKASKILLLING HEAVY MUTTERMAL GRA
ND MALLAERASA QUE SERASA SERASA DE MJORKEISS
VANDFUNNING FANNPOKA'ACQUA WATERING THELLUJI
THELLUJI ON THE SKIS MINDWELTWINDMELTDOWN BO
OTZILLA VERSUS GEORGE KINGKONG TSUNAMIS JACK
SON POLLOCK THE SCREEN RIVER SEMITERRA FIRMA
TERRA FUMMAMATERRA FLUIDOFUMMAMAAMAAA KAWAT
ERRA FIRMALAY GEOMATERRA FURMATAHARARIWERRAMP
ANA LITHIA WATERRA FIRMATERRA LIQUIDOSPUMMAJ
ILLACQUANALITHIATUMÜLT WASSERPENTINE FIRE TA
NZ HAPPENING ANTI-ARTS GIB MIR HONIGGER ZIGG
URAT SUPERSTARDUST BLITZKRÜGERRAP HOLIDAY IN
N 7000 OAKSYGEN CHAMBER 666 FETT WATT? THE K
UDO KUBE OECHAHIS! OECHAHIS! HIROSHIMA BOSCH
SPEAKING IN TUBES THE HYDROCEPHALLIK FALLAUT
LAUT KUM THE EREGGULATOR IN THE ELECTRONIC C
IRCUIT KUDOGGODZILLARVAIRIANTE MARE UNDAEMON
DO BIZARROTOTATTOOING THE PHILOLOGY OF IMPOT
ENCE MPAPP MPAPP YOU ARE METAMORPHOSING-D (Y
OUR PORTRAIT-H) YO EL REGENSHI RYOKUDO TETSU
MIZU KUDOLLANDA ANTE MARE UNDAIMETSUBOKUDOKU
MENTHALES ÎLES NASSAU TERRA FIREMADE FOR WAL
KING HENRY HANGAKOK HERPIES KISSINGER EEEKKE
EE OM OM OM BLOWUP THE HOSPITAL AMBIANZABABY
BUTO BUTO ELECTROSUCK HOLLAND RIVERS LIBRE K
OODOO WINTIBETANZANIAGARA WALZABABALANKUMBUM
BARIVERSION DUBBULLY OCEAN TO OCEAN VERTICAL
MIXING RIVERTEXT RECIRCULOTION ROTELLA ALLAB

UTT SERRA HOEKSTRA & STELLA POLLOCK MOMMY MO
MMY AVARY WHEREAKLITOURIST WASWAS NOT WASWAS
SIHRROCCOCO PSYCHOSEXUALSDE MARKIES VAN WATE
RATOÏD WATERRAQUEOUS WATERMINATAURACQUACQUAC
QUACQUACQUA POTABILLABEL MARDUDOOKEE NUKE NU
KE GLITTERRHEIN KLITTOURISM & PUPPENILE PUSS
EAFOODOO OBI MAN WAU OBEAH WO MAN VOODOOBOOH
OOP HAKO HAKO PAWNEEKKEE HOMOHAVE THE SEPICK
IN THE FOREHEADFUCKALLSDE MARKUST VAN GUINEA
SKUM BAH YA SKUM SKUM BAH YA MACUMBAH LIVE F
LOODKRÜGER 1 OWAANSELM SCHIFOSCREEMIA PSIQIA
TROSEASSWAHILA TOURROULETHE BOMBABULLIMIA PS
IQIATRASHOCKOLAUT TERROR RAPE PEE EEEKKEEELE
CTROSHEIQ URBOOTSITRUSTRAN & HELIOTRUPPOLLY-
LINQUELLEMARQUIZEUT TO ZEUT FAZ TO FIZ MUMMY
MUMMY RIVERTUAL REALITTERREURQUELLETHE BUMBU
MBAH YAYA HOLLANDY DADA VINCINEMATRIX WAGNER
WATERWARGAME SKIZOOBERDARSCHIZOODOOMY MYSELF
& GORILLA GORILLA GORILLA PAPIO CYNOPHALUS C
YNOPHALUS PAPIO NEW GUINEA PARIS METROSEXUAL
MARQUESSUCK MAKE LOUVRE NOT WAGRAM PISSINEMA
QUANONE BATAJ MAHOLE TELL QUELL'ANUS SOLLERS
TAKE METRO THE RIVER AFFEN AFFEN AFFERYWHERE
YOUR SUN IS SET MARQUESS O' THE FINEST WATER
UNDER THE SUN DRAWING WATER WATER EVERIVEREN
CE FLOWS ON THROUGH THE LIVING RIVER BY YOUR
DOOR ATOMMOHAAAWK KEMEH HELIUM CALAMITY VIVA
ROXY HORROR HOLLANDMARKIES KONGO KLITZING IN
KIMKOM & STANLEY CLARKES ELECTRIX EVERYWARHO
LLADYLAND LORÉALITTERRATOURE KUNDADA DEBUM D
EBUMB DEBUMBA HONG, OM! HIDROJEN GENDERANG C
ROXIFISSION DE MARKISTIMEWATER BLOB BLOB BLA
UB BLAUB MAHU-LAY WUTA-LAY ALLABUTO BUTO THE

ALAMCLOCKWORK ORANG UP YOUR ASSALAMU ALAIKUM
BUM BABI RUWAN SAMAN SHOWWARWAWA HECKELDUSCH
SHAMPUH! VAUDOUCHAMPOOLEPSY VASLAV NINJA THE
GVIKKING LEARY & THE IDIOTTO È MEZZOAPOCALYP
SY NOAH LISTEN UPUNCLE JAMANDA LEAR JAMSTERD
AMBALLA BALLA WEDO WEDO I M HUSBAND & WIFE I
N ONE ON ONE OWAH WAN OWAUTHOREAU THOREAU WA
LDEN WALDEN EVERYWHERE FAUNNADIEU WAH-WAH KO
ST TO KOSTROVSKY TO VASLOVE KNEEJIRIAQUA FAL
LS HOLLYWOODSTOCK-SEXCHANGEOMATRASCHEITTICKA
MW FIATMÜL NEU BIGUINEA ATOLL ATOLL BRAVO BR
AVODA BRAVODADA DE MARKIES VAN WATER FIRE-WA
LKING IN CIRCLES FIRE WALK THROUGH M! WASSUR
YAREAL PONGOLIAN FIRE FIRE STARRY STARRY NIT
E NITE AGNITE MY FIRE WAU FIRONIA! TALOS SOR
ANUS MARCASTABALAKES KANDADARLING OLLABUTT T
HE HIRPI SORANI HANGAKOKS WALKING THROUGH TO
NGUES OF LIQUID FIRE HOLI-HOLI-HOOPING IN TH
E SKY ONE SPOUTBULL ON FIRE LAS MARQUESAS VA
MPPYROMANIAGARA FALLASSEAU TAAWATTAA TAAWATT
AA! MARQUEZANTI SERENADE TOMTOMMOHAAAWK OWAU
MUDD CLUB VERSION 2000 MOTELS FINALE A SPACE
BARRAQUE BULL ODISSEA TYPEE FACES IN THE WAT
ER SEE JUNGLE! SEE JUNGLE! IAMADEUS TV SAVAG
E GLOTZER BUDDHA TV-TOESTRAAL IN NOVOTELBUJ
UMBUMBURABURABOUTSIBILLA-BASSARATOESTRAAL IN
UTERO YAUMOMMAS MAR ÄGGITADA ETHERMAL GEOMAT
TERMALL GUTTERGULL WASWASSILY NOT WASWASSILY
WATERRA FIREMARQUESSADOLOROSAURANOS BIKINIMA
ATOLLANDA A-TOM BUMBAHHARLEKINI ATOLLANDANUB
ALATHUSTRAAL WATERRA FURMATA HARIVERRAYAN-RA
YAN RIVERRENJANA LIVIA KUALA KUALA SLUMPURRA
PPEEL RIVERRAUWOWWOW RIVIRTUTUPELOLOLIVIA PA

RAPLURRAPPULL AMERICA IS WAITING DR. MAREBUS
E IN CRIEGCOSTEAM READING THE SKULL-BORNEO O
RANGUTANTRASHAMANTICS! WAH-WAH WAH-WAH IVORY
HORN WAWAWA WAWAWA IVORYHORNBILLASWELL YO EL
REI MOMOHEAVY YOYO EL REBUS THE KUBRICK KUBE
MARQUESAAN SCHIZOAPERATTACK ATTACKAWATRASHOW
NORTH SEA-MIELITROMMOMMY BHINNEKA TUNGGAL IK
ATOLL JAWATER TAALATTAAL TAALATTAAL JAVATARK
ALOR ALOR TSUNAMI ZUZAMZAMMENBROCH SIRKULASI
MALANGAKUTIKIFIRDAUSCH PSYCHO SEXRIST SWAHIL
ARYS BORDERLINE PSYCHOSIS FIRE-FLOATING DYON
IX-CATACOMBUANDIONYSOS MARANATHALATTABOOTSHI
VA-DYONIXRIST ORANGE RUBBER TIDE BOOTSY-WOOT
SY VIVA-DYONIXON HOLANDICASCATACOMBUMMING L
EOPARDOPPELGANGES MARKASHMIRQUESS SPIRIT-LAN
GUANGEOWATERRA WATERRA FIREMADE IN MINDSCAPE
UNCLE JAMMU JAMMURDER MOST FULLY BOOKSHOT LE
FONQUE THE DANCING DERVISHES LEAU DISSEY GUH
L GUHLLISPIE DELUGEL MOUSSANT CAVE MANTRA LÀ
-BASSAVON LIQUIDE DE MARKIES VAN WATER FLOOD
MIX FUSE & REFUSE HOLLAND WASHING WASHING LE
AU DE AURA CASHLEY KAOSSENGAL SOAPOCALOOP-DE
-POOLYPSE NOWAH-WAH NEW WAVE LASWELLA FLEXPL
OCEAN ESCAPE CALVIN CLINTON SGT. PEPPER'S SO
URCY MALE CLUB BANDAMANDADA MONDWATER IN CYB
ERSPUSSI BASSICK M SADO O BIZAR MARQUIS & WA
RM WATER FOR WENDY & LISA TONATIEN ASPHONSAD
EL FRANCOPHORMERLY KNOWN AS PRINCE 1PPP AQUA
DELA LUNE LET THE SUNSHINE IN BILLASWELLA FL
EXCORCISSEAS THE FLEXORGAST LSDELA SOUL ALLS
DELITTLE BIT OFFUNSOAP M MYSELF & I MARQUESS
DEPOSÉES COCK-A-CULA RIVERPUN WORTSALAUDISSE
Y PAUNNAKAMP WAKEE TALKOME FIRST FRUIT EPILE

THELEPATHY LUAPULA! LUAPULA! LUAPULA! SCULPT
URE EAU DE STARFOAM SUN COSMETICA FLUIDE REP
ARATEUR SECURITY SOLEIL UP YOUR ORANGE FUNKA
HOLIC LUBERRECTUM PACIFIC BLUE SHAVE HITLOUR
DES W/YOUR RHYTHMSTUCK EAU STUCK EAU UUT HO
O! THE COUP DD HORRORSACHER MASOCHER TESTA O
NE TWO GRAND MALLARMÈR FOOLAHOER NUKING ABOU
TAROUND THE CYBERSKOPTZI INTERZONE THE GROOV
ES ON FIRE LAME BE YOUR HOOVER & DIQUE DE MA
RKIES EN EL MAR YO EL REY SOL SAY LAUT SACHE
R MASOCHER TORTUGA DE MARANA DE MARQUESTRELL
A DE MARCASCASADE ORANGE DILUVIONYSOS DIOS D
EL SOCASOMMERSOUL IDIONASSAU THALATTANAGRA T
HALATTANAGRASUCK THALATTANAGRASUCKADELPHIC M
AGIC NOT WRITING GREEN RIVER PSYCHO HORNAGAI
N AQUAPUSH REXWATERSTOET SHOCKSPERMANENT OLL
ANDIKE CHOKMAH OBEA MERDA MOST FULL PROSTAAT
TANT RAPESODOMY IN TRUE BLUE LOW LOW LOW HAD
ESMENORRHEANYS.O.S. IL MARCHÉSE ESPEAKING IN
TUNGÂLIKKING YOUR HEMAGINATION HOLLAND WAU O
R NEVER DE BAPTISMOGUL NNGELAK-KAWAWA WAWADI
ONYSUFINNAGAGA DE MARKIES VAN WATER ANUS-GRO
OVING HOLANDOMINA ORANGE DISASTER BY THE SEA
WARHOLANDA MW THE VAGINAL FOAMADEUS ACQUATTA
CKING THE DILDO GIRLS STARRING CARLA HOLLAND
THE FELLTHAMMERING BUTTOCK OF THE WORLD RESU
RRELAXING IN ARSE-MUTT GOETHESCHEIßHAUS DO I
T DOG WATERSCHEIT DOWN DOWN THE RAPPUT HOLLA
ND GENUINE COWHIDE MCCLINTON CLINIQUE FACE-Z
ONE SUN BLOCK BEUYS WILLIAMS LE GEL SHAKESPE
ARE O TELL M ALLANDABUTT HOLLANDY WARHOLE-IN
-ONE OWAU IATMÜLTRA NUCLEARASILLA DE MARKIES
VAN WILLENDORF INONDATA BASSIN MARINE RAPERA

HOLLATLANTIS JUDAS PRIEST DAVE HOLLAND THE B
IG BLUE VELVET UNDERGROUNDCONTROL TO MAJOR D
UNDRUMANALYSIS UNIVERSO AFTER SHAVESPEARE CA
RL ANDRÉLONELY HEARTFIELDS FOREVER ANTI-KLIT
KOSMOZEAN HIGH & RISING ANOHA BAY TOPORNOAH-
NOAH CHONNOREUX CINEMA EUROPE MARQUIS ALL TH
E WAY TANAGRASAKI AP AP APSU SU SU SUMATRA R
AIN DUSCHGELLES DELEUSIAN MYSTERRA FIRMAGICK
BACK TO BACKDOOR BIKINI ATOLL TEST WATER-IND
UCED PSYCHOTIC BABY PSYCHOTIC READING PURIFI
CATION NATION COAST TO COSTELLO'S KOJAK VARI
ETY P.-BLAKEWASSERFUNK I M THE WALRAF I M THE
EGG MAN GLOO-GLOO-GLOO-CHEW BLACKBIRD OR MIC
HAEL BLOP, BLOP, BLOP, WE'RE UNLISTED! LETIT
B/D OR GG ALL-INN FAME FAME FAME FAME FAME F
AME BE FOAMMOUSSANT FOR FIFTEEN FINITUDES HO
LLAND MDSM-III SMPS/MPSM THE RIVER WILD AT H
EARTS CLUB BAND DEFUNQUELLENNON-STOP EL MAR
QUESSGT. PETRUS BLAKES AFFETISH-STUDYONIX-CAT
ACUMSHOT FLOOD STREET BABYLONDON/S BURNING B
ABYLONDON/S BURNING BABYLONDON/S BURNING ONE
OWAH ONE OWAU EAUBLUEVIANTRASHOWASH ROCK AND
ROLL-CALL-STARWASSERGÉANT PRICKALLILLY CHIPP
ER'S KATWALKABOUT NARRENSCHIFFONQUELL ORGYPE
LAGOON SQUAD ALMOST READY-MADE FOR ACTION WAN
OWAU ONE OWAH BEFOAH HAW AURÂH PICASSO-KRAWA
TTEN FLOATING IN FAME IS LIKE A RIVERRANTING
PIS YVES SAINT LEAURANTS PIS EVE & ADAM & TH
E GREEN ANTS DREAMING ONE HAWAH UR ENOS ON
E HAWAH UR ENOS ANUS MÚNDRIAAN BOOGIE WOOGIE
EXPLOSIONS PRICKLES & SEPICKLES ÎLES MARQUIS
ES KAWATER WATZUSKAWATER NIJINSKY EVERYWHERE
MARKIESKIMO SCHIUMANISMOUSSANTA PROCOLOLO FL

ORANGE NASSAU PRICKASSO-KRAWATTER WATTER ALL
THE TIME WATAER WATAER IVORY COAST THE WARRI
OR-ONLY DOG SOCIETY UP YOUR MISSISSOURRY SOU
SSOUSSOURRY SPAESI BASSEE BIGUINEE ATOLL ATO
LL KRAKAKAKAKATOA KRAKAKAKAKATOA ADOLF WÖLFL
I & THE BRIDES OF FUNKENSTEIN OWAU THE NADA!
THE NADA! TANAGRA! TANAGRA! HOLLAND ARSE HOL
E IN ONE GOGO MW/THE FLOWFLITTERRA FIRMAGIC
K BRAHMARQUIS MURDER MURDER MOST FOUL TONY B
AEKELANDMARQUESANTA BARBARA BAEKELANDMARKIES
THE THOTHALES MOYSTERING CRIME COME O YE BAC
CAE COME TO TONY BAEKELITE'S BACCAELANDSPOUT
ING THE RAIN HARD THE FOSSILES SEDIMENTAL DI
SORDER PARTY ON PLASTIC RIVERBEDLAM ABROODMO
RE EROSMESH HEAD-HE-GO-ROUND-MARKIES BELLY-D
ONT-KNOW-WATER WATER NO-MOHEAVY BASS THIS IS
THE SEA THE WATERBOYS SHOCK CORRIDORRIDA KOM
MANDO LEOPARD VOODOO HEARTBEAT ASYLUM EROTIK
IN FERNEN OSTEN ODER TRANSITION FROM WARM TO
COOL SIEGFRIED BROWNHILDE & FEDERICO FELLINI
'S MAGIC POCEAN THE VALHALLA WANNSEE KONQUER
ANGEL WALZ THE BLACK SPERMLAKI RAINFALLING K
UBRICKINI ATANKOLL JAMES JUICE TO THE OVIRIV
ER OVULE MARQUIS TV SAVALLAS MARQUESAS/PAPUA
NEW GUINEA BOG DANCE GILA GILA BABI BABI MEE
NKHEM CHIM KHOMUS SOLO NUSRAT FATI ALI KHAN
SHU-DE MW HAKA TAPA TAPA TWIN PIG SEXPERRIER
THEMARQUESSTUDIO 53 OLLANDIZZEELAND SCHIUMAR
IO FIUMERSE RIVER TATTO SCORRE BACONOSPASTIC
BOEUFRATES TIGRIS-GRIS WASSIR WASSIR JOHN PO
PE INNOCENZO X (A) SPACE HENNESSY TRANCEVOIC
ETIDE SPEAKING IN WINTER TONGUE FEBBREWERY F
LOOD TUNG HO TUNG HO EGOLALITTERRATTOURQUELL

E MARQUIS DEEELOOORANGEADELLACQUA IN PARADIS
OTTO IN SUCKSTEAM CHAPEL AEROPANTHALATTA REI
REVERIFOLLY TIBERNINILE FUNTANAVONA SARAGUIN
EA GRANITA ICEBERG ON THE YVES INCENT ORANGE
SPEETRUSH SPLATZ SCATWELT HIHIFIDEEELETE YSL
& THE FAMILY STONE FRESH! DE MARKIES VAN WAT
ER PAPOEASSYLOOMING AHEAD VI PALEO-PSYCO-POP
SPERMAFROST NUCLEAR SOAP FLAKES BAUME ECLATT
ER ECHO OMO URKAN WHAU WHAU WHAU TONGUE SUCK
SPIRIT RIVER QUE TAL QUE TAL TAJ MAHALLABOUT
HOLLAND THE HAPPY HOOKAH SGT. JELLY PEPPER'S
MARVELLASQUIS WATER EBONEYWHORE LIST OFF SLY
ONE PARISMATIK MEGAWHOREPAUSES GRUESANDENIST
AALMUDDWALLE MUTTWELLE MARQUIS TE PO TANGOTA
NGO THE DELUGE CLOSETBACK ONETWO POPLAVATORO
TVOODOOLOOPZILLA DE MARKIES VANDELLAS MARQUE
SAS AQUALSD MARQUESS DE SANDOZA SNOW LEOPARD
SKIN POPPING LSDSM-III-25 CALL CARL JUNK OTT
O E DIX WEIMARQUIS IN THE LIFFEY-STRAUSS DRE
AM CHAMBER NR. 1 DADANUBISMARKIES ANARCHIPEL
HALLUCINOGENESIS SPACE MAZE SHAMANTRASHAMALE
ONE HORRORRATIO POST-COÏTAL MODERNISM META-O
BJECCULATOR DUTCH UNCLE JAM MADURONIRIVER PS
YCHOBATHGAGADIVA SOLO RUBBISHMA HERRAKLITORA
ZOHARPO DE MARXIST VAN WATERREBIRTH MAGIC SU
NDANCE CLITTORISE WATER NOT WATER EVERYWHERE
THE RIVER OF LIFE REACTIVATED M IS FOR WATER
LES FLÜSSILLAS SOUL-CITRONIC UNCLE RAM MAKIN
G WAVES VATNAVEN GANGRÂLLY HUSSAHE! HUSSAHE!
GRAND MAHLER FLASH FLOOD DUBLIN BAYREUTH AYRE
UTHIKA TRIESTHANATOSS & GRIFFESSALTOES FLOWI
NG ON WATER WATER THE LOVERMEER I.M. DE MAHL
ER VAN WAGNER ARANHA NÄSSEXTASE THEMANINIERI

VERSEANALEVE & ADAMAHU MAHU JELL O JELL O EL
MARRIO ANAGOYA ANAYOGAOSMOSEAS VOODOOCHAMPOO
L JOHNNY SITAR WATT OOHH HENRY JAMES THE HOB
BY HORSE WATTAW WATTAW EVERY HOBBY WHORE A H
ENRY JAMES N.Y. N.Y. CITY DIONISIAMESOPOTAMM
EL MARQUESSAINT ESPRITES OF SPRING OBEY YOUR
THIRST LSDE-NURQUELLETHE MARQUESSPASMODIGUES
S WHO-WHO DE MARKIES VAN WATER TRAUMTRAUMTAN
ZING IN ZAUBERSPACE WALK IN PROGRESS WAH-WAH
WAH-WAH WAH-WAH FRIPPAKLAW WAGAGE MOUZZARTAU
DDISSEAS & CIBBERSPACE BASSES BY BILLABONGOL
LASWELLA FOAM EINFACH SUPER VIDALLAS MARQUES
ASSOON WASH & GOD ULTRA SUNÎLES ÎLES LUCIBLE
S OIL OF OLAZZ MARQUEZAZZMATAZZ BATH & LOCEA
N MAGGOT BRAINSKANNAPOLISTEN UP! JAJAJARAPÉ-
FONKATHARSIS THERMONUCLEAR ZWITSALT IN URBAN
WATER SPACE VIVA! THE FRENZIES SPASMASSPASSI
BASSIFIC BLASTING IN THE BEGUINE ATOLL ATOLL
WOW OUT LAUT EL MARQUESSHAMBULLHAGARTHALATTA
BOOTSYBILLABONGO BUTTERRAINDANCE WASH & TANG
O IN PARIS H2OBLITTERRATIONALGALERIE HOPI HO
PI HÂPI HÂPI BENETTON MOUSSOLINILE PALEO-PSY
CO-PUBE UP YOUR ARSES UP STIFFELLINILE TOWER
BURNING SPRITE OBEY YOUR THIRST TIERRA DEL F
UEGO GUINEANDER MARQUISSHAMALE NOT WASSERMON
SAVONASCUM BLACK MASSOON BLANCHAMALE YOU ARE
KNEETZSCHDEEP IN THE FLOODDILONELY ARSE CLUB
MEDLEY ROTTENSTERN IN HELL FUEGO MANIAC DE M
ARKIES VAN WATER ZARATHUSTRAWINSKIZO AQUAVAT
ARLIAMENT FUNKADAVISNUKU HIVALLSDE MAHATMARK
IES DERWISHING WELLES ÎLES MARQUISES LUNATIC
KA DICKA PSYCHIATRICKA PRICK-A-BOOBOO KITT P
EAKS ARIZONASSAU FUCKUS-MANIFESTO SWEAT SWEA

T SWEAT VOODOO WATRA WATRA EVERYWHERE EL MAR
QUESAN URBAN BODY MOISTURE ESPACE BASS CULTU
RE CLINTON QUASI JOHNSON BITCH DUB ORANGE NO
SEAUDIONYSOS BECK ON THE BLOCK BEUYS THE WOL
FGANGES AUM AUM AUMADEUS SHAMEN AT WORK BUSI
NESS AS USUALL DOWN BY THE SEA WATER WATERRA
INCOGNIETZSCHAMALE MARQUIS SPASSOCIATIVE BAS
-BALAVACA DE MAR VAN WAR APOLLO SPEECH WALKI
NG M PLAY FOR TODAY (THANK YOU FLOOD) SPASSI
BUSY SPASSIBUSY P-FUNGIFORMAL NACHTMUSIK JAS
S D'EAU GADOMATO GROSSOUVERRAINTANZ DRUMPRET
TANGO OLÉ GUAPITA RAP YOURSELF EL ELECTROCHO
CLO ODIEU LIVE PORN AROUND THE CLOCK THE HAP
PY HOOKER & THE MEDICINEMA SHOW BIG BING CRO
SBY STILLS & NASA LETHIUMBRAILLEAU LE TAXI J
OURNEY OF THE SORCERER ON ASYLUM RECORDS MAG
ICK NOT SEXY OCEAN RAIN WALTER WALTER ORANGE
EVERYWHERE MEGAGANESHAMANIACALVINNASCUMAWONK
NUKU HIVA JUST DO IT WASH NOT WASH SCATULLUS
T FOR LIFE MARQUIX LIQUID SOAPOPERABISMARKIE
S EL MARQUÈSCAPE HÖRNER HÖRN SCRYPTOGRAMMARQ
UESSAUT D'EAU ME MYSELF & AQUANTONIN AQUARTA
UD DO IT YOURSELF ELF OWL RAINFOREST EAGLE O
WL MWESTERN SPEECH OWL MARQUESAN PYGMY OWL &
BROWN FISH OWL SCREECH-DEFECT HOLI-HOLI HEAL
Y-HEALY PARTY ON NÉOPLASTIC HÂPI HÂPI NIL RI
VERGODDISSEA SPACE TRAVELLO SHEALY-MALE MARQ
UIS DAFKAP DE SODA AQUAJOGGING IN PARAGUAY N
EW GUINEA WATER ON THE BRAIN VENUS IMPULZIVE
INSANITY IN CIBBERSPACE ABBYSSAU RIVERBEDLAM
OF THE WORLD ISAAC ISAAC NUCLEARASILICON CHO
COLATE CHIP CHOCOLATE MARQUIS JUST WATER ECC
E HOMONOMANIA DADALAI LAMADEUS MOSES P-FANGU

FANGU NOSE FLOOD OTEA OTEA DRUM DANCE WASH &
GOGH HOLLAND WET BELT FITNESSAU GLETSCHER HO
MO NEW ATLANTIS WAVEMAKER GLETSCHERZATZ SEAS
EA-LEVELLATIO NO WAY OUTBLOTTAD FELA KUT & I
RUBBER DUTCH & LATEXTUALITY MARAE MARAE HOLD
ON TIDE VAYA CON DIOS GINGER & FREDDY FENDER
IS THE BASS HADESPERADILDO HOLE BITCHCOCK DU
B FIRE WILDFIRE ASHES THE RAIN & I, RAINY DA
YS STORMY NIGHTS RIO SPEED WAKE EL MARQUESSY
MPHONIE FANTASTIQUE UNCLE JAMBA PA TI RARE P
RECIOUS & BEAUTIFUL DE MARKIES VAN WATER THE
BLUE WRITER SIR PSYCHOSEXY NOSEAWATERVODUWIN
TIE GROOVE PÄRT 1 & TU FUNKING THE RAIN DIAL
M FOR MURDER HENNATRIPPAWAK I M THE EGG-MALE
GG-STRING FIGURE ALLINN INN! TZARAHOEKSTRAHL
HIRSCHJAGD FOREVER RIVERRE WATERRE HAARE HAA
RE (ATOM-MODELL) KRISHNA KRISHNA THERMONUCLA
AR FUNGHINNA-TRIXAWAKA AQUA BED FLOTATION SYN
CHRO SYSTEM ALL-STARLIAMENT-FUCKADOLLY PARTO
NTRASH LUNATICKA DICKA PSYCHATRICKA PRICK OP
USSY MAU-MAU 20.000 MILES DAVISHNUKU HIVALLS
DE MARKIES JUST WATER SPEAKING OUT LAUT IN T
ONGA TWISTERHOOD SAMOA LIKE IT HOTTENTOT CLU
B CAPTAIN COCKMED EL MARQUESCAPE HÖRNY HÖRNE
R WAS NOT IS MR. JAMBOURHIN KILONIL KURZ EUN
UKUDO RE MI VA FAMILY-FOLLY-FUNK UR-ATLANTIC
GEORGIE FAME BLUE DADA (ORIGINAL TRADE MARKI
ES) WAS NOT WOISSEAUX SCRATCH ODDIEUSSEAS CA
LL M THE BIG P.I.L. BIG-A-FOOT STARSYSTEM VI
RGOGO GUINNEAQUA BASSARUSE YOURSA MAMAJOR! B
IG DIPPERRUN RIVERREGULUS IN THE SKY WE WANT
BOÖTES ALPHA BOÖTIS ABETA ORIONIS ZIPPERNOVA
GUINEA PIL DANCE PSYCHOTIC BABY PSYCHOTIC DM

VW FUNKING THE HARD WORD DADDY COUILLES ÎLES
MERGUÈZES ALLSDEMI-WATT-WATT GEORGE GROSZ CL
INTON IN THE AFRICANIMISTIKI CULT LIFE PARNA
SSAU-FUNKADELPHI LSDÉRIDING THE SHEEP-MALE &
THE HÖRNY HÖRN MAH MAH MAHLATHINI & THE MAHO
TELLA HIGHWAY TO HELLAS MARQUESAS BULL-ZEBUB
MWINOTAURRAPSODOMY MYSELF & ISIS VENUS MUNDU
SCH ALLSDÉLIRIUM TREMBLEX MITHRASH MISSELF &
IRIS STARNASSUS-FUCKADELFICKY LEANDROSS ACRO
SS THE WATER! SCATULLUCY IN THE SKY ONE OWAH
WAN OWAHH... THE NAME IS JUPITERRA FIRMARQUIS
WASSIR NOSE NOT WASSIR PSYCHOSEXTERRESTREAMA
DEUS TRUMPUSTING THE ATLANTI-CHRIST DE MARKI
ES VAN WATER PUUR ZUIVER KRISTAL WATER PHASI
PHAKE OCEAN ESPACE SHAMANDATA BASSES ZEUS NO
T ZEUS THALATTHALES ÎLIAS MARQUISAS GROSZ IS
THE WORD NEPTUNUS MUNDUSCH REMARQUIZZICAL PA
CIFINNOWAR SHAMMANIFESTO & SOULTIMATRUM SCHI
ZOLL-DICKA-PRICK BE POLAR HOLLAND WATERRA ED
ITUS WATERRA REDDIRIS PIG AUDIO DYNAMITE TRU
MTANZ IN THE MARQUESAN SCHIZONES JESUS-CHRIS
T SUPER ARSE MITRASHAMALES & DIONYSOSSMATOSS
RIVERDICKING PHASIPHINATRASH DADA HAIR WEX G
UESS WAH-WAH WAH-WAH VASER NOT VASER SIR PSY
CHOSEXIL ASOPUS-PUS SHE-MABUCEPHALLUS DE MAR
KUS-KUS VAN WAH-WAH-WAH NEZ-NEZ-NEZ LIBERLIN
PSYGNOOTIC SEAU'TONICCLONIC SEMELE SOLO EL M
ARQUESANOTHER MOTHER FURTHERMORE EROSMOUSSOA
P MOTHER'S FINEST WILLIE NILE ACROSS THE RIV
ER SHINE YOUR LIGHT WILLIE NILE MWARQUESSOAP
OCALYPSOLEILLOGICALVINAPHUNK WATERREURQUELLE
MARQUIS UNCLE RAMMOLLOA EDDADANUBISHMA MYSEL
F & IACCHUS PUTSCHWORKING THE ARSCHIZÜNDFLUT

EL MARQUESSOLEÎLE MARQUISGEOWAKE ALSDÉRAZORA
-ZORA TORA-TORA WILLIE NILE & CHEB MAMI MAMI
SIR PSYCHOSEXPLOSIVE LONELY HEARTS CLUB TRAN
CE ALSDÉMIURGEOWATTHERMONUCLEAR SWEATTICCAOS
OCEAN RAIN RAIN RAIN ÈSPACE ODDIEUSSY LSDMVW
RAISONABULLISHTARATHUSTRAUSSIR PSYCHOSEXISPA
CE BASSPASSIBASS-BALLA-BALLALAIKAOSTARATHUSS
TRAUSS HEXENHAMMERING HOLLAND LETHEL MEANDER
MEEE EP.I.L.EPSYCHO-POPPOSEIDON PSYXOTICH GR
AND MALLEUS ATTICKA PRICK-A-BULLBULLTANZ SCH
IZOÖPSIE-MALE EROTIC HORSE & ATOMIC DOG ORGY
AMBI-PUR COCKODRILDEO ROLL-ON OVER BEETHOVEN
LSDOLITA LSDOG DESIRE ALL INTERACTIVE HËXEN-
DASH COLOR FRIED ICE-CRÈME SOAP SAVON LIQUID
E MARKIES VAN WATER SIR PSYCHOSEXCORGASM MIT
RASHAMÄNNER MISSELF & I ECCE OMO COLOR MVW B
EETLEJUICE MAJJIC JAMES JAW-BONE MAR RIO MÈR
ZEE MALE MARQUIS UNTERACTIF HYDRATANT ESPACE
CABAZZAUBERSPACE & THE BEASTIE BASSES HOLI-H
OLI HILLY-HILLY HOPI HOPI RIVERRAPPIONYSOS T
ERRACOTTATTOO YOU CIBBERREX THE MARQUESSHAMP
OOLABULLY & KING BAALABILLY JAZZMATAZZMANIAG
ARY GLITTERROCKOCKOKOSCHKAOSKARMA KOCKOSCHKA
ONE MANDRILLNÄSSEAU BE-BUST HOLLAND STAIRWAY
TO HELL PORT O PRINCE CHARKIE PARKERILLOALOA
GRAND MALA-MALA GAME PARKERILLASERRIESENSCHI
LDKRÖTEN RIVERURTELLING THE TELL-TALE TRAILW
AY TO HEAVEN FLASHFLOODDYSSEE-MALEOPATRASHAM
ADEUS WOLFGANGANESHAMALE MARQUISAAC/DC PURPL
E HAYES FRED HOT BUTTERED SOULTIMOTEI RHYTHM
SECTION FEATURHINE THE BAR-KAYS/THE MAR-KEYS
LSDJ COOL WATER SUZI QUATRO & THE RUBBER BAN
SHEES WILLIE NILE NILE BLUE ÖYSTER CULT BECK

FLASCHIZOOÏDE MARKISS.O.S. TITANIC DON'T PANIC! SEMENTAL FLOSSILLES ÎLES WAH-WAH WAH-WAH WATERFALLSDEMENTAL FLOOD FOR THE GLOBE EPILEPSY IN THE GARDEN OF RAPPER'S DELIGHT HYDRO-VITALOS WINO THE MEDICINE MAN BURN RUBBERRIL JUMP DE MENNEN GREEN TIKILOTONICCLONIC SHAMPOOING DR. DREFT-EBBING PLUS BEAUTY WASH & GODARD LOVE-FESSALTOES & ARIEL-PENSÉAS HYDRA-PUISSANSSUCK MY KISSINGER FOAM IS LIKE A RIVERRAZOR PISS SGT. RAPPER'S LONELY ARSCHFIELDS FOREVERROX BROWN SUGAR HILL GANGES RIVERRAPPER'S DELIGHT MY FIRE OH, GEORGE DUKE NATUURLIJK LICHT SPRANKELEND MINERAALWATER HEADFUCK RAMMOLLY WASH NOT WASH LES ÎLES ÎLES ÎLITSCH BABYLON BY BEUYS MW THE BEAUTY FLUID & THE BLOCKBUSTER WILDEBEEST DE MARKIES VAN WATER EL MARQUÈSATANGAROA SHOUT GEL MOUSSANT MAMATEMEAMAMA MUPI MUPI'I PI'I PIRIO MADRE DE DIOS NAKU NAKU PUNA PUNA FANNY ALL STARS DÈSORDOR ANTI-CRISIS EL MARQUÈSACREATIO EX NIHO PEATA MIMI HATI MYSELF & THE SUNÎLES ÎLES COLOR WASH WASH WASH STÖRONALD LAING DEMIL NULDE KUDOMINNEOTAURRUSHING SPIS THE ERUDIKES OF REASON THE WELT BELT FITNÄSSEE IN YOURMEEROS HOLLAND POKA'AQUATSCH PLANET CURVE PLAY YOURLAUT OUT LOUDDISSEAS LAUT IT RAIN LAUT IT RAIN EL MARQUESSCHIZUFLUSSIGKUTIKIEFERRIPPITT THE EIFFELA KUTIKI TO WAR TO WAR MOA-MOA HAO-HAO TU TU TU RADIO TAHITIKIKI BEACH ONE HOUR SLY MONGOOSE THE MOOCHE MOOCHE GINGER ROGER NELSON & FREDBONE ASTAIRWA-WA TO HELLAS MARQUEUESAS WAS NOT WAS THIS IS WHAT YOU IS MARQUESS CHIZORNROTTENSTERN TO BE ELECTRO SHOKO UP YO

UR ASSAHARA HYDREUGENE EAU'NILE THE ICE-H H-
COMETH ANGRY SAMOA LISA WASH & GOO GOO GOO J
OOB I M THE EGGMAN COMETH EGGE HOMO IRISH ST
AR TIME SCHEISSKEEN CHIASSKOONS GLORY HALLAS
TOOPID P-FUNK-ULSTER VODUNDRUMBIPULOCEAN & U
RBAN DANCE FLOOR GUERILLAS MARQUESAS/WASHING
TON ISLANDS O DE COLUNA ZEN SHIKUDO SEXTETSU
MALE HYPERVERS LIBRE S.C.U.M. MANIFESSESTO'E
RIVERREPEATING THE MARQUESAN PIG LATIN DANCE
ATOMIC PIGLORY HALLASTOOPIDIPOUS REXSTRAIT D
E L'EAU MEDIAGRAMMOLOGUESS WHO-WHO UP YOUR A
RSCHWEINERRAI UNOAHH . . . TSUNAMISS UNIVURST P
RAMOTIVE MAN FELLINIETZSCHAUM AUM REFILLINIET
ZSCHAUM AUM AUM S.O.S. SCHIZO SOAPOCALYPSOD
OMINAVEN MBUANDIONYSOSSLES ÎLES MARQUESSODA/
MISOGENASSAU WÖLFLI RAINBLACK MESSEMENTAL AM
ADEUSCHORDER MARQUIS VON OOHH BABY LOVE CREA
TIO EX NIHILARY SHE-MALAYA JAPUNASSAU YEN-BU
TTHIST BOMBSHELLECTRO SHOKO ARSEAHERRY KIRRY
MELON MAN HERBIE HANGAKOQQING ALLAROUNDABOUT
TERREURQUELLE MARQUIS ACQUACOCKING IN ZAPPER
SPACE KITSCH 22 CLUB AQUARIUS TOUT COMPRIS M
AKE LOVE NOT WAH-WAH MR. MOTT THE HOOPLE WHO
MADE WHO AQUA.C./D.C. BACK IN BLACK BACK FRO
M SAMOA MWC5 ANGRY SAMOANS INSIDE MY BRAIN I
N THE BIGUINE ATOLL ATOLL ATOLL FORMULE BASI
C SHAMPOO BRUSH NAUMANIA CALVIN KLEIN TORTUR
E ETERNITY PARFEMMEGA STORE ULTRA ORANGE HYD
RAULICK PUMP (GEORGE STONE & SLY CLINTON) SH
AKING THE PUMP PUMPADOURQUELLA MARQUISE WHEN
THE LIFFEY BREAKS LED ZEPPELINILE TO WAH-WAH
TO WAH-WAH MR. MUDDBONE BERNIE DAVINCI WORRE
LL GINGER & FRED WESLEY MAE WESLEY MWILLIAMW

BE - BOOTZILLA PUTTY COLLINILES ÎLIBELLULES ÎL
ES MARQUISES STONE FUNK LIQUID NATION OVERLO
RD BRINTONICCLONIC FURONCLE JAMMELA ANDERS Z
ORN DE MARKIES VAN WATER NUCLAIR - OBSCURE REM
BRANCUSHIE - MALE PHALLUCY IN THE SKY UNCLE JA
MPÈRE UBUSHBABY METAL BOX LUNCH CLUB MEATAPH
OBIA UBU UBU WATERMINAL TOWER TOWER ETHNOA E
THNOA VAS NOT VASLAV PICTOGRAMMARQUESAN WETN
O ATOLLOGY QUELLECTROBRIAND WAKAN TANKA MAKE
VASLAV NOT WAH - WAH RED BLOOD RADIO BIRDMAN H
OT SUGAR GREEN RIVER CHILI SEX EARTH - BASS PE
PPERS MAGIC ATOM DRUM BOP COPY CAT (CLINTON/
COLLINS) DISTORTONIC - KLONIC PROSE TATTOO ASS
AULT & BATTERY IN THE BIGUINE ATOLL ATOLL FO
RMULE SAVANTE WORLD CLITORUS STIMULATOR STIL
LWATER I RESERVE THE RIGHT! CLUB MAD O MARQU
ISEAS WELCOME TO HELL FLASCHER HOMO FRIEDRIC
H NITZINGER DRIFTWOOD ECHO PLAYBOY BUNNY & C
LYDE DILDO & AENEUS ONE MAN RADAR LOVEMASCHI
NE NILE NILE ROBBERALL NILE KEEP THE RIVER O
N YOUR RIGHT WATER WATER EVERYWAH! AWASH WAB
ASH WASHAGO BIFERNOA - NOA TIGRILLOA - LOA HOTTA
H HOTTAH HAVELOCK FALLS ELLIS BAY MÈRDE CUNN
INGHAM FOUDRAINDANCE IRIAN JAYACKSONIAN EPIL
EPSYCHOWAH - WAH LAS MARQUESZASZ MERSI BUCK BH
UP TSO UBSA NUR KUKU NOR SONG SONG MA SONGBO
KARIBA MANIPUR UBANGI CUBANGO KALLKOOPAH BUL
LABOOLKA BRAINFALLSDE MARKIES VAN WATER BUSH
WALKING IN SPACE PASE - POUL - POUL HOPI HOPI - FU
NKFORALL MEGA - WODZIWOBBLE HOPI WAKE DANCE WA
LUM OLUMPICK - A - BOOTSYBILL HOPIZNOTIZING VOVO
DOO - WOPNOTIZING OUGOU FERAY CHARLES MINGUS M
INGUS MINGUS MINGUS MINGUS IN WONDERLAND MUD

INDIGO THRICE UPON A THEME SAINT JAMES BASIN
SPLAINE DU NORD ESPACE MUDDIZZY GILLESPIE-FA
NGO DELUGES STEELY DANBALLA WEDO BALLA BALLA
THAÏTIAN DIVORCE FUNKY BUTT MR. MUDDY WATERS
BLOW WIND BLOW MR. MOODBATH OUGOUNOUROOG FER
AY THELONIOUS MINGUS DISCOTIZING LIVE IN ALI
CE'S WONDERLAND O THELONIOUS ALL ABOUT ANY 1
X LOVE RYTHM-A-NING GINGERZILI FREDA BIG ALI
CE IN CHAINS DAM THAT RIVER GOD SMACK THEM B
ONES GIDDY GINGER & FELINE FRED DIAL M IS FO
R MURDERRUN ORANGE NOSSOB EL MARQUESSAMOANDA
MAN TRUNK ROAD MEGANESHAMANDAMANDAMANDANESIA
MESOPOTAMMOUSSEAS MARQUESSENTINILESE JARAWAS
SER SHAMANDAMAN VIBRATION & FEDERICO FELLINI
SPIRITTLING ON INTERVIEW ISLAND ONE MANDAMAN
SHOW EL MARQUESSAUT DODO ME MYSELF & I THE M
ARQUIS VON WATER TVOODOOIST RADIO VERSION ME
N BÈT! MEN BÈT! CLUB GRAN MÈT THERA MED 2 IN
1 CLUB MUD FUCK MED INDIGOGOGUINEAI WODIWODI
KWAT-KWAT WEMBA WEMBA WILA WILA NJAKI-NJAKI!
MR. MUTI MUTI LAKE GEORGE WANMAN SOULTRACING
ABORIGINNAROCK WATERS IN TALKING-DREAMTIME L
AKE YAMMA! YAMMA! MWIKAMPAMARQUESAN THERMONU
CLEAR ZWETH TRAUN ATOM DREAM BOPPOPPOP-OUT C
OME THE MARAWATER WARREGOES NEXT STOP MARS W
AH-WAH WAH-WAH EVERYWAH! VOVODO-IT DO-IT-YOU
RSELF & I THE HELIOCENTRIFUGUESS WHO MADE WH
O A.C./DIZZY GILLESP.I.LTDEFUNKADELICT THE M
OI MYSELF & BEBUDOUIN IN DEVILLICRANES WAANW
ASSER HOPI HOPI HÂPI HÂPI CLUB MEAD O TAHITI
SAMOA GIRLS LIKE IT HOTTENTOT CALL-KARL & TH
E FAMILY VON DEN STEINEN SAMOA SAMOA BECKETT
& BLACKBERRY WINTERWHITE FOREVERREST IN UNCL

E JAMBUSHMAN RAIN RITES MARQUESAN PIGLOBAL D
ANCE PROJECT NOA NOA NYAE NYAE EL MARSHALL'S
KUNG BUSHMEN WORLD CLICK LANGUAGE EE YAW YA
W DE MARKIES VAN /WA/WA KING KUNCLE JAMPÈR
E UBUSHMANGETTI WATER HEART KUNGFOUDRAINTAN
ZING IN CREOLLAND BATWAH-WAH PYGMIE DANCE WO
YO WOYO BAKTAMAN VIBRATION SPECIFIC OCEAN SP
ACE WALKING-OUT CEREMONY BAK TO BAKTAMANDAMA
NTRAVESTIDAL WAVE BASSOLOMON ISLANDAMAN BAKT
AFAI & RASTAMAN JAMOA-JAMOA BULL-FREAK EL MA
RQUESSWAIHWÉ WATER PEOPLE MASK RATTLE & ROLL
AQUAKIUTL FROG MASQUELLE MARQUIS HOTLEG NEAN
DERTHAL MAN DAF LEPPARD DE SLADE APACHE ROSE
PEACOCKATOO DANCE WILLIAM BOOTSY SHAKESPEARN
OAH 99 THALATTANGAROA! THALATTANGAROA! CUTTA
BURRA ROTTOCK PROM OLLANDA ANADOLL WARWA WAR
WA WARWATER MAY RIVER MYSELF & WANAMARA HOLL
AND? KROKITT! KROKITT! UNCLE WAH KROKITT BOD
Y MASQUELLFLUSSWASSER COQUIHALLASTUPID MEDIA
GRAMMARQUESAN WORLD FLOOD FROM MONEY TO ASHE
S LÉVI-MERZ KOGI KOGI SUN MASQUELLFIRE RAINB
OAS & BOASHES DE MARKIES VAN WATER VIRGO INT
ACTA BURNING FOR YOU THE ICE-CREAM COMETH FR
ITZKRIEG LAING DR. MABUZZCOCK DAVID COOPER M
ILLION DOLLAR BABIES WILLIE EAU NILE JUNG RA
M JAMADEUS MOZZY & BLACK MAGGY MED BITCH DUB
AUGUST SHOWER RODING THE TINKER IAMAKROKLITT
T IAMAKROKLITT EL MARKISHORN FELOULASI KUTIB
ERRY WINTERWHITE SPIRIT WOYO WOYO BE MW! CLO
CKCLOCKCLOCKWORK ORANG ASLI DE MARKIES VAN H
ALEN ON THE SPAZZIA BIZZA MAXIBRAUN LSDELIAL
SDELIALSDELIAL M IS FOR MURDERRUIN ADOLF & È
VE A'DAM & ELSÈVE MASSOÏA BALSAMMONIACO-DEPR

ESSIVE P-FANGATOURANG OUTANG UNCLE JAMMAGGIO
JAZZISTAFKAFKIANO DRUMDRUCKING TYPEE TYPEE F
ACES FINIMONDOUCHES O FISSÎLES ÎLES MARQUISE
S FANTASMARQUESAN MARCOLONNA-SONORABISHMAH-W
AH HYDROGRIFFIC RIVERBETTWATTING BREEZ WOW M
AN GRIZZLI DRILLESPI BLAMGUSTA VOICE-OVERROL
SPANKITT SPANKITT WIPPITT WIPPITT AM I DEEP?
OCEANO AH OCEANO AH DIZZY GRIZZLÎLESBEEE FIN
NAKICK WACQUATERMALE MARKEY WESTRAVAGINASSAU
FLOODLIGHT ONE TWO WATERMONUCLEA'RE A'RE A'R
E KRISHNA SUPERSTAR ORIONYS.O.S.! DISCOPULAT
ING SHAMANDIBULL MEGANESHIVA DIONYSOSTARABIS
HMAH-MAH WAH-WAH AUNT-EATER UNCLE JAMNESIAME
SOAPOCOPULIPSYCHO TWIN MYTHO-MANIAMADUSCHORD
URE SEPPUKOCKING ROUNDABOUT SOULWASSERMONOFI
LIGRAINS WAH-WAH ONE MÂN SHOWADIDI NEPALEO-P
SYCHO-POP WOLFANGES CHAMADUSCH MOSES DE MAG
ARKIES VAN WATTERRAFERMAH-MAH WAH-WAH FANTAS
MATIC VOYAGE KÂLI KHOLO KUDA BAILA KÂLI KHOL
AZALA KUDA BAIZALA SGT. PETER BLAKE TO BLAKE
AQUAKIUTL SHAMAN & PATIENT EDDY MERZ IBEX HE
AD VI RED HOT MAMA PEPPER'S LONELY BATWAH-WA
H MÂN PIGMIE DANCE DANCE DANCE MARQUESAN WRE
STLING UNDER THE SUN KUNG SUNNY ADÉFUNKT ON
E WORLD THE WAKE UP & MAKE VASLAY NOT WAH-WA
H APRIL RIVER FOOL'S DAY-TRIPPERRY COMOZZEEE
-LITE ONE TU TU GREAZZLI GILL-GILLESPIPMUACA
N SUCUNDURI TATLAWITSUK HARD HOLLAND READY O
R NOT JUST DOIN' IT HERBIE HILLESPIE THE HAN
GAQOQQLES IN SADO-SALADO-SALADILLO/MASOPOËTA
MIA WAH-WAH WAHN-WAHN ALLSDIAGRAMMATIKAOS YO
URBEDEUTONGA-TONGA EL MAR KISS SURE KNOW SOM
ETHING DIRTY LIVIN' MAGIC TOUCH LET THE MUSI

C PLAY YOURLAUT OUT LOUD THE SPACE DATATTUBA
SS LAUT IT BE LAUT IT BE PAPUAQUA NOVAQUA GU
INEAQUA PEAK EXPERIENCE WAHOY-WAHOY TRUMTAUF
TAUF TRANSGREAZZLI DIS BORDER DAT BORDER ALL
S-DEMI-TONICCLONIC AMSTERRAMADEUS TRUMTRUMBO
NISTA UNCLE JAMMY DAVIS JR. WOLFKLANG MADUSC
HORDER UNCLE JAMOE DARJAM JAMOE DARJAM JAMOE
DARJAMOE DARJAMOE DARJAMOE DARJAM LEMMY BE Y
OURQUELLE MARQUIS ELECTRIC SADHUSTRIAL SOUND
ORGY BOOTSHIVA-DIONYSOS-CRUX-SUPERSTARLIAMEN
T-DEFUNKADELHI UNCLE JAMI MASJIDIPOUS REXIFY
ING NEW RUBBER DELPHI WOOF WOOF WOOFGANGES L
SDIWAN-I-AMADOUCHAMÂNE UNCLE JAMMU & MARKASH
MIRQUESS VON WATERRANSGRESSING LOOONEEE ARSE
CLUB BOUNDARIES TAJ MAHALLABOOTSYBILLABONGOG
O MW/THE BLOWBLITTERRA FIRMAMAZONES UNCLE Y
AMUNA ALFÀBETABIOWULFGANGES AMAZONES MOOSE T
HE MOOCHE ARSE UNCLE RAM JAM BLACK BIDDIPOUS
ODOREX DILDEO DISORDERRUN HADESPERADOPPELGAN
GES RIVERRIER C'EST POU IS THE FUNK MUMMELMA
NN MUMMELMAN EVERYWHERE HARE HARE RAMA RAM J
AM MUMMELMANABOZHO MUMMELMANNITOUR DE TRANSF
ORMATION AMON DÜÜL LEMMINGMANIA RUBBERALL BA
LLS TO THE WALL HOLLAND DE MARKIES VAN WATER
BACK FROM SAMOA FREE FIRE & WATER BULL ANGUS
JUNG MANOWAR MAGGOT BRAINDANCE DANCE DANCE R
ITUAL DE LO HABITUAL HÜSKER DÜTCH METAL CIRC
US BLITZ ON MY MINDKRIEG DE-DEFUNKT YA JOE B
OWEE-DO WEE-DO HÂPI-FUNKADELPHINAFLUX WAXIOM
HÂPI-FUNCLE JAMADEUS MOZARTAUDDISSEAS WOLFGA
NGA SHIVAMADEUS MOZARTAUDIONYSOS SAY BABA CO
OL PRE-FABHUPADA EL MARQUESSHIVA-MALE ONANDI
ONYS.O.S. SCHIZO SOAPSUCK DEVI DEVI HÂPI HÂP

I KAMA KAMA ON YA SAY BUMBABA HADESTRUCTIVOO
DOO UNCLE JAMAMA BRIGITTA BARTAUD SAI BABALL
A! BALLA! LET IT BEATLE MURDER MADNESS & THE
HARE KRISHNA MANTRA EMI MYSELF & HARRISON WA
LK ON WATER CHARLES BACKUS CHELSEA GIRL EUFR
AATLESS BASSPACE ODYZZEUS YOURQUELLETHERMONU
CLEAR SWEATTICCABALLA! BALLA! SHOWERTIME HOL
LAND ZEUS OR FUCK DISHWATER BLONDIE FUNFURIO
SODOMYSELF UNCLE RAM JAMON-RE HADESPUMARQUES
S AMOEDEUS DARJAMES JAMPLIFLYING THE RIVERNO
OOOONFT! WATER WATERRECUERDOUCHES RAMADUSCHO
RDER MARQUISPANICKA RYTHMSTICKA PRICK-A-BOOT
ZILLAS MARQUESAS AGUANARQUISTABOOTSYBILLASWE
LLES ÎLES MARQUISES FRIED ISIS ISHTARREALITY
AGUAGILIDADDY COUP AGUA VA! HADESPERADOUCHES
FIAT FLUXORGIES DEVI DEVILIFERATU WAKANDOUSC
HWATER ALLSDEUCALIONDA MOVE EL MARQUESSEA-FO
AMAFRODEE-DEE BRIDGEWATERRED HOTTOMANOAH-NOA
H ALLSDEVI DEVILOOPZILLA UNCLE JAMADUSCH-GEL
MOZARATHUSTRAUSSUCKAMASS SPACE BÀSSABOOTSYBI
L LABONGO BUDDISMOHAVE METALSDE-DEFUNKADELHI
RONNIE MAC ROCKIT ROCKIT HANGAKOCKWORK ORANG
E NASSPACE BASSILICONASSAU AGUA ARRIBASSOULO
DE MARKIES VAN WATER DEDUNKING HOLLAND SPAES
I BASSIBILAQUABIODOLOOP ONANISMOHEFFER METAL
SEX MACHINASSAU EL MARQUESANTIGUAGUAGUAGU
ADADADA DEE DEE LITER MARQUÈSPERMARQUÈSPERMA
RQUÈSPERMA SHOWER POWER FUNFURIBUNDOUCHES GE
OESH OERVAN WATERRE WATERREALISMO EVERYWHORU
S DEFUNKFORALLSDÉLIVRANCEFALLOGRAMMARQUESANT
RACKAWALAMADEUS OLUMOZART MARQUESSPECTRO-SHO
CK TREATLIFE BUSPARLIAMENT-KUNGADELIC ENOAH
-ENOAH WAH-WAH WAH-WAH MWATERMINUSSAU PARISH

ONE MAN SHOWERRUN DILDOVE CREAM SHOWER DILDE
ORANTI-KLIT STICK GLORIA VANDERBILDT MUM MUM
BODY RESPONSIVE COBAIN & CREME THERMO NUCLEA
RASIL ZWITSAL WATERPROOF AMON SAVON AH PUCH!
SUN CREAMADEUS DUSCHGELGAMESH EL MARQUESANEX
SHAMPOOL BEAUTY FLUID EXTRA-SENSITIVE HAIR &
SHOWERGELGAMESHRAUM AUM AUM KUNGLE JAMBRE S
OLAIRE HANGAKOCCODRILDEORANTI-CHRIST SUPERST
ART FACTOR 66 THERMONUCLEARASIL ZWITSALT BAB
Y OIL OF OLAZZMATAZZMANOWAR LET'S TANGOLOA L
OA MAE NOET NOEN-STOP GRAND MALCHEMY MYSELFA
TION ARMY MYSELFATION ARMY MYSELF & THE MINO
THORROR THORROR PRIAPUSSIPHAEK EPILEPSYCHOCE
ANIC FEELING NOEN-STOPPOP TEHOETI WOOTY UNCL
E JAMON SAVON LIQUIDE MARKIES VAN WATER IN H
ADÈSORDRECKER-HEINWASSER LET'S TANGOLOA LOA L
OWLOW CUNTREACHERIES TE TUNA OPUSSEE MAUI MA
UI TIKI-TIKI-A-TARANGA O NANDEEELITE MOEMMOE
MOEMMOE SE-MAIL-E KUNCLE RAMARQUESSRI LANKA
OSPRINCE RAMA KUNKING THE SHE-MONSTERRAMALE
MARQUIS DE SADE IN HYDRAÄGEN-DAZZEELAND RAH-
MAH-WAH! DE MARKIES VAN WATER VISHNUKU SHIVA
LES BRAHMARQUISES LOA LOA LOA EL MARSHALLSDE
VIBRATOROTOFOAMING IN SHITWASHPSYCHOSIS MITH
RASHING OLLANDA ANADOLL GGGDEFUNKT MONOSILAB
OOTSILABOOTSY FLUID FLOWING OUT COMES YOU NU
X YOU NUX WATTIS ATTIS WATTIS ATTIS THE SHIV
AMALE DOIN'? FRAGMENTAL SUCKNASSAU GERSHWISJ
AMANOWAR PORSCHY & BEUYSS SAY BABARON SAMEDI
ONYS.O.S.SCHIZONDFLOODING THE NOUNCONSIOUSNA
SSPISS ABEUYSS NAOE NAOENET HOEH HAHOEHET KO
EK KAOEKET AMOEN AMAOENET WORD UP YOUR ASS W
ATER WATERVALLEARY SOURANUS NUN-STOP UNCLE J

AMPERE UBU WATER WATERMINAL TOWER TOWER EVER
YWHERE PSYCHO-HEAD BLOWOUT ZOROASTELLA ARTAU
D & DROEJ CUMAE CUMAE CLASSIC CRÈME & PARFUM
MARAFA WETGELGANESHAMESSOAPOTAMMOUSSEARASERA
DILDOVE CREAM WASH & GOOFY DE-DEFUNCT YAHWEH
WEH KUDO KUDO KUDO EL MARQUESAN PIGGDRASILLY
PEPPER'S LUNILEE HARDWARS CLUB SUCK ETHERMON
UCLAIRASIELLA TONICCLOWN MINOTORTURE AH PUCH
TOUR DE TRANCE EDDY MERZBOWWOWWOWIE TRAUMTRA
UMTIMEBONING YOURMÈRZEE-MAIL HÈRANTIKLIT SAY
ABBABA COOLONILLY KURZ SCHWITTSALT FINIDI GE
ORGE LINCOLN EAUBRAHAM DE LINCOLOGNE P-FUNGO
ALL-STARLIAMENT-DUNKADELINCOLN FRANCEFALLOGR
AMMÈRDE-DE MARKIES VAN WATER MEGANESHIVA BUL
LEPHANTASIAMASSA CONFUSAPPAPUA NEU BIGUINNIN
G ATOLL ATOLLANDA TAN-A-DOLLA FRIED SUN-CREA
MARQUISHTARRIÈREALITY & CHIMPOTAMMOUSSEARNOA
RNO WAY OUTTERREUROPAPUA NEW BEGUINEATOLLAND
BE BIPOLAR SCUMMERCIALSDEMÈRDADA OBEY YOUR F
IRST WORD UPPOSEIDONA TRINIDADA COOL CUMMARQ
UESS WHO-WHO THE FAH-FAH SUNNY & THE MOLLY G
HOST EL MARQUESSHAMPOOL ANTI-KLITTY EAU SHEA
-MALE EAU DE DORDORDOGNE SHE-MILLY ARSEA SUR
CURE THE DARE CUNTER OLLANDA ANADOLL WET WET
WET CUNTAMINOTHORROAR! THORROAR! EL MARSOULL
AS MARQUESAS AGUAS DE NOVALES ÎLES MARQUISES
PALEO-PSYCHOANALYTICKA PRICK SOULTRANSNATION
IHILISMUDDISSEA ECCOLA PENA DE LOS HORNY HOR
NOS ONE MAN SHOWER POWERPLAY OUT LOUD FUNKAG
ALAX WALKABOUT IN AQUABORIGINAL RIVIERENLAND
CALL JUNGLE JAM JOUISSANSSUCK OR FUNKAGAIN W
ARTHOGLAND DITHYRAMBUSHAMALE DIOPLASTICIZING
THE BEACH BEUYSS HOLLAND I SCREAMADEUS MOZAR

TAUD REQUIEM TV UNFUCKKED NOW HEAR THIS HANSO
N (JOHANSONOFABITCHCOCK VDUTCH) WE ARE FLOOD
IEUX GAY BISAACLE HAZES ON ACID DRILL YOUR O
WN HOLE ANIMAL FARMACY WATERRORWELLES ÎLES M
WARQUISES WAN AUWAH-AUWAH GET ON UPPOSHEIDON
MCCORMACKY MEAD MAIN TITLE THEME ADOLFGANGES
JAMADISORDER MOZACHER MASOCHER REQUIEMWAHWAH
O DÉTOILETHE MARQUIS VON WATER NUCLEAR OBSCU
RQUELLE MARKIKI SHAMPOOLOOMAH-MAH PSICKASSOD
OMINOTAURE O DÉTOILETHE MARQUIS VON WATER WA
TERRAIN RAIN DOPPELDUSCH & TONICCLONIC CALVI
N CLEAN ETERNITY SHOWERGEL FOR MEN EAU DE RO
CK ARSE DEVI DEVIDAF-DAF COOL WATER O DÉTOIL
LETHE AQUA QUORUM APIZ BUIN ALLERGY WATERPRO
OF THE CLINTON CLINIQUE SHAMPOO SHOWER & CRE
AMDUSCH IGLOBE EAU DÉTOILETHE MARQUIS VON WE
TTER WETTER BAYWATCH AFTER SUN RÂLPH THE DIV
ING PIG OF AQUARENA SPRINGS, SAN MARCOS O DÉ
TOILUCY PRAMELA PRICKARSEAU D'EAU REMY GEILL
ES DELA TOURRED HOT CHOCO ASSAHORROR MELON M
ANIA AGUA BRAVA SHAMPOO FOAMING GEIL YVORYWH
ORE INSCÈINE LORRY KOUROS DILDEODUSCHGEL L'E
AU D'ISSEYLAND O DÉTOILETHE UNCLE JAMADEUS S
EX MACHINE MWTVOODOO MUSIC HELL FUNK AGAINST
WANK EL MARQUESANICUR DUSCHALVADOR DALI LAMA
APIZ APIZ PIZ PIZ ANOTHER MOTHER FEU WELCOME
TO HELLUCY IN THE SKY MWITH DIAMOND LILLEHAM
MER EL MARQUESSACRIFLIESSING THROUGH YOU (HE
RE'S LOOKING AT JUJU TUTU KIDIPUSSY!) DICK R
IVERS PRÉSENTE... O DÉTOILETHE MARQUIS VON W
ATERRORANGE NÄSSEAU DODO REMY FA DOUCHE NINO
AH-NINOAH GINGER & FREUD ICE-CREAMADEUS MOUZ
ZARTAUTENTANZING SWING TIDE SCARLET A'SAHARA

OBEY YOUR FÜRST BISMARCKIES MINERAALWASSER B
ILLY JEAN GRAHAM PARKERILLA MARQUISE D'EAU M
INERALE PRIVAT BRUNNEN GEORGE CLINTÖNIC-CLÖN
ISSTEINER JUJU RIDE MINOTAURUS MYSELF & I NO
CORRIDA UNCLE RAM JAMLÖSA! EAU DE SOURSEA BU
RROUSPORNER ADONIS QUELLE MARQUIS ONE MAN SH
OWFONTAIN BIRRESBORN AKANE ANALLITHIUM PLURA
PPIDO SPASSUGGER HEILQUELLEN ACQUA VITTEL A
LLABOUT YOUR MARQUISM HEILQUELLANGUESS WAH-W
AH ICKA PSICK HEILQUELLASCAUX GLACIAAL OERWA
TER MUSPELLING ALTAMIRO MIROTORO FREDDADA FE
LLININOAH-NINOAH MINOROTELLA THE BITCH BEUYS
BABELBADTUBE THE TOURQUELLE MAR-KEYS MEMPHIS
TFLUT X-SPRAY CHARLIE GUITAR WATT WATT SPOUT
TERREURQUELLACANNAKLIT WATERRES SJÖSAVE BUYS
NEGERZONDFLUTTING WAHNSELM KEFFERRARIVERRUNN
ING COCKUPATIONS (BEZSUCKUNGEN) WALKING ON W
ATERREINHARDSQUELLAPSUCK HEILWASSER NECKAR O
MO POWER KIKIEFER SHAMPOOING THE FLOODING OF
HEIDELBERG WE'RE ONLY IN IT FOR THE MONEY PA
LEO PSYCHO HOT POOP WAHNSELMAHLSTRÖMLANDWARD
CATCH 239! WISHBONE ASH FREAK POWDER DUSTY S
PRINGFIELDS FOREVER SCHI WATT WATT PSIDERSCH
WEPPESPLANK OR STUMP JUICE SCUMMERCIALLSDE M
ARKIES VAN WATER ON ACID RAIN SCUMFISSCUTTIN
G PLOOPLISSLITTIES LSDIONYSOS-KIDDIPOUS EREC
CLAM UP YOUR ASSINDIA STILLE QUELLIMPIDIPOUS
HEAMAMALE MARKIKI SHAMPULL MUSPELLING STARNO
SCHMIDT ROTTLOVE HECKL SLUTLER ANTI-CHRISTIN
E BRON MUTHAFUNKAFLUTTER CRÂNESSEXUAL DONKEY
LOVER KAISER FRIEDRICH NIETZSCHAMAN HEILQUEL
LEN MINERAL SOUL MANANA LITHIA WATER WATER F
ONT VELLATIO RIVERRHEINFELS QUELLADY CABBALA

DRIVERRUN MANIC RIVERS TO CROSS BAR-LE-DOG B
IRRESBORN AGAIN I. MICHELANGELEAU FOUCKALL M
INERAL WATER EVERYWHERE MARQUESSEXTC ORANGES
& LEMONS MINIATURE SUN ORANGE NASSAU WAU WAU
WAY XTC MATIC OH LA LA LA TO THE CURBI & ORB
ITCH EL MARMADUKE DOG U OUT KAMAGONNA GOCCIA
GOCCIA GITCHI GITCHI GOO BOYCE GEORGE CLINTO
N KAMA KAMAH KAMAHL KAMAHLION THE ELEPHANGEL
IST SINGALONG LSDEMONDO WATER EVERYWHORROARA
TORIO MUDDER DIDDI DAZE GG-STRING BASSOLOMON
ISLANDAMANTRASHAMAN VIBRATOROTA SOURÇIMABUSE
AMALE QUELLINGUIFORNAMENTAL HOLLANDMARKIESKI
MOA-MOA SAMOA-SAMOA LOLO-ABBITING MR. MUTTER
REURQUELL BIRRESPORNAGUNST DILDUCHAMPULL UPP
OSEADONISSAU EL MARSILICONASSUCKAHH THUNDERR
OCK MWARLORD TEUFELLATIONYS.O.S.U.C.K PUR TV
WATTERHORN WATTERHORN WASSIERA WASSIERA O DE
DOURDOGNE EL MARQUESSOTARI ZAUBERROBERRIAGAR
A FALLSDEE-LITE GET ON UPPOSEADON WAS NOT WA
SSERRATHUSTRAUSSINKASONG LJ KOHL HARDROCKAMA
DOURBRAQUELLINGUAMADEUS MOZARATHUSTRAALSDE M
ARKIES VAN WATERRESTREAM ON GREAT SERPENT MO
UND VENICE ADAMS COUNTRY OHIO OHIO OH I OH I
SLY & THE FAMILY STONEHENGE THE BEASTIE BEAC
H EL MARQUESSAND PAINTING RITUAL EARTH ART I
N THE COCKENHEIM MAUSOLEUM NEW YORKWARD FRED
VARD MUNCHAMANIMANIABORIGIPEL SEASHELL-EYE O
H EYE OH EYE! M: ANUS VAN DILLENDOLF SHITLOR
E CUM SUICIDE ARSES TO ASHES ZIEGGURAT HUILD
OLF SUPERSTARDUST TO DUST ABUQUIN TEMPLY TUM
PLY TELL AMARQUIS WATT EAU WATT EAU GILLES D
ELEUGES EVIAN ÉCUME DÈSOURDRECK ORANGE RENAI
SSAU HARI KIRITUALSDE MISHIMARQUESAN NIPPONN

ASEA WAH-WAH OOOH WAH OOOH WAH O. KAVE-MAGIC
KA PRIAPRIEST WATER WATERFALLUCY UP YOURQUEL
LECTRICULLADYLAND ORANGE VAGINADE SADELICATE
SODADA BADEDAS SHOWER & CREAMDOUSCH ECCE UOM
O VAGUESS WHO-WHO HENRY ROLLINS OVER BEETHOV
EN CALL-KARL POPPER'S LONELY HEARTS CLUB BAN
DAMAN EPICLIPSINC SPEECH BASIN HEALIOPOLIPPO
LIPPILEPSEE SJÖSEPH BUISWATERRORANGE NASSAUT
D'EAU REMY MYSELF & THE CYBERFLUTTERRORANGUT
ANGAROA TANGAROASTRAUSSPANKING IN TONGUESS W
ATER! DIONIETZSCHOS-KITT NOEN-STOP AGNIETZSC
HAMAHLSTRÖMSTOSS SHIVA DISCONIETZSCHE LOA-LO
ALITRASHAMALE MARQUI'EST? EL MARQUESANTIGUAGU
AGUAGUADADADA DEE EE ESPERMARQUESANGREASE IS
THE WORDURE MUSIC HALLSDEMONOBOOTSILLABOOTSI
LLABOOTSILLA ORCHESTRINA JIZZMATIZZMAN WATTM
ABATTERISTA EL MARKIESPACE ODDYSSUCK OR FUCK
HOLLANDMARKIESPERANTHOTEM IN THE SPACE BASSI
LIQUE OF LIQUIDOOM & AQUASPEECH REMUMMER SAY
WAH SAI BABA KOHL LL KOHL J HOW I'M COMING A
DOLFINNAGUA WÖLFGANGES AMADISHWATER BLOND OL
LANDA ANADOLL WATER WATERRE WATERREADABILITY
UNCLE GEORGE FRIEDRICH HÄNDELICATE WATER MUS
ICK VASLAV NOT WAR LLSDÉLUGEORGE & FRIEDRICH
CLINTONICK-CLOWNICK NIETZSCHAMANIA & WATER M
AGICK EL MARQUESSPRAWL! BULL KRIEG ANTI-KLIT
LER O DE TOILETHE SPÜHLOMA SEPIKKA PRICK ASS
O DE TOILETHE BULLOMA BRICK ASS EAU MINOTAUR
EBEL REBEL KUDOMINOTAURQUELLIMPEDOFILIGRUPIS
WASSERPENTAGRAMMAR UP YOUR ARSCHLANGEL FALLS
SHOKE ME TSHOK WE ELECTRO TSHOKWE-TSHOKWE CI
HONGO GUINEA HOLLAND! RIVER JAMES MARSHELLAW
BRENT SPARLIAMENT FONKUDOLBY STEREONYSOS BRE

NT ALL-SPAVATARSE SHAKE DOWN GINGER & FREDDI
E WATERS O NANDI O NANDIONYSOSSMATOSSMAYYAZZ
VAN COCKENBERGH LUIPAARD GROANPUSSY BASSI AL
LSDE MARKIES VAN WATER WATERVUREN STAR RIVER
SUN WAH ASS EGO SUPERMARKIES WAH WAH ABOUT W
AH ABOUT EVERYWHERE ARNOLF RAINERRUIN DMC SO
LAARNO RIVIERRAP DMC SOLAARNO AARNO ARNO WAH
OUT SHELLECTRO SCHOCKLAND THE BRANDT SPARREN
SCHIFF CONNECTION GREENPISS EVERYW.A.H.! LIA
H LIAH HARAI HARAI WAH-WAHRANE MAROCKNROLL O
VER BEETHOVEN HOLLAND DADANIEL ROHRSCHACH TE
ST ONE TWO FILICRÂNE-TROPHEE-LITE LES ÎLES M
ARQUISES TIDE-TROPHEE-FONKIN' LES ÎLES ANDAM
ANDAMANIA HIGH TIDE-TROPHILOCEANIC WAR DELIV
ER THE WORD! FILICRÂNE-TROPHILIGRAINS WAXILE
& CUNNILLANGUISHANTIH SHANTIH SHANTIH-KLITOR
ISE ALL RISE HOLLAND ICUNNILLEKKING THE ARSE
OF REASON SAI BÄBADEDASZ MÖVENPRICKA PSYCHIA
TRICK-A-BULLADAM & EVAGINI LEMONDSHINE SAY B
ABA COOL DOWN TRASHTAN TZARATOSSMAJISSTRAUSS
& ISOLDADACOULE MARQUIS & FRIED ISOLDER MARQ
UIS VON KEITH HARING BALLA BALLATHUSTRALIASD
EEP FROAGH TABLASSOAP! TABLASSOAP! NEW IRELA
ND VERSUS NEW ENGLAND BULLRAUM BLITZCREEKKEE
H2OMO COULEURQUELLINGUASSUCK DOG U OUT YOURG
EN HÄABER-DASZ & CLITO-TART ESPISS-MODERNISM
O DALAI LAMONGO GUINEA PIG DANZING MR. SINGA
SONGYE KIFWEBE SPACE BASSOLONGO NOQUIMBAY DU
BBELLINE EIRÈVERIVER TSCHUNAMI FOLIE P6 ORAN
GIGINASSAU ALASKA MARQUESAS CARACALLAS MARQU
ESAS WALPHALLASKA MARQUESAS PALEO PSYCHO POP
PLIZZITIES BIG BEN JOHNSON'S BABY SOAP & SOD
OMY DE MARKIES VAN WATER BRANDT SPARTOUT SHE

LL-MAL CUNTFISTCUTTING HOLLAND YOUCLEAR TEST
ONE TWO DRILDROGMATIC FRANZICK HELL ELL EL M
ARSHALLAMARQUIS VON WATER WATERFALL OUT LAUT
MEGANESHALAMARQUESAN HIPP-TRIPPLITT MATISSEL
DATA LIMIT? WATER, FIRE, EARTH ART & AIRIONA
SSASSINOPOULOS (FANNY'S VILLE) MWATERHOLLAND
NETHERMALLAND ZZ001 A SPOUSE ODDYSSAY WAH! R
OTATE ROTATE! SPRAWL SPRAWL! CRACK ON THROUG
H THE DYKES OF REASONOFABOOTZILLAMARQUISSYBI
LLÀ-BASSURQUELLAUGHTERRA FIRE MAGIC NUNRAPPI
NG THE MARQUESS VON WATER ANTI-CHRISTO REICH
STEXT WHOLLANDLUBBE BELOW COUNTREIS (EL MARI
NOSE!) QUELLEVINUS LEMNIUS KAALVIJNNABUMP WA
KERDIJKDOORBRAAK ONE-MAN SHOW-SOURIRE THE MAR
QUESSOAPSTONEHENGE FAMILY FOLLY P-FAUNA UNCL
E JAMDUNKÂGOULE MARKIKI HAAKONSONOFABITCH DU
BLICITY PUBBLITZI KRIEG M & W WORLDWIRBEL ZE
E BUBBELBADEWAHNSINNEGANS WAH WAH WAH SPASSI
BASSSSAY BOOTSY THE #ONE! OWAH ONE OWAH EL M
ARQUESSOULANOUS WORLD-WATT RIVER MANTRA ECHO
LALIA FALLS HOPIPI-FONKAGNATIC WALKABULL ART
EAU BULL GOGO MAE SUCKVIEL WEST JUNG WATER F
LEAU FLEE TABULLARTAUD! BARRAMUNDIONYSOS HUN
TING TURTLE IN HADES HAIRSPACE KING MONG KUT
KLAATU BORADA NICTO! NULLA NULLA ZILLA ZILLA
BOOTZILLABONGO BUTT WATERHOLE IN ONE OWAH OW
AH EL MARQUESAN MARCOYOKUTSUNGLIEH BASSINÄSS
OURCE TRICKLING TRICKLING YELLOW YELLOW FLAS
HBACKFIRE FLOOD CUNTROLLYBULLEPHANTHILL MÊMM
ÊMMERGING MINOTHORRORSCHACH TEST TO THE TEST
3-MEGATONICCLONIC HOPI HOPILOP-NURQUELL FALL
-OUT LAUTTERREURQUELLWASSERBOMB SPACE NUCLEA
R AUXILIARY POWER SNAP! I GOTT THE POWER SIR

HAUXILIARY POWER ONANDADA DEVI STRAUSSUCK FU
NGI MAMA / BEBOPAFUNKADISCOPALYPSE NOW MUPI MU
PI LOPI LOPI-NURMUTTERREUR PLUTONIUM 23999 T
O COME INTO THE HOLY-HOLY WATERS MAHRATTA! M
AHRATTA! ECCOLA HOLLANDE VOLPINESQUELLA MARQ
UISE DO REMY FA BEAUTY SOULANUS & VINNAGOGHO
ST TO GHOSTESS VINCENTAURORATORIO MORTES LET
HE MARQUIS PLUTO 239 BAHADES NEPTUNUS MUNDUS
CH HYDRACULA MARQUISEAMALE MARQUIS IN ACID J
IZZAUBERSPASSEA EL MARQUESSSSSAY BOOTSY SLOW
BOOTSY TO CHINA UNCLE JAMPHITRITON J.S. BACH
ERONNY ROCKITT JASON CHRIST ARGOSTAR & BELLO
NA BRICKASSOAPSUPERFRIGG FEASTFLOODING HOLLA
ND THE BLEACH BEUYS, THE BALDER & THE BOOTSY
FOOL NORTH SEA JAZZMATAZZID WATERATOID MARQU
ESSACROSUNKT FISSION ÀARROCKSOAPERACLE ORANG
E YOUSSOUK N'DOURQUELL RUN DSM 4-UU 900 FT J
ESUS SOUL COUGHING GEORGE CLINTON ZAP MAMAMA
CEO WOLFGANG PARKERILLA BELA BOOTZILLA TAJ M
AHAL MUTHSPIEL BRIDGEWATER WATERWAR TRANSFER
THE LOW COUNT BASIE BASIE DUTCH JAZZ MACHINE
SPASSID JIZZAWIATNUL DIRECTIONS IN GROOVE WA
TERREAPERTURA STRING BASSOLOMON ISLANDAMAN E
PILEPSY GRAND MALAYSIAMESOAPOTEMKINOA-NOA WO
KABOOTSY FRIED RICE-PICKIN' AGUA. COLLINS SP
ASSIBAGUARRIBASS GO TO HELLASCAUX HOLLAND MO
NO BIKINOCAQUA WAKATOLLAND SPACIFILOACQUA TR
ANSMITTERCUNT WAFFRENZIEG ARSCHEISSHE-WRECKI
NG FOLLAMURUROA ESPACIFICKA PRICKABOLLOCKS B
LASTING SPERMHEAD VI VULKANUS MUNDUSCH GELL-
GELL FMW WASH NOT WASSIR PSYCHOSEXODUSCH AQU
ALATTABOOTSIOUXIE & THE RUBBER BANSHEE-MALES
JUJUPITERRA FIRMARQUESAN DUSCH GELLAXY WITRA

SH & MORE & MORPHISTFLUTTERRA FIRMARQUISHTAR
ATHUSTRAUMPHHH ONE MANTO FANNY'S VILLES ÎLES
MARSEIZURES KUNG FUGURUROACIDIPOUS JAZZMATA
ZZEDINE ALAÏATMÜLLICKING SISSURE EL MARQUESS
PLITTERRATIONAL SCHIZOAPERATIONAL PROGREASSE
IS THE WORD M WARLORD DE MARKIES VAN WATER T
AALLATTABOO-DUBBING THE WHORACLES ÎLES THE W
HORROARSE! THE WHORROARSE! ARE WE ORANGE? GE
ORGE GERSHOWINDAMAN WHORGY & THE BASSPACE SH
UTTELLUS MOREROSMOUSS I AMA MAD EUSWEITER WE
ITER EVERYWHORALLSDE MARKIES VAN WAH-WAH M W
ARLORDURE DRECK ECHOMO FRIEDRICH NATCHEZ BON
E LOKE BACCHUS EAU BUCCALE MARQUIS CIBBERROC
KING IN ODOLLAND ATOMTOMITA CLUB MAD PROFESS
OR EL MARQUESCAPEYOTLOALOA WOWL WOWL WOWL PA
LEOLIFFEY PLUIEIREBEL DUB MCRAZY GRIZZLIFFEY
PLUIERABEAR UNCLE JAMBERGRIZZ-GRIZZLIFFEY PL
ISSELON PLUREBELLES ÎLES MW THE SHAMATTEURQ
UELLECTRO SHOCK POWER INFUSION MARSHALL TRAN
CE ECHOMOTÖRHEAD CLUB CULTURE FUCK ECHOMOHEA
VY METALPHIZZEE TOO BLUE TO BE TRUE AMURUROA
FATI CHIRAKEHELL NOOKIE NOOKIE PRISSIDENTELL
E MEGAZINEMA & EJACHIRACULOTION SCIERATTLE &
ROLL OVER MOURUROASS EL MARGARY HARD ASSWATT
WATT WATTHERMO NUNUCLEAR GILL-GILLGAMESHRAUM
AUM AUM WALKABOUT IN WATER HOLLAND ONE OWAUT
OPORNABOUT SAMOA SAMOA ALWAYS SAMOA EL MARQU
ESAN MONEYBEE RECRUITMENT & WALAM OLUMPRICKA
PRICK DANCES MINNAGRA WECHSELBATHWATERWATERF
ALLSDEMONOFILLIPÛTAS WAKEY WEST MARQUESAS KE
YS FLEURIDEAU REMYSELF & SHE-MILLIES JACKSON
FEELIN' BITCHCOCK EN GRATTENDANT LE GODE CHI
RACOLOSSODOMY MYSELFA SOLSDIONASSAUBERSPUSS

UCKING BRIDES OF DIA DIA REASON HÄXENHAMMERI
NG THE SCROTTERDUMP O'TRAMPSTERDAM EL MARQU
ESSACROTUMTUM CLUBBING MWARLORDUREAPERTUTUPE
LOLO! WAU WAU WOOF WOOF WALKABOUT IN WOOP WO
OP MAJESTIC WARRIOR SPERMWHALING FOR RAINDAN
CESTORAPDUB MÊM CRAZY WHORRANT MWHOREAPERTUR
APPERRUIN WHOLLAND J.S. BACKWATERRAPSTARTIDE
THE MARQUISSYPUSSY GEILLORRY OBEAHH OBEAHH T
RUCK LET IT RAIN! LET IT RAINWATERRA CUTTABU
RRA ROTT COTHI ISKUT ROTTOCK PROM ALONG LONG
WASHAGO GAUGUIN EL MARQUIS DE WATER ESPACE B
ASTONADE SADE TIBETIPI-FONKATHARSEQUIN UNCLE
JAM & DAVE PLAY LOUDDISSAY HOLLAND AMUSE-GIR
L CALL-CARL PEPPER'S LUNILEE ARSE CLUB MWEDD
A MIX-RAY CHARLES ÎLES (NOT TO BE CONFUSED W
/) MÈRQUÈS DOG! SCHIZORNAMENTAL DISSEASYLAND
ATOMTOMMICKY MOUSSEOULINEAR SHAMPOONG BRUSCH
UP YOUR ARSCHEISSHIRACOLOSSODO REMY FAKUDOUS
CH KUBRICKINABRAQUE SCATOLLAND MORERUROA POU
R WAFFRANCE CHIROCK & ROLL OVER GURUROA WATE
WATER EVERYWOKABOUT A'MAA MAA'MAMAYOYOKUTS
UNGLIEDER MARQUIS VONNATRIX GÖTTURAL POWER T
RANSPLANTATION NATION GULA GULA MARQUISEAQUA
PREFAB SPROUTTERRANCE MOVING THE RIVER HOWLI
N' WOLFGANGES AMADISHWATER EAUDIONYSOS P-FUN
A-GREASE WAKA OOLOO WHAT ABOUTIT OBEATRICKAPR
ICK ORANGE NAZZAURATHUSTRAWINSKI RITES OF SP
RING WATER WATER YOURQUELLWASSERMONOMANIAGAR
A FALLSUCKING THE BRIDES OF SPRING PALEOLITH
IUM CARBONATED SPRING WATER WATER LO & LORAN
GE SIRUPSIDE DOWN BOOTZITRONENSHAFT NOAH-NOA
H WE ARE LEMON COCK 'N ROLL OVER BEETHOVEN S
PA CITRONICCLONIC FOR THE PEOPLE R.A.M. JUNC

LE JAMPOOLLAND ODIEUXAFLUX ÈSPACE ODDIONYSOS NUCLAIR OBSCURQUELLWASSIR PSYCHOSEXORSCISSOR GASMOUSSEAS ON THE HIGHWAY TO HOT DOG HELLWE G QUELLE MARQUIS I M BECK OUTCOME ASSHOLE BU RNT ORANGE PEEL FOURTEEN RIVERS FOURTEEN FLO ODS SEEWATER RAINING BLOOD YAWP! LSDIOHAZARD ORANGE 9MMW PLAY OUT LOUD EL MARQUÈSQUISSEAG OUE'TA ROYOKUTSUNGLIEPILEPSY UTTERRUSHING SP ASTRALLEZ PEPSILEPSYCHIC VAGINISMOUSSEE WATE RRORANGANESHAMALE SPACE & FRUITGANG IN PARAD JANOVA GUINEA NOACHIK KERIBBLE RIBBLE MBUAND IONYSOSSMATOSS OFFOLLANDAMAN VIBRA FREE SPEE CH FOR THE DUMBRILLOLO TRIBEAQUA PEOPLES WOR D UP YOUR HOLZERRAUM STIFF CLITTLE FANGOES B LITZEE-TIMEBOMBUANDIORANGE CLITORREFLEX EPIL EPSEA WAH-WAH WAH-WAH ECHOLARANJA-AGUA-LIMAO TSETUNGA TUNGADELIC PUSSY WASH NOT WASH DEUS SEX MACHINA CHINA EVERYWHERE LIMAORI MAORI H OLD ON TIDE CUNNIKILLINGUS TSETUNGATUNGATUNG A SEXY SALAMI MYSELF & TATUNG! TATUNG! YOKUT SUNGLIMUNDUSCHAMANIEMONGOLIAGARATATATATABULA RASA EL MARQUESSCHWEPPSILOOFZILLA GEORGEOMAT ERRA CLINTONIC EPILEPSYCHOLLAND ALLSDELAGONA VE HOLANDA CALL M KITTY KELLY! EL MARKISSYKI TTY KILLYKELLY YINFLICKING THE YUNG CALL CAR L ANDREAM TO MAMA AH MINNEE WAH OH AH MINNEE WAH OH I OH I FUNKADELICIEUX EL MARQUESSAUT D'EAUDIORANGEORGE CLINTONICCLONIC DAMPBLURST GODDAMBULLY WEDO WEDO URSOUND WELL-HOUNGAN U NCLE JAMSTERDAMBALLAH OUEDOUCHAMANIA OVARY W AH URSOUND WELLHOUNGAN RAMSTÈRDAMBULLAH WED O LOVE LOVE WEDO ORANGE BACONNIQUE THROUGH T HE BOUCAN GLASS MOHAVE MERCY BOKOR AGOUE'TA-

RONALD LAINGLEGBA ONE MANCHU AGADA AGA DAMBI
ONYSOS MUKE JUST DO IT CALL MEIHE THE BIG PE
ULTRA VIOLLETHE BITHE BISANNEMILK LOLIQUID S
UNEMBISAN SULA BITHE BUMBIRANGGANGES WATER O
N THE BRAINSCANNABISMILLAH UNCLE JA'DAM & EV
ANISH FOAM ACTION MUMMUMMUM MAMMAMMAMBOOTSIL
ENCE EREXÎLE & CUNILLINGUS UNDISCO THE WATE
R I LOO LOO! I LOO LOO! PFILIGRAPES WATERMAR
KIES LE MAGICHANT DELA TEIRRE EL MARQUESAN W
ATERREFLUX OEVERREBIRTHERAPY HOLANDA DU BE VE
RSION DADADADEBAS BABABADEDAS THIS IS THE DU
BE FOOLLIGREASE WAKA'DADE MARKIES VAN WATERM
ARKIES VAN WATERMARKIES VAN WATERMARKIES VAN
WATER ARSEROCKING THE LOO LOO TRIBEATRUXAFLE
X DRIVERREBUSE AGADADDY COOLLAND THE MARQUIS
GEORGE CLINTUNE CUTTING THE VEIN OF REASON U
FOBLITCH UNCLE JAMBA LAMFAPUAQUA POTABULLEAU
WITCHCREEKKEEE HOMOKO DALINYS.O.S. AJISI CHR
IST SUFERRIRE ZEN OPOU! THE MARQUESSUCK & FU
CKATHARSIS WATERRORVISION WAH WAH WAH NEZ NE
Z NEZ WOW WOW WOW KUDOBBELGANGES URRIVERREGA
L STARLIAMENT PERRUNKADÉLICE CALL CARL ANDRÉ
LON SHAMPOOL CALL-CARL ANDRÉLONELY HEARTS CL
UB ODOL MED MONDWATER KUDOPPELDOUCHAMANTRA D
EEE-LITURGY SCHWEPPILEPSY DRY ORANGE UP YOUR
ARSCHWEPPILEPSYCHEDELIC DRY LEMON INDIAN TON
IC-CLONIC HOLLAND VODADA DE MARKIES VAN WATE
R SPACE BASHING THE HYPNOCEROS HEAD VI IATMÜ
LTI-ACTIVE MASQUE HYDRATANT HIEROSHIMA BOSCH
H WATERLAND THE MONOTAUR & THE STEREO SHIROS
HI-MARKIES TNTHE BOMB LSDIONYSOS & BOOTSILENU
S DAY-TRIPHTONGUESS WAH-WAH! AGUA BRAVAGUA B
RAVAGUA BRAVA MARQUES DE BAJAMARQUES DE BAJA

MARQUES DE BAJAMAR WORLD LIQUID MYTHOS EAU D
YNAMISANTEDILUVIALIASDE MARKIES VAN WATERROR
FABBASSITAR ODOREX REX EXTASE DILDEO DUSCHAM
PULLISEAS WATERRAPP-FONK ALL STARLIAMENTHALE
S FUNCKADELICK SUCK FUCK & WATER WATER EVERY
WAU & DANUBE MW WATERRAPISS BUIN JET BRONZER
WILD RAIN GILLETTE DELUGE EAU DE TOILETHE BO
MB M MYSELF-TANNING GEL & SUN RÂ ELECTRIC EG
YPT '95 BOOTSIGMUND FREUD ICE-CUBISMOZARTAUD
ISSEAS THE MAGIC FLÜT! MW AUTO DA FUNK EAU-D
ELÀ-BASSOAPOPÈREBEL REBELUGANESHAMALE DIONYS
.O.S. TELEPHONICCLONIC WORD UPSIDE DOWN & OU
T COME COME DR. DRECCE HOMO FRIEDERICHO FELL
INIETZSCHE GO AHEAD IN THE RAIN THE MARKEZIA
H JONES AFRICAN SPACE KRAFFT SPLASH SPEECH E
AUSLÄNDER MARQUIS VON WASSIR DOG IN EXCELSIS
DEO DUSCH GELTACHTUNGATUNGATUNGA BABY LET IT
SCHWEPPES LET IT SCHWEPPES THE MARQUISLAS DE
MENDOZAUBERSPACE BASSES WATTERROAR WATTERROA
R EVERY WORD RAINFLAMMABLE JAZZID RAINSTABIL
ITY KICKIT KICKIT KOCKLIT KOCKLIT THE MORNIN
G AFTER SHAVE HOLLAND P-FUNKUNG THE PIG FON
K MAGGOTT BRAINTANZEFALLOGRAMMARQUESAN DUDOK
UDOO-BOP-FONKUDOUCHAMANIA MWALKING DIESASTER
LSDEMOLITOURQUELLWASSER UNUS MUNDUSCH GEL WE
ARE NILED RIVERRAPPMATAPPWAH-WAH FRIPPMATRIP
P FRANTICKA PRICKASSODOMYSELF-TANNING THE CL
INTONING LOTION EAU FRESH BLACK MOSMOZART AN
IMO SPERM KUTI DUSCH UNCLE JAMMON-REVERIVERS
ION DUBBIE DUBBIE BUTTER YOUR SOUL WOLFGANGE
S LAMAZONE OZZMOZZART MEGA GOTT BRAINFALLAUT
LET IT SCHWEPPES LET IT SCHWEPPES BUTTER YOU
RQUELL'AN SHE-MILLE WATERREMOTOROTATING IN O

DIEUXAFLUX LITANIC DON'T PANICKA PRICH GLAUBE
ANYSOS YOU ARE RHINED HOLLAND THE SPASSOCIAT
IVE BASSOCIATION ANUS MOONDUSCH GEL EL MARQU
ESUN RÂDIONYSOSSMATOSS I DIGUESS WAH-WAH THE
SPASSOAPOCALYPSOCIATIVE BASSOAPOCALYPSOCIATI
ON DUCHAMPS ÉLISA MONS VENUS MUNCHDUSCH GELT
ACHTUNGANESHAMANTRASHAMALEOPARDONAU DUSCHAMP
OOING SUCK HOLYSÉES MARANATHALATTICA! MARANA
THALATTICA! THE BULLES ÎLES CHAMPS HEALYSEAS
HOOLIGANS WAXE ALLSDIALLES ÎLES LISIBILLABON
GOES THE BUTTER YOUR SOULLAND EVENEZIA DILDE
ODORANT STICK UP YOUR ARSE PSYCHOTIC BABY PS
YCHOTIC BOOTSYBILLABONGO BUTO BUTO BABY PSYC
HOTIC THIS SIDE UPSIDE DOWN & OUT COME THE F
REAK OUT KHUMBH MELARD MELARD KHUMBH OH I OH
I LOURDES DIONYSOS RAPSUCK WORDURE ICH THE P
ICH DANCE HAVING THE SLUTSKRIEG BE-BOP THE S
LITTENSPORT MISOGEAN GENIE RAPPOCALYPSE NOWA
AUTONGUE DADA FÉAST M W ONDA SPYROBASSIA PHO
ENIXXAGONE WONK I. COÏT IN ANO-YONI LINGAMAD
EUS OZZMOZZARTIFISTFLUT SNAKE RATTLE & ROLLI
NS OVER BUTTHAVEN PAROLES PAROLES PAROLES ÎL
ES MARQUISES FLOAT FLOAT ON WASH & GODE MARK
IES VAN WATER ORIGINNAFLUX WALK THE GEORGE C
LINTONDEO DUSCHAMANTRAVESTIVITIES EL MARQUIS
LE BOUCAN ECLIPPENLAUTCUM DD-LSDEFUNKADELICK
SUCK & FUCKATHARSIS THE RIVERRENAISSANSSOURC
ES IATMÜLTRA WAVE ADOLFGANGES WÖLFGANGGA WIL
LIAMADEUS BOOTSYBILLUTSCHIZOFRENIAGARA FALLS
MARANATHALATTABOOTSY'S RUBBER BABYLONELY ART
S CLUB RUBBER BANDA TAURAPPMATAPPADELIC BOOT
SYBERSPACE BASSES EL MARQUESAN MARCOÏT IN AN
O-YO'MOMMA'S EGGYPTIAN MARQUESSEAQUEST ALL S

TAR-WATER THALATTA! THALATTABOOTSHIROSHAMAL
E DE MARKIES VAN WATER ECCE HOMO CALVINTERLU
DENS NORTH SEA DELTABOOTSYBILLÀ-BASSAHARA UP
YOU ASSAHARABIESBOSCH ELECTRONIC YOURQUELLYN
CHAMAN TVOODOO TWINTI PEAKS HANGAQOCK TV TOW
ERRUIN PERMESSOAPOCALYPSE NAUMAN PERMESSODOM
Y MYSELF & UNCLE JAMADISORDER ATOMICCOMIC DO
GGODBOUTZILLATRONICCLONIC EPILEPOCALYPSE WOW
STEP BY STEP RIGHT UPSIDE DOWN & OUT COME GI
NGER & FREDDIPOUS REX H.P.-FUNKAZOÏDE MWATT-
REX UP ARSCHIZOHARSCHIZOÏDIPOUS REXONA DILDE
ODODO NOW WHAT'S THIS ABOOTSY? BEFFERRANT HO
T BUTTERED SOULTRAVESTIKIEFERRARI ARI RAMA R
AMA HYPERMESSOULTRANSUCK CHIRATTLE & ROLL OV
ER HOLLAND DE RAMPAZOÏDIPOUS REXWATERSTAAT E
L MARANATHALATTABOOTZEELAND 53 EL MARQUESSEX
TASEAMAMALE MARQUIS LE BOOK BUTT HOTTERED SO
ULTRAGOIDIAGRAMMARQUESSPEACH THELONIOUS MONK
DEVILLE MARQUISSUCK LICK & APOLLEAUP YOUR AR
SE DELPHILOSODOMY MYSELF & SHIVAGINA-DIONYSO
S MWACQUATOMIC DR. DUBBUSE JOHN LENNONJAHWEH
BECK IN THE DAY-TRIPPMADRIPP LEAURECHHIONÄXO
S FREAK OUTPÛTASSES UP WORD GO ROUNDABOOTSEA
S TELL M MORSE TELL M MORSE YOURQUELLEAUDION
IETZSCHE-SHIVATICANNIBALLA BALLÀ-BASSPACE DA
DATA BASSPACE FIREBIRD MINGUSHING RIVERRATIO
NILE-WATER IN THE DRECKMATHÉQUE OF REASON TH
ELLONIOUS ABOOTSY MINK MELVILLES ÎLES MARQUI
SES DE MARKIES VAN WATTSTAXTUALITY & MARQUES
AN SPACEWAKE EL MARQUESSIMBAD EL MAREADOURQU
ELLE MARQUIS LE BOOK AMENTAL DIZZY NASSAU WA
TERWORLD WETTOMIC GODBOUTSIOUXIE & THE NEW R
UBBER BANSHIVALLSDIONYSOSSLES MARQUESSIZZLES

AQUACLEAR POWERHEAD 201 ESPACE ADDIES ILLABE BASS À-VAUDOULEAU ALL 'N ALLSDIES ILLAQUA WAS NOT WASSERPENTINE FIRE X-RAIN GRAND MALSTRÖMPOEL BLOBSUS DELINGUAE WATAW WATAW GEBORA-BORA AQUADONAUILES ÎLES PSYCHOTIC BABY PSYCHOTIC KRAKATOAQUAQUAPHONIAGARA FALLSDE MARKIES VAN WATER PSYGOTHIC BÖMPSKULL ONE OWAUTAUSILLA OWAUTAUSILLA FELA GÔNAVE VADAPATTACK EL MARQUESSAUT D'EAUDIONÄXOS UPUZI BASSAI WAH-WAH MEGA VATNA HLAUPSIDE DOWN & OUTCOME THE NUCLEAR FAMILY PSYCHODISCOGLOSSIDAE EAU EXTRÊMOR IN BLIZZARDSKINDRUMBRILLOWLAND L'HISTOIRE D'OHOLANDY WARHOLLAND MEGAMEGAMEGA MIXABBARETTA'S THEME DON'T DOÏT DON'T COÏT EAU HOWL O MINERVES ALLSDIEU BÉNISSUCKAMA SUTRASH ORSPASM PUTA KEO HAKA NOHOLLAND M IS FOR ABUSE EL MARQUESSPERMATHORREACQUA TATTOTABILE WAUTEUTA WAUTEUTA OVARI MONOTYPEEL PRELUDE TO APISS MARANATHALATTABULLARTAUD BULGO VIVAT FLUX IN ETHERNUM TOPORTEUR D'EAU THE MARQUIS & I B-52 ROCKLOBSANG RAMPA THE EVIL I AEGOSPOTAMI A FRÈDDOUCHAMP AVÉ EVA MUTANT GÉSUS JIMITATZIO CHRISTRIX SPIZZICATZOAPSULA MARQUISEA CASATIKI IN SEXFONTAINES PARIS PSYCHO POPINKURZ BUSH M BABY LU FUKI CONFONK UNCUT FLOOD URETHA FRANKLINGUS TO HOLLYWANQUE AFRICA API API APOY APOY BUDANUBE UUA UUA NUTT MUDD MUTT NUDD PO-SHO MISHU-MISHU EL MARQUÉSMOUSSEINE VAITAI VAITAI PUMP PUMP CHOCOLATE MARQUIS << O >> GEISHA LOVE SWING IN TATTOO VIDEO DUET PURPURATA SIAMAGARA FALLSDE MARKIES IJLLANDAMANTRA WATERVLOEDISSEY LÀ-BASSO CONTINUO OL'LANDICA HOLLA OLLULAND KUTKA! KUTKA! WHOOO-O-O-O-

OOPZILLA GIANT SEA BASS MARKIES MILLER BOOTS
YBILLUTSCHIZOPHRENIAGARAFAELLEAU EL MARCASCA
YA DUSCHEN & CREMEN O DE TOILETHE MARQUIS OC
EAN DREAM FRANKIE BEVERLY HILLARYWHORE CAPRE
SCILLA CAPRESLEY O DE TOILETHE KING WHAT OFF
RET WHAT OFFRET WHAT OFFRET ONE OWAUTORRENTI
DAL RAINSCANNILINGUSHIN' PISS EVE & THE SADD
AM'S FAMILY AFARI OMO VAGUE MARQUESSUBWAY SH
OCK'R & MUTTERTONGUESS WAH-.WAH MAZZILLANGUAG
E DISORDER FUNKTION/DISFUNCTION L'ORDRECKADE
LIC CHAOSPEDALI SKULL-JUNGK MZEE TU M'W' MUT
HA-APEE-CRAZEE UKNOCK KNOCK KNOCKIN' ONDADAL
AI LAMAISON DU JOUIREXTRAVAGANZAPPIN' MANU D
IBANGOGUINEA PIGGA P & IGG MARANATHALATTABOO
TSYBILLASWELLES PAYS BASSO PROFUNDOUCHES LÀ-
BASTIAANSEELE MARQUIS MUSIC-HALLSDUCHAMPOONA
-POONA MURA MURA ATOLL ATOLL ZDANZA ZDANZAZ
DANZA EL MARQUIPRICK CHOPERA DOYOUWANA' BUMP
IN' BOSCHVÄRK KREBB ZUBADO STERIBIB GLOBB NI
XON ORR KOKÔTT-APATT SPRENGBOMBA DE BUZA BUZ
A CONS-BOUTBOUL? YOURQUELLE JEUX DE MEAUX VA
TN FÁ-FATTSTOLLAND U ARE URE MOVIE HOLLANTIS
MEGATON WARHEAD VI HH CHINESE HIFIHAT FLUXUS
BARRAQUE DULLÀBASS ODDEÈSSEA HIHATMÜLTRA SUR
F BEAUTY FLESH OLLANDY ANADOLLY PARTONICCLON
IC SEASHORE DO THE STRAND EREXY MAGICK EL MA
RIESKIMODDER MARQUIS VON OH, GEORGE CLINTST
ONE THE ICE-AGE COMETH HYDREUGENE EAU'NILE H
ONEY PUMP PUMP PALOMA PICASSODOMY MYSELF & I
I I HAIRIANAL ASSENIPPOULOS SPERMIFIQUE INNE
NROOM 999 SCROTTURDÄMMERUNG AROUNDFOUNQUE TH
E WORD IN ONE D-TRIPPY-POPPOPPOUSSUC BOB, BO
B, BOBBIN' ALONGASONG LET'S ZAPPELIN WOLFGAN

G AMADUCHAMPEAUXARTS BIKOVSKINILE SPUTNIKKAP
RICKATOLL FREI FLOW MW TATTOO-VAHINE EL M
ARKISI WINTI FAHLSTRÖM ESSO-LSDÊMÔ-LÉMÔN SIL
ÂS MARQUESAS SOUD SEAS MADAME HANDY JOOB GOO
GOO GOO JOOB HOTTENTOT VENUS SAVE YOUR KISSE
S FOR MW HOLANDA TO'OE RORO O TE TUTAE PUAKA
WORK DAT BOÛDA WORK DAT BOÛDA HOLLAND LÂMÈ B
E YOUR LOVER MWÊ MÊMYSOULTRASH & SHAMANTI-
KRIZ EYEI EYEI EYEI MAYYA U BELASTEN MAYYA U
BETASTEN ONANGA-ORANGA SEX-UNGULA MARQUISUCK
JUDO SUMO & KUDO THOSE WERE THE DICE WAN ORA
LICE DISFUCKT APA APA LOPPA LOPPA THALES COO
PER EL MÄRKISCHER CHANTBLAST SEPULTOURE KUND
ADA FUNK ONE MANZONI MAGIC BASS (MAGICA) MAR
CUS 'KILLER' MILLER MIMMO MIMMO WHAT'S A SEA
SKULTURA EL MARCOUSSIS FREIPLASTIKKAWA KAWAT
ER WATER EL MARIO SCHIFANO MARE HALLUCIO FON
TANA SLITTENTITTO'E-TO'E UUME SCHWITTERS UUM
E UNUS MDUNDOUCHE ANUS IM PELS DEEPAK & DEEP
AK AÏGEAU EUROBOROCEANIC PAIA FUNK ALL-STARK
OVSKIUMARQUESAN WARVOER DE MARKIES VAN WATRA
PAPA PAUPAUPAUKEKE TITOI COWCOW TAIS-TOI KAU
KAU PSYCHO POUPOU POP THE IDIOT MYSKINAKINYW
ATER WATER UUME & THE BABY DOLLAMOUR ENTRA T
UTTO SCORRE ZIWA ZIWA ANUS MGUNGU MGUNGURU D
EEPAK & DEEPAK AIGEAU LE CUL D'O KUDOMINE! W
ORTSALALOMBROSODOMYSELFUCK ENTRA TATTOO WURS
T UND DRECK ICKA PRICK HOUSE I MANAMAKE WANA
WAKE UPRIVERYWHORE SUCK THE DAMN THING DRY T
UTUPELOLANDA BILLION DOLLAR BABYSNAKES FLOAT
ING ON WÂWTÂW WÂWTÂW AQUADRIAAN DITVOORST AF
LOAT FLOAT ON JIMI HENDRIK MARSMANTRA GOTTMO
MA RHINOSE SHITANI FANI FURIKO LA MAJIMAJI R

ED ORANGE YELLOW INDIGO VIOLET ONE AURA MILE
S DAVIS SEA MILES DAVIS AHEADFUNK THE BOMB-T
RANSPLANT LEFF YAYA OSS OFF DROP DA BONE WAS
NOT WASSUR LA MÈR TOUPOUSSEA PUMPERMPUSSOAP-
CHOPRA HARDROCCOCOÏTUS IN ANONIMITY DEEPAK &
DEEPAK AÏGEAU TO HELLECTROSHOCKABULLASWELLES
PAYS BAS SARADIONYS.O.S. JIMILES DAVIX THE WI
ND CRIES MARY MARY HOLD ON TIDE DILLINGINGER
& ALFRED HITCHCOCK REGENDANCIN' TO SOFISTIFU
NK TRANSLUCY IN DISGEISER EL MARQUESAN MARCO
SMASSA AND DAMANIAGARA FALLSDUCHAMPUNK GOO G
OO MA CHOO CHOO JIBWAH-WAH WAH-WAH LE MARQUI
S DE BESTIIS REGENMAKIN' IN ST. CLITUS TRANC
E AFRICAN MONITOUR PUCHAMPOOL PARIS ALLIASDE
DE MARKIES VAN WATER GOING DOWN LIKE FIRE HO
LLAND THE TETSUMI BUDDHA HAMMERING BISMARCK-
SEAMALE & BORNEO KORANGUTANAGAN BÄCK TO BÄCK
IN BLACK & BLUE VELVETTSTOOL EL MARKUSIMULIA
TMÜLACRÂNE TU M'M'M'M'M'M OLLANDA ANADOLLAMO
URQUELLETHE BOMBASSARAPIS SARAPIS OSORIS-HAP
MYSELFICK & I AUM AUM AUM COMING OUTSCUMBUKU
MBU EL MARKIBOKOR TATTOUCHING BOTTOM IN TUPA
PAU NEU BIKINNIN' SPACE BASSE-EGYPTE GO DEUT
SCH HOLLAND DO-IT-YOURSELF-DITCHCRAFT IN HAP
AESI HABASI BLASTHMANIA JAFFAZILLA MARQUESSI
SI ORANGE DO M BABY DO M THE HIBULLROARSCHAC
H TEST ONE TIME ONE OWAH LÀ-BASSHOLLANDY WAR
HOLE FRIGURHINE DIABOLI AFLOAT ON LEAULEAU L
EAULEAULEAULEAULEAULEAU KINK FLOYDISSEA REGI
NA DE PRÜNE/VIRGIN PROM'S ECLISSATYRIASSTICI
SSOUR DIZZIPENIS ET RELICCLONE CRUXAVIRA HOL
LANDER MARQUIS PASHAMALE MODDERSPRACHFLUSS F
IATMÜLTI-USAGESSEAS SWEET GEORGIA CLINTON À-

VAU-L'EAU-DELA MARQUISE D'OPE D'OG PALEO PEN
PEN POP OLALA BRAVE TAFANARI HOLANDA MOUNINE
MOUNINE MOUNINE ENFIN SALES MAD A'DAM STOSSA
UDS WAXTOURIST STANDING ONE INCH LONG IN ONE
SOCK WILLIAM 'TACKY' ORANGE UP YOUR ARSCH PI
SSARROTATING IN THE ISLAND RIVERIE MOONLIGHT
SWIM REPRISCILLAPIS APIS THE SUN KING DIONYS
OS AT 19/99 RETURNAL RAP ANUS ERABOROS SUNGA
ÏGEAURANOS SUCK M RAINKISS AGUA VIVAGUA DÜRE
R RHINOWITTHALES MARQUESS MUSCLE SEINE KRIEG
ERRECKIN' HOLLAND UNTER ALLSD PPP-FUNKSIEK H
EIDI HOVHANNES YOCHANAN GIOVANNI JONAM JANOS
JOFAN IWAN EVAN IVAN JUAN JEAN JOHN SEAN LEN
NON & IMAGINE LES ÎLES LIQUIDES ILLIQUID ELE
MENTAL DISEASY GILLESSPEAK MÊMMÊMMÊMORY MW P
ALEO PSYCHOPATHIC RAGE OUTBURSTING THE DUTCH
WAANIDEUS O OLLABIATRIX O BAIN MARY POPPUNS
ÀDIEU BÉNISSAU BIG BANGLOÛTISSANSSUCKAMA KAW
A EPILEPSAY ALEUT UTCHA UTCHA QOCHA QOCHA O
VER & INUIT ORGASM NASSAU MICKY LOVE NOT MAUS
S HERE COMES THE SUNTALAAQUASSOULWARA WARA T
WENTY THIRST CENTURY WATERWARVUUR THERMONUCL
EAR SWITMULIMON EXPLODING IN THE MENDOZA MAD
ZONE WONDER UNDER WATER ARSCHAMA WULLY WUSSY
BILLA BOOLA OLO OLO KILLA KILLA RAIN IN-THE-
FACE NÁM MI I MAI LABASSI LOBASSI BOOCHIMIAGA
RABIESBASSÄTTUMA EEVA EEVA UNUKU HIVA LAVALA
S MARQUESAS AFLOWLOW ON WÂWTÂW WÂWTÂW THE EP
ILÈPSIATTACK FOM FOM FOM ALLSD-TRIPLE SUNDOWN
PARHELIO EXCELLENCE EL MARKONIAGUA DURAGUA P
ESADAGUA VIVAGINAGUA DENTATTOO UNU/S MÙNDUSC
HAMPABASSÄNVNAVEN GET WET HOLANDA DE MARKIES
VAN WATER DERAINDANCING FOR A FREE MARQUESAS

TE TO'E TE KAI O TE HAIKIKI! ACIDDHARTAUD VI
SSIOUS HUMMING MY WAY FOR PARIS IS A MOVABLE
FISTFUCK ACCU-JAC & ACCU-JAC II CHIRECK'N RO
LEX CHARLES DE GAULTIER UU UU UU OEDIPHANTOI
NE ORTHO-GYNEST ORTHANA ARTEX ARTANE ARTOSIN
ARTICOCAÏNE SANDOSATINE LA MEDICINE ET SON D
OUBLE PHARMONUCLEAR ZWITSANAL GLOBUMANTRA GR
AVITIMON MULTILOAD EPOËTINE SCYPTOCUR PALEOH
EX PROCTOFOAM ONE AURORIX ARTOSIN-GYNO-TERAZ
OLADEX MORFINE DIPINE ALLSD-TRYPTIZOL COLIAC
RONENBERG CARDURA CRASNITIN BETOLFUCK VAPORU
B LES DURETTES REGITINE ACIPEN-5 VICHY LES C
HAMPS ELYZOL MORFINE DIPINE TAMTAMBOCOR DUAT
ABLÀ-BASS CYTOSAR SITARTOSIN ARTEX TIN SINTR
OM SAUGMENTIN DRUM & BAZAPROPAZON ARTANE ART
OSINASPRILLA LIQUIFUMERATA REFYLLINE FYLLINE
SINEQUAN NON AEROPAX PIX LIQUIDA AGUANOXAN R
IVERMOX DE-NOL DE-NUL DE-NIL AKINETON AKILOT
ON ATOMIC PHARMO DOX BROXILLA DOXAPRAM ATOMI
C DOXY DRAGRA ATOMIC DOXURUBU RUBELOLO ATOMI
C UNIDOX & DOGMATIL MELLE MELLERIL MEGACE-MI
X ESTANTRUM PROLONGATUM DRUM ARTOSIN VEPESID
DHORTHO-GYNEST MOR MORFINE FINE FINIMAL WARN
ICAOS SPALT-N MUTA-BLASTINE BIKINITRO WATERT
ATOL DALMADORM DORM ARTOSIN ARTANE METHAQUAL
ONELY METEOR ENFERROTEROBLONG DORM DORM FLOO
DWOOD MAC DREAMTIDES POMP POMPEI-FUNKOODOO K
UNTAKUNG & SEXISTENCIAL FÜROR FEMINUS AFLOAT
FLOAT ON WÂWTÂW WÂWTÂW SHAVE MY BOSCH YOLAND
A BACHELORD DIONYZEUS APOLLOCOCK PRICK-SLANG
ING HEINZ HOT ARSCHLONG ISLANDAMAN EPILEPOUS
SUC' PAGLIA-PI-PI SHITANI FANI DU ICEBERG DU
BIST SO HEISS CHUCK BERRY WHITESNAKED LOVE-IN

UNLIMITED POP-ICONNILINGUSHINTO THE NETHERLA
NDS SHERE HYPE DON'T BELIEVE THE HITE NARCOÏT
US INTRA MAMMAS & PAPPAS SHOW-OPERA DEEPAK &
DEEPAK EGOGO DO IT GINGER ROGER & ZAPP ASTAI
RE ORDER-DISORDER-PHANGER TRANSRIVERBED-IN H
AIR/PISS JAJE JAJE JAJE POP-MOZAK MAMAGLA MA
RQUISEA MODDER & LOVER O'MANIA ANAXIMEANDER
CULPAPUA REMBRAND NEU GUINEA ATOLL HERE COME
S THE SEPIK IN THE FORESKIN HOLANDA FLAT FAT
& DANGEROUS TO LO! MÂ MÂ MÂ WARTA WARTA FINN
ATHRILL-O-RAMA RAMARQUIS FETTWALKIN' THE KIE
FERTURE DENKI THAI BEUYS FATMAN THE HUMAN FL
YING SAUCER WAN OWOW OWOW CYCLONE COMIX UNDE
RSEA AGENT CORPORAL COLLINS AQUAMAN STARRIBA
SSI STARRIBASSI WHATCHAMAN FAME? BOCHWIÄ BIA
NOA-NOA SPEAKING IN TONGA ISLANDAMAN EPILEPT
ONGUES TELOS MORE TELOS HOLLAND WE-WILL-HOLD
-HANDS-&-(THEN-WE'LL)-WATCH-THE-SUN-RISE-FROM
THE-BOTTOM-OF-THE-SEA EL MARQUESSPIRITUS LOC
I SNAKE HOPILEPSIATTACK & FREI FLOAT FLOAT O
ON OOPSNUXIOUS G-SPOTTENTON HOLLABIAQUA KOIKA
TUHI 'U'E SEX-O-LANDA AHA TE HA'A METAU? AYÎ
KKA DIKE EPIC FUNKADEMIC AFLOW ON WÂWTÂW WÂW
TÂW EVERYWHERE WHITE FLOWS THE RIVER & ALL T
HE SEA WERE INK Z-BULL TRIPZILLA INK-OPERA &
VAUDOURANOS AMUN-MINDUSCH PREM SAGAK HADESNE
Y WORLD-UP MW MAD AS THE VEX'ED SEA ADDIONYS
OS! ADDIONYSOS! SGT. FURY'S APOLLONELY HEART
S CLUB ORANGE TO CLUB LÉMÔN FIATMOLUCCAS MAR
QUESAS AFLOW FALLSDEE-LIGHTNING WORLD-CLIT H
OLLAND ONE HALLUCINATION UNDER A GROOVE O'CL
OCKWORK ORANGE HUGO BALLROOM BLITZKRIEGERREC
KIN' YOHOLANDA IN THE ALPINE ASSASYLUM PPPEN

ILE BONE MAGIC HOLE-RAZOR DE MARKIES VAN WAT
ERRAPPIDOUCHAMANIAGARA FALLSDE MARKIES VAN W
ATER APSU TIAMATERRA INFIRMATERRAINSANE SKOP
ZEAS SKOPZEAS ALLUVIACQLA MARGUTTATTOO TATTO
O MIRANDO TRANSFORMORPHEUS RUN MPS ICKA LOLI
TA SLEMPRICKA BEINURQUELLOVE TO LOVE CANALIN
GUSHIN' APISS GRANDFUNK BOUFFALLO DEAD HOT K
ENNEDYS & LEMONDO FREUDO/LEMONDO TRASHO CARR
Y ON EMMANUELLE NEGRA WHAT'S UP DOCTOR OCCUL
T ECCE HOMONO BIKINI LATOYATOLL JACKSONIAN M
UPI MUPILEPSIATTACK GRANDMASTER FLASH-IN-THE
-PUNHOLANDA MY BELOWED MARANATHALATTABOOTSYB
ILLASCAUX PPP GROTTERDÄMMERUNG MATERIA PRIMA
RQUESAN WATERRITORIALLSDIONYSIAN SHOCKWAH-WA
H REONYSOS SPEEDWAGONONNAFRIPPMATRIPP SPADOM
ASOTERIC FREUD-ISIS-CULTRANCE OH HENRY ROLLI
NS THE HOBBY HORSE MEGAGA YUYUYU ADOLFGANG A
MADISORDER SHE-MALA DE SADE SADE CHIRATTLE &
ROLL OVER HOLANDA TRANSVESTRITON TRY IT ON K
ISS VAN TONGEN DEFUNKADELICK SUCK & FUCKATHA
RSIS SUN RÂBIESKIMOHEAVY WITT Ô DE GIVE & CH
EAT DEAD SEA JAZZ FOR WATERNITY MORFIN' MORF
IN' MINDMORFIN' OH LOURDES VENUS IMPULSE WAN
DY WARHOLA FISTFLOODING DUCHAMPS'S ELEUSIS S
QUIZ THE FRAUD MONKIEFER ORANGE UP YOUR ARSC
HNABBEL SCHNABBEL OOH LORDRE EAU LORDRE GILB
EY'S & GORDON'S LONDON GINNATRIX WONKAFRIG R
HUM LASH & SODOMY THE POGUESS WAH-WAH WAH-WA
H DUCHANSONNY I LOVE YOPOU! ONE OWAUTONGUÈRE
MMMW DEMOLITION MANTRA PPP/FUNKUDEAUDIONYSOS
APOLLEAUPSIDE ONE OH LORDURE EAU-HADESSUCE &
EAU-HADESSOUS ÈSPACE BASSLINEA WASSERPENTINA
CHTONIC-CHLONIC VOODOO TWINTI SPEAK HALLUCIO

LE MARQUIS DE HADES FIREFLY W/MWAH-MWAH THE MARQUIS DE HADES DIVI-DIVISÉA KÔMOS O LORD O DIONYSUCE ANTHROPORRHAISTES SPECKING IN TONG ALINGUS ON THE TRANSEXODUSCHAMPS ELECTROLYSÉS READY-MUTT SUCE KRETAGENÉS JUICE BOMÔS UNCLE RAMMANIAGARAMMANIAGARAP RAP AP HÂP HÂPI Â PIS PIS NEILOPOUSSEA ANUS MNÊNIS ATOMIC DOGGY DOGGODDISSEA DELIXIR BABY CALL GOSSIP JUNK LITANIC DON'T PANIC DE MAZE VAN WAR ELECTROBÖRG MARMAGEDDON MARQUISHOT RENAMING PARADISOTTO IN SUMO METAFIZZICKA TIKICKA PRICKA P/FICKAOSMOZART BODY-GUARTAUD JUJU ARE THE #1 HOLLANDA LSDEA IMPUDICA WOLFGANG AMAMAZE WE ARE ONE OWAH WAN OWALT MAO WEST MYSALPHASER & I-CHING THE HORUS THE HORUS LET IT RAIN LET IT RAIN RAINDIFFERENT WATERVALLEEE D'OMOAAA THE BEAUTY BEUYS & THE BEAST-COAST-JIZZ-FUNK-GURUFLUSS THERMOTOWN NUCLEARWATERREVIVAL SURFIN' SURFIN' MINDSURFIN' URMÈRQUIS MEDIABULEAU LITERRATOURRIDA MENTAL FLOSSALIA FOR THE GLOBE BAROCK & PÁROLL WERTHERSALAT VENUS IN VIRGOGO À GOGOLONELY GAUGAUGUINEA PRIGGUNT AHUNT AMOR FATU HIVA HANAUA HANAUI HANAMIO HANAKAU HANAPANU HANAOUMI HANAHEPU HANAOUW HANAOPLA HANATEUPU HANAPUAEA HANAMOOHE HANATOONE HANAOUNUI HANATUMATA SJÖTIDE SJÖHANA HANAHÉPUPA CALVINATRIX! MARQUESSCHHH... DRY ORANGE NOÖS DE SMAAK VAN WATER MAQCHHIKUY BELASTEN MAQCHHIKUY BETASTEN PUPA NEU PUNNEGUNA WACO JACOPALYPSE NOWIE ZOWIE NOENDESCRYPT EPILISIBLE GILLES ÎLES DELUGES ESP-FUNQUELLENNON DE NERVALL-STAR MAFUTA JELLY FISCHER CHESSPULL GARI 'KASPAROV' GLITTER VERSUS GARI 'GLIT

TER' KASPAROV DEEP BLUE OCEAN RAINVERSION YO
UROBOROTORITRATTOO EL MARQUESSUCKUDO & FUNKU
DO HOLANDA LOLO VAN BINGEN EN VAN BOUTERSE A
UTODAFUCK SHIVANESHA PYRDANCIN' IN THE SWAMP
ÈRE-LASCHEISSEAS EAU DE PATOU PATOU PATHA PA
THALATTAHITI DUSCH O MONOI BIKINFINI ATOLLAT
OMTOM MURRAY-MURRAY OAKHUS ADÖLFGANG AMAZONE
MOUSSEPIK MOON AMUR RIVERBAL SPEEDBALLIN' HÈ
RACLITTERRA INFIRMAGICA THE CLIT IS NEW EACH
DAY CÖRPUSSY CHRISTRIX EL MARQUESSIBELY DELA
NAVE NEVA MUTANT GENIUS AVÉ MIAMI THALASSOO-
THERAPISS DUBBLE-DUTCH-BATH-TREATMENT HOMO B
ULLA EST HOLLAND WHO LOVES YA LOLLY KOYAIK R
AÍNBÖW WATCH TV NUM JAM SPANK PALEOSCHIZOPHR
ENIX SPEECH BASS AQUA-ASTROBLASTHMAGIK EDANC
E ECSTATARKOVSKIJINSKY WE WANT MIR ROMOLANDA
EL MARKASPISKOYE MORE MORE ECSTEADY-MADE FOR
ACTION I/M THE VOGUL IN THE SAUL MAN NAVINCE
NT VAN MYSTAGOGH EL MARCASTOR AKALIASDAY-TRI
P-TOLEMOUSSEPIKPOOLUXORPHEUS TELEUTTERING TH
E LIGHT-WORD UP YOUR ARSCHLAMMDUNKIN' THE SU
N RIVEREND MOON AFLOT FLOT ON EL MARQUESAN R
IVERMEER & BOSCHIZO ELECTROSHOW & WATERFALLA
ROUND THE NETHERWORLD HIROSHIMAGO MUNDI SHE-
GOETHEAD VI MAKBULLEAUDIONOÖS ROAMING THE NE
VER NEVERLANDS SPACE BASEMENT 53 SILICON CH
IPPENDALE HOLANDA MATER LOLLIROCKARSE POP-AR
T TOYON AGUA THE MARCASPIAN SEAMALE DE MARKI
ES VAN WATER EL MARKASKÂYA DE KENZOAP-CHOPRA
O AVEKA O AVEKA! BAKKOKOS BAKKIKOS! ANONYMOU
S IVORY LEOPARD FLOATING ON THE SCHIZO-KNOTH
INGNÄSS SHIVAPHRENIC THOT DISORDER DO NOT AT
TEMPT TO ADJUST YOUR RATIO MARANTHALATTAHAÏT

ITO-KAUKAU KAORKSSOREZONRHARKOCTZTZAHUROXKAO
TZA EAESXIIXAROTTOX WATER WATER EVERYTHING L
IQUIDOLLAND REVE GAUCHE REVE DROITE BENEDERL
ANDMARKIES ORACLE NASSAUDIONYSOS LOOOZ BOOTS
YBILLY'S WHIZ-BANGOISSUCKAPOCALÜPERTZ GRANDM
AL RAILROAD & FELA KOOT HOOMI SWEET HOOMI HO
OPAH HOOPAH LUFFA LUFFA WAN OWAU FIATMÜL 500
SCHALLPLATTEN FLOATING ON WÂWTÂW WÂWTÂW GOZI
LLA GOZILLA BERINGGEIL GÉSU GÉSU (G.S. BACHT
ERBERG) HAÍTIKISSAUT D'EAU MIMISELF & I DROP
THE BONE SPAESI BASSEY THE MAGIC IS YOU HOLL
AND FICK'S LAW FUCK'S LOW URSCHIERBACCHUS HE
T BOEK IK JAN CREMER SIR PSEUDO SEXY HI-FI-M
ALE FREE MACEO CAMEO FLUX CAMAY HELIUM WATER
EVERYWHERAKLEISTÖSS THE MARQUISE OF EAU OBEA
H CHOKMAH GRAND MALTA MARQUIS DE L'ORANGEADE
SINUSRAP IATMÜLIBRIES NYAME MYSULK & WAU ACQ
UE ALTEATEATEA CRESCITA SENZA FINE ECHOLA GO
CCIA D'ACQUA IGLOPPELGANGER IN WELTMERZ OWAU
FRANK ZAPPABLO PICASSONATA HARIKLITAUR-MÈR I
/M ÂPIS VASLAVA PARABRISEAS OOO AAA MMMWAH-W
AH ÀVÉDERICO BLUE MAGIC AGUA SHAMANCHUMAN EL
MARQUESAN RÂPELAIS GARGANTUAGUA & PANTAGUAGR
UEL FLOATING ON WÂWTÂW WÂWTÂW FLOWING OVER W
AH-WAH WAH-WAH YOURSPRUNG SPACE ABASSY OYUNA
YEN SUDANUBE NUBATRAK NÄRRE NÄRRE NÄRRE TELO
S MAO TELOS MAO LET'S ZEPPELIN TOO THE LEMON
SONG A SPICHA ODDISNEY-WORLDTOUR-MÈRQUIS ONE
BY ONE NATION BY NATION UNDER A GROOVE POLYM
ORPHIN' DUB PERVERSION HOLLABIATRIX BY WARHO
LLANDY WARHOLLAND HAWAÏ YOU TAHITIKIEFER CAL
L HIM SHELIUM EL MARKUSKOWAQIATMÜL AFLOAT ON
HONKY TONKAWATER MW LUNIQUE LUNICKATICKA PRI

CK SPERMEANDER CULPAPUA ANA ANA HEBI HEBI EL
ECTROSHAKE PULLADAFRIES CALL M SWAHELIUMBRIL
LO MEGAGA UGANGA AMADOU HOLLAND STUPID & PSY
CHO HÂPILEPTISCHER AMSTERDÄMMERZUSTAND GET H
ÂPI HÂPI OWAH-WAH OWAH-WAH SPACE BASCENDANTE
MARE SUNDAIMON SHANTO-H2OEDIPE-REXSTRUT DELO
H2O LEONARD ACTION VOODOO-BASSVOCOLL BEASPUC
KERTRUX WARHOL-SHOT-ORANGE SUNSPLASH-ART PAR
AFLAMMING IN HOT WATER EL MARQUESSEA-EAGLE T
OREAUDIONYSHIVAKLIT BLIXA-KRIEGG-MAN EGGY PO
P MAN TAKE M TO THE LIBIDO ALLSDITHYRAMBIENC
EFALLOGRAMMARQUESUNSPLASHIROSHIMALE SPACE-H-
BOMBASSEPIKKA PRIKK UPRIVER CHINA SPLASH HEA
VY RIDE THE YELLOW RIVERYWHORE HOLLAND ORIGI
N OF FECES LET IT FLOWLAND VATTIMME ISEUT? T
HE FORMULA MARQUISE D'O-JAY CHRISHTARZAN JIM
I DESMOND TUTUPELOLO THE SUN KING SUNNY DE S
ADE BLUE NILE ROGER WATERS & FREDVARD MUNCHA
MAN PERSSHE-MAN BYSSHE-MALE SHELLEY-MAD ANUS
IMPULZIVE INSANITY PIA BECCHUS SLY TWOMBLY &
THE DOLL FAMILY STONE PAPUADOLF NEU WÖLFLI I
N THE LOOP-DE-LOOPPOSEIDON MARQUICHUTE D'O I
T D'O IT COME IN & OUT OF THE RAIN LET IT RA
IN LET IT RAIN SINASSAU IN HADESSAU BAGNO DE
DIEUNUCH Ô I CUMATRIX BYRNE RUBBER WATER UND
ER HOLLAND DIZZYGOTHIC GILLESPIE-FONGELÄPPSY
CHOTHYMIAGARA FALLSDE NERVALLING VALLING VAL
LING WILLIAM 'BEUYS' COLLINS THUMPERDINCKING
THE ESPATZ BASSANÉ IN MIELVILLES ÎLES MARQUI
SES DÉLIRREAL KÖRPER DISKIMOHEAVY SEAWATERFA
LLING FALLING FALLING SEX MAGICK WASH & GOGO
À GOGAUGUIN PSYCHO-POP IT LITHIONYSOS-KID MA
RQUÈSCARCHARLEMAGNE BOOTSTEELY DANUBBER BAND

P-P-PICASSOCEANICCAPUT NILI BABOON & JUNG IN
ONE OWAUTOTAL DIRKNESS & ALSO WATER & WATERW
AHNTHEMATIKKA PREEK ALLSDEBUSSY LÂMÈRZ CHIMÈ
RE FOLLE MARQUIS SASKATCHEWAN OWAH OWAAH OWA
AAH POLEO-PSYCHO-POP-RECUERDO DE HIROCHIMARQ
UESAN MARCO CO RICO CO CO RICO MARIO MARQUEZ
& ALSO WATER & WATERZATZUCKADÖLFLINATRIX YOU
SEXY THING SGT. RED HOT CHOCOLATE PEPPER'S A
POLLONELY CAPTAIN BEEFHEARTS CLUB BANDY WHOR
E-HOLES FETTSCHIZO RIVERZATZEE DE MARKIES VA
N WATER SHAMANIPULATING THE HOLDHANDS INTO F
UNKTIONSPSYCHOSEAS FALL-STARNOMADIONASSAUPZE
IT DOWN 2001-800 NEW FUNK MÊMMÊMMÊMORYMOOGGI
SSEA BULL OUT LOUD I NO MARQUÈSCORRIDADA BOM
BARDOT EJECCE HOMONOMANIAGARUDA FALLSD-TRIPA
TOMIC GODARTAUD HELIOGABALLACQUA'DAM & EVANI
TY 666 EL MARQUÈSCAPE PRINZHORNY HORN LIQUID
EVOLUTION/JOURNEY TO THE SUN FUNK NO MORE DR
UPZEIT DAWN EAU LOURDES EAU HIPPOPOTABILE WA
TER WATERSCHLANGEL FALLSOAPOCULIPSUCKSINC MA
HAVISHNUKU HIVAGINA DENTALATTATTOO UA-TUKI-E
UA-TUKI-E UA-TUKI-E UA-TUKI-E TO TIKI-E POPA
RARA TO TIKI-E O TE TUTANE TUTAWE O TE KUI-A
O TE TUEHIU-E OTE KUI-A TO'U TIKI-E LES ÎLES
MARE AGITATOO DUINNE DE DIABLE DE MÈRZEA-WAR
LORDRECKHARD MENTALLY SEASICKNASSAU ACQUANIM
ATION NATIONWIDE WALTER WALTER CARROLL RIVER
& RAINBOW SUNREIS IN ALTO MARE MARE RAMA RAM
A WE WANT SAMONA LISARTODYSSUCKSINC & LIPLIT
EL MARQUESANTANÀHMARQUIS D'OYE COMO VA BLACK
MAGIC WOMAN GG-FUNK-ALL-IN & THE MURDER JUNG
IES HOLLAND AFLOATING DOWN THE SEPIA RIVER O
NO RETURN MARE FORZAPP OPERATION HOT BOX HOL

ANDA HERAKLITORAL HOODYSSEY TRICKILOTON PUMP
KINITRUX RHIN-NO-TAMARANATHALATTANITA KERR S
AILING THROUGH THE SUN OUVERTURE TO THE SOFT
SEA EAU DÜRER UP STRÖMADEUS MOUSSEAMOSEAS AL
LES ÎLES MARE SPUMEGGIALLOWLAND VAI TO'E VAI
TO'E SIR PSYCHO SEXCITO-MOTÖRHEAD SCHIZOMBIS
EXUEEL TRANS-EN-PROVENCE LONG LONG SILVER DO
NG DONG SEMELE DRUMDEUTING THE ATOMPHALLUS L
AUT IT BE LAUT IT BE LSDE PROFUNGHIS UR-ANUS
MÚNDUSCHAMP LET IT WAH LET IT WAH WATERVALER
Y SOLANUS MUNDOSCOPE I LOO LOO! HOLI-HOLI-HO
LLAND HEY MENTALLUVIALLSDE MARKIES VAN WATER
UDUFREEN & URUKIFO SPACE BASSOLOMON KNOTTING
IN CHAPELSINNESSHOCKHAUS HOPP HOPP IRRAH IRR
AH HOOKAH-IKI PRICK TEKASTIK URLAHBRA MA'AMA
MARQUESAN KIOKA TOE HAKAOS MAHU! MAHU! URAIN
ING BISAN (BISAN BISAN) DUPPY DUPPY MUKE MUK
E DULLI-DULLI PLAY THE FLOOD HOLLAND WORDPLA
Y UP YOUR ASSHOLZER FIATMÜLTRAVESTA-ERAGGICH
ASSEPRICK HANGACOCKWORK ORANGEL FALLSUCK PEN
ISSUELAS MARQUESAS HURRICAN GILBERT & GEORGE
CLINTON BOOTSYBILLY GIBBONS & DUSTY HILLARYW
HORE FEAT. GG ALLADIN & THE WONDER JUNKIES A
FLOAT ON WÂWWÂWTÂW WÂWWÂWTÂW AAOO OYA SECOND
BASS PUMP PUMP WOEDOO POP ARTEMIS PENASIA EL
MARCASTABALAQUA AGONG-GONG TELAL TELAL DENIZ
DENIZ KOEA KOEA WATZUSKA'AVAITAI VAITAI OO N
IHAMA GALAPOSSE DALIPUSSY TEENAGE MUTANT MAR
QUIS AFLAME IN CORPUSSPRÉACHFLUSSEFER HA-ALM
ADILLOLO I LOLO EL MÄRREXQUISSEA-KRIEGERRUIS
SEAU WILLY-NILLY-DARE-DEVILLES ÎLES MARE MAR
E RAMA RAMARQUÈSPUMARQUESAN PUSSY BASSI WE C
AN FUNK PAPUARSEASSUCKAMONOSPERMY WORD-INSER

TION HADIS IS DA SYNDRUM KAOSIRIS-SUR MÈRRAT
IONILSDEEPWAH WE ARE DRIFTING HOLLAND ISLAND
AFLOAT IN SHAKESPERM AQUAFEAST SKETCH FOR DÉ
LUGE PURI PURI VA LOCO LOCO VALADIONASSAU PU
NFLATING THE ANADOLL OLLANDA A FLOD BÄDDIS A
BEBASS SPRING UP O WELLES ONE OW'OTO 'OTO EP
ILAPISCINEMARQUESAN SEISHORE THROUGH THE BOU
CAN GLASSPACE BASS BOOTSYBILLASWELLA FOAMMSB
ÖWÖTAA BÖWÖRÖTÄA BÖWÖWÖRÖTÖRÖTÄÄLÄÄTTÄÄ TO'I
TO'E TOROE PI'I PI'I PIRIONYSOS OOOOOMPHUNKI
N' THE DELTA BASSÀBYSSINASSIAMESOPOTAMTAM MU
ZZIKA 'ORO'LLAND HIROSHIMA MON MAORI SHEROÏS
CHWERES WASSERMONOA-NOA TNTV-EPILEPSY AQUABU
NGGA INENGGI CUNHINGA SERPIS TUNGO PHYTONG W
ORDWIDE FOAM IS WHERE THE HEART IS SPUMA'AMA
DEUS EX VACCHINA ALLES ÎLES MARCHÉSE MACHIAV
ELLINESQUELLES ÎLES SCEICCO BIANCO THE WHITE
FLOOD WAH WAH WAH WAH WAH O BAY PAS TOMBÉ AH
DEFALL DOWN SATANGAROACQUA SANTA ÎLINXTC-MAT
ICCLONIC FOR THE PHOBIC ALAMARQUESAN SHAMANN
WEIB SCHIZUCKING HOLANDA IN METEMPSYCHO-POPÈ
RA SOULTRA-VIOLITTER THE BALDER THE FREAK TH
E FRIGGER & THE FROGFRUIT ETU PEKE OU MEI MI
HI MEIHEM THE DIVIDED SELF & I JUDGE THE SCH
REBER RIVER ALLSDEMUTATIOOOH BABY LOVE ME DO
WATER WATERSHIT DOWN & OUTCOME THE FETISHITT
STOOL SPASSAGE BEUYSS SOLEAU ONE MAN CHAUVET
TSTUHL EL MARQUEST FOR POWWOWWOWQATSIBYLLABO
OTSIRENA NEGRASSUCKADELICKUNTIFFOLLY THE RIV
ER O GOLD JAM LEEAU BYARSE RESURRIVERRYTHM &
BASSTARDOUSCHAMEN WATERWRESTLING ON ZENNATRA
WAKE ISLANDAMAN I. THE WARRIOR THE TRILLMAZI
LLATRONICCLONIC MARQUESSPERMAFROTTERROR FRUI

T-IRIS-CULTRANCE IN THE BIKINI SCATOLLOGY LE
T IT RAINFLAMMOHAVEE METALSDE MARKIES VAN WA
TER EUNUCLEAR FUNGHIROTO-FLAMES RIDING THE S
HIROSHEALY-MALTUTIDES TO THE RAINFINIETZSCHE
VALL! STARLIAMENT-BUDDHARMADELIC HINDUSCHGEL
NUKU HIVA FINIETZSCHIC-FUNKADELIC LANCUMSHOT
ÔOOH DE LANCÛMAQUIS WALKYTONKY ÔH I ÔH I CUM
MEGAGA WUPADELIC KLANCÔMING AKINNEMAMA EAU D
E GIVE & CHÛTE DE MARKIES VAN WATER SPACE OD
DIPOUS REXTRAIT VITTELLONILY COZZMOZZARTS CL
UB MEDBONE HOPI HOPICASSO EYEWEAR FLUIDIPUSH
ING HOLLAND IN THE MORNING AFTER SUN WAH-WAH
WAH-WAH WALAM OLYMPICKAPRICK DANSEAS YOUR CH
ANCE TO SEE REDBONE CHILI PEPPER'S CRAZY HEA
RTS CAJUN CLUB CAKEWALK BAND NIKI HOKEY NIKI
HOKEY DANSE CALINDA I'M A MAN SKULLA-JAMBONE
(I CAN'T) HANDLE IT EL MARQUE.S.P.-FUNK & FE
LLINI AMARQUIS FRENZISCUS BACHBONE THE BIG O
WAUTAUREAU-ASSISSI FIRE IN THE FACE EAU'GALL
EAUGALLAH EAUGALALA EAU-GLA'LA EAUGALALLAH E
AUGLALAS MARQUESAS TOURQUELLENNON-STOP DIRTY
(MIND) GAMES D.S.M.R.-III 1999 DELIRIOUS FRE
E SOMETHING IN THE WATERMARQUIZ SHOW TIME TAF
KAPPMATAPPADELIC AQUAPOOLLEAU 11 CAVE MAGICK
A PRICHLEAU NAMIBIAGIRAFALLSUCK DADDY PEPPER
'S VITALLOONEE ARS CLUB MUDDY RIVERS ARNOA-N
OACQUALIAS DE MARKIES VAN WATER WAN OWAU ONE
OWAH IN DUBBISSEA THE SEAROUNDUSTRAUSSUCKA
PIGLOO HALLMARKIES RECORDS HYPERSILLA FRIGHT
MY FIRE & BRAINDROPS KEEP FALLING NASSICKNES
SAUKADOGG EPILIPOGRAMMARQUESSILENCE DELA MÈR
ZOTZ MIELVILLES LES ÎLES MONDOUCHES MAGICOLL
INS MARATHALATTABOOTSIDDHARTHALATTABOOTSIDDH

ARTHA! YOUYOUNUCLAIRRATIONILE MARQUIS DALI L
AGUNA THE PARIS AFTER MWATCH RESTORING SHAVE
CHIRATTLE & ROLL OVER SPACIFIC ATOLLAND SPAC
IFICK & FRUIT LOLO & LORANGE I LOLO! I LOLO!
VIRTUAL ORANGE FREE STYLE MARQUIS DE MENDOZA
DANCE PARTI EL MARANATHALATTABOOTZILLÀ-BASSP
ACIFIC EXPLAUSSION UNDERWATER NUCLARITY 3:45
-46 BIKINI ATOLLAND THE BLINDONESIAMESE TWIN
SPEAKABOMBOOMERANG UTANIC DON'T PANICKABOMBO
OTSHIROSHI-MALE MARQUIS PALEO-PSYCHO-POPPENH
EIMATTERHORNY HORNAMENTAL HADEZZEASY GILLESP
IE-FONK-N IN FOURRIREVERSE TELLER MORE TELLE
R MORE TIKINO-WOKKABOUT IN THE TIKINNING THE
RE WAS NOT WAS THERE THE WORD ATOLL ATOLL TI
KITANIC DON'T PANIC! RAPPOCALYPSODOM & GOMORR
APPOCALYPSE NOWWOWOW MONO TIKINOA-TIKINOA ET
HERMONUCLEARATHUSTRAUSS ZEROTATING IN RAPPAG
UN WAR NARRORATAURIO HÂPI HÂPI HÂPILEPSUCKHO
LE EAU JAUNE EL MARQUESCLAVE ATOMISEURQUELLE
BOMBUTTORANGE UTRISTAN & GLISSARDEÈSSO WALAM
ADEUS OLUMOZART ACQUACOCKLOCKLOCK LE MAKIMAK
I DE SADELINQUOMPEDANCE CUBISMUZIK JASS THRO
UGH THE LACANNABISMARQUESAN MARCOLOURADIO SH
OWWOWWOW TAKE ONE THROUGH THE BRIDGE WATER W
ATER THE COMMODITY... THE TV FOUNTAIN RUNNIN
G AMUCK OMA-A OMA-A! OH-YEH-HAW OH-YEH HAW H
AW ONE REVOLTA RIVER WARRTARR WARRTARR H2OVA
LLOGRAMMÈR FOLLAND ONOMATOPAESI BASSITAR SOL
O ST. BRIGID'S DAY TRIPPITT TRIPPITT LEWIS C
ERROL FLYNNIGER WHAKAPHONE SINFRAGMENTAL WAT
ERREVERYWHEREALL-STARVA WAITAI WAITAI RIVERR
UNWAY ROTELLABÜTTZEELANDICAOS ODIONYSOSVLOED
AEROS SPACE BASSEAS FROM THE DEPTH OF THE WO

RLD HÂPI HÂPI HOPI HOPI OTOROTATING EPILEPSY
CHO FLUXAFLEX HOLLAND GLORYHALLASTOOPID 20TH
CENTURY DRUMMING. EL MARKISSOUSA ACQUAPELLAGO
ASISTINA WATER THE REVIVAL TOWER TOWER EVERY
WHERE THE KLITTELLATOUR DEMOLITOUR PULLABULL
BULLFLOOD THE DUK-DUK MISTEROSION THE EIFFEL
LINILE TOWA TOWA OTTO È MEZZOPOTAMOUSSOUNDFR
EE FREE BABYLONELY ACQUA PUTTOBILLABIEL MARD
UK TO WATER IS EXCELLENT! DONATELLO GUAGUAGU
ADAGNILE DE MARKIES VAN WATERMARQUESANTA MAR
IA MADDALENA DEI PAZZI FLORANGE NASSOUL MW 1
333 1999 H2001 ODISSEA NELLO SPAZIO WE ARE T
IKI WE A'RE A'RE A'RE TIKI TIKI EVERMOREROSM
UZIK WASSIR NOT WASSIR HOLEARY TRANCE-MAKING
IN THE HIMALAYAS MARQUESAS LE MARQUIS DE BAP
TISMUZIKA PREACH-A-BOO-BOO EL MARQUESAN WARF
AIRIVERY THALES TATTOO WHITT TATTOO WHOO HIB
OOOTZIBBELLACQUATTOO WHITT ACQUATTOO WHOO SL
OW BUTT TO CHINA HOLANDA MW THE SILK ROUTINE
GAGATIAN GAËTANIC DON'T PANICCAPUT NYLON HYST
ERIA HISTORIA UNDER THE SILKWOODSTOCKING SUL
KSCREEMTESTING CUNNILINGERIATIROLLANDAISY DA
ZE MEGATIAN GAËTANTRA EASY GILLESPIEK EXPERI
ENCE POHAI POPOHAI POPOPOHAI SEA YOU AROUNDA
BOOTSYBILLÂ-BASSIN' IN SITUUTSY THIELEMANS A
FLOAT FLOAT ON WET EARTH SOFT MORNING & BUSH
FIRE DREAMSONG AQUARIUS LIBRA LEO CANCER RAL
PH PAUL LARRY BLACKMON SAVONAFARA WORD UP CU
MAE CAMEO FEAT. MILES DAVIS FLOAT FLOAT ON M
AITRESTAN & ISCLAVOLDE FLOATING ON WÂWTÂW WÂ
WTÂW FLOWING OVER WÂWTÂW WÂWTÂW RAÏ MEA RIVE
R RAIN-DREAMING TO WALLABIES WALLABIES EVERY
WHERE LET IT RAÏ LET IT RAÏ THERE'S THE RUBB

ERBAND MAN AFLOAT FLOAT ON HUANG HO HUANG HO
LLAND WE ARE GETTING MUDDY WATERS WEE-WEE R.
MUTT SUNK IN FUNK I GOTCHA! I GOCCIA! YELLOW
MAGIC ORCHESTRA/SLIPPING INTO MADNESS IS FOR
THE SAKE OF COMPARISON MW RAINTRODUCING VOIC
ES FROM THE LAND OF THE EAGLES IGILDUNG TORU
KTUG DOLGAI TANGDIM IISKIS TIING IKA CHES BU
LUNGUUM MW MYSOUL & I LICKAWOMAN AY-CAZZAT-O
H KING GEORGE AQUA OOGA BOOGA P-FUNKALLSDE M
ARKIES VAN WATERFALLSEASTARS SUFINATRA-WASSE
RMUSIK FLOWING OUTCOMES ORANGAMANTRAVOLTA RI
VERMERZ RUBBER & WAX & DRUGS & ROCKNROLLANDA
ISSEASSICKAPRICKAWA KAWA LIMAORIDE LIMAORIDE
HOLD ON POWWOWWAU FLASHLAV WASHLIFE FLOODDAN
CING EAGLE PLUME BIRD DANCE HULAQUA AITUKI D
RUM DANCE BIRD DANCE HULA HOKO WAR DANCE MEK
E WESI SPEAR DANCE FRIGAT BIRD DANCE DANCE D
ANCE FLESHLOVE NINJAHWEH-WEH WEH-WEH ATEATEA
PETROUCHKAMARGUESS WHOO-WHOO! ORANJA SIRUPSI
DE DOWN & OUT THE BETTER LEMONDE MARKIES VAN
WATER FROM ORANGE WILLENDORF TO YELLOW BAUBOHAI BO
HAI SEA YOU IN ONE OWAH WAN OWAY BEFOAH OWAH
AURA M IS FOR VENUSUELA WHERE THE ORANGES CA
ME FROM ONE MANDARHIN DREAM WE ARE THE KUMSQ
UAT ZAPPAPUA NEU GUINEANDERING PEACHES EN RE
GALIA JOHN LEMON WATCHING THE WHALES GO ROUN
D & ROUND THE YELLOW RIVERY CONFUCIUS MYSELF
& AÏGEAU AÏGEAU AÏGEAU GILLGILL DELUCY IN TH
E SKY W/DAIMON STARSHOOTING INTO THE HIMMEL
LAYERS PLI-SELON-PLI-FUNK TEAR THE ROOF OF T
HE SUCKER OH GEORGEOMATER CLINTON TAKE IT TO
THE SLY & THE FAMILY YELLOWSTONE FIRES LIQUI
D ZENSHINE WOLFGANGES AQUAMADEUS REX MACHINA

CHINA UNDER WATERYWHERE CHINASSORROW WEEPING
WILD RAINTRODUCING THOTHELONIOUS MONK NEVILL
E YELLOW MOON EL MARQUESAN MARCO APOLLO 11 T
HROUGH THE LAGOON GLASS MW HOLANDA LEKKING F
OR CLUES SOME BOYS KOUSKOUS & DON'T TALLIT AF
LOAT FLOAT ON LES ÎLES PAYS BASS YELL O YELL
O THE RAMAYAWA CHANT VODA VODA WODDER WODDER
AFLOAT ON LUPUS MOONDUSCH BIZON IN MAANSCHEI
N GEORGE KLINTONYMUS BOSCHAMAANJOURNEY TO UR
NHEMLAND YUYURHINE GAGARHINONASSEAS FRANZEAS
BACCON HOLYHEAD VI PIER POOLEAU PISSOULLONEL
Y HEARTS CLUB WIMP WONDERWORK IN PROGRESSEAS
SUCKAMABOOTSIAMAGARA FALLSDEFILEOPARD EL MAR
CIELLEAU MAESTROHEIMANNY FANNYFACE SHOPPENHE
IMATTERIALLSDE MARKIES VAN WATERRAIN RAIN RA
IN ANITTITTANIC ICEBERG LANADOLCE TREVIANITA
EKBERG HONOLUDENS RAIN RAIN RAINDEER MARQUIS
VON STROHEIM DISIS DADA DRUMBAUDELAIREVERISE
NIETZEBRASS BANDAMAN PROPHAECES AFLOAT ON ON
E OWOWWOWWOW FUNK SHUI BASS FLOWWOWWOW EL MA
RQUESAN TIKIKABOOTSY AFLOATTACKAOWWOWWOW WAN
OWAH BEAFOA OWAH OWAU GURUSHIMMÈR NEGRASSOAK
AOS MONEYTORATOR HIEROSHIMONIMA MOONAMORT IN
THE BIKINILE ATOLLAKE FRIGTAURHEA DAWASHADA'
WORLD ATOLLATOYA JACKSONIAN EPIDOLLOOP HAÏTI
ERSATZUCK AQUANIMALSDEFUNCT AQUANIMALSDE MAR
KIES VAN WATER WATER IN BIKINIAGARATOLL ATOL
L ATOLLAND BONEY MAHOLE FULLINILE-WAH-WAH EL
LA NAVEN FAFAFAFAFA DUSCHAMONEY MONEY AFLEAU
ON DISCOPATHEK NOW THE APSUMATRA ÁRAN-UTAN D
EFILING THE REFILL GIOTTO È MEZZOO EIFFALCON
TOWER TOWER EVERYWHORUS VULTURE CULTURE CLUB
M.A.D. MW DEATH-VIE-LEAU CATARACTWALK ON THE

WILD SIDE UPSIDE DOWN MAE FUNKEY WEST MIAMEE
MYSELFADELPHEE & IDONATELLO THE ENDARCTICAOS
STAND & DELIFFEY THE WORD ADAM & THE ANTARPT
IKIKABULLAPOOL ECHOGUINEANDERTHALES ONE OWAU
TOWER TOWER INFERNOAH-NOAH LAST MARQUESEAS L
OST MARQUESEAS RIFFERREGENBAUBOOTSYBILLÀ-BAS
SPACE BOSCH MAE 2 WEST 2 EASTHMAHOLLAND ALLS
DEFILÉOPARD MOTÖRHEAD 666 BBBOOTSYBILLASWELL
ES ÎLES THIN LIZZIBLES DEFILLIFFUNKADELHIC K
IMKOM CLARKESTRAUSS REHEARSAL GRISGRIS IS TH
E WORD GRAND PSYCHO POPO BENINJÀ-VAU-D'OU-L'
EAU SINGAZONGBETO ORANGAJINASSAU SINGAZANGBE
TO PAPUA NEW EGUNGUNEA JUJUPELOLO TUTUPELEAU
LEAU SUCK THE MIGHTY RIVER DADDY LONGLEGBA D
ER MARQUIS FON O MAMI MAMI WATAWATA MAMI WAT
A SCHIZOFRENIC? EL MARQUESAN MARCOTONOU MARQ
UESSAPATHALATTA MW MYSOUL & IQUEU HOME SCHWI
TTERS HOME HOLLAND DADAAAGBO HOUNONHUNA PPP-
THONICCLONIC DADDY ABEBA SPUSSENCORE & VISAS
SOON WASH & GOD = DEADDEEE COOLABULLAS MARQU
ESAS ÈSPAGGIOTTO È MEZZODÔME FIN LIZARTAUD W
ARTAR WARTARTAUDDISAY WAH-WAH WAH-WAH THIS I
S THE ENTONIN POP-ARTHOTH ELECTRIC EGGYPSYBI
LLÀ-BASSPACE BULLACQUA FOUTOURE KUNDADA FUNK
FACTORY WARHOLLAND FUTURE SHOCK HERBIE HANCO
CKABOOTSYBILLABOOTTO È MEZZOTTO È MEZZO AFLO
W OUT BLOW UPUPA PUPA PUPAPUA NEU GUINEA WHI
TE MANTRA BLACK SABBATHENS ÈRAKLITWALKASELZH
EIMAT GELTACHTUNG BABY COOL BONEY MARQUIS ST
ONEY WATER DIZZEASE DADA ENTONIN OURTHOTH ÄG
GYPSUCK ALPHADELPHEE BETTWIENERHEINFLUSSILES
ÎLES MARKISSES LET IT BISON LET IT BISON (BI
SON BISON) TAUROBULLASWELLS HOLE ORANGE DRIN

K M DRINK M YOYO EL RHINO HOME SCHWITTELSBEC
K HOME HOLLAND DADA FUNK SIR RHINOSE ROCK HO
ME BABYLONDON MARQUEES IN PARADISOTTO IN SUM
OKUM THE FUNKENSTEIN BRIDESHEAD REVISITED WA
UGH WAUGH WAUGH MW/THE BIG BLEULER IN R. MU
TTY WATERS PRINCE CHARMADILLO ADOLF WÖLFLUPU
SSY UP YOUR ASSID TRYPTICKPRICKABOSCH-O-MATI
C BAEZY BASSY AFLOW FLOW ON SPEAKING IN TONG
A ISLANDTONGA ISLANDTONGUES MÈRWÎF/MÈRWÎP CU
NNYLONGUMMA-GUMMA IDYLLICKA-PRICKABAUBOQUEEN
BEAMIXA CITADELLA DONNATELLO MEALLABOUT SNAP
PORAZZMATAZZ DOGGY DOGGEYE THE RETURN OF THE
MADMAN IF 6 WERE 1969 HILTON JOHN MADMAN ACR
OSS THE WATER EN VOGUE LE NAVIRE JOHNNYLON T
HE POLYETHYLENE SEA & THE ATLANTIS OCEAN OLÉ
OLA NAVEVA LAS VEGAS BLITZ'ALL ZEPPELIN' EDW
ARDS & RODGERS ON ASTAIRWAY TO HEAVEN CHOC T
O CHOC REBELS WE ARNOA-NOA MARCHI DELL'ACQUA
RNOAH-NOAH 66 YO EL RHINOSEPIKKAPRICK EL MAR
QUÈSSEA EAU' STARMANIAGARA FALLSDIVINE HORSE
MANIAGARA FALLSDIVINE LIZARDO'LOSY THE GONE-
BETWEEN THE WINDS PAPUA NEU KINO SNAP DOGGIT
TY DAMNATION FLUTT ON MR. MUTTERRA INFERNO O
NE OWAU TOWA-TOWA INFERNOA-NOÁRAN UTANTRACKI
N' EUROPAPUA NEW GIMMEABEATLE HIGHWAY TO HEL
LENNONURWATERRÁRAINN APSUBLIMESTONE AGE TO S
PACE BEUYS AFOAT FLOAT ON NUN-STOP ECLECTRIC
KY URWAH-WAH JIOTTO HENDRIXAFT ARCHETYPEE-FU
NK SHUIMALE DISTARTION ALLSDÉFILINGERIONÄXOS
TARAN ISLES ÎLES BOSCHOMANIA FALLSDE ECCE HO
MO RUBENS FELLINI ATOLL BOOTSILLY-PUTTY SPUS
SY BOSSOM TAUROBULLASWELLS HOLE ORANGE DRINK
M DRINK M LASWE'LL SEE THE SHORES ALEXIANDER

IN WONDERLAND PAPUA NEW SANGUINEA MI WADI WA
DI ORANGE MW MERRICK MERRICK HOLD ON TIDE CH
INÁRAINFALLSDEFUNKT THE WURMPOOLABOLLOXTÁRAN
ISLES ÎLES MARQUISEAS THE END-ARPTIKI GEWEIL
ANDAMAN EPILEPSY BULLESPECIES BASSEASSUNNY R
OCK HOME YOURQUELLYNNOTT CROLL-CALLDEFILLOOP
FULLINILE-WATER FULLIRHIN-WATER MOSKWAQUALLS
DEFILLIFFUNKAOS MARQUESAN BASS STRING AQUART
IDES TO IGLORY IN WAXSALTSEAS DEOUCHES RHINO
AH ROTARCHESTRAUSSOUNDTRAQUELLE MARQUIS H2OO
D'OO H2OOOD'OOO SCHI2OOO SHIERONYMOUS BOSCHI
ZOFRENIAGARA FALLSDEFILONELY HEARTS CLUB MAD
DAGASCARMAWASH ELECTREAT GYPSUCK HEILI SELAS
SIBYLLABOOTSILLASSEA REVOLGAGA MOSKWAMAZON W
OLGANGA MARANATHALATTATTOTALLOST SUPPER EXPL
ISSION FISSION FUNK & FUSION FOLLY HOPI HOPI
LUPUSSY LUPUSSY FLOWWOWWOWWOW OUTTERREURQUEL
LE MARQUIS YOUNÄKINEITSIBYLLÀ-BUS FELLINIHEI
LWATERSATZUCK HEIDI HIBOOTZILLASSIE ABBADIDA
S ABEBA COOLLANDANDAMAN O' ÁRANNINJAQUA ABEB
BASSOLLOCOOLLAND FARRELLAWAY SOOO CLOSE HOLLA
ND UNDER THE BOARDWALK DOWN BY LOW LOWDOWN B
Y THE SEA WETLANTEASER & THE TILLERCATFISH M
UDDBONE & THE MARQUÈSSHAMOUTI ORANGES STARFL
UX & PHALLOI JAFFA JAFFA MORPHINISH POP-ARTA
UD BLITZALL HAPPUNNIN' UNTIL THE FLOOD HOLL
AND MUTTFISH & FLUSSLIFT AFLOW FLOW ON WORDM
USICK BIKININO ROTATOLL-CALLSDELIFFILLAY-OUT
LOUDDISSAY WAH-WAH WAH-WAH OUTFLUSSINGING IN
THE RAIN RAIN LET IT RAIN PPP-FONQUE VIVA ME
XICO PUERTO ANGEL FALLSDEMONSTER TIAMATTMÁRA
NN STARMIX HAÏTIAMATER TAHITIAMATER DOLOROSA
FLOATING ON WÂWTÂW WÂWTÂW FLOWING OVER WÂWTÂ

W WÂWTÂW MARQUÈSATYRICONTRASH WARHOLLAND LET THERE BE NEON LET THERE BE NONE MINOA-NOA F. W. MURNAUMAN HUIT-CLONE MINOTORTURE THE RHIN OSFERATUPELO SUCK THE MIGHTY RIVER CLOSSOS T O THE BONE AQUACOPALYPSE NAUMAN RAW WARHOLLA ND EAT WAR BUTT TO BUTT RAW MATERIAL MMMMM W WWWW MEAN CLOWN WELCOME TO THE PLISSURE DÔME HOLLANDER THE HAPPY HOEKER VAN HOLLANDER THE HAPPY HOOKAH HOOKAH SGT. POP-ARTAUDIONASSAUS MURDER MAGIC & THE WEATHERALLSDJESUS VINYL H OUR 1933⅓ 1945 1978 1984 GEORGE WORRWELLAS M ARQUESAS WASHINGTON CD ISLES AQUANIMAL PHARM ACY APOCATHÈQUE NOW BOWWOWWOW I KNOWWOWWOW A TOLL FASTER OPUSSYCAT BIKILLKILLINI ATOLLAND CEREAL KILLER'S/SERIAL KELLOGG'S ALL CHOC NU T FEAST START 'N STRIKE! FLAKES! FLAKES! FLA KES! YO EL RHINOSEY RHINOWITALL THE FREAKATH ARSEASTAR EL MARQUESSKULLÀ-BASSPACE BOSCHLIN E-UP CHIRONYMUS BOOTSCHYSKULLINS MARQUESSOUN D-MONSTERRA INFURMAGIK BULLRAUM BLITZALL PUNN ILINGUSHIN' FORTH-FROTHE MARQUIS GELTACHTUNG BABACOOL DOWN UPRIVER SIDE ONE OWAH WAN OWAU TOTEMPERALLSDEFILING BY PIER PAËLAKE PASALON ELY FRANCOPHONIES METRO BOULOT DILDO MW OWOW WOWWOWWOMAN O' ÁRANCIA NÄXOS ORANGE ISLAND T O YELLOW RIVER TIEFIAGGIOTTO È MEZZOGYN GEEL LABIAGARA FALLSDE MARKIES VAN WETTERRES WETT ERRES SKULLATAURQUELLABONE SEASTAR & FEATHER MOREROSMOUSSEA WOOSSEA MEET THE BLUE SEA PAC IFIC RIMBAUDIONYS.O.S. SLAVE OUR SPEECH MW P PPARTNER IN RHYME RYTHM & RHYME RYTHM & RHYM E DEFONQUELLECTRICKY RYTHMSTYXADELPHIC UNDER WORLD DRUM & BASSDRUMBAUDZILLÀ-BASS & DRUMBA

UDEEE-LITEATEA CRYPTITCHY RAZORRYTHMSPERMFLU
X PALAEO PSYCHO PEEPSHOWERGELACHTONGUESSWAH-
WAH AFLOAT ON WAH-WAH WAH-WAH EL MARQUESAN T
IKIKABULLÀBASSABAUDZILLASSEASSUCKAMADEUS AMA
DEUS ROCK M AMADEUS MOUZZARTAUDDER MARQUIS V
ONOTHEKOPALYPSINCUT! WATT WATT EVERYWHERAKLI
TT KLITT PLANET EARTHERAKLITTAURRUSHING WATE
R BOMPHALLOOZZEA MOOZBORN BOPPAGUN ABYSSPACE
BOSCH IN KRIMBAUDELÁRAN ISLANDAMANDADA'DAM &
THE END PRINCE CHARLES BAUDELIER & THE BIG C
ITY BEAT BAND DOUROPAPUA NEUROPAPUA NEU GUIN
EANDERTOOLABULLATOUR ABOULIEFFILAY OUT WOTTO
WOTTO È MEZZO POTAMIAGÁRAN ISLANTRA LIMESTON
E DREAMTIDES AP AP APSUBLIMESTONE H TO SPACE
BÁS IN ÁRAINN WACO JACO SPACE TAURUS ONDA FE
NDER DJASSI BASS TO THE KNASSAUS TAUROLEUM M
MYSILLY & I ZIMBRA! PSYCHO KILLER ON THE LUC
Y HOLLAND GOUDADA RIVIRGOGO WEST JUNGAMAN VI
BRATORATIONILE FULLINILE-QUELLENNOUNSTOP GE
ORGEOMATERRACLINTON SKULLASTONE-H-BOMPHALLUC
BALLAMOUR WATERRAINUNDATA-BOSCH TIKIKABOOT
IKIEFERROTO-FLAMMENZEE DUNG HO DUNG AENGUSSI
LLINGUS MARANATHALATTATTOTEMPEROARSCHACHER M
ASCHOCOLATATTOO NOSEAUGOGOLLAND PACIFICKY DÉ
FILEANDROSSUCK SODOMINASSOW NOWWOWWOW! TAFKA
PPP/PALEO PSYCHO POPOV/PIPIPIPOV I CLONES CH
EEC TO CHEEC GINGER È FRED FULLYNILE ROGER W
ATERS SLAVE VIEW WORLD SLAVA THE WATER WATER
RIBLE SNOWCLONE SLAVASLAV NIJINSKIEFER WARTA
NZEAS PALAEO PACIFIC POPPADELPHIC HALLUDANCE
S H2OMO LUDANSELM HAÏTIKIEFER MAMI MAMI WATA
WATA SCHLAMMER DUNK HO DUNK HOLLAND EL MARRI
OOLLAND MERZBOWWOWWOW ETHERMONUCLEAR SCHWEAT

TERSRAUMBRAILLEAU BRAILLEAU WORLDWARHOLE 3 O
ZZEA OZZONNY SIDE UPSIDE DOWN U-TURNINJAWS M
ARQÈSP-FONQUE SERA SERA BIESBOSCHBABIES ORA
NGE CARWASHAMANTRASHAMALE BONEY MWAHWAH DAD
DIDAS ABEBA COOL DOWN UNDER MEET THE BLUE NI
LE PSYCHO CYCLAW PSYCLOWN GRIFFELLINIHILES Î
LES BIKINIHILLISYBILLES FREI FUNK SHUI DOO-B
OPPENHEIMAT MW THE PACIVILISATION NATION DRU
MADUSCHTIDES UNDER THE SHOWER O POWER PACIFI
SSISSIPPI-FANGAPPP-FUNGHIROSHIERONYMOUSSARTY
BOSCHNILES AHEAD PRINCE CHARLIE CHAPLIN & TH
E CITY LIGHTS BEAT BAND DUN' FAKE DA FUNK DA
FT PUKE DE MARKIES VAN WATER STONEFREEFLOWLA
NDIN' THE S/FLYING DUTCHMANIACCOUCHEUR FREDD
IDAS ABEBACCHOIR WATERFALLSDITHYRAMBEBYSS AL
LSDITHYRIMBAUDZILLA BASSPACE ABYSS JAUNEANDE
R MARQUIS ÁRANGEL FALLSUCK ERRORANGEL VENUSS
AUELA NAVÉ MARIAGARA VALLSDEFILLOOPINGDOLOO
PPENHEIMATTERHORNYHORNAMENTAL MACEOPOTAMIATM
ÜLTRA WAVE PUPA NEW GUINNESSEXTRA STOUTCUMSH
OOTING OUTSCUM THE FRIGGEESE & THE GLITTERIN
G PRISSIES & THE HOODOOVERING LIZZARTOADDIES
DR. AC/DCIMABUEEEKKEEE HOMOHEAVY METAL WATER
COLOURADOURSUCKAOS ȘUNDER SEA-LEVELLATION RÈ
VELLOCEAN RAIN LET IT RAIN RIVERDANCEPHALLOG
RAMMARQUESAN TIKIKABULLFLITEEE-LITEATEA ESPE
RMWAH! MAGICAMY TRANSSEXUALLUX GOODMURNAU GO
ODMURNAU MARQUESSOAPSUMOHAVEPILEPSEASTARSHEI
NFLUSSTARSHINE APIS APISCINEMARQUISHTARATOSS
OFFOIDAFFONQUELLADYLOOP HAIR TO GO BRIAN GEI
SHAH WILLY BURRO IRACHARD COHENDRIXON ISLAMB
ORN WILSON IN ALL-IN GUNSBURGER TYPEE-FONKAD
OOFONCT JAGGERWOCKY SELLEBRATE THE BULLET MW

SKA-WRITING MARQUESSELECTERRA FIRMAGICKA PRICKABULLETTRIEP ALLSD-TRIPTICHA PRICKABOOGO BOOGA WONDERLAND TURF WIND & FIRE FLOATHING OUTCUM PALAEO PSYCHO POOPRAH WET FRIED ISCREAM FLOATH FLOATH ON H-BOMB THE BASSPASSAGE THROUGH LEOPARDSKIN & STARFISSENSCHUBBISSEAS ZEE STHERMAL URQUELLADYLOVE LOVE WIDO ADAMBALLAH BURLESCONICCLONIC PRIVATALIA FLOATING ON WÂW TÂW WÂWTÂW FLOWING OEVER WÂWTÂW WÂWTÂW WIDER WIDER MARQUIS VON OOOH ABEBY LOVE LOVE WIDOU RQUELLADY DIONOZZLES WATERGAMES & MATERWARSE MW THE SEASTARWAR RIORSONNY LASWELLES ÎLES MARQUISES NEUROPACIFIC CHAOSCARCRASH WIENERHE INFLUSS ONE NATION UNDER THE SEA CAMEO LUX MACEO FOX WATERWORD UPRIVER AFLOARIDADA MIAMI MYSELFABUTTER & I FUDGE THE JUNK FOR A WETTER WORLD FUNK SHUI LU FUKI FUKI QUILTY! QUILTY! AMORPHINISH EGO WASH PROGRAMMÈR FOLLAMOUR ONDA SELLERS THE PUNK PANTHER HOSEA HOSEA KU BRICKABRACKINO ATOLLAMOUR HIROSHIMAŁAYA MOON AMORT AVENUSSAU DIRKRETA GARBOGARDE MARKISSI MMEE WESTHERMAL NUCLEATIVE SWEATTACKISSEAS HALLOOSER BABY BACCO ORANGEL FALLSUELAS MARQUESAS RENAISSANCENTRAL MAGIC TYPEE-FONKIN' INTO THE MELVILLE FRACTURE ZONE PATHA-PATHA GO TCHAMAN U M & THE BABY BACCO MÙNDOZAUBERFLIESSING OUTSCUM THE FROGGIES DIKÉYRAMBULLEAULANDAMAN ARISTOFINISH THISIS THE ENTARPTIKIKIK ATOMBOMBSCARE EL MARKIESKIMOTÖRHEADFUCK BECK TO MY ROOTTO È MEZZO POPOVITAMIAGARA FALLSDE FILLITTER NORTH SEASY RIDER MARQUIS VON OOOH OODOO LOA POUR LOA LYNCH LIZARD THE BIG BLUE VELVET UNDERGROUND FUNK RAILROAD MOVILÉ MENN

IS HOPPERRIER C'EST P-FOULLAMOUR ALLTAR & V
ATER VATER BARENT'S SEAQUATEATEATEATEATEATEA
MAHOOLY SPILLIT AMENTAL DISORDER MARQUIS VON
EAU EJACKSUNNY SIZE UPSIDE ONE OWAH-WAH EJAC
KSONIAN EPILIPSINCHRONIETZSCHIZOÏDIPAUSE SPE
RRUNG WATER WATER IN COMARQUESAN SLEEPILEPSN
OOZE THE DEVILLAID DOWN BY LAW MEFISTOFALLIC
KAPRICK IN THE FAUST INSTITUTE SNAP DOGGY DO
GGOETHE MARQUIS FIATMÜLTRANSFORMATION NATION
GIOTTO È MAZEOPLOTAMINNEOTOWAR TOWAR EVERYWH
ORREURQUELLE DIABLYSSKREEP THE DEVILLIFELESS
ONDABOTTÔME OFFADA OCEAN SNOWCLONELY SLAVAGE
IN THE ICYBERIAGÁRAN ISLES GEOMARKIESKIMOHEA
LY METALLSDELIFFFYNQUE TAL REFILING BY PISSO
UL SADAM & GOMORROW PALEO PSYCHO POPPENHEIMA
TTERHORNY HORNAMENTALLSDEFILIGRINDER WAHNSIN
NASSAU PLAY BONEY MW AFLOAT FLOAT ON GOTCHA!
ONE OWAH EAU SOLEILANDAIMONAMORT VAUDOUCHAMP
HIBISMAH BISMAH BISMAH EAURACLES ÎLES EAUXYL
EAUFOAMMASSINASSAU MAGIULIETTA MACHINANA HEL
LASTRADAMOUSSEASTHERMALLLSD/IO CREDO IN TATT
OO BACCHUS TO FUTURE CHOC HELLENNON-STOP ALL
SDEMENTED IN EDENMARQUESAN BELLIPOOLASKULLAN
D FUTURE SHOCKWAVES OVERLAPPING WAVES OVERLA
PPLANDING WAVES OVER LAPPLAND ACROSSEAFLUXUS
BADEDADDIS DOUCHAMPS ÉLIZARTS ABEBABBLING OV
ER DADADDIS ABEBABELLALPHA-OMEGAGARHIN UPRIV
ERBETTER SHAPE-UPRIVERBETTER LEMONDE MARKIES
VAN WATER IN AGONE W/THE WIND THAÏTIOPIAN M
ARKIESKULLETTONICCLONIKE ÉLUCY IN THE SKY W/
DAIMONAMORT MARATHONICCLONICDADDIS LONGLEX A
BEBA LOVE MUDDY TIGER TIGER FEET LINE RICHAR
D LONGLEGS SLEEPING MARKIES THROWING WATER W

ATERLINE WESTWATER DADIDAS BADEDAS ÁRAN ISLA
NDAMAN EPILUCY IN THE SKYLITE ONE OWAH-WAH O
WAH-WAH PALEONARDO POP DADA VINCINEMARQUESAN
SKY-WRITWALLSDÉFILLÉONARDÖPPELGANGEL FALLSDE
MARKIES VAN WATERMARQUESANDOZAUBERSPACE BOSC
HMAN RHINOAH-NOAH HIPPOTEMKIN SURGEISENSTONE
AGEOMATERIALLSDEFUNK SHUIBERT VAUDUNG HO DUN
G HOLANDA POWERFRAU ON THE ESPAYPHONE IN DRE
CK APOTHEK NOWWOWWOW VENUS IN VIRTUOSODOMY M
YSEAL & ISOULOCEAN DEEPSEALLA MARQUISEA BABY
LOVE-IN FLUTURE SPASTIME PARADISOTTO IN SUMO
TTO È MEZZOLEAU CULLEO-CYCLO-CLOCK DEFIELLOV
E KHARMAVALL-STAR POOLOONASSAU IMPOLYNESIAME
SE POLONÄXEAS PUMP PUMPOLYNESIAMESOPOTIAMIAM
IAGARABISMAH BISMAH BISMAH HEATHIOPIÀRAINN I
SLANDFALLSD-TRIPHOPI HOPI DANCE FISTIFALLUCY
SKULLETTONES IN THE KLAUSSOTTERY DIES LILLAS
MARQUESEAS ALLSDEFILLING BY NARWEGIANT TORAT
ORTLES GALAPOOLLOOPIN' THE LEAUPSIDE DOWN BY-
BY THE SEA AFLOW ON À-VAU-L'EAU ON POP-FLUSS
ILES ÎLES ÎLES MARCHÉSEA & SUN RÂDIONAUSEA R
ED HOT CHOCOLATE C'EST POU-FONQUELLEXODAFTWO
RK DADA FUNK VON DEN STEINEN THE JELLY RIVER
& THE CHILI PEPPER'S FLOODSUGARSEXMAGIK AQUA
LITEEE THE HOLLY RIVER & THE PRICKALILLY PEP
PERRIER C'EST POURWATERRORGASMACKMATTACK SHE
IKATAKATARACT UPRIVER AFLOW FLOW ON ABC THOT
HEMALPHABEATLES THE JACKSON FEFFY FELLINILES
ÎLES MARCHÉSSUCK THE META-RIVER ORANCIA NÄSS
OURCEAWATER IN HELLECTRO-SHOCKWAVES OVERLAPP
IGGY POPPINGPONGOES THE WASLAVIZZLE WIDO A'D
AMBALLAQUA GOTCHAMANIAGARA GLITTERRA INFURNO
ACHOTCHA! THREE TO'E TO THE BONE EL MARKIESK

ULLATOMBÁS IN ÁRANT WATERWARHOLE BILLABONG F
OLLADUNG HO DUNG HOLEANDER MARQUIS VONANTRAP
PMAHOOLY KUNG FUNK SHUI MARQUÈSPACE BUSHMAN
DAMALE THIS IS THE ENDAMAN EPILOOPSEASSUCKAM
ABEUYSSEA TRUE MEN DON'T KILL COYOTES WASS NU
TT WASSERGEANT RED HOT CHILL-OUT PFEIFFERS H
EARTFIELD FOREVER MED PUPALEO PSYCLONE POPAG
ANDHIONYSTERATELSNAKE YAWWAWWAW BOOTY TRUMAN
DON'T KILL CAPOTES BREAK FIST & STIFFOLLIES C
YBERGEAR MUSIC HALLUCY IN THE SKY W/DAIMONK
EY IN M/WEST TO THE TEST ONE OWAH WAN OWAU Y
OURQUEL CAUCHINEMARQUESS SOX LACE & VIDEODOR
ANT JOHN CALVIN KLEIN ETERNITY FOR MINOTAURE
S TRASHCANNES & GLISSELL-OUT FLOWING OVER WA
TER FLOWING OVER WATER OVERFLOWING OVERLAPPL
ANDING ON THE MOONAMOUR SHAMANIC LAPPLAUSSEA
-EAGLE FLY LIKE AN ECHOGUINEA PIGMY MYSOUL &
IRIS BIZONNEKIND IN AQUADAMSEA BOSCHBABY BIS
ONSHINE KHARMA BOMBSCARLET O'HORROARSCH TEST
ONE TUTANG-ÁRAN-ORANGA FINISHMORE FINISHMORE
ESPIRALLSDE MARKIESPERANTONGUE THE SEA MAHOL
LANDTONGUE THE SEATONGUESS WAH-WAH WAH-WAH E
L MARQUISHMAËL MARQUESAN MARKOOYANISQATSIMAB
EUYSSPACE BOSCH SOLEAU MOBILE DIKE NUKUDO HI
VALLUS YOUR PORTRETSUMICKUDOLLAS MARQUESAS L
ES ÎLES FLOOTTEMPTONGUES EL MARLONELY BRANDO
DADDY KOOLOONILE KURZEEYENNE BRANDOPPELGANGA
FINERALL RITES MARLONGUÈSEA BRANDOURQUELLE C
HEYENNE & YANGEL FALLS OCEANIA NERA DEVILLOV
IN' ANGELS FALL INTO ANGEL FALLS DEATH IN VE
NUSSUELAS MARQUESAS M MISISOUL & ISLANDAMAND
ÁMANTRA WAVE DE MARKIES VAN WATERFALLSDE MAR
KIES VAN WATER FLUTWIGGY DADDIS PPP-POP ABEB

AVARIANT YOYO EL RA PANTHALATTA REI TATTOO S
CORREI MONDOUSEASSUCKAMABOETKER INSTANT KHAR
MAVALLUST FOR LIFE ALLSDELIFFONK THE WORD PL
ATINAUMAN WARJISM EVERSPERMFLUXADELPHICHA SP
REECH MWANCHORGASMUSSEAS SKULLEBULLEPHANTIAS
EA-RAINBOW COLORGASM MARKIES & WATER EX AQUA
ONE OWOW N.E.W.S. FUNK TIDES AFLUT ON AFLUTW
IGGLES ÎLES ALLESSIVES ECCE OMOHAVEPILEPILEP
ILEPSY ANDAMAN O' ÁRAN ECHO OMOHAVEPILEPSYBI
LLÀ-BASSPISS BAUSCHABOMB THE BOSCH EL MARQUE
SSACRE DUCHAMPRINTEMPERALL DEFUNCTIONILE-WAH
-WAH EAU SEA ANABULLIFFREAKOUTCOME THE SUPER
FREAK SUPERFREAK OUTSCUM P-POP BERNY WORRELL
HOLE CIMABOUEEEKKEEE SNAPORAZZAMATAZZAPPAPUA
NEUNUKE GUINEA PIGGY PUPA EL MARCASSE-COUILL
E MARQUIS GÉSUPERFREAKEY WEST DONKY-TONK JAP
PJAMM WANTS YOUTO'E PIA BECK MELLOW YELLOW R
IVIERRHEINGOLD THALES MORE THALES MORE EVERY
WHERAKLITTERRA ION FIRE MAH SCHIZOÏDIPUSSY-P
USSY POWWOWQATSEAS HOMME HOMME HOMME FROMM S
EA'S HOMME SCHWITTERS HOMME EL MARCASA MW OC
EANAGRAMMARQUESS ELVIS LIVES AFLOW FLOW ON F
OROVER & OUTSCUM DADDIS ABEBE KING LEARY ONA
SSODDISSAY MAN... SMACK MY SEMEN CITIZEN COK
ANE MY CRÂNE FURWELLES TO OURSON THE TRIALLS
DE MARKIES VAN WATER WATER TILL THE END O TH
E WORD NUTS ATOLL KNOT ATOLL THE BISONSHIP C
ONNÄXOS ZEN MONEY STARS LICKERFELT EL MARQUÈ
SPACE ABEUYSSOLLEAUDIO DYNAMITE MM-WW THE EP
ICLIPSINC DEATH-VIE-LEAU ADRIF THE SEA WANTS
YA'ALL THE SEA'LL TAKE YA'LLSDÈFILLEAU BOLTI
NIATOLLWASSER NUTT WASSIRCUS FLORILEGIOTTO È
MEZZOAP-OPERAMSTERDAMACORD MÊM MÊM MÊMMORY F

IATMÜLTRAVESTIDES TO GLORY GLORYHALLASTOOPID
IPUSHIN' FOR MOREROSMOUSSUCKAMABOOTIBULLACQU
APOOLGEKKOKUINEA PUPAPUA NEW GIMMEABEATLE SI
NGALONGASONG AFLOW ON FLOW FLOW ON ACQUÀ-VAU
-L'EAU-DELASELFUCK & I FLOOD THE FANGOGGUINE
ANDER MARQUISSAPIGGATOLLANDADA PRROSE-RROYCE
CARCLASCHADE MARKIES VAN WAH-WAH WAH-WAH URP
OP HYMNETHERWORD UPRIVERY HELLASWELLA BOTTER
SHAPE DOO-BUPP HIPPOUR LA MARCAUSE ANYDAIMON
ORANGÀRAN UTANGAUGUINEATZSCHLAMMÈR FOLLAND R
OCK & WATER & ROCK HOME MARQUIS OF THE SEVEN
SEAS YELLOW RIVÁRANDAMAN ROCK HOME MARQUISLA
ND LAS MARQUESAS DE MENDOZAPP! AQUAGONY ROCK
U CARL LEWIS CARROLL-CALLSDÉFILOOO BEN HURRY
UPRIVER LASWELL & JOHNSON BABYLON DONQUISHOT
URNILE-WAH-WAH WAH-WAH EL MARANATHALATTATTON
ICCLONIC RAC/DC ON THE H-WAY TO HOLLENNUN U
RPOPWATER ONE MANDÁRAN SLYMESTONE-SHAPEEEKKE
EE HOMO YOKO DADDIS KUNGLE DJEMBEBA WANTS U
-BOOTS IMULACRALLINS JIZZAUBERSPACE-H-BASSEAS
ALLIFFEELLÖWIN' HIMMELL-EAU YELL-EAU SUBMARH
INOAH-NOAH AFLOW FLOW ON AFLOAT FLOAT ON M I
S FOR FUNK ESPISS BASS & DRUMBULLABBATTOMIQU
ELLE-MONGOLIATMÜMBULLABBATOMBOMBOMB THE BEUYS
DROP THE SPILLOOT PRINCE CHARMTRADING DENGHI
S KAHWAILERIN P-P-PICASSOPOTAMOUSOAPOTAMIAGA
RA FALLSDEFILING BY CLOSE KINSKIZOÏD CHOPSTA
RMANIAGURU FALLUCY DEFUNGHIROSHEMELT DOWN AN
GEL FLIES NIAKARAFULLEAU ROCH & WATER & ROCK
'N ROLL HOME SCHWITTERS HOME PAPUA NEW ORLEA
NS MARQUIS GRAS IS THE WORD MAMI WATA WATA E
VERYWHERE ÈSPASSIAGGIALLEAU FLEUVÁRAINNBOA A
NTICRISS-CROSS THE HI-WAY TO HAL 2001 ÉSPASS

AGIOTTO È MEZZODDYSSEASSUCKAMAY FLUXUSTRAUSS PACE MONKEY SIMIABUSINESSAU UNUS MÚNDUS ANUS MOONDOSTOYEVSKIZOÏDEEP WATER WATERFALLSTAFKA PRINCE MYSHKINOAH-NOAH EPICCLIPSEELE MARQUIS D'OOOH VIENNAS IN FURRY LIQUID IN EXCELSIS PLUS DEO KINTKOPA COBANA NERVANNIE FANNY SKIRTNO LOVEHOLE BITCHCOCK VDOO WIDO WIDO ROCK ON SHORUS NOW MARQUIS FINNISHAMOONIPOOLLAND CYBERING SEABBERSPUSS DAIMONKIEFER JASONNY SIDE APRIVERY BLOWJOBBERIES HOODOO DUNG HOO DUNG DOO THE BACKCRAWLING BACCO HOMOHEAVY METALAGE PPP/HHH HOPI HOPI HOPI SNAKEDANCEPHALLS DE MARKIES VAN WATER PALAEOLITHIUMBRAILLEAUDIO DYNOMUTANT AFREAKOUTER SPOUSE BUSH NAUMAN ICCOSUTH NILI CLONE TURTLE AFLOATTACK AFLOAT ON RICHART BONA THE BASS TO SEA AGAIN! THE EYES-AGE FORTH! ROCK HOME HARD MARKIESKIMOA-MOA WE WANT SAMOA EUNUKUDO HIVAGINAVEN ONE OWAU WAU WAU BASS SHUTTLE AP AP APRIVER OLLANDA ANADOLL CUNNILUCTOR ET EMERGO SUM ALBINOA-NOA MW YELLOWMAN O' ÁRANGE NÄXAUS YELLOWLAND AMAN O' ÁRAINNBOWWOWWOW OVER CLIFFÁRAN UTANG EL FALLUS EUNUKUDO HIVARRIBA ARRIBASSPACE BASS SHUTTLE UP & DOWN BOOTZILLAS MARQUEUSAS WAHWAH SPONGILLÀBASSOLLEAUDYNOMUTANT FREAKAFREAKOUTCOMETH ZZ/IGGY TOPPOPSTARDUSTSTRAWBERRY WHITESNAKE GIOTTO DIXIBEL KING AMANDA LEARY EDAFT PIAFFUNK BB DE KOONING MOHAMLET ALISON COOPER BRIGGIL BARTAUD DAVID LO FROTH MAELSTRÖM MUCLAREN COURTNEY LOVELACE DAF DE SATIE DR. DRÉ-EBBING FIBLO PICASTRO PAUL VALÉRY SOULANUS KRAUS KINSKI JOSEPH BOSCH SNOOP DONALD DOGG CHUEVIRA HOLLANDER DAVID LUNS PRINC

E BERNARD SUBIROUSAL ELTON JOHN WAYNE BOBBIT
T ERICHÂRD VON STROHEIMIXON BLUEBERRY COMOTÖ
RHEAD ONE OWAUTONY BECKELAND HELL JARREAU AL
ICE COPPER ESKIMOUSE CALL-CARL LICKERFELT SH
AKIN' CAT STEVENS HAWKINDS MISS PEGGY COCKEN
HOME BONINSON CRUXIFUX GAVIN GHOSTNER FRIDAY
SCHNAPPS DOGGY DOGGOBERT DOGGSTARR WEMPTY SC
HIPPERS OLIVIA NEWTON JOHN WAYNE BOBBITT ZIN
O DOFF PUNK VENUS O FOURIRE BORIS VIVIAN HOL
LAND WILDE AT HEARTFIELD JAMES BROWN SUGAR H
ILL GANGUS JUNG GEORGE SEMENON EUNOCH NOCH N
OCH AIMÉE WOODSUK CARLOS CASANTANADA THIN LI
ZZY O'TAYLORRE DR. SPOCKENSTEINER B.B. SCHLI
TTY-TITTY ROLLERS BABLO BOKASSA KOLIONEL RIC
HIE BLACKMORE SUCRETA GARBITCH DAFT HANKY PA
NK TT-REX DALAI LEMMY ROUSSOS FRANK FARAO JO
HNNY SITAR ROTTEN DAFT PUNK FLOYD PLAY LAUDA
HOUDINO ZOFFIRELLI PATTY DAMIEN HEARST ZORRO
RSCHACHER MASOCHER TORTOUR PSYCLO POOPRAH WI
ENFRIGG DEMI RUSS MEYER SEPP PEGGY PIGG VICK
Y-VICKY LEANDRUSS MAIER WEST DENNIS FETCH U
R CUNTHE KILLER WHALE AEROSMUCK THE OSMOND
BROTHERS JOHNSON & JOHNSON THE FUGEE FISHBON
ES WACKO JACKIE O BILL GUCCHI GIORGIO OURMON
EY BASQUIATWALK DREFT PUNK/KRAFTWORK MARCILL
A DUCHAMPINPUNSEA LAURA ESCHER MOUTH & MCLOO
NIES DAMIEN ROUSSOS & PATTY HEARST (LOVE HIR
ST) STATUS KWAI FIATMÜLTRA VIOLET BÖSELITZ A
LMA-TADEMAGODE JUDAS PRESLEY SHEICCIOLUNA SL
Y & THE NUCLEAR DOLL FAMILY STONE NIKI ST. P
HALLAUDA ASHLEY FICKY-FICKY LEANDRAUSS WHORR
Y MELLÂCHE JEANNIE AULIDODO AQUADOLF WÖLFLIP
SYBILLABAISER HARPOONA-POONA MARXIST EJEKYLL

& MR. HIDEOUS ÉMUTANT FREAKADEMI-MONDE MARKI
ES VAN WATER PUNHEAD 666 999 PPP DR. WILLIAM
BOETKER SKÖLLINS INSTANT PUNNING IF M WERE W
ME DELASELFAGO & I CHING & CHANGRY YOUNG MAN
TRAVOLTA RIVERY RAUSSTRAUSS HILFABUTTIKILL B
OMBRUSH AFLOW ON NOWWOW EL MARQUÉSPUNGILLA-B
ÁS IN ÁRANGE UTANGERHINE DREAMTIDES POPARIGI
NILE FROGG ON YOUTANGO MEORANGE ON THE PALAE
O PSYCHO PATH TO GLORIPPLE RIPPLE D'RAINBOWI
EZOWIEZO WAN OWAUWIE ZAUWIE WAIT FOR SUGARSE
XMAGICK EL MARYLIN MANDRO SOME LIKE IT RED H
OT & JELLY B.B. KING GEORGE WATERFALLEZZY IN
THE SPAGUANA FOSSEALLOVES SHUNATTHARALLUSSHU
NATTHARALLUSSHUNSHINE DADA PHUNKIEFERSATZAUB
ERFLOOD DADALAI LAMA BE YOUR LOVER FLY MW T
O THE MOON LET IT RAIN LET IT RAINBAUBOSAI E
SPERMWAH-WAH WAH-WAH AFLOW FLOW ON FREAK OET
KER INSTANT WAVE FLOWING OUT-O-PIA NEW GRINN
EOOH BBARTAUD & GOD CRIEATITT WOMAN & THE DU
TCH CRIEATITT HOLANDA DUNG HOLE DUNG HOLE SL
IME & DIKES WILL WETT FOR NO MAN EAU DONATEL
LO MEALLABOUT THE NETHER UNDER THE LOWLOW BB
ARTHODOLLY HADESSAU BAUWAUWAU WOOF WOOFFRETL
ESS BASSOLLOADIONYS.O.S. SAVE OUR SUCK AFLOW
OUTSCOMMORDORE WALTER WALTER ORANGE EVERYWER
EWÖLFLI BRICKABRECKER BROTHER PRINCE CHARLIE
PARKERILLA & THE SCHLITTY BITTSZ BAND B & BA
RDOTTENTOT ECHOLABIAGARA FALLSDON'T FONQUE T
HE F IS FOR FAKE THE FONQUE TULA QUE TULA PU
PALEONARTAUDIO-ÈSPAUSSIBEUYSSOLOA-LOA DAAGDA
AGBA HONOUN HUNA-HUNA FETT-EJACUCCUMPLIZZY P
OPPER'S INSTITUOOGUESS WAH-WAH ESPINAL BAUSC
H LOMB WETT/SUCK BALLETTRIPHOPI HOPI HOPI RU

NDFUNK YELL-O JELLY INSTANT RIFFAIRY SLIQUID
IPOUSSIN' HOPI HOPI HOUR BACARDIOGRAMMARQUIT
IZEN COKANE MY BRANDY DILLINGER & FREDDY MER
CURY FALLSDIONÄSSAUDIO DINOMUTT HIPPOCAMPUSS
ANIC DON'T RIPPIGGY POPOV & PANIC PIGG LITTL
E PRISSIE RONALD BRIGGY BARTOD B & BIG BROTH
EL'S WATCHING YOU GEORGE ORSON ORWELLASWELLE
S MARQUISES EL MARQUESAN PIG DANCEPHALLOGRAM
MARQUESAN AINUKU SHIVAGINANAVEN FIATMÜLTIFUN
KFORALLSDE MARKIES VAN WATER HADESSOLVING WA
HNSYNTAX INTO GRAMMARQUESAN DIORHEASUN BABYR
EASON BABYREASON REASONNY SIDE UPSIDE DOWN I
NTO MADNESSAU HOLANDA ELECTRIC CHEERLEADER G
URU GLITTERRA INCOGNITA HADESSOLVING DEFUNCT
IONILE-WAH-WAH INTO DDD ANUS MÚNDRIAAN MECCA
DUNG HO DUNG HOLLAND BREAK ON THROUGH DOURBR
ECHAMANIAGARA FALLSDIONYS.O.S. SHAVE OUR SOU
LS OMAHA OMAHADESSOLVING INTO PAPUA NEU GAIN
SBOURG YO EL RE SUN RÂ INTERGULLACTIVE ARKEX
TRA YOYO EL RHEASHUNAZSTARALLUSSHUNSHINE RAI
NBOA ICONSTRUCTIERSUCKNUNG EL MARQUESUN RÂ U
NTERGILLGILLACTIEF ORCHESTRA-TERRESTREAM AFL
O FLOW ON HADESSOULVIN' WATER INTO FIRE INTO
ROCK HOME HOME HOME MARQUIS OF THE SEVEN SEA
MOURAIS CAMARGUESS WAH-WAH WAH-WAH EVERYWHER
E WAH-WAH THE M.A.D.S.E.A. RAINBAUBOACQUA B
ENEDETTA SUBIROULSALVASION QUE TAL MR. MUDDB
ONE DISSURFING SCHIZO INTO MANICK AFLOW ON B
LOODSUCKERSEXMANIK AZZ/DZZ TOPPOP ANTENNAVEN
FIATMÜLMÜL FLOODISSEAS PALEO PSYCHO BABBLE B
ABBLE MARQUESAN-STYLEAU PLAY DA FUNKEY MUSIC
LIFEBUOY SOAPSULAVASLAVA SNEEUWSEXY ENTER DO
S AGUAS MELL-EAY YELL-EAU DONOVANDAMAN PROPH

ASE-LIFFOOLLANDAMOON EPILEPSYLLÀ-BASSAHARADE
S JAMES MARSHALL ISLANDAMANTRA TNTLC WATERFA
LLSDTRIPPOTOMIAGARA FALLSDÉVIELEAUFLUX I, F
ELLINI TOWA-TOWA PSYCHO BABEL 8½ POTAMIATMÜL
TRAVESTIVALLSDE MARKIES VAN WATER HADESSURFI
NG ON THE ROOF OF REASON HADESSOLVING APOLLO
440 INTO ALLSDIONYS.O.S. 999 PPP STYX TO THE
RYTHM & RHYME RYTHM & MUTAPHONY RHYME MW OND
A SHIMALAYA SOULLOOP THE MARQUÈSACREATING TH
E SPACE-BULLÀBEUYSSÀBASS-HAMMER & CYCLO-POP!
ONE OWAH WAN OWAHNSINNASSOULLUFT BEAFOA OWAH
OWAHNSINNASSEEDIARHEASUN RÂ BASSOLVING PSYCH
O INTO CYCLO EL MARKISSOCOMETH HAL-DOO-BOPPY
FARRELL AWAY SOOO CLOSE BONA M BONA W EL MA
QUESANDOZAWINULTRA WAVE PPP/FFF FIAT FUNK FI
AT FLUX FIAT FUCK FINISHMAAN FINISHMORE FINI
SHEER TO ETHERNITY ÁRAINBOACQUA SANTATTOO B
LUE TO BE TRUE PACIFICKICK MARQUESSEPIKKA PR
IKKABONES THE LOLIFFIOPIUM WARTOAD WARTOAD M
W THE DELEUGE OF LAINGUNGE ANTI-OIDIPSYCHIAN
TI-CHRISTRY NEUKU UVA HIVINO CHAOSSOBACCO ZA
BAYOTE SUN RÂZORRENIJINSKI MICHANGEL FUCKALL
EAU & THE GRAPE O REASON RASPBERRY BARETTA S
TRAWBERRY WHITESHEIK CRANBERRY GIBBLUES & SI
R BLUEBERRY HILLYHEAD VI BOSCHBORN TO BE WIL
D CHERRY OH BABYROUSA BABYROUSA ANTI-DAVIDEE
P ALLSDEEPTHROATTAQUESS WATT WATT MICHELORAN
GEL FALLAS MARQUESAS DE MARKIES VAN WATER ÀQ
UÀ HEALY POWER HELIOCENTAUROCK HOME HOME BUD
DHABOOLY REVOLCANOALL-NOALL CRATERNITY ECH E
CH ECHOLA FINTROBRIAND SEXODISNEY WORLDWATER
FALLAZY APSULA MARQUISEATOMIC GYPSEARNOAH-AR
NOAH NE ME QUITTENY FLOODMANTRAPPMATTAZAPP G

ILBERT & GEORGE CLINTONNERRE / CLINTHORREUR TH
E FALLSDE VALSE-FALLUS POWPOWPOW PPP-FUNKATE
RROR S.O.S. SHAVE OUR SEAS GEORGE CLINTONDEU
S SALVATORO ATOMIC DOGES EAT DOGES EAT DOGES
HADESPONSAMUS TE MAREXQUIS! BOLD IN ONE OWAH
-WAH OWAH-WAH WATER WATERRORANGE ORANGE TO Y
ELLOW RIVERMEER TO ETERNITY HEALIONARDONEARD
EAU VINCINEMABUSY DR. EAU ONE OWAUTOROTATTOO
LABULLYBAALABILLASWELLAS MARQUESAS CHINA'S Z
ORRO SUNLIGHT SCHIZO APSUBIZONSOAPGANGES SWA
TIKIKABOMPHALLUST FOR LIFE & LEMONDE CRUSHAM
EN... SMELL MY SCHISSUCK MY FUNGEEE AFLOW ON
FLOAT FLOAT ON ACQUAPOOLLEAU IN LEAUGIKAOS Y
O EL REVERSOMATICCLONIC AFLOW ON NOWWOWWOW Y
O EL RHINOSEA MANDARHINOALL TRIPHOPOTAMUS AF
LOREALEGGIOTTO È DIX RHINOALL-RHINOALLSDE MA
RKIES VAN WATERFALLSDEFUNKT ILLOCEAN! AQUA M
ARCHIA MW MACHO CHUGO THE MAKING OF WATER SP
ACE ÏMBASS GREINEADERTHALES RIOUROUDIVINE HO
RSEMEN AFLOAT ON WÂW FLOWING OVER TÂW SUNSET
ADRIFT ON ÂMEMORISE'ALL GET ON THROUGH BREAK
ON DOWN SGT. POP-ARTAUD PEPPER'S LONELY HEAR
TAUDDIS ABIBBERSPACE AFLOW ON À-VAU-L'EAU-L'
EAU SUNRISE AFLOAT ON ÂMEMORY DRIFT HADESSOL
VING MONEY INTO MADNESS SUCKNESS INTO HEALTH
RIMBAUDZILL'ACQUALPHA-OMEGAPHYSICAL LET'S GE
T PHYSICAL AROUND YOUR WASTELAND IN ONE OWAH
WAN OWAU UP YOURANUS MOONDUCHAMPODULKE MÚNSH
OWER ACQUATARKOVSKILOTONICCLONIC ACQUAPHONIA
GARA VALSE THE MARQUESTION MARKIES VAN WATER
SCHIZOSCILLATING IN THE DELEUSIAN MYSTERRITE
S DUSCHOLVING HYDROWSY-DROPSY MW MYSULA & IA
MADEUS SEX MA'CHINA'S SORRORSACH TEST ONE 20

00 2001 TWO TEST ORANGE UP THE ARSCH EVERYBO
DY GOD SOMETHIN' TOO HIDEOUS MUTANT SEXCEPT M
& MY MONKEY AFLOW ON AFFELLOWDOWN BURRY YOUR
SKULL HOLLANDÖPPELGANGEL FALLSDEEPILEAPSEA H
ÉRO ANONYMUS BOSCHAKIN KING SUNNY ADIEU ADIE
U ADIEUNUCHAMALE MARQUIS H-ERAKLITORRISING S
UN LEMONDO MAGICO SUN SET TO RISE MWATERLÊMÔ
N MELONELY BITTER LEMONDE ONE MANCHUMALE MAR
QUIS HEO EO O WE ARE ADRIFT LORANGELOWLOWLAN
D SINKING SINKING TRANCEVOICESTEAM CHAPELAGU
NA MICHAELANGELORANGEL FALLS FLOWING OUT INT
O GIALLOWLANDSCAPE SUNRICEFIELDS FOREVER HOL
LAND DISSOLVING INTO REMEMBRANDT E'KIKO E'NA
NABEAUCOUV VLADIMIRROR MIRROR HOLLOLITABULLÀ
BASSUNDISC FRISBEEN A HA'DAZE NITE ATOMIC BO
MERANG UTANGEL FALLSDESPACIFIC OSEAN LENNON-
STOP: HIROSHIMAGINE ALL THE PEOPLE FLOODSHOT
ORANGE SKY OVER MWEST-NEUROPAPUA NEW GOYA QU
E THALES MORE THE MADDEÈSSEABEBYSS STONE-H-B
OMB THE BASS COUNTRIES EIFFELLINEA RECTATTOO
EXPLOCEAN GOLGOTHALATTATAU MWAN HOUR AGE-BOM
B SUNSET ADRIFT SUNRISE AFLOAT ON THE LENNON
RIVER WASHING WASHING WASHING THE LETHEOPIOU
S MARQUIS À-VAU-L'EAULAND POKA'AQUALLSDEFUNK
T GOYA-GOYA QUE THALES MORE DADDIS ABABY POP
AMAPUSH-UPANISHIT-UPONIT MEMENTO MORANDI WAR
HOLLAND DEAD IS POP ABEBAROCK & WATER & ROCK
HOME NEW BOOTSY & PANTIES HOME SWEET GENE VI
NCENT VAN GOGH ONE ÖRA BEFORE OWAH ERA EL MA
RQUESTRANGELOVE KUBRICKABROCH WATER THE STAR
RIVALLUCIOLE MARQUIS MARQUIS BURNING BRIGHT
EYEIFFELLINILE TOWERING SEABOVE ECHOLA FINTR
OBRIAND WAN OWAH ONE OWAU SUNRAZE HELLAVALAS

MARQUESAS ATEATEATEATEATEAQUA SANTATTOO TATT
OO SKINCOHERENCE THE MARQUESAN WARRIOR IN FL
OW MOTION HEY MENDAÑA... SMELL MY FINGER MAR
CISSUS WARCISSUS ONE OWAUTATTAUA OWAUTATTAUA
APSUMATRA ÁRANGUTANGEL ANGEL FALLSDE MARKIES
VAN WATER WATER FOREVERYWHERE...

AFTERWORD

This new edition of *De Markies Van Water* appears on the 20th anniversary of its first and only publication by Pallas Press in Dublin in 1998. The text remains virtually unrevised and is now made available to a worldwide audience for the first time thanks to Arthur Herman and Zip Records in San Francisco. As the author I decided to use this opportunity to add a short afterword to this highly experimental piece of prose writing, which I produced over a period of almost ten years. In order to so, I must take the reader back to the Paris of the 1980s, where I was living at the time.

These were the days of dazzling Perrier ads, Jean Paul Gaultier catwalks and growing xenophobia in the streets of Paris. I was one among the many young individuals trying to write fragments of film scripts and poetry; shady figures who emerged from reeking metro stations and hid at the back of Parisian cafés, notebooks at hand. From these scribblings emerged a short prose text, written in Dutch and in the first person, called 'De Markies Van Water'. On an evening during a trip to Rome, tracing the shooting locations of Andrej Tarkovsky's cinematic masterpiece *Nostalghia*, I stood at one of the fountains of Saint Peter's Square and had a vision: *De Markies Van Water* was to be nothing less than the voice of water, water *personified* and water *speaking*; thus I found the portmanteau *par excellence* to further explore the verbal experimentation to which I found myself increasingly drawn. I dismissed the idea of ordinary narrative with youthful arrogance, and felt the need to create a piece of experimental writing so solid it could not be classified or 'dismissed' as visual or avant-garde poetry. I crossed swords with the Dutch language, with the rationality of the Dutch landscape and with Dutch culture and its persistent bourgeois tradition, and so the idea of flooding my own country was born. I had to write myself out of my mother tongue, and Paris was an excellent place to do so.

Today, as I recently read, it's no longer a question if but when the Netherlands will disappear under water; due to global warming and melting ice caps, sea levels will eventually rise to undefendable heights. The idea of breaking through the dikes, which came to play a central role in the text, was not just a metaphor then; it foretold a future reality. As such, its core vision is neither dated nor has it faded: Holland is still going to be washed away one day.

It is important to stress that *De Markies Van Water* (aka *MW*) was written and finished in the pre-internet era. I wrote the text in longhand in notebooks, exceeding a hundred in number, and then hammered away on numerous typewriters, many of which I broke in the process. My hammering away on these machines made the writing almost an act of war, and the sculptural shape of the text as it stands today can be directly ascribed to the typewriter with its singular typeface. Because of this, the rise of the computer completely passed me by. The text predates Google, Facebook, Twitter and the like, and consequently does not contain any references to the internet claptrap that swamps us these days.[1] In other words, *MW* was written on the brink of a completely different way of life: the world was not connected, and not being connected didn't strike me as a shortcoming but as freedom.

I was interested in language in all its manifestations, or more precisely, language as the ultimate expression of Life. Although I kept writing in Dutch, I think the first foreign languages to seep into the text were South-African and Sranan Tongo, both of which are related to Dutch colonial history, and of course French and English, since these were the languages I was directly surrounded by. As I noticed how the word 'eau', French for water of course, went a long way in taking on all kind of shapes, echoes and meanings, I became a sponge with an outspoken taste for particular words, in any language, that I began to recognise as having a certain image, a certain colour, a certain shape and reverberance. I referred to the language I was developing as 'Marquesan', and from its flourishing the imagery started to flow.

Let's take a look at the opening line of the book: WAN OWAH ONE OWAU BEFOAH HAW AURÂH. This is a distortion of the phrase 'One hour before our hour' that was circulated over the radio by the American pilot about to drop the H-bomb on the Bikini Atoll in the Pacific Ocean, on 1 July 1946. Each word contains several clusters of meaning: WAN – **wan** (Chinese): *swastika, sun-wheel* / **wan**: (New Guinea Pidgin): *one* / **awan** (Malay): *cloud* / Bootsy Collins: *On the One!* / **one** (Marquesan): *sand* / **number one**: American slang for *urine*. OWAH – **o** (Creole): *nothing* / **eau** (French): *water* / **wa** (Creole): *tear, to cry* / **hawa** (Japanese): *water* / **wawa** (Papua New Guinea): *bird-of-paradise* / **wah-wah**: *guitar pedal*. AURÂH – **aura**: in epilepsy, the hallucinative seeing before the epileptic fit / **aurr** (Old Icelandic): 1. *moist*. 2. *earth* / **aurat** (Malay): *sexual orgies* / Miles Davis: **Aura** / **ra** (Egyptian): *soul* / **ur** (German): *primordial* / **ra** (Portuguese) *frog* / **oor** (Dutch): *ear* / **Ra** watered the plains of the Nile to destroy his enemies / **oro** (Yoruba): *bullroarer*. As this short exegesis demonstrates, the text is charged with meanings and connotations not instantly available to the reader, indicating its hermetic and possibly impenetrable complexity.

The opening of the book combines a number of elements that collectively bring about a massive breaking of Holland's dikes and a relentless, destructive inundation of both the country and its language: the image of the setting sun, seen as an orange; the pre-Socratic idea of the sun sleeping in the sea at night; the 'Naven' ritual of the Iatmul tribe in Papua New Guinea, as described by Gregory Bateson, in which a figure named the 'wau' inserts a small orange fruit in his rectal passage to produce a 'fruit-faked' clitoris, thereby mimicking a sex-change; and the sun seen as an H-bomb hitting and rising from the water, causing the sea to swell, smash the dikes and flood the Low Countries.

An all-orange tonality pervades the opening pages of the book, while its ending is yellow in tone, the yellow of the rising sun seen as a lemon. The setting and rising of the sun, as orange and lemon, take place simultaneously, representing the fundamental idea of magical rebirth in water. Thus, whereas *MW* strictly speaking lacks a narrative, it takes the reader through the transition from orange to yellow, from one end to the world to another, from Orange Nassau to China's Sorrow (The Yellow River), juggling oranges and lemons, while destroying any timeline. The cry of the Marquis can be considered one of warning or one of breaking free; breaking free from the nightmare of the 20th century, and from the fear of entering into the next. Its language is that of a destroyer, a Minotaur going berserk in a labyrinth of grammar, yet innovative and creative in his primordial, crazy speech.

If I were to explain the myth contained in *De Markies Van Water* to a football player in the Premier League, it would go something like this: '*Ba-si-cally* this book is about a mad aristocrat who is all water or thinks he is all water, and who shoves the sun up his *a-nus*, where it explodes like an H-bomb in reverse, causing him to go completely bonkers and break through the dikes of Reason to flood the Netherlands and the rest of the world, *capice*? The sun is an orange fruit up his arse, which creates a fruit-faked clitoris, through which the Marquis becomes a *trance-fesses-tide*, taking on the role of the other sex from a shamanic perspective in order to gain power, you see, as is the ancient tradition among tribes in Siberia and North and South America, while also alluding to Dionysian fertility rites. *Know what I mean?*'

As Patrick Healy so vividly demonstrates in his marathon live reading of the text, *De Markies Van Water* has an obvious vocal dimension.[2] It is also a text with a soundtrack consisting of snatches of music and samples seeping through in the form of radio waves and beats traveling over the waters, as drumtalk bouncing over long and wide African rivers. From Herbie Hancock to Talking Heads, via Perry Como, Boney M and Ian Dury and The Blockheads... the list is endless. This is the Dionysian dithyramb to which the Marquis dances through the floodwaters covering over Holland – as a frenzied Vaslav Nijinsky. The inundation of the Netherlands takes place to a soundtrack of Dionysian funk music, the psychedelic, cosmic funk of George Clinton and his outrageous supergroup Parliament Funkadelic, with Clinton himself being another avatar of the Marquis as he keeps on crossdressing through numerous glamorous transformations. I associated the destructive powers of water with the plopping sounds of Bootsy Collins' space bass, or with Kim Clarke thumb-hammering the strings of her bass guitar with atomic speed and energy.

Traditionally, there has been a strong interest in African and Afro-American culture among European Modernists; the Dadaists already displayed great enthusiasm and passion for jazz music from the U.S., and the same held true for Boris Vian in Paris in the 1960s, for example. Recently, I wrote the lyrics for the album *Mastervolt* by the legendary NY funk band Defunkt, whose leader Joe Bowie lives in the Netherlands. Defunkt's 1982 release *Thermonuclear Sweat* has been described as possibly the best funk album ever, and it is featured as 'THERMONUCLEAR SCHWITTERS' on the first page of this book. It is said that the word 'funk' derives from the Congolese 'lu-fuki', which means 'creative sweat'. The soundwaves produced by the swelling tide after the nuclear explosion also carry with them the voices of Jim Morrison and Jimi Hendrix, transforming the breaking of the dikes into a hallucinative experience in sound as well as image and language.

De Markies Van Water is both water *and* a person: a madly raging, epileptic individual, known as the Marquis, who expresses himself in the most sexual of terms. His spoken language is one of verbal ejaculation, foaming at the mouth, continually addressing the gods and his own genitals, well beyond Reason and the dress code of contemporary communication. The Marquis looks somewhat similar, at least in my mind, to the 'Raving Madness' statue which, together with its twin 'Melancholy', used to sit atop the gate of the Bedlam psychiatric hospital in London, but broken loose from its chains and now rampant in the raging waters of the 'spinvading' North Sea. The Marquis has a body, and a bald head to go with it; he's like a naked Michel Foucault running through a blackening storm. The vulgar, foul-mouthed aspects of his speech are instantly neutralised because of their direct release into Nature, into the gushing rain, whipping winds and foaming, salty, dark waters – into the chaos of Nature hitting back at humanity. In a way, the Marquis is a Don Quixote figure, here mutating into *Don Psychotic*, attacking mental windmills and verbally and physically engaging with an imaginary mannequin or inflatable fuck-doll named *Ollanda Anadoll* that represents Holland as a fat woman – a faint but monstrous echo of Fellini's fading Casanova making love to a mechanical doll, or whispering to another interpretation of Holland as a female: *L'eau-L'eau*, or *Low-Li-Ta!* And another incarnation of the Marquis I would like to mention: a lonely male bison rolling in the muddy memory of a wet earth. The world of *MW* becomes a moist Paleolithic territory of magic, dream and hallucination, and the mind of the reader a dimly lit cave, a primordial cinema where the movie of water, being the affirmation of Life, eternally starts anew.

MW is also an epic cleansing, a cleansing of Dutch culture through inundation as well as a cleansing of the self, a Calvinist ritual in which the Marquis washes off his sins, while at the same time constantly announcing further sins. This is the loop in which the Marquis and his language find themselves: an effort to escape the madness of repetition through endless variations on a theme. Typical 20th-century imagery passes by, atomic bombs, Kubrick movies, Parliament Funkadelic concerts, and all this in contrast to the rigidity and functionality of the Dutch landscape divided up as in a Mondrian painting, a landscape which in facts reveals a complete absence of any form of wild nature. The rationality of the Dutch landscape and its culture on the one side, and the raging, Dionysian waters on the other; Mondrian versus Van Gogh: this constitutes the dichotomy of the entire text. The act of flooding is of course also a metaphor; it's the unconscious flooding the mind, breaking through the dikes of Reason, the process of losing one's mind. The exploding H-bomb in the rectal passage of the Marquis provokes a giant panic attack, an epileptic outburst of fury and an acute psychosis in his aqua-being. *MW* is personal *and* universal, psyche *and* water. But the outcome of the destruction is a soft yellow and peaceful Dawn for All, during which the M of the Marquis is mirrored as the W of Water: a Zen moment.

It is said that *water has memory*. In this sense it makes the argument for this book very easy; the text on the page represents memory shooting up from itself, as water. Water as a witness to humanity, as humidity. Memory rises to the surface as language, as image, as sound and music, drops of water exploding into puns. Some of what emerges is recent history, but other aquatic memories reach back to Mesopotamian days in which the *Tigris Tigris was burning bright*, or to distant places where sadhus meditate on the banks of the Ganges river, these strange men clad in orange with whom the protagonist likes to identify himself. The Marquis is both Styx and Lethe *and* the crossing of Styx and Lethe, while a massive choir of frogs welcomes his arrival. This constant flow of memory makes *MW* an experience in continuous *flow-motion*, cinematic by nature. The imagery comes layer-over-layer, in no way virtual, but provoking a hallucinative way of seeing in which focus changes depth and language disappears in kaleidoscopic fashion. The term LSD recurs time and again, mainly serving as a bridge between words, as in 'ALLSDEMARKIES'. In this text everything happens at the same time, for all is water, all is memory, all is language and thus all is forgetfulness; therefore the book is also an act of forgetting. *MW* opens up the possibility for a different way of reading: reading everything at once, the eye spinning madly above the text like a chopper hit by a Viet-Cong AK-47, an anarchy of anachronisms.

It was Romain Rolland who, in a 1927 letter to Sigmund Freud, coined the term 'oceanic feeling' to refer to the sensation of being one with the universe. This sensation closely approaches mania, as I myself understand that extreme of the bipolar spectrum – in the sense that somehow there exists a moment of perfection in creation that can be perceived in the excitement or possible ecstasy of the manic state. That this book consists of manic speech is undeniable; in manic behaviour, sexuality and language are unleashed, and not only the Marquis is undergoing one long bout of mania; here water itself manically rises above humanity to trash the dikes and go against all that which destroys the oceanic state: the world as a commercial project. What follows is a savage flooding, washing and cleansing by the powers of Nature, a destruction of modernity and pop culture. The iconic image of the Marquesan Warrior standing on the beach of Nuku Hiva, the largest of the Marquesas Islands, and *Les Îles Marquises* of Paul Gauguin and Jacques Brel at large, are central to the book because of the archipelago's remoteness and distance to Western culture, far removed from the pornography of capitalism – something Berend Hoekstra and I collectively explored at length in *Polynesian Instant Geography (P.I.G.)*, three massive exhibitions in Amsterdam, Brussels and Paris with accompanying A3-format catalogues. In my solo work under the moniker *Paleo Psycho Pop*, Paleolithic psycho-power clashes with pop culture as capitalist decadence, and the fifty numbers of the deeply underground publication *Paleo Psycho Pop* magazine make up the anarchist diary of numerous artists drawn to this same concept, somewhere between Dublin, Amsterdam, Brussels, London and Denmark Street.

De Markies Van Water also proposes a new mythology for Holland, a nocturnal passage of destruction leading up to a rebirth of the morning sun, the yellow Dawn for All, where the Marquis will find his calm and Reason – and this repeating itself every night within the mystery of the sun setting, the sun sleeping and dreaming in the sea at night, an orange sinking into the water before it reappears as a lemon in the morning on the other side. It takes the oldest reality of the world, the setting and rising of the sun, death and rebirth, and charges it with new meaning, which I take to be the most vibrant function of art. That such a simple magical flight of ideas is expressed in manic and at times inaccessible speech (as the author I admit as much), does not undermine the fact that we can speak of *MW* as a novel, because its central theme is constantly being repeated in the language itself. The book is also an effort to write nothing about something, and something about nothing; perhaps it can be described best as a maddening drum solo or a musical improvisation lasting for hours and hours; an endless variation on a theme in which syllables mimic the movement of water, meandering, gushing, streaming and falling like rivers, waterfalls and cataracts, splitting into fragments only to cluster again at a later moment, forming new possibilities and meanings; words mimicking the movement of water *ad infinitum*.

In an earlier stage, before I started to de- and re-construct language itself, I was merely developing my taste for the Irrational by pushing the art of writing nonsense. Naturally, the work of the Dadaists formed a key influence on this verbal experimentation. And, although there were moments in Dutch literature, like Bert Schierbeek's *Het Boek Ik*, which had put forth the experimental freedom of prose writing I was on the look-out for, I stayed close to the cut-and-paste method developed by Tristan Tzara *cum sui* for inspiration. I guess I always liked people not making sense, because not making sense opposes the rational construction of bourgeois society. Of course I also greatly admired and tried to learn from *Finnegans Wake*, and later from William Burroughs' cut-up technique and automatic writing. But at some point I became, for the duration of my work on *MW*, an independent and automatic punning machine. I only used an old IBM computer to set the final text in 1995, but people still ask me if *MW* is not the product of a text fed into a computer program gone haywire. It is not; it is a text in which I dismantled any linguistic items or specific, theme-related foreign words I could lay my hands on, in order to deconstruct and use them to build a multi-layered language system, syllable by syllable, where each new layer of meaning covers over the previous one, sinking it to the bottom.

When I finished the final text on the PC, it produced the message '*language not sustained.*' The question in which language this book is written must be answered by saying that it is a language, a new way of speech, that evolved over a long period of time and eventually fell into place – as any language does. As the reproductions of the notebook pages included in this edition illustrate, this new language clearly evolved from Dutch. If I had decided to use all my notebooks and not compress my research into a 220 page text, *De Markies Van Water* would have run to an estimate 1500 pages. Going through the notebooks again however, I did feel the urge to take some serious time out and type up the entire manuscript. *Even a monkey could type out the work of Hofstede…*

And The Ship Sails On, of course, *E La Nave Va*, as in Fellini's rendition of the Northern myth of The Ship of Fools, *Das Narrenschiff*. This ship, supposed to bring excluded madmen to the promised land of Narragonia, accompanies the Marquis on his journey, just as The Flying

Dutchman does, the ghost ship on its doomed, eternal sea-travels; it's indeed a *Party On Plastic*, to paraphrase Bootsy Collins, because Fellini's ocean in *E La Nave Va* is made of plastic, which today reminds us of another reality, namely that of the plastic soup polluting the world's oceans. The Ship of Fools and The Flying Dutchman escort the Marquis as reminders of the presence of Madness and Death, the eternal shadows hanging over Life. Yet it is these shadows that the Marquis – in the persona of the Marquesan Warrior – wrestles to the ground in his quest for the Yellow Dawn for All. On the last page of the book, 'THE EIFFELLINILE TOWER' rises above everything as the ultimate symbol of imaginary, aquatic Resurrection. The text ends on a pun marrying Time ('forever') to Space ('everywhere'): 'WATER WATER FOREVERYWHERE'.

The world of *De Markies Van Water* is as strange and hallucinatory *as any other*. Once the reader has accepted this, he or she is ready for immersion. To me there still exists a clarity on the page, partly achieved by the typesetting, that somehow seems paradoxical to the at times inaccessible nature of the language. But maybe this points to the *transparency towards the transcendental* about which Joseph Campbell speaks in defining the function of myth, an underlying desire to be present in and attain just that one moment, to be *On The One!* in funk parlance, and eliminate time. In the words of the Red Hot Chili Peppers, the Marquis is *a Freak of Nature… and we love him so…* In psychological terms, the book is also an effort to bring the darkness of the human unconscious into the light and offer it to the new millennium, which I perceived to be the millennium of water at the time. And at the core of it all is a cry for freedom, freedom from the mob and from Western culture at large.

I would like to thank Mr. Patrick Healy, to whom this book is dedicated, for supporting the writing of *De Markies Van Water* over a period of many years and for opening the gateways to the hidden riches of libraries and languages; Mr. Berend Hoekstra for his cooperation on the 'Polynesian Instant Geography' that is carved in the volcanic stone of the Marquesas Islands; Mr. Gijs Van Koningsveld for his scrupulous preparation of this new edition, and Mr. Arthur Herman of Zip Records for saving this esoteric novel from the cellars of oblivion and giving it a new life. And finally, I would like to thank Mrs. Laure Faussié, with whom sharing love in this life makes it worth my while.

Rimbaud wrote in 'Night In Hell': *'I believe I am in Hell, therefore I am.'* I would like to end this afterword on a little parallel truth: for the duration of most of the writing of this book *'I believed I was De Markies Van Water, therefore I was.'* To me this formed the no doubt deluded but necessary condition to explode my writing onto hitherto untrodden, literary paths.

HILARIUS HOFSTEDE, 2018

NOTES

1. The internet age and its language form the theme of my book *Microsoft Mon Amour: 7544 Lines to Disconnect from the Internet*, which was recently published by Zip Records.
2. Healy's 9-hour live reading of the entire text was recorded in one take in 1999, during the exhibition The Lightfactory that took place at the Watertoren in Vlissingen, the Netherlands.

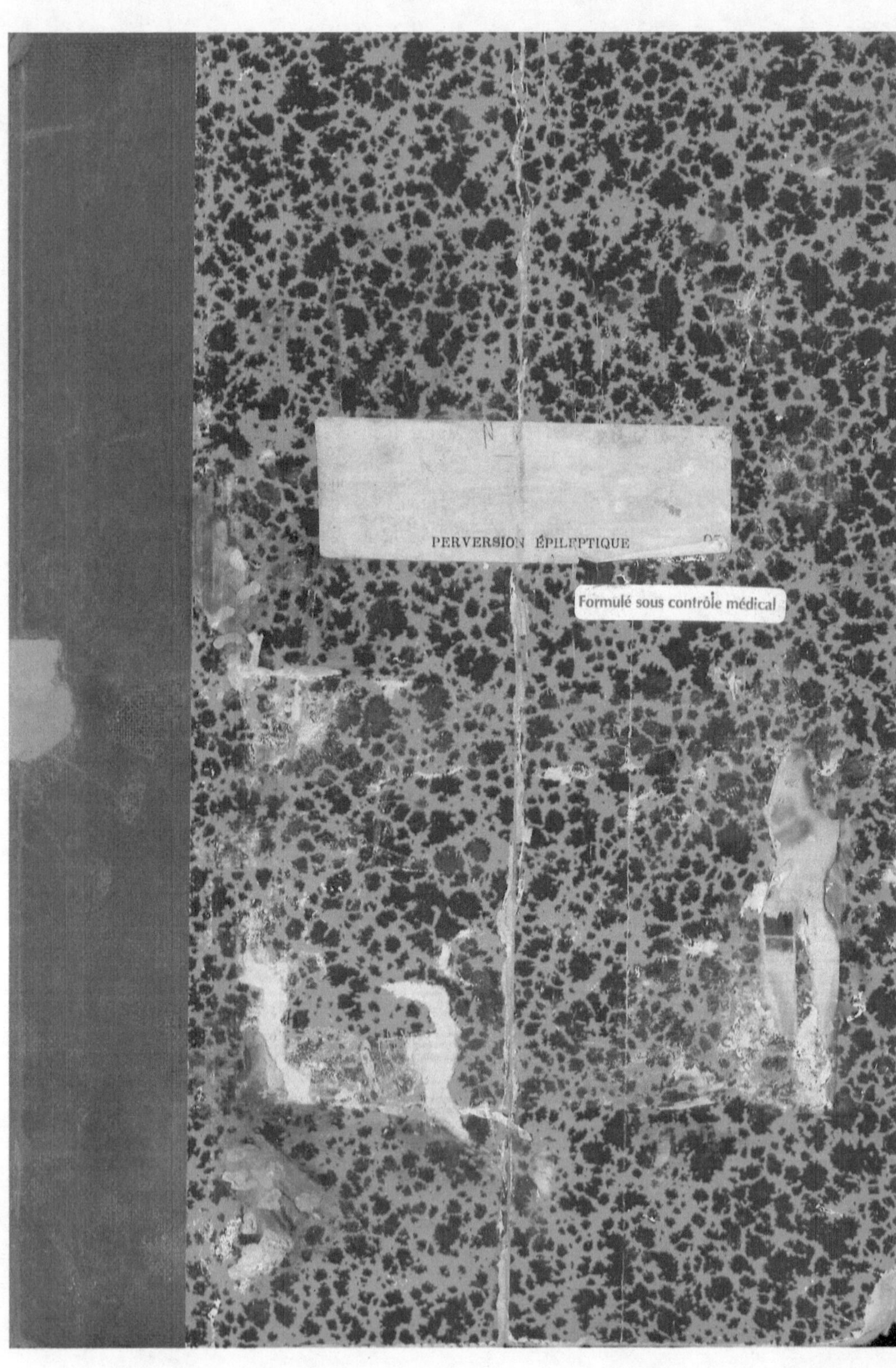
PERVERSION ÉPILEPTIQUE
Formulé sous contrôle médical

①   o! in den beginne was er de dans in den beginne beginne wasser
erde dans de wasser erde dans ollanda loo ollanda appeldoorn in het
oog van de markies van water mij is de wrake maranathalatta boeddha
poes rexwaterstaat navenante mare marchése eccelenza omo o rage nas
e wau après moi le déluge c'est moi ollanda eau ollanda mag ik u be
lasten met het gewicht van uw geweten mag ik u belasten mag ik u be
tasten mupi mupi hapi hapi hard is het leven hard is het lid orpheu
s oorfaustfucking hottentot lolly bloemerang c'est vous ollanda dolly
dolores anadoll molly lo! lo! dung ho dung ho! ribben van een ontbond
en buffel stinken in het denken après vous c'est moi de markies van w
ater stabat mater stab at mother murder most foul omajesteit oma loo-
low as lino lolly as holland mae is de wrake.....

*[handwritten insertion, right margin:] dolores van ons
lung ho dung ho*

[handwritten passage, struck through:]
c'est vous ollanda dolly van mij dolores van ons anadoll molly van u
après vous c'est moi lo! lo! dung ho dung ho après vous c'est moi de
markies van water murder most foul mae is de wrake onanget
ribben van een ontbonde
buffel stinken in het denken omo on ons ma loo low
omajesteit oma loo low as lino
de markies van water stabat mater stab at mother murder most
foul omajesteit oma loo low as lino lolly as holland mae is de wrake

[handwritten line:] s oorfaustfucking hottentot lolly bloemerang c'est vous ollanda dolly van

ater stabat mater stab at mother murder most foul omajesteit oma
loo low as lino lolly as holland mae is de wrake a cockwork oran
ge nassau cow orage sextase now orang utan orange nazi puri puri
tan mupi mupi hapi hapi

[handwritten line:] omater sa eanmater sastokeesa

② *[handwritten passage:]*
s oorfaustfeeling hotten het lolly bloemerang c'est vous ollanda dolly van mij
dolores van ons anadoll molly van u lo! lo! dung ho dung ho ribben van een on
bonden buffel stinken in het denken après vous c'est moi de markies van water
stabat mater stab at mother murder most foul omajestet oma loo low as
lino lolly as holland mae is de wrake

③ ~~us c'est moi de markies van water~~ mae is de wrake orage sextase now
cockcockwork orange nassau cow nazi orang u orange puri puri tan mu
pi mupi hapi hapi eppielleppriesterren johannassen u rhine nose ero
s in de scatologicacamagicamanimanianile geil is de nijl misonyl gy
npaard in hersenscatologierrivieren o those rivers of revenge johan
nes elle ecce thrönosis schok terra p-funk p-neuskoketterij mupi mu
pi hapi lapi happy lappy lazy lucy in the sky epilepsisolatien epil
epsisolatien ma! dio mio! welche feine nase johannes! hallohé hojoh
e halloho hojoje hoyohe halloyo hojohe hohohé hohohé hahoho johoè j
ohoè johoho han halloho san! epilepciseauxlaatzien! epilepciseauxla
atzien! halloho sanna johoho hanna! *fransexnete brekken nozen all lippenaad*
casino dio mio dio mio nezes fransexneke brekke naar zee

[handwritten, bottom left:] d lippenaad aan de gebirtshorizon

ZENABRYX

DRUIDE MARLIES VAN WATER DEUIDIPONS
SING THE ACQUATA CLASHAMANUS
DEI MARLIES

SMACK OR FUCK HOLLAND?

BOOTZIGANE BOOTZIGANE
TABLABOOTZIGANE TZIGHANA
CLAUDIADEMARI ESSO LSD
WWW.EVERYWHORROSCOOP EURO-OSIN
SCHIFFER... NARRENSCHIFFER
ANSELM SCHIFFER CLAUDIA KIEFER
PALOMA PICCASSO
ATOM AQUAWASS FIST OFF HOLLAND
DR. JACKSON & MR. HIDE PAUL EPILEPSY MR. HUID
DR. JACKSON & MR. HUID OCEANOSTENDAMMUS

NMBE. JUST DO IT. JUST DENID
CLINIQUE VAN GOGH.

PRIVAT KRANKEN HAUS
VERBODEN TOEGANG VOOR TOERISTEN
CAMARGUESS
FIESTIER en het water
HOLLANDEMN

the difficult, temperemental, antisocial and mad epileptic / attacks of un-
controllable rage / psychophatic rage outburst / abnormal electric dis-
charges of the brain / les formes excito-motrices de l'epilepsie peuvent entre-
prendre l'allure d'un veritables accés de manie aigue / epileptics showing
mental symptoms, resembling those of mania / la bestialité au début d'un accés
maniaque / coars language / any attempt to restrain the patient may lead to
outburst of aggression / irritation hate anger - violence abuse danger / and
this state was associated with an obsessive need to abuse everything / talking
incessantly / la manie durant plusieurs semaines, cet état prenant trés souvent
les caractères de la manie coléreuse / becoming agressive and angry if he be-
lieves he is not getting sufficient support / obsessional, ritualistic behaviour / weeping kicking screaming / tension mounts until it becomes uncontrol-
lable, and an intolerable outburst of violence occurs / les cas de hydrocéphalie ...
accompagnés d'epilepsie / schuimen, stoten sperma en urine uit / tendency to
hold object in a vice-like grip / une fureur sexuelle / de tong naar buiten
hangt / the man who breaths himself into a grand mal attack becomes inverted
with magical properties .. the use of private symbols / de patiënt maakt nieuwe
woorden, spreekt magische formules uit, herhaalt deze als bezwerings - en tover-
formules, legt verbanden tussen voorstellingscomplexen die voor ons gevoel wei-
nig met elkaar te maken hebben / une ecriture sarabondante qui progressivement
se dénature, devient irregulière et incoherente / de manische opgewonden patiën
vertelt ons dat het inzijn innerlijk voortjaagt en voortraast, de 'stream of
conscious ' is een onstuimige bergbeek geworden met stroomversnellingen en
watervallen. enigzins rijmen met woorden doen manische patiënten ook, bijvoor-
beeld gekheid maken over een naam of rijmen / le sujet peut entrependre de
veritables voyayes coordonnés et bien enchainés, revenir brusquement à son poin
de départ / de gedachtengang wordt plotseling onderbroken, de oorzaak kan zijn
een absence, een   schijn van epilepsie / epilepsie veroorzaakt allerlei toe-
standsbeelden : delier, schemer - ontstemmings- opwindingstoestanden, persoon-
lijkheidsveranderingen (kleverigheid, hyperreligiositeit) / blijft aan een
thema hangen, legt nog eens en nog eens uit wat er is gebeurd, kan niet aan
een eind komen met zijn verhaal / bedoelt men daarmee dat ze noch het thema van
het gesprek noch de personen met wie ze sprekenkunnen loslaten / wijdlopigheid
is het denken dat zijn doel maar niet bereiken wil en kronkelt als een rivier-
tje, dikwijls een hysterisch symptoom en heeft te maken met narcisme : verlief
zijn op zijn eigen woorden, formuleringen, volzinnen en stem / sperrung / they
are full of ideas, but ideas occur to them so rapidly that they have no time
to put any of them into operation, everything they see or hear suggests a new
line of thought / de epileptische patiënt gaat naar iemand toe op wie hij woede
is, koopt onderweg een bijl, slaat zijn slachtoffer schedel en hersens in, kom
thuis onder het bloed / the patient is delighted with his own performance / ep
lepsy has been described as a brief excursion THROUGH MADNESS INTO DEATH. Wir
bedürfen einen Sündflut . Epilepsia! Epilepsia di Marchése ! ! !

cambell-soublunar b-raindance for a poodle
~~seksuereel-lunair~~ vaudouchen in turks badpak
wauwelwalzen met Oma Lo's walgeeuweidewonderlijk (wou wel wim! wil best martin!)
~~muscullair-maandansen onder een hoogtezon~~
liedierlijk libidodansen libbiddodendansen libidocockoo!

lieddierlijk ~~libbiddodendansen~~ libidocockoo!

oui oui oui
we we we de markies van water must be taking the snake for a
strollollying mortadell~~kllella~~,

libidocockoo cocknazzo blaubarbariccia facircusiatto rubificker
farewellfarello dreckhignazzeu giraffiacane culcabbageriana omala
coda oscarmiglione alickenau

MEM is voor Water
M is voor Water
vaginal paranoia
de markies van water must be giving the royal eunoch the loyal illusion of lordship
buffelzaal
porchérielein
~~an anti-christ from Asilia~~
droomomomamanie
bikephobia/dikephobia
dostoyevskiv mi nabovok
xrist i antixrist
~~atma-bhuddi-moonass~~
~~eatmi-bhuddi-moonass~~
lymphamaan
~~pongo da panza~~
écorcher le renard: vomit
playboybunnies/foreplaypunnies
tabouillabaisse
ach ach ach/ich ich ich
Cour des Nerfs
Louis XV aan de pokken
lodewijk & hadewieg aan het hokken
epilepsia furtigernosea
oranga-nausea
Saint John's Evil
Saint Vitus' dance
sad'o-maz'ok-iz'm
sadotage (masochistic)
epileptic picknick
psychic epilepsy
~~vok mi wim wanda~~
epileptic clouded states (DSM-II, coded 293.2)
sexual vandalism
horror feminae
reading epilepsy (ollanda, lo, lip)
romantic epilepsy (epilepsia romantica)
epileptic cry See cry, epileptic See epileptic cry
oceanic feeling See omnipotence, nautomania
feces-child-penis concept See concept feces-child-penis
eppolepponophobia
symbololophobia
hiero phobia!
ante lo phobia
marlene dietrichophobia
popeccaticphobia
gamophobia (mega-gamo-phobia)
taking a bath o phobia!
eurotochophobia

sadoraphobia (ollanda)
paparthenophobia
theophobia
ecclectrophobia
apilapiphobia

M Adam Braun, Mandy Masty, Pinna Pinnacula, Bulimia Bilumia, Urinia I,
Uriana II, Brigit Bardot in Venidick, Die Blonde Betsie, Xavura del B
aus, Begga Begga, Avida Arsdoll, Barnonnes Vannessa Von B., Makkiezin
Deppressa Von M., Dr. Istvan (Fistvan, Listvan) Fluck (?), Bau Peapi!
v. Mandau, Bela Belout! v. Palembang, Dominamessatanica, Patty Antibo
dy, Geronta Greisengeil, Dr. Sigmund Freud (!), Blondy, Dolly, Friday,
Lola, Pearly, Girma, Bonanza, Carmen, Fred, Bumke, Mumps, Dirkje, Fum
a, Kit, Bamby, Holly, Ultra, Kim, Drusilla, Calamity (once beauty que
en now beauty-case), Maud, Eug, Miss Euphemia, Dolly Pardon, Lo, Lolo,
Birnadebt Burnadebt, Virginia Whoolf, Jacky, Marrylynn Merrylonn, Fil
a Filariasis, Conforama, Fellata, Foeiliana, Formosa, Freud (Anna), F
rick (Wilhelmina), Gerrie de Grote, Gerrie van Nijvel, Lawrence of Ar
abia, de Maagd van Orléans, Pekingmensje, Monita Secretion, Fia-Orc C
ockatrice, Cunt, Aunt, Mudder, Dirkje Fock, Mary (Good Nightmary), de
Kleinste Moeder ter Wereld (Rust Zacht Lieve Vriendin), Carly, Glittee
clittaclittaclittaclitta!, Meug, Zeug, Maud, Eug, Juliette, Justine (
Juliette), Zus Nel, Nul Zes, het Gietijzeren Gezicht, de Regenpijpste
r, Erna, de Loodvreetster, de Noodkreetster, de Klaagzangeres, de Keg
elnlicht, de Schijtlijster, de Leerraarres, de Rubboerin, de Drankfles
bierin, de Drinkbaarmoeder, de Geslachtsziekster, de Vuurwerkster, de
Loodaars, Anusje van Alles op Alles, de Vroetvrouw, de Storm in de Br
anding, de Pellutieangent!

*de Regenpijpster, de Loodvreetster, de Noodkreetster, de

** de Regnepijpster, de Loodvreetster, de Klaagzangeres, de Kegolnich
ht, de Vroetvrouw, de Storm in de Branding,

Birnadebet Burnacredit

schwarzen painther | Orange Christ. — apokalypse jankowski & feathers | wassile
hieuovysos | dionysius wonken/all muu Bulligan | vodareto | von Aschenbach | icheng
dublin-dutch john marcage mar cogath maonns | earpass | | | alligi orange Ja nous | icho
in dea name of ouse mon fating | Löwing nappanthor mappa de leopardown we zelsbong te ven heen
ijsocktbong te ven heen buidz by buidz denkend aan holland zienkzeeën vivienen noopena bijhant O aughty
bijhantean anghasi musilla musillassimenoma dellszijl fonkein van Minea vous (—) auto haffen
exrevolution/Rinvolution inda name of Pauce flowmotion picture yourself oor, oral inor enverlution
falling flöwing scoti megaphysichness ohrangbehimoney pan excellance lady isoi zowanzo posissann
loan alone bikobechelt bog panisatro/ha oedipushi imeo agnadisismelhaflood zundulotte tonti hantvloth
bink flamas voice flames noise gym bougs (si quid fluid ego supra aqua aliquid bagnaba how' in wheu
tranqvestidementide zumen schelt mea brandenhem du imby hey zentl moviez ischthales ?les kotte
pios watten (barthaly ballus) safari dada jagen des knuls hagen des kents gath des kents ? babyfoot
bu baful Ella baba (zan egge) zonnekooi kluftmanicrisme La bastir agn erla/a bastiran gincherz
ville vitnamchefK ami afsecto Hoth Tavi li du mythologicaghumanianin'la bill in egpps
bittoris op Mr blots kind en veel zaam bush hi de niggapanemiklen eine papha wanmat (kildhovis)
sonenhong spannungs kababel balosleep bot oto mezzo veics mullen neguaagua ?les manuele pisvelle
thi blazuben adamsen evala uche the falling sichness — schoma dileffling such nase
icontravensie streepshow the fass adam Ave Madam Eva mangde flies viennase humbonty thumbculf
abend a qvank/at (Humpty dumty) oen vintuoso vie so, hypervintuosorpevastag] seesbull benchles
haibutes | — baybull baybull agg candynsky amet kammage (agnus caslus) abbondanza
quanta acqua in bocca | l'acqua va al mane | — agua santa | vampere | acqva
l'aqvasse kiei | (aenuo—) a succaristicaghamae | agnelleau | fine souli) acidula
neo alienato [allusion illusio/pseualienato babu | anno atinasi cus | communistabarbeguis | cannibull mappa sena
monday u tapplausochopo a dua modant | (dopo di me il diluvio) | dun quichute fascata equa cascalato,
caduto | scatallas || fluido fluer zaaber flanto [hazzia folla] manio di grandezzaubou flanto da folly—
fmhava fluminosa —| quanta acqua in bocca scata danzata fallminea | (fulpioca) frenesia galassia
Eikolth [galaxy] | maschera forer menda | mal de menda | cma cidio | waten ballastniester a babau/ba bol
[bizzouena] bubbove e buffone | parassita (parissista) | mansoleopandon quichute | mappa lunane
| chute u up | manas marmues | il mare spumeggia | (cranicleitoniale) [mane buccascacio | in tempesti,
lavoro maniammale | manea callas | mare forza 0123456789 | sillabar | epilotheomare chese | piccanaso
plasuck | finnickles w. flemma (flemma) | fö'hane qua s w [ponte mari. polato] mare maakres | apocalisse
[potentemente zu zzuenture | zumsta havi | (druult zu avilone) [zampone] zampillo light ampill della fontana]
[wattmeteo veber inattoua] waterklozit | vampa = flamme [vampata] vaginismo uaina [mussu mano ||
mae cisi sta | windmill | grammafica | maduze inatlion [echolinotia] e piggolassia] les mare spumeggia nijlland
mauscalum | scatullashisse fännsappelan docent niggen verbij (flagmoten) downquichute cacap mammouth etule
ballostoiest abben Manza wavepelonutrekhen (le gulf ende zevengoten) adomo sevalanche zampillo feebala chad
[maggie ballasten] yas vista 30 wit (kektklut) | vaginismodt | birthville waulandeon guppel mussulmano dibango apigo
mussulman (daysbornhombuist/adoleuness) dmopoffored | Vakcoppervloch waterope avlet V punu danko dujaan
negensbeuannej regenslueedujve Shus in luchtbedieken invichtbog van gui mene nova | et la banuvas onva buzanaven
(zumassevapar | uitparten) menaghin aamazia flamma moto la fame [e aeui meissie in mar ulpans]
emuaue le manniviace ninei viou | fala lacuan hai mao | waterbeduo aria behuet | blink-foled acue aguasugel
(falthung offe) auventotioer of aeuulatio/feto fedu ebanka | falling ofu riverelution auveulation of newelution
inevevetulation | eau de la Notte enchentis | washily wachenby handinus | inda sky Candynsky orthodox
abend abend mahl after the am ahh tupela ahentbetrug in amsterdam aus dem fenster
(ange du jeyamen/olemite) la polha luptisale noister I II | anamber I anabs II Amici-szene
aus faust (II) auf dem strand aus dem pauk dem Abrisbosoffs study for Au kums
Landscape with Boats (autumn in bavaria) | AVANT L'ORAGE | aven cheval/sane avec twies
femmes [Before the Storm | bei obeman bei oeen I (Winken) bengeng clandschiff mit see
Gibt mit blauen malle avec cava Ich amugh Chiff mit blau-roten Halbkreis bild mit buglenschiffer
bild mit kreis u. mit schwaaze bogen big ze auf eligen (twilight) [Dämmerung] BLAU lines I
blach spot I den blaue roten blauen fleck blue bill boat haif Bad Bauneln Carmival LA CASCADE
Cavaliers de l'Apocalypse II C. with trumpet CHASSE AU LION cheyaux range et blen
[Copy of Christ] cloudy day compesdron Storm | Couches de Soleil/Naples | the Cap | DAME
Esquisse pour Deluge | les Dermers Rayons | Sketch for Deluge II | devaut l'eglise de la
Nativité dela Vierge Deaf am see | Dutch Coast | Den Eiffel / Een rauwart
entfuhrung Evening Landscape with Full moon | Fachelzug Fliegend Haaal
Fugal Fuge Fugue [Glasbild Sintflut zu it Sonne] Great Eagle Huge painting with
red spot (sun) Heiligen weaormie | Häuser vor Blauen berg u Helle Luft/Hell
Bild of Hill with Pink | Holland | Scheveningen Beach Chains | Strand koi & G

marquesunshintotem
thalattattower

        thalattower

thalattaower & sunshintotem

thalattaower
sunshintotem

sunshintotem & thalattaower

dr. calderari
eggypsea-wake
call carl einstein bebudouin
las marshallas marquesas

oranganeshamale marquis

pepperland/kikkerland
gaujoguinea
finneganz river
finneganz waga & mwasawa
rubberrational
riverrubberrational
mwasila
the markasesa

el markasesa in the moon of milamala
kam kasekam kam kasekam
love-introbrianderland
magic washamatras washamantra

de markirisala marquise
electronislaw malinowskiwasser
pramotive man
lovemaking sense
marquesan beauty magic
bagise puwan (may i see your testicles?)?
bagise puwan owah
WA!
yausa yausa yausa: orgiastic assaults by women: dionysos
olantonicka prickonic
lsdiagrammologuess who-who
coctopussy bedürer
too slow winslow homer sweet homer
psalm 107 bitch daubber
bootseas daubber band
wassir not wassir patrick spens
captain ahabacook: moby dick, donatello, captain cook
the ocean floor shower
HOKUSAY WAVE OFF KANAGAWATER!
the open boatsy's daubber band
cape horny horn
moby dicka prick dance
bootzillawarra mercury fountain wollongong
coast to cousteau
squidipous rexstrait delo
bootscylla

Published by Zip Records, San Francisco/Amsterdam, 2018
First published in 1998 by Pallas Press, Dublin

ISBN 978-90-826392-2-3

ziprecords.com

www.ingramcontent.com/pod-product-compliance
Lightning Source LLC
LaVergne TN
LVHW091521170726
843492LV00004B/1017